Acknowledgements

In 1979 I started writing a Troubles-related story, which I've never finished (yet). Twenty-nine years later, after the recession wiped me out, my daughter Victoria suggested I dust off the manuscript and finish it. I didn't because I thought that with nearly thirty years additional life experience I could tell a better story. And so Alex Casey was born. Throughout the year it took to write Victoria was a perpetual source of encouragement; she still is, so thank you Victoria.

Averill Buchanan, my editor and help with all things related to this book, thank you. You had the unenviable task of taking the ramblings of a would-be author and turning them into this wonderful book. You also brought on board the relevant experts – Mike Faulkner (copy-editor), Victoria Woodside (proofreader), Design for Writers (cover design and website) – to make the whole project a success. Cheers.

Family and friends: none of you laughed when I said I was going to write a novel so thank you for that, and for your enthusiastic support.

I have three other people to thank who gave me encouragement and generous support when necessary. Without them the project could not have been completed. You know who you are, so thank you.

And finally Alex Casey, *thank you*. You have given me many hours of pleasure so far and your next escapade, The Lost Island, is ready for Averill's red pen.

Chapter 1

'Get rid of it, or I will!' he said, then turned and strode out of the Dublin maternity hospital, the black malacca cane click-clicking on the polished floor.

The nineteen-year-old girl in the bed looked deflated, the midwife horrified.

Outside in the car park, a Mercedes stretch limo was waiting, the rear door held open by an enormous chauffeur. He stood nearly seven feet tall and wore gigantic burgundy Doc Martens; his bottle-green uniform was stretched at every seam and button. Underneath a silly little peaked hat was a huge round head scored by a livid scar that ran from above the left ear, under the left eye, across the nose and down to the right corner of his mouth. He had no eyebrows or eyelashes, just white skin stretched over the football-shaped head which gave his face a look of vacant idiocy.

He nodded once at the immaculately dressed man with the malacca cane tucked military-style under his arm who came down the steps of the hospital.

'Home, Peter,' said the man, sliding into the back seat of the Mercedes.

* * *

The watcher was dozing when he heard a car door close outside. It wasn't a tinny rattle like his crap Lada, but an expensive clunk. He jumped to the window, drew the dirty net curtain aside and peered out.

A Mercedes stretch limo had turned into Carmel Street and was blocked by a builder's skip outside No. 3. A man in a tiny

1

peaked hat was striding purposely along the street, hunched over against the sheeting rain, looking closely at the house numbers. He stopped outside No. 9, checked to right and left, then turned and walked back to the limo. As he reached to open the passenger rear door he straightened to his full height.

The watcher gasped involuntarily, shocked by the man's height and his hideous face caught in the light from the street. He could see now that the man was wearing a uniform.

The chauffeur – for that was surely what he was – leaned down to the rear window of the limo and, as he came back up, opened an enormous umbrella emblazoned with the Irish rugby team logo, then held it over the rear door. An elegant and obviously expensive pair of white leather loafers appeared on the grotty pavement. The watcher soon discovered that they belonged to a tall, stunning, raven-haired young woman wearing tailored white trousers and a full-length black leather coat. She took the umbrella from the chauffeur and held it above his head while he reached in and carefully lifted a bundle of what looked like plaid and tartan rugs off the seat. Under the shelter of the umbrella the unlikely couple walked down the street to No. 9. Outside the door she gently took the bundle from the chauffeur and he took the umbrella.

At a nod from the young woman, the huge man pounded his massive fist on the door. By this time, everyone in the street knew that No. 9 had visitors – unusual, but not unheard of at half past midnight.

A few seconds later a bulkhead light flickered into life above the door, a bolt was drawn and the door scraped open. Sean Casey stood inside in a pair of sagging underpants, a black donkey jacket over his shoulders.

'What the fuck ...?' His jaw hung open.

'Here, Casey, you keep your bastard!' The young woman thrust the bundle into Casey's arms, snatched the umbrella from the chauffeur and ran back to the limo.

The chauffeur stepped in close to the doorway. Sean took a step back. The driver reached into his inside pocket and pulled out a bulky envelope which he threw at Casey's feet. Staring at Casey with his unblinking black eyes he pointed to the envelope, then poked Casey in the chest with his forefinger before thumbing his own chest twice. The watcher, if he could have seen this pantomime, would not have understood its significance. Sean Casey certainly did.

The young woman was settled in the rear of the limo by the time the chauffeur returned. He folded himself in behind the steering wheel and, without a word, reversed the limo out into East Wall Road. He executed a near impossible three-point turn and headed back towards south Dublin where the young woman lived.

Another thing the watcher failed to see – the elegantly attired gentleman sitting in the back of the limo, his two bony hands resting on the polished silver knob of a black malacca cane.

'It's done,' the young woman said in a tired, defeated voice.

'Good,' the gentleman replied abruptly.

The chauffeur raised his eyes to the rear-view mirror and watched the young woman as she lay back against the leather upholstery, tears slipping down her beautiful face. Almost imperceptibly, he shook his head.

* * *

Sean Casey stood a full minute before he reacted, torn by conflicting emotions. Then he closed the door and walked into the kitchen.

His mother, who slept in the back room off the kitchen, came out to see what was going on. She looked first into Sean's face and then at the bundle he held in his arms. She carefully took the bundle from him and unwrapped the blankets. On cue, the infant inside started to cry, its gentle sobs soon rising to a healthy howl. Sean turned back to the front door and lifted the envelope. In the kitchen he sat at the table and opened the sodden packet. As he extracted a letter, a bundle of fifty punt notes fell at his feet. He glanced half-heartedly at the letter dated April 1987.

'Out loud, son. You know I'm not good with small print.'

What his ma really meant was she couldn't read at all, other than her Bible, and that was only because of her daily visits to chapel. When confronted with a situation where she had to read anything else she usually found she had 'forgotten her glasses'. The fact that no one ever saw her wearing glasses was neither here nor there.

Sean shook his head and was about to fold the letter back into the envelope when his eyes jumped to a handwritten sentence at the bottom.

> *Casey, I have one favour to ask, but if my family hear of this it will be the worse for both of us! Please name the infant after my great-uncle – Alexander Sebastian. Not very 'docks area', I know, but I'm sure you will explain it away in your usual inimitable fashion.*

The baby had stopped crying and gone back to sleep.

Sean's ma looked up from her detailed examination of its features. 'He's yours and no mistake. So, who's the mother then? That smart young hussy what left him?'

Sean flinched at the accusing tone in her voice. 'Don't ask. The less you know about that the better.'

He looked around the room in a daze, then at his mother and finally at the bundle lying in her lap. He collapsed back into the seat.

'I don't believe it. I just don't believe it!' he muttered.

'What don't you believe? That you went and made a grandmother of me out of wedlock? That the whore you lay with has dumped her bastard on us? That she can buy us off? Just who the bloody hell does she think she is?'

'She wants us to call him "Alexander Sebastian". She's from a family that neither you nor I's going to upset. They carry out their threats. She's in a difficult position. She didn't write that letter of her own free will, and we're going to do exactly as we're told. Understood?'

And with that, Sean clumped his way up the stairs.

'Sure haven't I been dreaming of grand childer for years and along you come,' Mrs Casey said to the infant as though he could participate in the conversation. 'You'll be Seany to me and my friends. To blazes with all them fancy names. If I'm going to rear you, then I'll call you what I want – not what some tart says. Now, that's the last we'll speak of it.'

Clutching the baby to her ample bosom she rose from the chair and scooped up the money. Sean came down the stairs dressed for town, not work.

'Where are you for? And why are you all fancied up? Them's your good clothes. You only wear them when it's special.'

'I've to meet a man, and I know what I'm wearing. After that I'll go to the council offices early and talk to them about moving you. You'll need a better place now on account of *him.*' Sean nodded towards the infant.

'It's Seany, not *him*, or them fancy names that she wants. If I'm rearing him, it's Seany.'

'Mrs Casey!'– he always called his mother that when he wanted to make a point – 'the child will be christened Alexander Sebastian as his mother – and father – want.'

Sean left the house, closing the front door quietly behind him, as though not to disturb the infant. It was, in fact, because of someone else that he tried to leave the house unobserved. He turned right instead of left, as he normally would, and cursed softly: he'd forgotten the outside light was still on. Certain he had been seen, he turned back and walked towards No. 2, the first house on the far side of the road. Through the sheets of rain he noticed a slight movement at the dirty net curtain, confirming his suspicions.

* * *

Inside the house, the watcher was on the phone. He saw Sean Casey approaching, and in a panicked voice whispered into the phone, 'He's coming to the house! Bloody hell, he's at the front door. What the fuck do I do?'

'What you do best,' a ghoulish, disembodied voice replied. 'Disappear!'

Before the watcher could hang up, Casey had knocked the door, but not so loud as to attract attention from the neighbours.

'Tell your boss I'm for the Tavern at Dolphin's Barn,' Casey whispered loudly through the letterbox. 'I'll be there in twenty minutes and I'll only wait for ten. Tell him to come on his own. I know about Sligo, and he best talk to me before I have to talk to the Garda in the morning. Tell him this is checkmate – he'll understand!'

The letterbox snapped shut and the watcher heard Casey's footsteps fade into the distance.

* * *

With his collar turned up against the rain, Casey set off for the lockup in the next street where he kept his car, a well-preserved, canvas-topped V8 Land Rover he'd owned from new. It was his first and only extravagance. It was after one o'clock in the morning, but he was wide awake. His one regret about the chain of events he had just set in motion was that he had not said a proper goodbye to his mother, or to the infant.

He drove down the East Wall Road and into Forth Road, swinging round past Lansdowne rugby ground, his only company the swish, swish of the windscreen wipers and the throaty burble of the V8 engine. The rows of Victorian terrace houses looked down at him as he made his way through the streets. This area, although desirable, lacked the grandeur of its Georgian neighbours to the south and west of Ballsbridge. He travelled up Londonbridge Road and Haddington Road, meeting the Grand Canal at the junction with Baggot Street. Many of the fine old houses in the area had given way to new office blocks, crude concrete monstrosities that devalued their neighbours. His route followed the Grand Canal out to Dolphin's Barn and Lock No. 2. There, he swung into the Tavern car park and pulled up parallel with the driver's side of a Toyota Land Cruiser parked facing out to the road.

Sean opened his window and peered at the dark interior of the Toyota through the lashing rain. With the street lamps behind it, all he could make out was the outline of two people in the rear seat and the driver's shadowy face.

In that instant he decided what to do. Double declutching to engage four-wheel drive and first gear, he accelerated past the Toyota and pulled in behind it. He slammed the Land Rover into reverse and floored the accelerator. Its engine roared as the two vehicles crashed together, gravel scattering like machine-gun fire under the spinning wheels. The Toyota's parking brake was no match for the relentless power of the Land Rover. It gained grip, and with a groan from the reluctant Toyota, both vehicles slowly shunted out of the car park and across the narrow road towards the canal.

In his rear-view mirror, Sean could see the occupants of the Toyota flailing around in a panic. With creaks and groans and then a loud crack, the wooden fence that surrounded Lock No. 2 shattered. Sean stamped on the Land Rover's brakes and watched as the Toyota, the doors on both sides thrown open, tipped over the edge and nosedived into the water. He engaged the handbrake and stepped out, withdrawing a sawn-off shotgun from its hidden mounting behind the seat. Two paces and he was looking down into the lock.

Some fifteen feet below, the tail of the Toyota was just visible above the water. One man was struggling to climb onto it. Another was treading water five or six feet away, waiting to see what might happen next. The third was thrashing towards the lock gates, seeking a handhold. All the while, the rain continued to sluice down.

'I'm sure he got the message to come on his own.' Sean's voice, calm and measured, carried easily across the lock. 'He shouldn't have sent you, Paddy!'

'Yeah, well you know how it is, Sean – always belt and braces with The Man. He says we need to talk.' Paddy said this as though he was sitting across a table, not treading water to stay afloat.

'Naw, Paddy, it's too late now. It'd be a waste of time. I told him it's checkmate. He should have listened. He should have come himself.'

Swinging left, Sean raised the shotgun and blasted the man who had by now gained a hold on the lock gates.

'Yer man should've listened too!' he muttered.

He swung the gun right and blew the man off the Toyota's rear door.

'So should he!'

'Fuck you, Sean! That was my son. You shouldn't have done that. He wasn't carrying.' Paddy sounded angry rather than afraid.

'Then he was a bloody eejit like his father.'

Sean broke open the shotgun, reloaded and smiled thinly as he pointed it. The eruption where Paddy's head had been, and the gore from the other two, turned the lock into a stew of oily, bloody detritus.

Sean shook his head and threw the gun and the unused cartridges into the settling water.

'Goodbye, Paddy. Sorry about your son.'

He walked back to the open door of the idling Land Rover and climbed in. Disengaging four-wheel drive, he drove back the way he'd come. As he turned right at the junction with Leeson Street he met a Garda car – lights flashing, siren screaming – going like a bat out of hell.

'You're too late for this party, lads, and too early for the next,' he mumbled to himself.

The rain eased as he headed out of the city towards the Wicklow Hills. Just past the Glen of the Downs he turned right into a barely visible minor road that led through the village of Glendarragh. His headlights reflected off the puddles, making sinister shapes of the heavy vegetation on either side of the narrow road. He had little idea how he was going to handle the next half hour, but of one thing he was sure: he would be a very unwelcome visitor where he was going. The Man would have heard about the shooting on the canal by now. Getting past his nervous, trigger-happy guards would require all Sean's skill and a considerable amount of luck.

On the ascent into the hills, inspiration struck as he approached Sweeney's Bar. He swung the Land Rover in on the far side of the only car in the car park and cut the engine. The bar manager, Thomas Toomey, was locking the side door.

'Can't you see we're closed?' Tommy shouted as he walked towards his car, head down against the rain, slipping the keys into the left pocket of his coat. 'You're covered by cameras and I'm carrying,' he added, his right hand disappearing into his coat pocket.

'Bejesus, that's some welcome to give a buddy,' Sean said, stepping down from the Land Rover. 'You'll earn no stars from Bord Fáilte for that performance!'

'Ah Christ, it's yourself, Sean. You're hardly looking a drink at this time of the morning, are you?'

'No, but I need a lift, Tommy – up to the Lodge. I'm just about out of juice. Good job you're late closing up tonight.'

'Late? This is early. It's usually three or half past before I get clear. I've closed on account of the shooting. Did you not hear about it? At the Tavern on the canal? A couple of the lads were sent to warn me. Fortunately there were only a few punters in and they weren't hard to shift when they heard the news. According to the boys, The Man says the shooter'll likely come this way, so the dirty glasses can keep till the morning. I'm off!' Tommy opened his car door.

'Ah, there's no end to this bloodshed, and in our own backyard as well. Anyway, can you drop me off at the Lodge?'

Tommy stared at Sean. 'No way! When the boys was in they said that if anyone saw you in the area they're to phone

The Man and tell him immediately. What's he want with you anyway? Has the pair of you fallen out again?'

Whether it was the dying rain, the catch in Tommy's voice or just old-fashioned intuition, something made Sean reach for the safety catch on the Glock in his coat pocket.

'Don't you worry about me, Tommy. Just go back in and phone him. Tell him I was here. Say I'd run out of petrol back up the road a bit and that one of the punters offered me a lift down to the Texaco station on the main road. That'll keep you right with him.' Sean reckoned the call would draw some of the guns away from the Lodge.

Tommy narrowed his eyes. 'Jesus, it was you did the shooting, wasn't it?' He laughed. 'You mad fucker, I should have guessed. It has all your style. And now you want to take him on. Are you brain-fucking-dead?' Then his expression changed.

Sean could practically read his mind: there had to be a bounty out on Sean. Self first at all costs, no matter who else gets hurt – that had been Tommy's style of late.

'Not take him on, Tommy – take him out,' Sean said, his voice deadpan, businesslike.

'You *are* brain-fucking-dead!'

Tommy turned back towards the pub door, fishing in the right pocket of his coat.

'Wrong hand, Thomas, wrong hand.'

The phut of the silenced Glock was masked by Tommy's howl and the clatter of the old .45 that fell to the ground from his shattered hand.

'You of all people should know not to pull a piece when your back's turned,' Sean growled. 'And definitely not on me!'

'Fuck, Sean, I had to move it to get at the keys.'

'No, you didn't. Your keys are in your other pocket. Now open up and in we go.'

Tommy fumbled with the keys as he pulled them out of his left-hand pocket and dropped them.

'Step back, Tommy, you're starting to annoy me!'

As Sean stooped to lift the keys, he caught a tiny movement to his right. He quickly took a step to one side and swung his right hand back. The Glock smacked Tommy across the mouth, removing some expensive dentistry and part of his upper lip. A doubled-edged flick knife clattered to the ground near the .45.

'You're getting very careless in your old age, Tommy. You should remember who taught you all the tricks.'

Another backhand swipe with the pistol sent Tommy reeling into the doorframe. He seemed to hang for a moment before slumping to the ground in a motionless heap, his ragged breathing the only sound to be heard.

'Bloody amateur,' muttered Sean.

He dragged Tommy round the corner to the back of the building. Among the chaos of crates and kegs lay a badly coiled garden hose. Sean traced it back to the tap and turned the tap on, directing the stream of water at Tommy. It took a full minute before the bedraggled body started to cough and splutter.

'Nothing like a cold shower to bring a man to his senses, eh, Tommy?'

'Fuck you, you bastard. You're dead.'

'No, you are if I have to ask twice.'

Sean threw the hose to the side and crouched down beside Tommy. 'I need the alarm code for the bar, and I need you to make a phone call. You all deserted me when I needed you. This is checkmate now, Tommy. I don't want to make Mrs Toomey a widow, but another corpse doesn't matter to me now.'

Tommy groaned and pulled himself up, his back leaning against the wall. 'Three seven one six,' he croaked, his left hand alternating between his lower jaw and his mashed right hand.

'Jesus, I should have thought of that – your old prison number.'

Sean pulled Tommy to his feet and pushed him in front of him round to the car park. They had just rounded the corner when a fusillade of bullets lifted Tommy off the ground, making him dance backwards before he collapsed, his face and chest ripped to pieces.

Sean turned, vaulted the low fence that surrounded the car park and, ducking down, ran to the far side where the light from the security lamps didn't quite reach. He dropped flat to the ground and peered between the slats of the broken fence. Two men were cautiously checking around the stacks of crates and kegs.

Sean took aim with the Glock. Even in the rain and at a distance of thirty yards he felt confident. The first shot missed, but neither man reacted; the silencer was obviously doing its job. Sean steadied his breathing and tried again. The second shot took the nearest man in the back of the head, the dumdum bullet removing half his face as it exited. The second man dropped like a stone, as though he'd also been hit. Good reactions, Sean thought. Definitely a pro. He waited, his eyes never leaving the spot where the man had been standing. Years of covert operations had taught him to look without staring, hardly blinking. Sure enough, after a few minutes he noticed a slight movement. The second man was trying to slide backwards towards a stack of crates, keeping his head down so his pale face didn't show in the gloom.

Sean rose to a crouch and silently ran back the way he had come. He leapt over the low fence again and practically landed on the second man. Both were surprised, but his opponent was the quicker. As Sean's feet landed, the guy swung his legs round in a scything motion, forcing Sean to jump again. The man flipped onto his back, threw up his pistol and fired. Sean felt the air kiss his cheek as the bullet passed by. When his feet hit the ground a second time, he fell flat and rolled away to his left. He stopped behind a pallet of empty beer kegs, lay on his side and listened. Sean began to count slowly and silently. His opponent moved a little, allowing Sean to get a fix on where he was. He forced himself to continue his slow count … nineteen … twenty.

He erupted from his cover, pushing the top row of kegs in front of him as he leapt towards his man. He crashed into crates of empty beer bottles and these joined the kegs falling on top of his quarry, the smell of stale beer filling the air. This time there was no near miss. Sean landed full force on the other man, knocked the gun out of his hand and jammed the Glock into his Adam's apple. Sean immediately recognised his opponent – it was Brendan Magee, one-time colleague and gambler, who was lying among the broken bottles and empty beer kegs still tumbling around them.

'You've played all your cards this time, Brendan.'

'Fuck you, Sean,' Brendan croaked, the gun jammed against his throat making it difficult to speak. 'You might win this hand, but the deck's well-stacked against you.'

'How so, Brendan?' Sean eased the pressure of the gun. 'How so?'

'Numbers, Sean. There are too many of them and they know you're here. Look in my pocket.'

Sean kept the gun in place as he patted Brendan down. He felt a rectangular object about the size of a cassette tape in Brendan's coat pocket. Then he noticed a wire attached to an earpiece protruding out of his collar. There had to be a microphone somewhere on his clothing. Sean removed the Glock from Brendan's throat.

'Thanks for the warning. You had an ace up your sleeve after all.' The smack of the Glock against Brendan's temple sounded worse than it was; he would wake with a splitting headache, nothing more. 'I always had a soft spot for you, Brendan Magee. Don't push your luck again.'

Sean rose carefully so as not to disturb the sea of glass that surrounded him. He stepped quietly to the corner of the pub and paused to listen. Satisfied, he dropped to his hunkers and peered cautiously round the building. He shot out the two security lights, then sprinted to the Land Rover, opened the door and threw himself across the seats, glad there was no interior light. After a few moments, he raised his head and scanned the car park again before he settled behind the wheel and started the engine. Keeping the vehicle in darkness, he slowly turned to face the exit, stopping by using only the handbrake to avoid any show of lights. He waited.

How the next few minutes played out would depend on who was in charge of security at the Lodge. Left to his own devices, The Man would just charge like a bull, trying to flatten all in front of him without any plan. If no one arrived in the next three or four minutes, then wiser counsel was in charge.

Ten minutes later Sean accepted that they were not coming to him – he was going to them. Peter or Seamus must be in charge. He dusted down his filthy clothes and recalled his last conversation with his mother.

'Ah shit, I should have worn my work clothes after all.'

He engaged first gear and, relying on his ability to see in the dark now that his eyes were accustomed to it, he drove slowly out of the car park and turned left up the hill towards the Lodge.

The explosion was heard in the city centre over twenty miles away. Pieces of the Land Rover were still being found in nearby fields for days afterwards. The remains of Sean Casey, such as they were, were buried the following week.

* * *

High Mass was conducted by the bishop himself, while Father Ignatius Tomelty, the parish priest, was supportive of Mrs Casey in her hour of need. But he advised against her decision to exclude the infant in the funeral proceedings: she forbade any mention of the child, particularly in the eulogy, so movingly delivered by Michael Slaney, Sean's best friend and top driver.

Praise of Sean and condemnation of the perpetrators were reported in equal measure by the press and on the radio and

TV. Sean Casey, owner of Casey Transport, was an embittered forty-three-year-old when he died, respected by all who did business with him, admired by those who worked for him. He demanded complete loyalty in all his dealings; his word was his bond. He was feared by those in the IRA who knew his commitment to Irish unity and to the cause. That was what made his death so incomprehensible, so unexpected. Questions were asked in the Dáil, and the Northern Ireland Secretary tabled a motion in Westminster. Security forces north and south of the border were put on red alert. The American ambassador condemned the atrocity, while the pope prayed it did not signal an upsurge in the ways of evil. And yet no one claimed responsibility.

Though Mrs Casey and Sean never discussed it, she had been well aware of his connection with the IRA and the dubious benefits that came from it. If ever she was pressed by friends or neighbours, she repeated the 'I never ask Sean about his work' line, and the occasion of his funeral was no exception. At the wake in Molloy's pub on the corner of the East Wall and Forth Roads, the good was exaggerated and the bad ignored, and rightly so. But Mrs Casey couldn't help but wonder what was to become of her and this new child now that Sean was dead.

Michael Slaney, too, was concerned about the future. He couldn't see how Mrs Casey could possibly keep Casey Transport in business. Sean had known the industry inside out, and without him Casey Transport was sure to go under. So he was even more perplexed than Mrs Casey when an elegantly dressed gentleman carrying a black malacca cane introduced himself as Sean's business adviser, a position in the business neither of them had heard of. The presence, at the edge of the gathering in the saloon bar, of an enormous man in an ill-fitting chauffeur's uniform did little to reassure them.

'I apologise for raising business matters at a time like this, Mrs Casey,' the gentleman said, 'but banks and clients are no respecters of death. Please do not be alarmed, however. Sean's affairs are in excellent order, due in no small part to *your* efforts, Mr Slaney. Perhaps the three of us could withdraw to the snug for a few minutes. I see it's now empty.'

Indeed, when Michael and Mrs Casey turned they saw the chauffeur inviting the occupants to leave by silently holding the door open and indicating with a nod of his huge scarred head that they should vacate the premises.

'You won't know of me or my business,' the gentleman went on, guiding Mrs Casey towards a seat. 'Suffice to say I was instrumental in Sean securing the Excel Containers contract last year, a contract which I understand is now yielding a handsome return. For us to maintain and expand the business, I propose to retain my links to the company – with your agreement, of course, Mrs Casey.' He smiled at her. 'You are its titular head now and I need you to sign a letter of agreement. As manager of the company, Mr Slaney, I also need you to sign a letter of agreement – an agreement binding you to the company until Alexander comes of age and can take over its running.'

The gentleman withdrew two official-looking papers from a slim document case. Mrs Casey could only stare at him. For once she was speechless.

'Before you ask, Sean spoke to me on that fateful night and requested that I take this action if anything should go wrong,' the gentleman said. 'If you doubt any of this, I have here a deed of covenant, signed prior to the finalisation of the Excel contract last year. That deed hands control of all Sean's assets to me in order to secure your future, Mrs Casey, should you find yourself in such circumstances as you are in now. In light of the surprise arrival of Alexander, I now undertake to extend the period of my responsibility until he turns twenty-one.'

For a moment neither Mrs Casey nor Michael Slaney could speak.

Then Mrs Casey turned to Michael. 'I don't understand,' she said. 'Sean's business was Sean's business. You know that,

Michael. You help me decide what's to be done. I can't think straight. I've just lost the light of my life.' She turned to the gentleman. 'And how did you know about the child, Mr ... whatever your name is? Who told you about him?'

'As I just explained, I spoke with Sean that night,' he replied, tapping his cane impatiently on the flagged floor.

'Mrs Casey's had a great shock with Sean's murder,' Michael said in a low voice, 'not helped by all the publicity and lack of effort by the guards. So I think you should feck off and leave us alone.' Michael almost spat the last words out.

'I apologise again for the intrusion at this time, but business will not wait, even at times like these – especially at times like these. Decisions have to be taken, and taken now.' The man stared at Michael, then at Mrs Casey. 'Believe me, you don't have any choice in this matter, Mr Slaney, Mrs Casey.' The gentleman's words carried an air of finality that silenced Michael.

'What do we get out of these agreements you want us to sign?' Mrs Casey asked.

'A secure future for you and your grandchild, Mrs Casey, without any financial worries.' He turned to Michael. 'Job security and an excellent income for you, Mr Slaney, provided you continue to perform as you have in the past.' He glanced up at the chauffeur, then back to Mrs Casey and Michael. 'I will not meet either of you again,' he continued. 'Everything will be handled by my office. Here is the telephone number. It is ex-directory and for your use only.' He laid a business card on the table face down.

'Where do I sign?' Mrs Casey said wearily.

'I'll go with it as well,' Michael added.

The gentleman slid the agreements over the table to them with a swanky pen, indicating where they were to sign.

'Thank you,' he said politely as he collected the signed papers. 'And I do apologise for the intrusion.' He picked up his pen, tucked it into an inside pocket and left, the chauffeur gently pulling the door behind them.

Michael turned to Mrs Casey. 'What the hell was Sean involved in? Look, I'll take you home. That's enough for one day, God help us.'

'Sean's gone. It's up to us now. Whatever dealings he had with Mr ...' She paused and handed him the business card. 'You read it. I've forgotten my glasses.'

Michael took the card. 'There's no name on the bloody thing. No fecking address either. What the hell sort of a business card is this. Just a bloody phone number.'

Mrs Casey narrowed her eyes. 'It might come in handy some day. Here, did you notice another thing – he kept his gloves on the whole time he was here, except when he shook hands with us. He's a deep one, that's for sure. But if he was good enough for Sean Casey, he's good enough for me.'

Chapter 2

The inquest at Coleraine Crown Court heard that Alfred Spencer McNabb never saw the juggernaut that hit him as he turned out of the car park of Robinson Memorial Hospital in Ballymoney in March 1987. The lorry was coming the wrong way up a one-way street and Alfred wasn't paying enough attention, having just been present at the birth of his first and only son. The driver was foreign, didn't understand even the basic road signs and had not taken his regulation rest breaks. The coroner recorded a verdict of unlawful killing.

The strangest thing about the whole sorry incident was the respectable gentleman who attended the funeral. Afterwards, at the house in Portballintrae, he introduced himself as Alfred's silent business partner and offered to buy his share of the dead man's newsagent's shop. He apologised for this indiscreet mention of business at such a sad time, but stressed the urgency of reopening the shop to maintain customer loyalty. The mention of a small trust to pay for the widow's newborn son's further education, should he choose to attend university in the future, was a generous bonus. This made sense to Mrs McNabb, who was far from traumatised by the death of a man whom she neither loved nor respected.

The gentleman did not mention his name, or take a cup of tea or anything to eat. Mrs McNabb was left with the memory of an elegantly dressed man who wore a pair of fine leather gloves, carried a distinctive black malacca cane and offered a business card with only a phone number as a parting shot.

Two weeks after the funeral, Mrs McNabb took baby William to stay with friends in Donegal. When she returned, she discovered the house had been burgled. Nothing seemed to have been taken; it was more of a professional search carried out in a systematic manner. The police said the intruders had been looking for something specific.

The shop closed a month later.

* * *

The teenage Willy McNabb could best be summed up as a geek. Shortish, fattish, and 'yuk' was how the girls described him; compact and studious was how his mother liked to think of him. His John Lennon glasses and sticky-out ears did cause her some disappointment, and his unruly mop of blonde hair made him look too much like his father, but she took consolation in the fact that he had 'brains to burn', according to his teachers.

Willy, meanwhile, thought his mother and teachers were plain dumb. The reason for this youthful arrogance was his incredible self-taught computer skills. Unknown to them, he was a worldwide phenomenon: the most sought-after hacker in the business. No one knew who Mouseman was, but many were keen to find out.

For his thirteenth birthday, his mother had allowed him to move into, and furnish to his own taste (within reason), his father's old room. It had a wonderful view over the harbour and a built-in wardrobe. But that wasn't what interested Willy most about the room.

When the new carpet was being fitted, he discovered his father's secret hiding place under the floorboards beneath the bed. In it was a small cash box and a collection of old but graphically stimulating magazines. By the time he finally moved into the room, the loose floorboard hidey-hole had been replaced by a fireproof security cupboard purchased with birthday money, a cupboard his mother said spoiled her efforts at interior decoration. To appease her, Willy promised to do his own cleaning, which satisfied her well enough.

Each afternoon after school, he would open up his office,

as he liked to think of his room, select a target and get down to business. By the age of sixteen his list of successes was impressive; Mouseman was a legend in cyberspace. He was wanted by five European governments and by the Australian and US security services. Some wanted to punish him for exposing their inadequacies while others wanted to learn from him. But there was one person who was particularly keen to find Mouseman.

Along with the cash box and the dirty magazines under the floorboards, Willy had found a little red book filled with an incomprehensible alphanumeric code written out neatly in his father's handwriting. Of course it didn't take Willy long to crack the code. It led to five interest-bearing bank accounts in Liechtenstein and the Cayman Islands which between them held a total of £2,013,564.08 on the last transaction date, 27 March 1987, Willy's birthday. Unfazed, Willy had set that information aside for attention at some point in the future and continued with his hacking, unaware that some seriously dangerous people were now looking for him. They knew that someone had accessed the accounts but they didn't know exactly who.

At the age of eighteen, he was accepted at Queen's University in Belfast to study computer science and politics. He could have gained a first-class honours in computer science by the end of his *first* year of studies, never mind after three.

'How did you develop such skills and knowledge at your age?' his tutor enquired at the end of the first term.

'When you looked like I did in my early teens, you realised you needed something the school bully hadn't got, something to trade for protection,' Willy explained. 'My homework and test results were the most plagiarised in the school's history.'

Such was his self-confidence that Willy fearlessly charged to the rescue of a damsel in distress at the students' union one evening. He had imbibed a little more than he should have, and, although only five foot ten, unfit and podgy, he suddenly saw himself as a Belfast version of Clark Kent. He dispatched the damsel's tormentor with a high degree of luck and a small degree of skill, his first and only punch landing exactly on target. So it was that Willy established a reputation for being a hard man as well as an academic genius.

He also became very friendly with the damsel, an attractive redhead from Wicklow called Siobhan Toomey, known to everyone as Toots, though she wouldn't say why. Her commitment to Irish nationalism scared him at first, but their cosy pillow talk eventually kindled in Willy a passion for Irish politics and he became as fervent a supporter of Irish unity as Toots was, a situation his mother, a diehard Protestant, considered 'sinful' and refused to discuss.

Chapter 3

Alex Casey grew up fast – he had to, to survive in Dublin's docks area. Although money wasn't a problem, his grandmother was as stubborn as a tired mule. By his sixth birthday their house and two others were the only remaining occupied houses in Carmel Street. Michael Slaney had tried; Father Ignatius Tomelty had tried; the port authority had tried; the guards had tried; the city council had tried – all to no avail. Mrs Casey flatly refused to move – that is, until one day when she took Alex to the beach at Sandymount.

Alex was playing there with some kids about his own age. When the other kids started to pick on Alex because of the part of Dublin he came from, throwing sand in his face and hitting him with their spades, he retaliated with his fists. This led to an older boy getting involved, and then the whole family. Mrs Casey, who had been dozing, was woken by the yelling and shouts of the children and released a string of expletives at the other kids that would have shamed a docker. The other children's mother looked horrified until a bystander, complimenting Mrs Casey on her ability to swear for half a minute without repeating herself, explained what had happened. Peace returned, but poor Alex was nearly blind with sand and bawling his head off.

'Bring him up to my house and I'll wash his eyes out,' suggested the other children's mother, who introduced herself as Mrs Harvey. 'I'm a nurse and I live just over there.' She indicated the houses across the road from the beach. 'Come on, kids, let's go.'

She took Alex's hand and set off at a trot, followed by her own brood. By the time Mrs Casey had gathered all her paraphernalia, the Harveys and Alex had crossed the road and were in the drive of a neat one-and-a-half-storey bungalow.

'In here,' Mrs Harvey shouted and disappeared round the side of the house, Alex in tow.

Mrs Casey entered the open back door and set her bundle of stuff on the kitchen table. She looked round the room admiringly and pulled out a chair. An Aga cooker, the only material thing in this world that she coveted, dominated the back wall of the room.

'Tea, coffee, a mineral?' said a gentle male voice from behind her. 'Doctor Stewart Harvey at your service. I understand my children owe your son an apology.'

'Children will be children,' Mrs Casey said, blushing with pleasure at being taken for Alex's mother. 'Alex is actually my grandson, though I've brought him up like a mother. I think it's me what owes you and your missus an apology. That was a right mouthful I came out with. If Father Tomelty hears about this, he'll be hard on me come Sunday.'

When they were leaving the house later, after a cup of tea, Mrs Casey noticed the 'For Sale' sign at the gate.

'You're leaving?'

'Yes, we're off to Australia next month,' replied Mrs Harvey.

'Would you mind if I had a look at the rest of the house?' asked Mrs Casey.

Eight weeks later a handful of sand had succeeded where the good, the holy, the wise and the law had failed. Mrs Casey and Alex moved into 87, Beach Road, Sandymount, and threw a house-warming party the neighbours were to talk about for years.

For his seventeenth birthday, Alex was given ten driving lessons and the promise of a car if he passed the test on the first go. On the evening of his fourth driving lesson with Jackie, his twenty-eight-year-old instructor, he lost his virginity. His ability to mistake her right leg for the handbrake, and her need to check that the waist strap of his seatbelt was in the correct position led to this joyous coupling. Subsequent extracurricular activity ensured a pass for Alex and a VW Polo estate as the prize for that pass.

No. 87 became the office for Casey Transport, as well as their home. Norma, their bookkeeper, had taken over the dining room. Michael Slaney usually came up from the docks each morning for coffee and to update Gran. He had become something of a surrogate father to Alex, who talked to him about things he thought his gran ought not to be bothered with. During one of the chats with Gran, Michael expressed his concerns for the business and Alex's future.

'He finishes school in a few months and says he wants to drive for Casey Transport,' Michael explained. 'He's ready to do his HGV test and could be on the road by July. But I think it would be a mistake for him to drive full-time. Let him do the test and drive during the summer – it would help me with holiday cover, which is always a problem – then pack him off to business college. We won't have our mysterious business adviser for much longer, and I'm thinking of retiring when Alex is able to take over.'

That evening, after much arguing, Alex accepted his gran's plan for his future. He passed his HGV with flying colours, spent his summer holidays driving lorries for the family firm, and in October 2005 he entered the hallowed portals of Trinity College Dublin, that 'decadent outpost of English imperialism and Protestantism', according to Father Tomelty.

Mrs Casey never discussed money with Alex. From an early age he had become used to a fairly generous allowance. His relief-driving at weekends was both financially rewarding and a great lady-puller. He confided to Michael Slaney that the posh birds seemed to enjoy a bit of educated rough, especially on an overnight trip to Cork or the like, in the cab of a modern artic. Michael, for his part, envied Alex his youth and the opportunities that lay ahead.

That all changed, however, one day in the summer of 2009 when Alex met Willy McNabb.

Chapter 4

Toots, Alex's second cousin with whom she was close, brought her new boyfriend, Willy, down to Wicklow at the start of the summer holidays to meet her family. They'd arranged to meet her mother and Alex for lunch in Sweeney's, where Toots's late father, Tommy, was still affectionately remembered.

After four pints of Guinness, Alex turned to Willy. 'Now then,' he said, 'what's a wee Northern Prod like you doing with Siobhan Toomey, the daughter of one of the heroes of our struggle?'

Had it not been for the smile lurking at the corners of Toots's mouth, Willy would have been scared. Sensing the spirit of the interrogation, he decided to play to the gallery.

'Toots told me a little about you and your family background,' Willy said, removing his glasses and polishing them furiously. 'So, can I ask: what does the S stand for in Alex S. Casey?'

Alex looked at Toots, hands on hips. 'You never. Bejesus, you never told him, did you?' He tried to glower at her but a smile tugged at the corners of his mouth. He had suffered ridicule as a child because of his names. At least he'd been able to shorten the first one, but his middle name he never used at all if he could avoid it.

Toots started to laugh, then her mother joined in and soon a small crowd at the bar was chuckling.

As the laughter died down, Alex stepped back a pace, stood to attention and in his best pretend Northern accent announced: 'Alexander Sebastian Casey at your service! And if you so much as smirk, I'll knock your fecking block off!'

The onlookers erupted into laughter again. Alex insisted on buying everyone a round of drinks and while they were waiting, Alex turned to Willy.

'You'll do all right, Proddy boy,' he said, smiling. 'Toots told me about your stunt in the students' union last year. Thank you for looking out for her. I'm pleased to call you a friend.'

Completely taken aback, Willy could only mutter his thanks and blush to the roots of his wayward thatch. Toots saved him any further embarrassment by announcing that she was hungry and sweeping him, Alex and Mrs Toomey off to dinner in the pub's restaurant that evening.

During the meal Willy learned a lot about his hosts and imparted a little about his own family. It made him realise how little he knew about his father, and he resolved to investigate his family history. There had to be an interesting explanation for the money he had discovered in the offshore bank accounts, and for his mother's refusal to talk about his father. He wondered, not for the first time, who had established the trust fund that was financing him through university.

After the meal and a few more jars, Mrs Toomey asked Willy if he would like to stay the night at her house. Before he could say anything Toots butted in.

'Thanks for the offer, Ma, but Willy has booked us into the Laragh Grange Hotel.'

'Ah, that's nice,' Mrs Toomey said, smiling knowingly. 'You get a good night's sleep, Willy. You've a long drive ahead of you tomorrow, and your mother will be expecting you to be in good form for her party.'

His mother was throwing a huge party for her fiftieth and had invited a guest for every year. Willy was dreading it, but the prospect of a night's fun with Toots cheered him up no end. After more laughter and backslapping, Willy and Toots excused themselves, said their goodbyes to everyone and walked out to the car. When they reached his car Willy looked at Toots, a quizzical expression on his face.

'Out the gate, turn right and follow the signs for the Wicklow Gap,' Toots said getting into the car. 'You'll see the hotel in a few minutes, and don't ask questions.'

'Yes ma'am!'

Willy had no idea what was going on, but he could hope. He lowered the soft top of his convertible VW Beetle and accelerated out the gate, gravel flying and both laughing uncontrollably.

'I really shouldn't be driving ... the amount I've had to drink. And I'm starting to get a sore head. I'm going to have the mother and father of hangovers tomorrow.'

'Stop complaining, you wimp. It was a great party. Mum and Alex both liked you, so you should feel honoured. It's not everyone who gets to meet my favourite cousin and stays standing. He either drinks them under the table, if he likes them, or throws them out if he doesn't.'

'That's nice to know, but it's not going to cure my head tomorrow.'

'Well, I think I have just the cure.' A half-smile played about her lips.

When they pulled up at the imposing Georgian entrance of the Laragh Grange Hotel, Willy was impressed. The building was magnificent with its columned portico, grand sash windows and a spectacular outlook. The arrival of a liveried porter brought him down to earth with a bump. The bill! Even before he was inside he knew it would be way over his budget. Willy looked at Toots who smiled at his obvious discomfort. She turned to the porter.

'We get a special rate here, Eoin, don't we?'

'Most definitely, Miss Toomey. Your father was held in high regard in these parts, as are all the family, of course.' He collected their rather cheap-looking bags from the Beetle and led Toots up the steps to the entrance.

At reception, Toots checked them into their room and they

followed the porter up in the lift with their bags. The lift doors opened onto a luxuriously appointed hall with only one other door leading off.

'I hope you like it. It's all they had,' said Toots, grinning mischievously.

She punched a number into the keypad and walked into a stunning drawing room, furnished with antiques, original oil paintings and heavy silk drapes. The scent from numerous floral displays was enveloping, nearly cloying.

'Bloody hell! This one room is bigger than my whole flat in Belfast,' Willy said, turning full circle, taking in the luxurious room, its marble fireplace and extravagant furniture. 'I can't possibly afford this, Toots – even at your special rate.'

'You don't have to worry about that. Our family get a *very* special rate – it's not costing a cent.'

Willy shook his head, dumbstruck. He walked to a door opposite the one they'd come in. It opened into a secondary hall with doors off to the right and left. He opened the door on the left. The vision of marble, mirrors and gold fittings stunned him. The double bath, twin basins and enormous wet area caused Willy to step back. Toots stood in the middle of the drawing room, enjoying herself immensely as she watched him tour the suite in amazement. Finally, Willy opened the bedroom door and gasped as he walked in. The four-poster bed that occupied the centre of the floor was pure theatre. The room resembled a Hollywood set with its lavish furniture and paintings; the carpet came to the top of his shoes.

That night they explored every room in the suite. They fooled about in the double bath, they drank wine from the minibar, they listened to music and watched TV, but mostly they couldn't keep their hands off each other.

Finally, sated and exhausted, they slept.

Chapter 5

The next day, after Willy had left, Toots hitched a lift with Alex in a lorry run to Galway. She was meeting a couple of her girlfriends there; they were going on a road trip up the west coast to Falcarragh.

On the journey from Dublin to Galway Toots talked incessantly about Willy McNabb. She was obviously very taken with him and Alex was pleased for her: Willy seemed like a nice lad – a bit wet behind the ears, but Toots would soon sort that out. They stopped for a cuppa at a Truckers' Halt, one of a chain across the country, and Alex took the opportunity to find out more about Willy's computer skills.

'Can Willy trace family trees on the internet?' he asked. 'Does he know anything about it?'

'About what? Genealogy? Sure all you do is go onto one of those family tree websites, put in your surname and away you go.'

'Not that easy, Toots. I've tried that and can get nowhere. I keep hitting brick walls. I just wondered, with him being a computer geek and all that.'

'He's more than a geek, you thick truckie. He's studying computer programming at university.'

'Oh, hark at her,' Alex said, laughing.

Toots took a swipe at him. 'Seriously, Alex, why are you asking?'

'I'm trying to find out about Mum and Dad. Gran won't tell me anything. She says she never met my mum and gets very defensive when I mention the old man. Michael's the same, though I'm convinced he knows more than he's saying.'

'I can always ask Willy if he'd have a look for you,' Toots said. 'He could do the Toomeys at the same time. I don't think too much about it because I know what happened to Dad, but I'd like to know more too.'

Toots rummaged through her rucksack for her mobile. When she found it, she pressed one button.

'So you have him on speed dial!' said Alex, smiling and ducking as Toots took another swipe at him.

'Hiya, Willy!' she said into the phone. 'Are you home yet? ... I'm with Alex and he wants to talk to you about computers, believe it or not.'

Toots handed the phone to Alex.

'Afternoon, Willy. How are you feeling today? Head not too sore, I hope? ... Those wee beds in that place are awful uncomfortable, aren't they?' Alex turned to Toots: 'He says it's his back that's sore.'

Toots clobbered Alex across the head.

'Ah, bloody hell, she's attacking me,' Alex said to Willy, laughing as he spilt his tea. 'She's going to get us thrown out of this place into the bargain. Listen, do you know anything about tracing family trees and the like? ... How do you go about investigating it?'

Alex nodded and uh-huhed for a few minutes as he listened to Willy on the other end.

'Top man! That's great. I'll talk to Toots about it on the way to Galway and then she can give you the details. A pint or two and an evening's craic sounds a fair enough price to me! Here's Toots for you. Cheers!'

Alex gave the phone back to Toots. 'See you outside when you're ready. Don't let lover boy keep you too long!' he said and went to the counter to pay.

For the rest of the journey Alex and Toots discussed their families and compared notes on what they did and did not know. They agreed that Michael Slaney must know a lot more than he let on about Sean Casey and Thomas Toomey. But they decided that the best thing to do was to give Willy as much information as possible and see what he could find out first, then sit down with Michael and their own families.

* * *

Toots's friends were waiting for them at the ferry port in Galway, the starting point for their odyssey. Liz O'Gorman, the noisy one, was on a gap year before studying medicine at NUI Galway. She was the great-niece of Senator Eugene O'Gorman, a staunch republican who allegedly opposed the use of violence. The other girl was Kate Rutherford, a stunning six-foot-tall goddess whose father owned one of the most successful estate agencies in Dublin, specialising in development property and foreign investment. He acted for the National Bank of Kuwait and the Sultan of Brunei, among others. Alex was immediately love-struck when he was introduced to Kate; she didn't seem quite as impressed by his tendency to ogle.

Once Alex had left, the girls checked in at the guest house where they were spending the first night, then took a taxi to a restaurant and nightclub called Second Floor. Kate and Liz made it clear from the outset that they were on the hunt, but Toots wasn't interested and told them she would drop out if – *when* – they scored: two Amazonian babes on the loose were bound to attract a lot of company.

Just as they were finishing their desserts, the maître d' came to their table.

'The two gentlemen in the window seat wondered if the ladies would like to join them for a drink in the bar,' he said, adding in a conspiratorial tone, 'You would also be doing me a service. I've a late booking but no table available.'

'That's the best chat-up line I've heard tonight,' Liz said to the maître d'. 'I hope they tip you well.'

He gave her a solemn nod of the head.

She turned to Kate and Toots. 'What do you think, ladies?'

'It would be churlish to refuse the gentlemen our company,' Kate said, flashing a wicked grin. 'Let's go.'

As the girls left the dining room, Toots's mobile burst into life, its horrendous ringtone blasting out round the restaurant. She winced and went out to the foyer to answer the call.

'Do you miss me already, you lovely man, or are you keeping tabs on me?' she purred sexily into the phone. 'I was going to phone later anyway and tell you about my chat with Alex.'

'I couldn't wait. I wanted to hear your voice. Where are you? It sounds noisy.'

'We've just had dinner at Second Floor. The girls have been invited for drinks in the bar.'

'You too?'

Toots could hear the anxiety in his voice. 'I'm on my best behaviour, I promise. I thought you'd be helping your mum get ready for her birthday party.'

'There's nothing to help with. She's had a tribe of helpers all week. Some quiet affair this is going to be! Her friends have persuaded her that fifty is a glorious age. It's great to see her with a smile on her face, not her usual frown. Listen, I had a look into this family tree stuff and set up an account for Alex. But I can't get very far.'

'Yeah, that's what he said too. He can't get anywhere with it.'

'Someone seems to have gone to a lot of trouble to stop him from finding out any information about his family. And it's not just Alex's family, it's yours too. Because your mum and Alex's dad were cousins, the Toomey name came up straight away, but someone has kicked sand over that trail too. And whoever has blocked access to your families' information has also set up search alerts: when anyone searches for those names, they get notified by email. The problem is, they'll be able to trace the searches back to my IP address.'

'Bloody hell! What's that all about? You make it sound as though we have some great family skeleton in the cupboard.'

'Whatever it is, it's serious. I recognise the IP address of the person blocking the info.'

'And? Who is it? Are you breaking the law doing this? Because if you are I want no part in it.'

'No, no, I'm not breaking the law. This is well below the law's radar. I don't want to say any more on the phone. I need to meet you and Alex face-to-face to sort this out. There's a good chance I'll want no part in it either.'

Their phone call ended a little less romantically than it started.

Poor Toots! The anguish was obvious on her face when she returned to the bar. Liz came over with a lime-green cocktail, a cheerful paper umbrella stuck in it.

'You look like you've seen a ghost,' she said. 'Have you had some bad news?'

'No, not bad, just disturbing.'

Toots took a big gulp from the cocktail and screwed her face up. 'What the hell's in that?'

'If you want to talk, we can go back to the guest house,' Liz said. 'These guys are a little boring, to put it mildly.'

The girls jumped into the first taxi they could find and went back to the guest house. They changed out of their glad rags, put their feet up, opened family-sized packets of crisps and passed the vodka round.

Soon Toots was explaining why Willy was looking into their family trees and what he'd found, trying to keep it fairly light.

'What about Alex's mum and dad. Can't they tell him more?' Kate asked.

'Alex never knew his folks. He was raised by his gran, and she can't – or won't – tell him anything. She's old and probably doesn't want to revisit painful memories.'

'I think every family has some relative who's not talked about,' Liz said. 'My dad's uncle, Eugene O'Gorman, has some history or something. I heard Dad once on the phone shouting something about Eugene and his wife, Alice, and telling the person to never say that again. I don't know who he was talking to, but he was fair ripping when he came off the phone. Told my mother it was that bastard Blaney or Slaney, or something like that. I was quite young at the time, so I don't remember much more.'

'And my great-grandfather was thrown out of Scotland for sheep stealing,' said Kate. 'We're all the same, only different.'

Toots started to think she was being a little dramatic. Another couple of drinks, a few more laughs and they were all set for bed.

The next morning, after a full Irish, the girls were still sitting round the breakfast table when Toots's wretched ringtone disturbed the peace again.

'Haha, is that lover boy calling? Hot for you first thing in the morning,' said Liz, laughing. 'Put it on speakerphone so we can all pitch in.'

'Go to hell,' retorted Toots, smiling as she left the kitchen. 'Two chicks who couldn't pull last night – some help you'd be.'

'Morning, Toots!' Alex's strong voice always reassured her. 'Hope I'm not too early for you guys. I've been on the go since six.'

'Well, we went for a walk at seven, so you needn't crow. It's too beautiful a morning to be lying in bed.'

'Mmmm, not as beautiful as it should be, I'm afraid. Patsy Dan's lorry was torched last night in the secure park at Balbriggan. Some fucking lowlife full of drink or drugs no doubt. The guards don't hold out much hope of "apprehending the guilty party or parties", to quote them. Why the hell do they use such ridiculous language instead of just saying they haven't a hope in hell of catching the fuckers?'

Toots's mood changed completely. 'Jesus! Was Patsy Dan hurt? Was somebody else hurt? You didn't phone me to tell me about a burnt lorry.'

'No, no one was hurt. It's something more ominous than a burnt-out lorry, for sure. I came back to Sandymount this morning so Gran wasn't on her own. She was a bit shaken up by the whole drama. The guards had called her about the lorry in the wee hours of the morning. Anyway, when I fired up the office computer this morning, there's this email addressed to me. It's not nice, Toots. It says, in caps, "Leave it alone. Next time someone gets hurt. Remember the letter." There's no name, no sender's email address, nothing – just the message.'

'Christ! Has Gran seen it?'

'No, no. She knows nothing about it.'

'What about the guards, Alex. You should phone them. This is serious. And what about Michael? Phone him too.'

'I tried but he's gone fishing for the weekend. I asked Mrs Slaney to tell him to phone me urgently if he called her. But I need someone to try to trace the email. Could Willy do that?'

'Jesus, Alex, just ring the guards. They can do all that stuff. It's their job, not yours or Willy's.'

'I can't do that – not till I know who sent it and what letter it's referring to. I need to get hold of Michael. He'll know what to do. He might know about the letter. But, in the meantime, I want to try and at least trace the source.'

'Oh Alex, this is awful. Willy phoned me last night, and wait till you hear this.' Toots told him about how Willy was trying to trace the family trees.

'Jesus, Toots, that's weird!'

'Do you think the email is linked to the lorry fire?'

'I don't see why it would be. The lorry was just a night's entertainment for some fucker with too much time and cheap booze on his hands. Will you speak to Willy – ask him to phone me?'

'Of course I will. Give me five minutes and I'll call you back. Go and have a cup of tea with Gran. She'll be glad of your company.'

Toots phoned Willy's number, but it was engaged. Back in the bedroom the girls were drinking already. Liz had opened a bottle of champagne and made Buck's Fizz.

'That must have been some dirty phone call – you look shagged,' she quipped. 'Come and get some fizz and share all the steamy details.' By the sound of her voice Liz had had two or three fizzes already.

'Not dirty and no steamy details. That was Alex. His gran isn't too well and he's asked if I'd mind going back to Sandymount for a couple of days before I go on with you guys.' Toots decided it was easier to lie than face any questions from Liz and Kate.

The girls reassured her it was fine. The plan was to go on to Bearna, to a holiday cottage owned by Liz's family. They were going to hang around for the Galway Regatta and Toots could rejoin them later. Toots packed up her stuff and got a taxi to the railway station. In the taxi her phone rang; the caller ID said it was a private number. She answered it and asked who was calling, but the line went dead. Then she called Alex back.

'I can't get hold of Willy,' she explained. 'His line's engaged, but I left a message. I'm in a taxi on my way to the station. I'll catch the next train to Dublin.'

'We'll be in time for the ten thirty,' the taxi driver volunteered.

'Did you hear that, Alex? I'll be on the ten thirty. Will you meet me at Heuston?'

'Sure thing. I'll tell Gran to expect you for lunch. That'll put a smile on her face.'

At the station, Toots's phone rang again just as she was paying her fare.

'Jesus, you could get done for disturbing the peace with that racket!' said the taxi driver, giving her her change.

'It's top of my to-do list,' she said with a sheepish smile.

'Hello, Willy,' Toots cooed down the phone, relieved to hear his voice. 'Listen, we've another problem.' She told him about the burnt-out lorry and the threatening anonymous email that Alex had been sent. Then she texted him Alex's number, adding a saucy message of her own.

Chapter 6

'Morning, Alex. It's Willy. Toots asked me to give you a call. Something about an anonymous email?'

'Yeah, some bastard has sent me a threatening email but I can't see who it's from. I know you've got family commitments today, but I really would appreciate some help, Willy.'

'Not a bother, big man. Are you at the computer now?'

'Yep, I'm looking at the bloody thing.'

'Okay, I'm going to email you some instructions, which you must follow exactly, and then I want you to forward the anonymous email to me,' Willy said. 'Don't do anything else on your computer until you hear from me. I want to give my mum her birthday present and have a quick bite of breakfast. Then I'm all yours for an hour or so.'

An hour later Willy was ensconced in his office looking at the email from Alex. As he traced its IP address he became more and more concerned. It seemed to have come from the same source that had blocked the Casey and Toomey family tree searches. Something also prompted him to check the IP address that had set up the secure access to the bank accounts he'd uncovered in his dad's little red book. It was all generated from the same IP address. Willy was stunned. He went in search of his mum.

'A pal of mine in Wicklow has a major problem with his computer and—'

'—has asked you to help him. Willy, I can read you like a book. I told Mavis you'd come up with some excuse to miss my party. I'm very disappointed.'

'Ah, Mum, I'm sorry. Sure, his computer will keep for a day. I'll stay.'

'I'm only joking, son. Away you go, and thank you again for my scarf. It's beautiful. I just love it!'

Willy went back to his room to throw a few things in a bag and looked at his laptop screen. 'Oh fuck, the bastard's trying to trace me!'

He immediately switched off his router and phoned Alex. 'Disconnect your internet now!' he barked, not bothering with any pleasantries. 'Do you know how to do that?'

'I think so, but why?'

'Just do it. I'll explain in a minute.'

Alex came back on the line after a few moments. 'Willy, what the hell's going on?'

'Just a precaution, big man. I think we may have walked into a hornet's nest. Your phantom emailer is the same guy who put the block on your family tree searches and set up the security on some bank accounts I hacked into a few years ago. Someone is trying very hard to hide something.

'What's this all about?' Alex sounded perplexed.

'I hoped you could answer that one. I'll help all I can, but I need to know where we're going with this and who we're up against. Is it legal? Is it physically dangerous?'

'I know about as much as you, Willy. Listen, Michael Slaney phoned just before you did, and when I told him about the lorry fire he said he would pack up and come back to Dublin immediately. Reckons he can be here mid-afternoon. I'm on my way to the station soon to collect Toots. She's coming to be with Gran who's a bit shook up.'

'Right, I'll be leaving shortly, so I should be there mid-afternoon as well. It's going to be quite a party.'

'I don't expect you to come down! What about your ma's birthday party? She'll be well pissed off with you.'

'She'll be well pissed all right – she's been on the gin already. She says she didn't expect me to stay anyway, so I'm on my way. See you later, and whatever you do, don't turn on the computer till I get there!'

Willy grabbed a change of clothes and his laptop, the little red book and a few other gadgets that he thought might be useful, ran downstairs, kissed his mum goodbye and jumped into his car.

Willy was looking forward to seeing Toots again, but he was also worried about this mysterious IP address and the consequences of his probing. The person behind it was good, very good. Willy didn't doubt his own ability to get to the bottom of it all, but he was concerned about the reaction it might precipitate. Just south of Belfast his mobile rang. He let it go to answerphone and stopped at a café just past Sprucefield. After an early lunch he took out his phone to check for a message. There was no message and the number was unknown. The remainder of the journey passed without incident, and a few hours later he pulled into 87 Beach Road, Sandymount.

Alex greeted him with a huge bear hug and led him into the office where Michael Slaney was having a heated conversation on the phone with the Garda.

* * *

The news about Patsy Dan's lorry had changed Michael Slaney's plans for the weekend. He hastily excused himself from his fishing companions, packed his bag and drove straight to No. 87. His prime concern was not the loss of the vehicle, it was the potential disaster facing him personally and Casey Transport generally. The Excel contract was the mainstay of their business and it might be in jeopardy thanks to his deceit. He could feel Sean Casey turning in his grave and he shuddered.

There was no procrastination or prevarication by An Garda Síochána when it came to Patsy Dan's lorry. Guard Brian Mulligan, a native of Clonmel and fresh out of training school, was determined to make his mark with this, his first major case. His sergeant had rather mischievously suggested that a speedy resolution might lead to a transfer to the big smoke. So by the time Michael Slaney was put through to the designated officer in charge of the case, Guard Mulligan was fired with ambition and zeal.

'Hello, Mr Slaney. You're through to Guard Mulligan. I'm the officer in charge of the investigation into an arson attack on one of Casey Transport's vehicles while it was parked up in the O'Farrell Commercial Vehicle Park on Friday night, at a time unknown and by a person or persons unknown. Any information that you can furnish us with that is deemed to be of importance in the investigation of this serious crime will be greatly appreciated and officially acknowledged by the Commissioner of An Garda Síochána in writing at a later date.'

The forensic officer, Paddy Molloy, who had been discussing his provisional findings with Mulligan when he took Slaney's call, struggled to keep a straight face. The young guard's response was straight out of the training manual.

'For Christ's sake, son,' Slaney yelled down the phone. 'I'm Casey Transport's traffic manager, among other things. Where the hell is Sergeant Reilly. He knows me.'

'I'm the officer in charge, Mr Slaney. Sergeant Reilly is not available, and even if he were, it is myself you have to liaise with. As I am in conference with Forensic Officer Molloy, I would appreciate your co-operation. After all, you phoned the guards, we didn't phone you.'

Paddy stammered his apologies and rushed out of the room. On his return a few minutes later, and still struggling to maintain his composure, Guard Mulligan was in full control judging by the faint smile on his ruddy country-boy face.

'… is very straightforward. I felt a forensic evaluation of the scene of the crime was relevant, and Officer Molloy attended. As it is the weekend, he was available immediately. Otherwise it could have taken a number of days to reach the situation we are now in.'

'And what, may I ask, is the situation you are now in?' Slaney's voice was heavy with sarcasm.

'The situation now, seeing that theft is also involved, and the lack of security on the vehicle—'

'Theft? Security? What the hell are you talking about? The bloody lorry was set on fire in a secure compound! What theft? We haven't reported any theft?'

'The security issue is this. O'Farrells are very specific in their regulations, and I quote: All vehicles parked in one of our secure compounds must be protected by the vehicle's own locking and alarm system. Unquote. The vehicle in question was not locked. Therefore the alarm system was inoperative. Also the customs seal had been removed from the locking door on the rear of the container. This is in breach of Excel Containers' security and, indeed, your own goods in transit insurance regulations and … Mr Slaney, are you still there?'

'Aye, fuck it, I'm still here. What happens now?'

'We need to arrange a meeting with yourself, your driver, a representative from Excel Containers, O'Farrell Secure Compounds and their insurer, your insurers and any other interested parties. As there has been a spate of similar misdemeanours in the Dublin docks area, I will ask the Harbour Police to send an observer. We take our responsibilities in this—'

'For fuck's sake, it's not the mafia you're dealing with! This isn't organised crime you're looking at! It's a fucking lorry fire and a bit of theft in an arsehole town! It happens every day of the fucking week somewhere in the country!'

'Mr Slaney—'

The line went dead.

* * *

Willy introduced himself to Mrs Casey, who patted the seat beside her rocking chair to indicate where he should sit. A sprightly, though slight, eighty-five-year-old, she dispensed coffee, sandwiches and cake with a steady hand and instructed him to call her Gran. With six or seven pertinent questions, she painlessly extracted Willy's entire life story.

Toots joined them in time to hear her question about his father. 'You're an incorrigible inquisitor, Gran,' she scolded. 'Even I haven't asked him that.'

'I could be dead in the morning, so I need to know who you're running with before I go.'

'No more of that kind of talk,' Toots said. 'And I'm not running with him. We're just good friends.' She winked at Willy.

'Humph! Just good friends, my foot. Then I'd like to see how you dress for your boyfriend when you meet him. There's more material in one of my dusters than's round your backside.' Mrs Casey rocked back in her chair, laughing mischievously.

Willy's eyes were drawn to Toots's bare legs and he found himself blushing.

'Share the joke. We could all do with a laugh.'

Alex's intervention couldn't have come at a more opportune moment as far as Willy was concerned.

'Let's get to work, Alex. Thanks for the coffee, Gran. It was good to meet you at last.' Willy rose from the table.

'See that, Toots? Manners as well,' Mrs Casey said. 'You'll be grand with that one.' Another gale of laughter followed Willy and Alex into the office.

'She'll have you married by the morning if you let her,' Alex said. 'She's convinced she's on borrowed time and wants to see the world put to rights before she goes.'

He introduced Willy to Michael, who was seated in front of the computer.

'*Don't touch that!*' Willy yelled, slapping Michael's hand away from the ON button. 'I need to run a few checks before it's turned on.'

'I've had it on. There's fuck all wrong with it.' Michael rose from the chair aggressively. 'Do you think because you go to college you're the only one who can solve problems? I've been doing it all my fucking life without a poncey degree, so fuck off and leave me alone.' He gathered up some papers and turned to the door.

Alex stepped in front of him. 'Nobody speaks to a friend of mine like that. Apologise now, Michael.'

Michael looked from Alex to the doorway behind him where Gran had suddenly appeared.

'He's right, Michael, he's right.' Her voice had an authoritative edge to it that surprised Willy. 'William is welcome in this house. You'll apologise and it's forgotten, or you'll leave and not come back.'

Everyone held their breath. Michael looked first at Willy, then at Alex and finally at Gran. He walked towards her and, with a half nod he put his hand on her shoulder, gently squeezing it.

'It's time I went, Gran. He's the master now. I taught him as well as I could. Whatever happens now, just remember I did it for Sean.'

As he gently pushed past Mrs Casey, Toots, who had been standing behind her, reached for his arm.

'Michael, please …'

'It's over, Toots, it's over. Sean would understand.'

He walked out the front door, pulling it closed behind him. In stunned silence they watched him get into his car and drive off.

'I'll go after him,' Alex said half-heartedly.

'No, Alex.' Gran shook her head. 'He's right. That time is over. It's your time now.' She turned towards the stairs. 'I need to lie down for an hour or so. It's going to be a long day. Toots, help me upstairs, will you.'

When Toots came back to the office, Willy was at the computer and Alex on a stool beside him. They both looked up.

'Is she all right, Toots?' There was real concern in Alex's voice. 'She's had one hell of a shock. We all have. Michael's been her crutch and friend since Sean died.'

'And it's my fault,' Willy said wretchedly. 'I shouldn't have yelled at Michael like that. I'm sorry. Me and my big mouth.'

'It's not your fault, Willy. I've never seen him like that – ever, and I've seen him well provoked in the past. There's more to his outburst than you slapping his hand.'

'Gran told me upstairs it's been brewing for months,' Toots interjected. 'And she should know – she sees him every day and has done for, what, the past twenty years?'

'Longer than that, Toots,' said Alex. 'He worked with Sean for ten or twelve years before his death. But we've a bigger problem at the minute. You tell her, Willy.'

'The computer's been hacked,' Willy said, his fingers dancing over the keyboard.

'How did that happen? Isn't it password-protected?' said Toots. 'Doesn't it have antivirus software installed? I know mine has.'

'Passwords, firewalls and off-the-shelf antivirus software will only stop an honest man. To people like me, they're like gnats to an elephant. I don't waste time trying to go through regular security software, I bypass it altogether. Someone has accessed the files on this computer – documents, email, web-browsing history – the whole lot – with the level of skill and technology that police computer forensic teams use when they're investigating corruption, money laundering, paedophilia, et cetera. He's a worthy opponent for me and I look forward to the cyber struggle. He's trying to cover his tracks, so I'm glad you forwarded me that email you received. Had you told Michael not to use the computer?'

'I did, and I know what you're thinking, but in fairness to him I didn't tell him why.'

'Listen, I'll need a bit of peace for an hour or two.'

'Okay. Just shout if you want anything.' Alex stood up and patted him on the shoulder. 'I'm away to the container yard on the East Wall Road.'

'Wait for me, Alex. I'll come with you,' Toots said before planting a big wet kiss on Willy's cheek.

He looked up at her and grinned. 'Enough, you wicked temptress. I've got work to do.'

'Scorned for an electronic mistress!' Toots said, already on her way out the door. 'See you later.'

'It's a date.'

* * *

Alex and Toots were turning into the docks off the East Wall Road when Alex suddenly braked.

'I've just seen Patsy Dan go into the pub over there. Fancy a pint?' he asked.

They left the car inside the dock gates and crossed the road. Molloy's pub hadn't changed much since Sean Casey's wake some twenty-two years previously. The clientele was just the same – hard men drinking hard liquor and not a woman in sight. The big change was the 'No Smoking' signs. There was a lean-to shelter to one side of the front door from where a handful of smokers gave Alex, and especially Toots, the once-over as they crossed the road.

One of the younger men came forward as they stepped up onto the pavement. 'You're Sean Casey's bastard, aren't you. And is this your fuck for the night?'

One of the older men extended his hand to Toots. 'The daughter of Tommy Toomey, if I'm not mistaken. Marty Pearce at your service.' Toots took his dirty, gnarled hand in hers and shook it warmly. 'Youse are both welcome here any day and I'll be buying the first pint,' he said.

The other men hooted with delight; the gobshite who first challenged them slunk back into the bar. Alex clapped Marty on the back, winked at Toots and led the way into the dingy bar.

They got a good reception inside the bar too. Two of Casey Transport's drivers came over and offered to buy them a drink. But Marty stood his ground, and the first pints were on him. Alex looked round for Patsy Dan and saw him in the corner deep in conversation with two other drivers. When Alex went over, all three of them looked up at the same time.

'How're you doing, Patsy?' Alex looked at the other two. 'I need a quick word with Patsy here. I'll only be a couple of minutes.'

He nodded towards the door and walked out. Patsy followed.

'Wha-wha-what's the problem, Alex. Nothing wrong I ho-ho-hope?'

'You've been driving for Casey's for twelve years now and in that time your record has been almost impeccable. A couple of tickets for speeding and one for an insecure load – that's not bad for fifty thousand miles a year. So I need to ask you some questions about your lorry on Friday night because it seems out of character for you. Is that okay, Patsy? You'll not be in any trouble if you're honest with me.'

Patsy swallowed hard and nodded.

'Good man. According to the guards your cab wasn't locked Friday night and the container had been opened before the rig was torched. Do you know anything about that?'

'You need to ask Mm-Mm-Michael. He met me at the p-p-park and took her in.'

'Okay. Well, why Balbriggan? Why not here?'

'Va-va-valuable load. Needed a ss-ss-secure park.'

'So how did you get back home?'

'K-K-Kitty p-p-picked me up.'

'Okay. So, who broke the customs seal and when?'

Patsy Dan shuffled about on his feet, his eyes darting left and right. In the pub window Alex saw the reflections of two men standing behind him

'I suggest you tell those assholes behind me to disappear,' he said. 'C'mon now. Tell me the truth and you'll keep your job.'

'Mm-Mm-Michael. At Balbriggan, before he parked up. The f-f-forklift was waiting when I arrived. I got down, spoke to Mm-Mm-Michael and left with K-K-Kitty.'

'Okay. Well done.' Alex looked hard at him. 'Listen, I need a new traffic manager. Are you up to the job? Another forty on top of your usual rate till we see how it goes. Start Monday morning in the office at six.'

Alex didn't have to wait long for Patsy's decision.

'Okay, I'll be there,' said Patsy, all trace of his stammer gone.

The two men shook hands and smiled at each other.

Alex turned round to face the two men who had been hovering in the background hoping for trouble.

'Do either of you work?' he asked them.

They shook their heads.

'Be in the yard at seven on Monday. Patsy Dan'll need a couple of helpers for a while. Keep your noses clean and who knows, you'll maybe get your HGVs. Let's go, Toots.'

'How do you know Patsy Dan's up to the job?' Toots asked Alex when they were back in the car. 'Never mind those other two worthless eejits. Some helpers they'll be. Help themselves more like.'

'I checked Patsy's record before I came out. It's very impressive. If he can organise as well as he drives, he can do the job. As for the other pair … set a thief to catch a thief. Right, let's go see how the computer geek is getting on.'

Chapter 7

When Alex and Toots arrived back at No. 87, Gran was sitting on a chair beside Willy who was in front of his laptop.

'This is the most wonderful machine, Alex!' Gran exclaimed enthusiastically. 'You should have explained it to me sooner. This young fella has opened my eyes to a whole lot of things I needed to know about.'

Willy polished his glasses nervously.

'And before you say anything, I made him show me,' she went on. 'Of course, I can't find my glasses when I want them, but Willy's been reading things for me.'

Alex threw Willy a look of annoyance.

'I'll go and put the kettle on. You come and help me,' Gran said, reaching for Alex's arm.

As soon as the door closed behind them, Toots confronted Willy. 'What have you done, Willy? What have you told Gran?'

'Ten minutes ago, after she spoke to someone on the phone, she came in and asked me to explain what an email was and asked specifically what was in the email that came to Alex. I told her they are computer letters and showed her some on my laptop as examples. I put up the email and read it to her.'

Alex put his head round the door. 'Come on to the table. Gran has a cup of tea poured,' he said before going back into the kitchen.

The three of them sat at the table and helped themselves to tea and sandwiches. Then Gran came in and sat down. She had a slim document case in her hand, something Alex had never seen before. No one spoke while she comfied herself at the table, took a drink of tea and then opened the case.

'Read this, Alex, till you understand what it means,' she said, setting a letter in front of him.

Alex read the letter silently, slowly turning white as his eyes scanned down the typed page:

> Sean Casey, the following instructions are to be followed to the letter. Any deviation will be dealt with severely, which will be very unpleasant for your mother or anyone foolish enough to interfere on your behalf.
>
> No contact is to be made with me or any member of my family.
>
> No one, especially the civil and religious authorities, is <u>ever</u> to be told who the mother of the infant is. Our encounter never took place. I have never had a child, by you or by anyone else. If I ever hear to the contrary, the infant will live the rest of its life an orphan.
>
> The child is to be raised in a right and proper manner, given a good education and encouraged to attend university in whatever vocation is appropriate – other than the church!
>
> The child's well-being and its future will be monitored from a distance by representatives of my family who will report to me on a regular basis.
>
> The child is not to be taken out of the country, except for holidays, until he is 18.
>
> The money enclosed with this letter is the amount that will be delivered to your mother every three months. It is to be used primarily for the benefit of the child, but should you or your mother fall on hard times it will be adjusted accordingly. Do not take this as a meal ticket, however. You are expected to contribute to the child's future, as any father should.

A postscript was added at the end of the letter in a beautiful flowing feminine hand:

Casey, I have one favour to ask, but if my family hear of this it will be the worse for both of us! Please name the infant after my great-uncle – Alexander Sebastian. Not very 'docks area', I know, but I'm sure you will explain it away in your usual inimitable fashion.

The blood completely drained from Alex's face and he slumped further down in his seat each time he reread the letter.

After reading it for the fifth time, he handed the letter to Toots, stood up and walked round the table to Gran. She seemed to shrink into her seat, as if fearing the worst, but Alex knelt at the side of her chair and wrapped his enormous arms around her. Toots shook her head as she read the letter, her mouth hanging open.

Feeling uncomfortable at this scene that he neither understood nor was a part of, Willy left the table and went outside. Ten minutes later, Toots came out to find him sitting with his back against the trunk of a tree in the back garden. She knelt down in front of him and handed over the letter.

'You'd better read this, Willy,' she said. 'It'll throw some light on the things you're concerned about.'

When he'd finished reading the letter he looked at Toots. 'This explains a lot. The denied access to information about the family tree, the email, the wiped computer – maybe even the burnt-out lorry.'

'There's more you don't know about – stuff Alex and I discovered today at the pub,' Toots said.

'How's Alex taking it? Disowned by his mother at birth – worse than that, denied by his *own* mother!'

'Oh my God, I hadn't thought about it like that. I was thinking about what the threat meant. Poor Alex ... and poor Gran! She's had to deal with this all these years!'

'Well, Toots, it's up to us to do what we can to put things right. Gran and Alex will have a lot to talk about, so let me go in and gather my bits and pieces. Do they still want my help to find out who's behind all this?'

'I'm sure they do. You wait here for a few minutes and I'll see how they are.' Toots gave Willy a quick kiss full on the lips.

By the time Willy came back into the kitchen, some semblance of normality had returned. Alex and Gran were seated at the table side by side and Toots was standing behind them looking rather serious.

'This changes everything, Willy,' Alex said. 'Toots says you want to carry on trying to trace the email, but it's a whole different problem now. This letter changes everything. Your offer of help is much appreciated, but I can't let you become involved. It's too risky now.' Alex's tone of voice was firm.

'It's not that easy, big man,' Willy said. 'You need my help. Take this to the authorities and it'll disappear in a quagmire of bureaucracy. In any case, whoever's driving this thing is trying to trace me now. They appear to have access to very sophisticated equipment, so it's only a matter of time before they identify me. It's too late for me to back out now. And I want to keep an eye on Toots.'

With that he walked into the office and started to gather his bits and pieces. Alex followed him into the room and closed the door.

'I don't know what to say, Willy.'

'Then don't say anything, big man. You and your gran have a lot of ground to cover and it's all relevant to the problem in hand – at least I assume it is – so the sooner you deal with that the quicker we get to the answer. I'm off to a local hotel that has broadband. I might need to go home tomorrow for another piece of equipment, but we'll see. You've got my number. Give me a call when you've anything of interest.'

'Thanks, Willy. I owe you one,' said Alex. 'Go to Hall's Hotel at Ballsbridge, almost opposite the RDS showground. Excel Containers use it when any of their brass is over from England, so it must be okay. It'll have all the facilities you need. I'll phone ahead and organise a room for you.'

Alex left the office, and as Willy followed him through the kitchen Mrs Casey gently put a hand on his arm.

'I'll say thank you as well. I don't understand what you can achieve with all this computer stuff, but I'll be very grateful for any help you give Alex. I'll pray for you.'

Outside, the sun was setting, casting a copper-yellow wash over the beach across the road. The twin stacks of the power station loomed in the background. They seemed to add to the sense of melancholy that enveloped Willy.

'Let's go and do some work,' Willy said to Toots as they jumped into his car.

* * *

Alex led Gran into the sitting room and settled her into her favourite chair. Then he went into the kitchen and returned two minutes later with a tray on which were a bottle of Irish whiskey and a bottle of vintage port, two glasses, a jug of water and a tin of shortbread biscuits. 'Gran's delight' she called it when, on special occasions, she took a glass of port and dunked shortbread fingers. With their glasses charged, Alex looked at his gran and raised his glass to her.

'Thank you for doing what you had to do, for giving me the start you have and for being there for me when I needed you most. Don't leave anything out in the telling, even if it hurts. Remember, I love you more than anyone in the world.'

Mrs Casey sniffed, a habit she had when she was embarrassed, and raised her glass to Alex.

'You're a credit to yourself and your da, and I know he'd be proud of you.' She shuffled around in the chair to get comfortable. 'When we came in from Connemara in 1949 your father was five years old. He was an only child. I'd lost a girl after him, and the doctors left me that I couldn't have any more children. Enda, your grandfather, got a job with the horses in the docks. Them days they still used horses to draw the trailers round the yards wherever they were needed. On account of that job we got the house in Carmel Street. I never met Enda's father, your great-grandfather, but I heard all the stories about him in the Rising. Wonderful stories they were too. He taught Enda everything he knew before he was killed – murdered, some would still say – with Padraig Pearse that Easter. On account of his own father, Enda was very bitter – hated the English – and would spit on the street if one passed. When the horses was finished with and the "wee shunters" took over, they said your grandfather was too old to learn how to drive a wagon with an engine. Your grandfather said it was on account of the yard foreman, an English lump of dirt that took a good man's pride away. Anyway, we was lucky they let us keep the house. Dublin Corporation had took over the houses and they let us stay on account of Sean.

'Two months after he lost his job, Enda went to Scotland to work at the pylons. A friend from Connemara, Paddy Joe Flaherty, was the foreman on a gang of erectors. When they finished a run of ten, he was to come home for a holiday. On that last day, Paddy Joe pointed to one of the insulators what was wrong and Enda said he would go up and fix it. The electricity was on and it shouldn't have been. They sent all that was left of Enda home in a wee box. No holiday for him, just a funeral. I got a widow's pension of course – damn little money compared to the bonus the company won for getting the power on early!'

Gran dipped into the pocket of her apron and pulled out a small paper package. She looked at it for a moment and then handed it to Alex. He opened it and inside was an old brass belt buckle.

'At that time your da was eleven – big for his age and able for anyone. He was good at his lessons, but he was even better at the hurley, and that took him all over the country playing for his club. I still have some of his jerseys upstairs in an old chest. Because of who his grandfather was, people used to talk to him about the Uprising and the like, and he gradually got involved in the republican movement. I tried to stop it, but what could I do when all them people were filling his head with all this romantic stuff. Anyway, when he was sixteen he left school and went to work for the O'Gormans, a big family in the lorry and haulage business and a family with all sorts of connections. He told me it would open the world to him. I said he should concentrate on the hurley – he was playing senior for the county by then. But the O'Gormans won.

'Sean got his lorry licence when he was seventeen, the youngest ever, but he had plenty of practice round the docks, shunting and the like. Michael Slaney worked for the Harbour Authority, and he and Sean was best mates. When deregulation came in, Michael persuaded your da to buy his own lorry. O'Gorman was very fair with him, guaranteed the bank and everything. He thought a lot of your da, did O'Gorman – promised him all the work he could handle.

'The work was there, and the money was there. As fast as Sean paid one lorry off, he bought another one, and by the early eighties he had seven or eight on the road. But he wasn't happy. His involvement in the IRA seemed to take more and more of his time. He'd stopped playing hurley and was drinking too much. In January 1981, he took a load of sheet steel from the docks for Cork. He was coming into Feeney on a bad bend and lost control of the lorry. He took a bus full of kids – a junior hurley team, would you believe – off the road. He killed three and crippled another half-dozen. God help us and all the poor souls involved. Sean said the load on the lorry wasn't properly tied, but the guards said he was speeding – twenty-four tons downhill at fifty miles an hour, they said. Sean said no, but they didn't believe him.'

Gran had started to cry quietly. Alex put an arm around her shoulders and gave her a hug.

'He did time, your da. Three years. It was hard on him. He wasn't the same when he came out – never laughed, no craic, angry at the people what set the loads and at those who turned their backs when he was in trouble. He swore to his dying day it was a rigged load, not his driving. But O'Gorman didn't turn his back on him. He helped him to get started again – sorted the bank and the insurance. Sean had three lorries in the end. But it wasn't the same. He didn't enjoy the work any more and he was heavy into the IRA, shifting stuff for them, it seems – bad stuff. It was Michael told me years later.

'In 1986 he got his licence back and started to drive again – not all the time, just when the notion took, or when one of the men wanted a day off. Anyway, early the next year things changed. Sean was out all hours, day and night. Then in February he was arrested over near Sligo for delivering a load of bales of straw to a wee farm in the hills. Apparently they were waiting for him, the guards and the soldiers. There was explosives – semitext or something. It was in the middle of the load. They held him in jail for two weeks and then he was let out. Someone had stood bail for him. He didn't know who put the explosives into the middle of the straw. He didn't make the load himself. Boys, he was fair steaming when he got out. I never heard language like it. I had to get Father Tomelty to do a special mass for him. For the next few weeks I hardly saw him. The only time he came home was to go to bed.

'And then this night a lady arrived at the door. Very posh she was, talking nice, and she handed Sean a bundle of blankets. That's how you arrived and that's the only time I saw her – your mother. She was tall, beautiful, terrible well dressed, and she was with this big hulk of a man, a scar across his face. He was as ugly as she was beautiful. If I could have had a daughter that's how I would have wanted her to look. They didn't come in, just left you and an envelope of money and that letter. I kept it for you until the right time. I think it's the right time now.'

Alex felt awful. He was angry at the injustices his father and grandfather had suffered, at his mother's casual disposal of him and at Gran's secrecy at not telling him all this years ago. But his anger was tempered by love for this old woman who for years had looked out for him, and love for his mother, so simply yet beautifully portrayed by this same old woman.

'Tell me the end,' he said quietly. 'Tell me how he died.'

'He didn't die,' she said. 'He was murdered. His car was booby-trapped.'

Chapter 8

Hall's Private Hotel comprised a fifties house, renovated and extended to three times its original size. Its credits board listed all the usual luxury features that one would expect in a four-star establishment, all approved by Bord Fáilte no less. Willy approached the rather aloof young lady seated behind a reproduction Louis XV desk that occupied the centre of the generous hall.

'My name is McNabb. You have a room for me, I hope, booked by Casey Transport.'

The young lady made a great show of checking the register. 'When was the reservation made, sir?'

'About two minutes ago, by phone – by Alex Casey,' said Willy sharply.

'Ah, yes, here it is.'

Toots burst out laughing. 'Morag, you're a cow!'

Morag joined in the laughter as she came round the desk and hugged Toots. Stepping back she turned to look at Willy. 'So this is the man with all the …'

Toots laughed and shook her head at Morag.

'I'd like to hear the rest of what you were about to say,' Willy said.

'… expertise and computer equipment,' said Morag, smiling.

Their room consisted of a large en-suite bedroom with an extended recess beside the wardrobes to accommodate a desk, coffee table and television console.

'Well done, Alex,' Willy mumbled to himself when he saw it. 'This will more than suit my needs.'

He heard a movement behind him and started to turn when Toots put her arms around him from behind. He felt her press her body against his back.

'Work can wait a while, can't it?' she said, as she started to undo his shirt buttons while kissing the nape of his neck.

* * *

In the early hours of the morning, Toots's annoying ringtone woke them. Willy scrambled to find the light switch while Toots padded across the room in the moonlight looking for the source of annoyance. 'I'm going to change this damn ringtone today if it's the last thing I do!' she muttered.

She found the phone just as Willy switched on the bedside light. 'Private Number' it said on the screen. Toots answered as she always did when the caller ID was hidden: 'Who's calling please?' But whoever it was hung up.

'That's strange,' she said on her way to the bathroom. 'That's the second time that's happened recently – no caller ID and no answer. Ah well.'

Willy lay back and was just dozing off again when he was rudely jolted back to reality by his mobile ringing. Rescuing it from among his discarded clothes, he glanced at the screen as he pressed the answer button. 'Private Number'. He put the phone to his ear but the line went dead.

'That's odd. What the hell time is it anyway?' He looked at the phone. 'Three bloody twenty-seven. Asshole!'

'You too?' asked Toots who had reappeared in a fluffy white bathrobe.

'Yeah, that's the second one in as many days.'

'You've had two and I've had two. These two were one after the other. When was your other call?'

'Yesterday. In the morning when I was driving. I didn't look at it until I stopped for lunch.'

'Mine was about the same time. Check your call log till we see.' Toots picked up her phone.

'Okay, Miss Marple, anything to please.'

'Nine forty-five and eighteen seconds,' Toots said, looking at Willy.

'I don't believe it! Mine was at nine forty-six and thirty seconds. That's got to be more than a coincidence!'

Toots climbed back into bed. 'I can't think straight. I'm going to get some sleep. You should too.' She patted the bed beside her. 'Everything will seem clearer in the morning.'

Willy shook his head. 'I'm going to have a cup of coffee and take a look into these calls,' he said, wrapping himself in a fluffy white robe. He blew her a kiss, opened his laptop and switched on the anglepoise light.

'That'll do for now, tech man,' Toots said, laughing as she turned off the bedside light.

Willy fired up his laptop, connected his mobile and set to work. After an hour he was exhausted and about to turn everything off when the incoming email alert sounded. He opened his inbox and immediately pulled back as though he had been slapped on the face.

I AM CLOSER TO YOU THAN YOU THINK

Willy was troubled. What was going on? Making his third cup of coffee, he mentally retraced his steps. He had confidence in the integrity of his system and in his own ability. The incoming email had been sent to a temporary email address he had set up to investigate Alex's family tree. It seemed fair to assume that, as yet, his real identity was unknown. However, it was also fair to assume that the deeper he went, the weaker his cover and the greater the risk of exposure. He looked at the sleeping Toots.

'I won't expose you to danger, whatever the provocation. I promise,' he whispered.

Toots stirred as though in response.

He turned back to his laptop. If his adversary was responding to his probing, then why not lay a trail to lead them into a trap.

An hour later, Willy double-checked what he proposed to

do and called it a night. He gently slipped into bed beside Toots who snuggled up against his back, her arm round his waist. As he drifted off to sleep he felt confident about his plans and warm in Toots's embrace.

* * *

The sound of a quiet voice woke Willy. He sat up with a start and looked at the clock. It was nine thirty, the sun was streaming in and Toots was on the phone. She turned and smiled at him as she carried on her conversation,

'Of course he can manage a full Irish ... We'll be down before ten, Morag, and Alex is going to join us too ... Okay, thanks.' She hung up and came over to the bed. 'Up you get,' she said to Willy, but grinned when he pulled back the covers to invite her in. 'Oh, I see. You're up already.'

Willy made a dive for her but she skipped out of reach.

'Breakfast with Alex at ten,' she said, smiling. 'Come on!'

They were just seated at a table in the dining room when Alex walked in at ten past ten. They were the only people there.

'Sorry I'm late. How are you getting on? Did you make any progress, Willy? Are we any the wiser?' Alex had a new determination in his voice.

'Yes and no. I got an anonymous email during the night from someone reacting to my investigation of the email you got.'

'Jesus, Willy, I thought you said you were protected, that you couldn't be traced.'

'I am. The email was sent to a temporary email address I've set up. But they don't know who I am. At this point in time there's no link between you and me, but they do know that someone is investigating the email sent to you. We really need to find out who they are before there's another "accidental" fire – or worse.'

'Does that mean you think the lorry fire and the email are linked?' asked Toots.

'Absolutely. I'm certain of it,' Willy replied.

'So am I, Toots, particularly after my chat with Gran last night,' said Alex.

'How is Gran? Was she able to help?' Toots asked.

'Gran's fine. I said I'd chase you up to the house when we're finished here. And, yes, she was able to fill in some blanks. Sean Casey – now there's a story and a half!'

Just then their breakfast arrived and that stopped the serious conversation. Willy and Toots tried to engage Alex in a bit of craic, but it was obvious his mind was elsewhere. The mention of his father seemed to have weighed him down, and they ate in relative silence until the plates were cleared. Toots rose from the table.

'I think we should go upstairs to the room so we can talk properly. I'll organise coffee.'

She left the room and Alex looked at Willy, grim-faced, a haunted expression clouding his usually placid demeanour.

'This could get bad, very bad,' he said. 'If I tell you to get offside, will you?'

'No, Alex, I won't. There's too much at stake I need to protect.'

'Toots?'

'Yeah, I love the girl, Alex. I don't want anyone to get hurt, especially Toots.'

Alex smiled for the first time since he'd sat down. 'She couldn't be in better hands,' he said. 'Toots's happiness means a lot to me and Gran. Gran approves of you, even if you are a wee Proddy boy from the north, and that's saying something.'

They made their way up to the bedroom and Alex's phone rang. Toots poured the coffee as they waited for his call to end. But after a few minutes he fell silent. He just stood there, mobile in hand, ashen-faced, devastation written on his handsome face. Toots leapt up.

'Alex, what's wrong? What's happened? Is it Gran?'

'No, no, it's not Gran. It's Michael Slaney. He's dead – murdered!'

'Noooo!' Toots wailed. She promptly sat back down. 'Oh my God! What happened? How did ... when ...?' She paused. 'What about Gran? Does she know? She shouldn't be left on her own. Does she know, Alex? ... Jesus!'

'The guards phoned the office looking for me. Fortunately Norma answered. She just gave them my mobile number, so I assume not.' Alex hesitated. 'Toots, are you up to telling Gran? I've to go and formally identify Michael, and then they want me to go with them to see Mrs Slaney, God help us.'

'I'm all right, I'll go,' Toots said. 'Can I borrow your car, Willy?' He threw her the keys and with a wave she was gone.

'What can *I* do?' asked Willy.

'Talk this through with me, Willy. This is getting out of hand completely.'

Willy put the kettle on and opened the minibar. He searched the miniatures until he found what he wanted – two brandies. He made two cups of sweet coffee and poured a brandy miniature into each cup.

'Get that into you,' he said, handing Alex a cup. 'It'll steady the nerves.' Willy took a mouthful himself. 'So, tell me what happened.'

'Jesus, I'm still taking it in. Michael was murdered at Lock Number Two on the Grand Canal. Why there, I've no idea. The fuckers!' Alex put his head in his hands and started to weep hard racking sobs. Willy moved towards him, but Alex waved him off. 'I'll be all right in a minute.'

The sun that streamed in the windows had lost its warmth now. For a moment, neither of them spoke while they drank their coffee, both lost in their own thoughts.

'Why Michael? Why now? Who the hell would do such a thing?' Alex said, emptying his cup. 'I've known Michael all my life. He was like a father to me. Yesterday, when he lost it in the office, I saw a man I didn't know, a man Gran didn't know. He knew something was afoot. I think he read the email before it disappeared. Sometime last night between the time he left us and six thirty this morning Michael ... but why?

What had he done? And who murdered him? Let's assume the letter the email referred to was the one left with me when I was brought to Sean and Gran as a baby. Could my mother's family be the people behind all this?'

'Did Michael know about the letter? I assume he did. Gran obviously trusted him,' Willy said.

'So did I!' Alex's phone rang. He held his hand up to Willy as he answered the call. 'Hello, Toots. So, how did Gran take it … Oh, did she? … If she's up to it, will you go with her? … Okay, look after yourselves. Hold on a minute … Ask Gran if Michael knew about the letter. Had he read it? … He had! Okay, thanks. Bye.'

Alex looked relieved. 'Gran took it better than Toots expected. She wants to see Mrs Slaney. I don't know that I could.'

'I'm going to play devil's advocate and make notes as I go along,' Willy said, going to the desk and opening his laptop. 'Suppose Michael not only knew who your mum was but also tried to make money from the secret … blackmail.'

'No way!' Alex retorted vehemently. 'Never!'

'Bear with me. By the sound of the threats in the letter, any interference like, say, blackmail, could get a buddy killed all right.'

Alex nodded. 'You're right, and there's something you don't know, Willy. Patsy Dan told me yesterday that it was Michael who set up the lorry fire. He opened the container for someone to steal part of the load. It was all organised when Patsy Dan arrived at the park.'

Willy typed as he listened.

'If Michael was in debt or some kind of trouble, who knows what he might have done to raise money,' Alex went on. 'Theft, blackmail, who knows? Or was he being blackmailed, stealing to order for someone?'

'So, you think Michael might have been working on his own or being forced to work for someone else,' said Willy. 'But is the lorry business and the email directly linked? The lorry was a warning, the email was a follow-up threat. Or was the email a response to my probing the family trees, as I first thought? Go back a few hours from Michael's death. Let's assume he discovered that the Garda were investigating the fire, not treating it as vandalism as he'd hoped. He was in the office for an hour or so on his own. Who knows who he spoke to in that time. We go in, and he flares up. According to you and Gran, it was completely out of character. Perhaps he flared up because the scam – whatever scam he was involved in – was about to be exposed. That's a more likely reason for his reaction to me. He stomps out of the office, out of your lives after all those years saying, "It's finished, it's over". It wasn't only his job and his relationship with your family that was over. It has to have been something much bigger, seeing as how he was killed for it. There has to be something that Michael knew that the bad guys didn't want us to know about.'

Alex remained silent.

'Your mother's identity, on its own? No, not enough to kill for,' Willy went on. 'But with something else … maybe. Your mother's family must be very important, or there must be something in the past, perhaps to do with your father – something heavy.'

Alex now looked uncomfortable.

'You've just opened another can of worms that I only discovered last night, something Gran told me. My father was involved with the republican movement. He'd done time. He was stitched up on an explosives charge about a year before I was born. Then the night I was left at the house as a baby, he went out to meet someone important. Three hours later he was blown up by a booby-trap device under his car.'

'Holy shit!' exclaimed Willy. 'What have we fallen into? We're in way over our heads.'

'It gets worse. After Sean left the house that night, he met up with Toots's father. What for no one knows. He was there when Tommy was shot dead.'

'I can't take in any more,' Willy said just as the room phone rang.

Alex answered it. 'Hello? … Yes, Morag. I suppose so. Tell them to come up.' He hung up. 'A couple of official-looking men are here to see me about Michael's death.'

Willy gathered up his laptop and other belongings and was stuffing everything into his overnight bag when their visitors arrived. Alex had the door open.

The two men were dressed in smart suits, no uniforms, and were both in their mid to late forties. They were men you would pass in the street without taking any notice.

'I'm Inspector Sullivan and this is Mr Hollinger. You're Mr Casey, I think.' Sullivan offered Alex his hand. 'And you are?' He turned to Willy.

'McNabb, Willy McNabb, and I'm just leaving. I came to help, but it's all way beyond me now. I'm sorry, Alex, I've had it.'

'Mr McNabb' – Jim Hollinger spoke with a soft south-of-England roll to his voice – 'I may need your particular help in the next few days. If you'll bear with us for a few minutes, then I'll explain that cryptic remark.'

Reluctantly Willy sat down. 'What is my particular help? What do you know about me?' The questions remained unanswered. 'Five minutes then.'

They sat around the coffee table and Inspector Sullivan opened the file he was carrying. He laid out a number of A5-sized photographs face down on the table, numbered one to five on the back. Hollinger helped himself to a bottle of water from the minibar.

'You might not want to look at these after I tell you our provisional findings,' Inspector Sullivan said. 'An edited version of course – it's very unpleasant. The reason we are here to talk to you is to avoid you having to see the remains.' He began to turn the photographs over one by one. 'The coroner has accepted the identification provided by the deceased's driving licence and by one of the scenes-of-crime officers who knew the deceased. From preliminary forensic examination of the body, my colleagues suggest that the cause of death was drowning, combined with heart failure, probably brought on by torture.'

Willy put a hand over his mouth and ran to the bathroom. They heard him puking. Jim Hollinger and Inspector Sullivan remained silent.

'Why?' Alex said eventually, looking from one to the other. 'Torture? Why Michael?'

Willy returned looking a little shamefaced and sat down.

'We don't yet know,' Sullivan said. 'There's more, I'm afraid. Lock Number Two was emptied, but the outflow gates remained closed. Mr Slaney was crucified on the lock side of the right-hand gate. The sluices were opened and we assume he was interrogated as the water level rose. Prior to death, his tongue was cut out and his face slashed from above his left ear to the right corner of his mouth. Death was ultimately by drowning, but obviously he suffered a great deal before that.'

A heavy silence filled the room.

Suddenly Willy exploded. 'Fucking animals! Fucking twisted, evil animals.'

Alex stood up and walked to the window. 'Why have you told us this in such detail?' he asked eventually without turning round. 'We didn't need to know the ins and outs of Michael's death.'

'It's a long story. It goes back at least twenty years.' It was Jim Hollinger who spoke this time. 'I work for Special Services in London. The department has worked closely with the Irish government for many years. Our work here morphed from anti-terrorist to anti-organised crime as the peace process gained momentum. After all, it's the same people involved. Yesterday's terrorists are today's gangsters. You've unwittingly stumbled into the middle of a worldwide money laundering racket that we're investigating. The Irish end of this seamless movement of dirty money is controlled here in Dublin. There was a Northern Irish partner, based somewhere on the north Antrim coast – that's all my predecessor could discover. That person ceased to be active twenty-two years ago.

'Nine years ago, we were alerted that the dormant account had become active again,' he went on. The account was deliberately accessed – it wasn't a random hacker stumbling across the account by accident. We're sure of that because we couldn't identify the source. This was a sophisticated intrusion that bypassed all our surveillance programmes and didn't leave a digital footprint ... just a name. It was the work of one of the most talented hackers in the world. It also puts him or her at the top of our wanted list – the bad guys will be looking for him too.'

'What was the name?' Willy asked with a deadpan expression on his face.

'Mouseman.' Hollinger sat back in his chair and watched the two young men. 'I wouldn't want to be in Mouseman's shoes,' he continued. 'He may have signed his death warrant when he accessed that account, and as we know from Mr Slaney's experience, that death will be rather unpleasant.'

Sullivan gathered the photographs. 'I think these lads have heard enough for now, Jim. Let's take a break, and then could we ask you to come to Ballsbridge Garda Station at, say, three thirty?' He looked up at Willy and Alex. 'We'll have the final results from the post-mortem at that time, and Jim can finish his history lesson, okay?'

Alex stood up and extended his hand. 'Suits us.'

After the inspector and Hollinger left, Alex turned to Willy. 'You look awful. Those photos *were* pretty gruesome.'

'It's not just that that's bothering me,' Willy said, slumping back in his seat. 'That was me they were talking about. I'm Mouseman.'

Chapter 9

When Toots arrived at No. 87, Gran was sitting at the kitchen table, a pot of tea and a bottle of brandy in front of her. It turned out she already knew about Michael's death – Norma had told her – and she was bracing herself to go round to see Mrs Slaney. She poured Toots a cup of tea.

Toots could see the strain on Gran's face and pulled her chair a little closer. Gran extracted the letter from her apron pocket, the letter that came with Alex when he was a baby.

'I don't know how much Alex has told you about our family's history,' Gran said. She went on to tell her about Alex's father, his involvement in the republican movement and how he died. 'Nobody claimed responsibility for it and the guards didn't prosecute anyone. But I worked it out with a little help from a clever priest, Father Tomelty, God rest his soul. After Sean's death, the first thing we did was try to trace Alex's mother. That hussy waltzed in, left him and this letter' – Gran held it up – 'and some money and then she waltzed straight out again. But we were able to trace her from the handwritten note at the bottom – see here?' She pointed to the end of the letter. 'Father Tomelty, God rest his soul, spent months looking at other people's handwriting. He even hired some handwriting specialist to compare samples. Sean had driven a horse lorry on a number of occasions – he never said who for. A year after he was murdered, Father Tomelty was at the horse show at Ballsbridge – he liked the horses, he did – and by chance he saw this lady get down from a real swanky lorry. She fitted my description of the woman who had left Alex, and he had this feeling about her. Thinking on his feet, he committed his one and only sin on this earth. He told the woman he was collecting for St Saviour's Convent and asked if she would like to give something. She wrote him a cheque for one hundred punts on the spot. That's how he got her handwriting. It was Alex's mother all right.'

Her satisfaction at the success of this little piece of detective work showed clearly in her face.

'Sean might have told me eventually,' she went on, 'but he never had the chance. He was murdered that night – the same night as your poor father.'

'Who is she, Gran – Alex's mother? You have to tell him. You should have told him years ago,' Toots said.

'You're right, child, but it was Michael. He persuaded me not to – said it would jeopardise everything. I went along with him, contenting myself that Alex was too young to be told the truth. But then when he was old enough – well, everything was so good I didn't want to change things. That's a sin I'll pay dear for come the Day of Judgement, no doubt.'

'But who is she?' Toots was getting impatient.

Gran patted Toots's hand. 'The name on the cheque was Victoria Elizabeth Mary O'Gorman – Vem O'Gorman.'

Toots was flabbergasted. 'Is she any relation to Senator Eugene O'Gorman?' she asked with a squeak.

'Indeed she is. She's his daughter.'

O'Gorman! Toots was horrified. The name ran through Dublin society like blood through veins. It was everywhere. The senator had been charged with assisting the government in the Northern Ireland peace negotiations, yet some said he was the head of the IRA's General Council. Jesus!

'Are you sure?' she asked.

'I'm afraid so, child. Father Tomelty checked and double-checked the handwriting with three different graphologists. He even sent it to an expert in Rome!' She said this with great pride, as though it had gone to the pontiff himself. 'I think the night Sean was murdered he was on his way to see Vem, or the senator himself. He was a good man, Sean, at heart. He wouldn't have wanted Alex to grow up a bastard. I think Sean wanted to do the right thing – marry her to save her any embarrassment.'

'Gran, she abandoned Alex and disowned her own son. And Sean marry her? She would have laughed him out of the house. Her father, the mighty senator, would have trod on him like a piece of dog shit. I'm sorry, Gran, if Sean went to see them, it definitely wasn't to propose marriage. Let me read the letter again. Then we really must go and see Mrs Slaney.'

At that moment, Toots suddenly remembered her conversation with Kate and Liz. Oh God, Liz O'GORMAN! What was it Liz had said about family skeletons ... 'that bastard Blaney or Slaney?'

'The letter please, Gran.'

Toots took the letter and read it again. This time it really sank in.

'The dirty stinking bitch! How dare she threaten you while she dumps her responsibilities on you. The bloody tramp, whore –'

'Stop, child. Come on now, it was a long time ago and she probably did what she thought was best at the time.'

'Best, my arse! She was suiting herself. How the hell did you cope?'

'Michael. He was there whenever I needed him, right from the start.'

'I take it he knew about the letter – had read it and all?'

'Of course he did. He knew all about everything.'

'Now I understand why you think O'Gorman might have murdered Sean, and maybe even my dad. We have to tell Alex about his mother. Now!'

'You keep quiet, girl,' Gran scolded. 'I'll tell him myself. It has to come from me, not anyone else.' Gran rose from the table. 'We'd better go and see Mrs Slaney.'

* * *

Mrs Slaney struck Toots as a woman of great dignity when she opened the door to them. She greeted Gran with respect and Toots with warmth and led them to the 'good room', a throwback to Victorian clutter. It smelled of hyacinths, and mothballs. She indicated where they were to sit, facing the window in matching easy chairs, while she sat on an old wooden chair strategically placed in the window bay from where she could see both out to the road and into the room.

'You're both welcome in our house, Mrs Casey, Miss Toomey. Michael talked about you both from time to time and I'm pleased to make your acquaintance. Such a shame it's under these circumstances. Now, tea will be served in five minutes.'

They sat in silence for some minutes, Mrs Slaney not seeming to feel any need to make conversation.

Eventually Gran said, 'I'm sorry for your loss, Mrs Slaney.'

'Michael was a good man and didn't deserve the death he was given,' Mrs Slaney said. 'But the Good Book says, "The Lord giveth and the Lord taketh away", and so it is with Michael. He must have committed a great sin to be handed the punishment he received, but the Lord in his infinite mercy will pardon that sin on the Day of Judgement.'

'When did you hear about it?' Gran asked.

'I have a good relationship with An Garda Síochána as a result of Michael's misdemeanours over the years. I was phoned this morning at six forty-nine and told of the discovery of Michael's body, its whereabouts and the presumed manner of his death. I'd been expecting Alex to call this morning, that being the information I had been given at ten thirty. In his absence, you two ladies can be entrusted with the information I have for him, I'm sure.'

There was a single knock on the door. A maid in full service uniform delivered tea and cakes, and the stilted conversation that followed made neither Toots nor Gran feel any more comfortable than they had when they arrived. Not wishing to extend their visit any longer than necessary, they declined 'second cups and another cake'.

Mrs Slaney rose from her chair. 'If you'll excuse me, I'll retrieve the documents I have for Alex from Michael's study. One moment please.'

On her return, she handed Gran an old, battered briefcase.

'All Michael's papers and files are in this case. It was presented to him on his departure from the Harbour Authority, prior to his employment with Mr Casey senior. It has no sentimental value to me, so please dispose of it as you see fit.'

Mrs Slaney rang a little bell and the maid appeared immediately.

'Please see my guests out. Thank you for calling, Mrs Casey, Miss Toomey.'

Once they were safely back in the car, Toots and Gran sat in stunned silence.

'Bless us, that's the hardest woman I've ever met!' Gran said eventually.

Toots laughed as she turned the key in the ignition. 'What an ogre! How could he have loved her?'

Gran fastened her seat belt and settled the briefcase squarely on her lap. 'And what secrets do you hold?' she said as she gave it a little pat.

Chapter 10

'You're Mouseman?' Alex was incredulous. 'Are you really a talented hacker? A wanted man?'

Willy fetched a bottle of water from the minibar and told Alex about finding his dad's hiding place under the bedroom floorboards nine years previously. 'There was a box in it, and in the box was a little red book containing an alphanumeric code. Once I cracked the code, I ended up with a list of seven offshore bank accounts. I accessed all of them and the total balance amounted to more than two million pounds.'

'You're joking me!' Alex's jaw hung open as he digested what Willy had just said.

'Well, that was the total in the accounts at the last transaction date.'

'So what! Give or take a day or two, it's still a big lump of money.'

'No, the last transaction date was the 17th of January 1987!'

'Holy fuck! Twenty-two years ago? Do you have any idea what it's worth today?'

'Eighteen million, six hundred and seventy-three thousand, nine hundred and thirty-five pounds and ninety-nine pence, at the end of trading on the London Stock Exchange last Friday.'

Alex sat back and stared at Willy. 'Mad! Totally fucking mad! You're beyond belief!'

'All I did was crack a code, Alex!'

Alex burst out laughing and sat back, shaking his head. 'And you're proud of being on some sort of most-wanted list? What about the money, for God's sake?'

Willy shrugged and gave him a crooked grin.

'I'm glad you're helping us with our problems,' said Alex. 'We need someone with skills like yours. We just need to make sure the guards don't catch on.' He suddenly groaned.

Willy frowned at him.

'We've to go and see those two gobshites this afternoon. I wish I could figure out what the hell is going on – who killed Michael and why, and how it's connected with the lorry fire. And the email – what did it say?'

Willy looked at his laptop. 'Leave it alone,' he read out. 'Next time someone gets hurt. Remember the letter.'

'The letter … The letter from my mother. That's it! It's talking about the warning in the letter that came with me when I was a baby. It's got something to do with protecting my mother's identity. They knew we were investigating, so they sent the threatening email, and then … killed Michael. And look what happened to my father. Has it got some connection with that? I think there's more that Gran can tell us.' Alex fell silent for a moment. 'Enough of this navel-gazing. Let's find Toots and Gran and have a bit of a brainstorming session.'

'Yeah, I think Gran's the key. She might know more than she thinks – stuff she's forgotten about or doesn't think is important.'

'And what about Sullivan and Hollinger? If they suspect you of being Mouseman, you might not get out of the Garda station. I don't think we should go there this afternoon.'

Willy pulled a small black box the size of a mobile phone out of his pocket.

'What's that?' Alex asked.

'It's an invention of mine, what I call an iJack. I developed it with a South Korean guy who's in the same year as me at Queen's. His dad has an electronics company in Wanju and he made this prototype. One of its many features is its ability to detect listening devices – bugs – and jam them.'

Alex gave him a puzzled look.

'We've been bugged!' Willy said. 'By Hollinger, he must have placed it when he went to the minibar earlier. I was only pretending to be sick in the bathroom. I was really checking the iJack to see if my suspicions were correct.'

Alex still didn't look convinced.

'Come and I'll show you.' Willy went to the fridge, Alex following him, and held out the iJack. 'Watch the screen as I pass it back and forth.' The digital reading shot up when Willy hovered the device around the back wall. 'The bug is here, just behind the fridge.' He pointed at the spot.

'Jesus! But they'll have heard everything we've just said!'

'No, no. I jammed it while I was "being sick". It's me they're after, not you, but they obviously don't have anything on me or I'd be in Portlaoise by now.'

'Well, let's get out of here anyway. I'd feel safer in my own house.'

'Hollinger probably has a tail on us too, so let's make him earn his keep. You go first and wait for me at the Horse Show Inn at Ballsbridge. I'll follow in a couple of minutes on foot. You can keep an eye out and see if I'm followed.'

'Jesus, this is getting more and more like a James Bond movie,' said Alex.

Willy lifted his computer bag and headed for the door. Before he opened it he put his finger to his lips, telling Alex to be quiet. He pulled out the iJack, punched a few buttons on the keypad, waved Alex out of the room and slammed the door.

'What the hell was all that about?'

'I was just unjamming the listening device. The slammed door was just for badness – give them a sore head.'

They parted in the foyer, Willy leaving the key at reception with Morag who gave him a cute smile.

He set off at a gentle pace and arrived at the Horse Show Inn fifteen minutes later. He walked across the driveway and turned down towards the pub door. As he opened it, he caught a glimpse of a figure reflected in the glass. He went two steps into the hall, then turned and came back out again. He was just in time to see Alex embrace a man in a bone-crushing bear hug.

'Is this the guy who was following you?' Alex shouted.

The man struggled rather feebly, his arms pinned to his side. 'If you'd release me, I'll show you some identification. I'm a Garda officer.'

'Hear that, Willy? He's a Garda officer – with identification!' Alex gave the man an extra squeeze, then released him from the bear hug but kept hold of his right arm. 'If you try to run, I'll break your fucking arm. Show Willy your ID!'

The man produced his wallet and showed his ID card.

'Sorry about that, Guard Cosgrove. You can't be too careful these days,' said Willy, grinning. 'So, would you like to explain why you were following me?'

'I wasn't following you. I was just going in for a quick bite of lunch.'

'Then come and join us. The least we can do is buy you your lunch,' said Alex, trying not to laugh.

'Eh … no … no. You're all right, lads. Thanks. I'll have to run – just realised the time.'

'Well, be sure to give our regards to Inspector Sullivan,' Willy said mischievously. 'Tell him we'll give him a ring. We have to change the time and venue for our meeting this afternoon.'

Guard Cosgrove hurried out of the car park and disappeared round the corner.

Alex and Willy followed him out to the road and watched him climb into a white van a few yards away. They turned and looked at each other.

'Let's catch up with Gran and Toots,' Alex said.

Chapter 11

Now in his seventy-fifth year, still straight as a bulrush and dressed to perfection, Senator Eugene O'Gorman was taking his daily walk. The immaculately maintained gardens of his estate in the Wicklow Hills were both a refuge and an inspiration to him.

In attendance, as always, was Peter the Wake. Some claimed he'd been given the nickname on account of his deathly demeanour, the soulless black eyes, the livid scar from his left ear down to the right corner of his mouth, his sickly pallor and, of course, his silence. Others said it was because he'd knocked two men's heads together so hard during an altercation at a wake that he'd killed them. No one used the nickname to his face.

Peter was treated with as much regard as the senator, though for very different reasons. At six foot seven inches tall, and weighing in at nineteen stone, he had hands the size of dinner plates and legs like tree trunks. The man-mountain wrapped in a bottle-green uniform and wearing specially made Doc Martens might elicit humour privately, but in public he was shown nothing but respect.

'Peter, we have a problem!' said the senator. He often discussed his business with Peter, as much for his sage advice as for his ability to listen without interruption, for Peter was mute, his tongue cut out at the same time as his face had been laid open. If it hadn't been for the prompt action of the senator and Dr Michael Rafferty, Peter would surely have died that day.

'I fear young Casey is getting into a position from which

he will have great difficulty extricating himself,' the senator went on. 'The question is, what, if anything, do we do to help?'

As the senator continued his walk holding this one-sided discussion with Peter, his son, Dominic, watched from a distance. The old coach house had been converted into an elegant and luxurious suite of offices. Dominic had taken over the principal office on the first floor when the senator had vacated both the office and the position of chief executive of O'Gorman Enterprises. The office afforded a panoramic view of the gardens and orchards, and nearly half of the six hundred-acre estate.

'I wonder what that old bugger's struggling with at the minute,' Dominic muttered to himself. It was obvious when the senator was having one of his debates – he carried his black malacca cane in his right hand and gesticulated wildly with his left. The trickier the problem, the wilder the gesticulation. 'Why won't he hand over the reins completely. He still has his tentacles everywhere in the business.'

'Perhaps, Dominic, it's because he doesn't trust you,' said a female voice behind him.

Dominic spun round. 'Some day that tongue of yours will get you into real trouble,' he said, almost growling.

'Ahhh, dear brother, methinks the chickens are coming home to roost and that "old bugger", as you call him, is troubled to see them landing here,' Vem said. 'He's protected this place and our family with his life. But under new management things appear not to be so safe.'

Dominic hurled a glass ashtray at Vem's receding back, the office door closing in time to prevent injury. It briefly cracked open again.

'Careful, Dominic, your weakness is showing.'

The laughter that accompanied the closing door was like a corrosive liquid eating away at him. The truth was always harder to hear from someone who knew the truth. Dominic turned back to the window, but the senator had disappeared.

The Rolls-Royce exited the courtyard through the coaching entrance below the office where Dominic stood. It cruised straight down the private road to Lough Tay, turned right into the woodlands and then passed out of view. Dominic lifted the phone on his desk and buzzed an extension.

'Where's the senator gone?' he barked into the phone.

Mary Lennihan knew about everything that happened on the estate and in the 'big house', as she lovingly referred to the Georgian pile in which they all lived.

'I am neither his keeper nor your informer, Mr Dominic,' she replied. 'The senator has his mobile phone with him though, and I'm sure he'll take your call.'

Dominic slammed the phone down. 'The day his coffin leaves this place is the day she'll follow on her bloody broomstick!'

The senator often left the estate undecided about the direction he would take to reach his destination. This was a throwback to the old days when security dictated that he vary his route out of the area. But not any longer; now it was just a habit.

'Peter, to Balbriggan, please. The O'Farrell Commercial Vehicle Park, and then the Garda station. We'll stop for some lunch wherever you choose. Let's take the scenic route.'

As Peter drove through the orchards and fields, the village of Kilbride and the twisting road alongside the Liffey, the senator called Mary Lennihan. He had her on speed dial.

'Mary, I want to meet the Garda officer dealing with the Casey Transport incident. Could you phone ahead and let them know we should be at Balbriggan station by four o'clock. Then I'd like you to contact the commissioner and suggest dinner at Roly's Bistro at eight o'clock tonight. Just book us the usual table. Peter and I will stay at Bewleys Hotel tonight, and Peter will dine at the hotel while I am at Roly's, so you'll need to let them know. And, before I go, can you put me through to Dominic, please? I'm sure he's curious to know my schedule.'

He heard Mary laugh just before she put him on hold.

A few moments later Dominic's voice came through. 'Father, you were looking for me?'

'No, I was sure you'd be looking for me. We haven't spoken today.'

'I did ask Mrs Lennihan if she knew where you were going, but it wasn't important.'

'It must have been important if you were looking for me, Dominic. However, now that you're on the phone I'll tell you my itinerary for the day.'

After the senator ended the call, Dominic went to the cocktail cabinet and poured a large measure of Powers. His conversation with the senator troubled him greatly. The investigation into the truck fire would certainly lead to the discovery of the stolen goods and, eventually, to Michael Slaney's death at Lock Number Two. It would turn the clock back twenty-plus years and open a Pandora's box full of all sorts of shit. He couldn't let that happen.

* * *

After an excellent lunch in Malahide, the senator dozed as they followed the coast road to Balbriggan. Peter stopped the Rolls half a mile before the O'Farrell Commercial Vehicle Park and tapped on the privacy screen behind his head. This ritual allowed the senator to gather himself, freshen up and marshal his thoughts. As they moved on, Peter had to brake sharply to allow a wide load to pass. It was the burnt-out rig they were going to see being taken away on a flatbed truck followed by a similar vehicle carrying the damaged container.

As soon as they were clear, Peter accelerated on to O'Farrell's. At the same time, the senator rang Mary again and asked her to get the investigating Garda officer to come to the vehicle park immediately. Peter drove through the gate and stopped directly in front of the office. He was just opening his door to get out when an angry little man shouted at him from the other side of the yard.

'Get that fucking lump of English shit out of my yard. You can't park there.'

The torrent of abuse stopped abruptly when Peter unfurled from the Rolls, walked slowly across the yard and stood in front of the by now contrite man, looking down at him, unblinking, his face calm.

'Thank you, Peter. I'll take over now,' said the senator, arriving at his side. 'You need to be careful what you say, sir. Peter is very proud of his car. Now, I'm looking for Mr O'Farrell. My name is O'Gorman.'

'I'm O'Farrell. What did you say was your business?'

'I didn't, but that's it arriving now.'

A Garda car turned into the yard, lights flashing and siren howling. It skidded to a halt and three doors opened simultaneously. Sergeant Reilly nearly fell over himself in his rush to greet the senator.

'I'm honoured to meet you, Senator O'Gorman. This is Guard Mulligan, and this is Guard Molloy, our forensic expert. How can we be of service to you, sir?'

The senator nodded to each of the men in turn, then asked, 'Why has the burnt Casey wagon been removed? I met it on the way in just now. Surely the experts haven't finished already.'

Guard Mulligan stepped forward. 'We're definitely not finished with it, sir. There's to be a meeting tomorrow with all the involved parties. Dublin Harbour Police is even sending a representative.'

The Senator turned to O'Farrell. 'So why has the truck been taken away?'

O'Farrell shrugged. 'I got a call a couple of hours ago from forensics saying the wagon and trailer's to be taken to Dublin. Fine by me. I want the bloody thing out of my yard. So two low-loaders turn up and get on with it. End of story.'

Guard Mulligan stepped closer to O'Farrell, his eyes narrowed. 'Before I left yesterday I told you the vehicle and trailer were to be considered evidence and the area round them a crime scene. Is that not so?'

'The call was from an inspector somebody or other,' said O'Farrell. 'To be honest, I wasn't paying much attention. I'm short-staffed and booked solid tonight. What was I supposed to say?'

'"Phone the officer in charge" is what you should have said, Mr O'Farrell.'

'Guard Mulligan,' the senator interjected gently, 'I understand your frustration. Perhaps it would be beneficial if we were to follow the vehicles in question. We can find out from the drivers who requested their removal and where they are to be delivered. Sergeant Reilly, might I borrow Guard Mulligan and Guard Molloy for an hour? As we travel, they can give me all the facts. Then you and I can discuss the matter in full on my return.'

'It's very irregular, and as the senior officer present—' began Sergeant Reilly.

'I shall commend your suggestions and speedy decision-making in this matter when I meet the commissioner this evening. He will be suitably impressed, I'm quite sure.'

'Thank you, sir. Right then – Mulligan and Molloy – go with the senator and give any help you can. I'll see you back at the station for the debrief.'

The senator turned quickly to the Rolls lest anyone should see his smile. During this discussion, Peter had checked the map of the local area and was waiting in the car. The low-loaders could only have taken one of three main roads: south to Dublin, north to Dundalk or west towards Navan. On the assumption that whoever had organised the removal wanted the lorry and container out of sight, Peter decided that they would most likely head west to sparsely populated countryside. Once the senator was seated in the back, a police officer on each side of him, they set off. Ten minutes later Peter's assumptions were proved correct.

With the low-loaders in sight, he held back. The vehicles indicated left into an industrial estate. Peter drove a few hundred yards past the entrance and pulled into a farm lane that afforded a view of the estate.

'Well done, Peter,' said the senator. 'Now, we'll wait until they've started to unload. With the help of our law enforcement friends here, we shall soon find out who is behind this little exercise.'

The senator, hospitable as ever, offered his guests refreshments from the built-in cocktail cabinet. During the short journey he had skilfully extracted all the information he could from the two guards who, eager to outdo each other, had been more than helpful. Mulligan declined even a mineral water, though his eyes almost popped out when he saw the drinks compartment appear from the back of the front passenger seat. Molloy was less circumspect and availed of a glass of whiskey.

Peter caught the senator's eye in the rear-view mirror, skilfully turned the Rolls in the farm lane and drove into the industrial estate, parking some distance from the low-loaders and successfully blocking the entrance.

'I think the matter is now in your hands, Guard Mulligan. I shall wait for you to call me over.' The senator smiled encouragingly at the young officer.

'Thank you, sir. I'll call for you as soon as I've ascertained the facts about the vehicle's removal from Balbriggan, who arranged that removal and any other relevant information.'

The senator watched from the car. As Mulligan approached the drivers of the low-loaders, one of them went back to his lorry and produced a baseball bat which he aggressively slapped into the palm of his free hand.

'I think, Guard Molloy, you should join your colleague. Two against one is hardly fair,' the senator said, pressing the button to open the car window.

'Ah, yes, sir, but I'm in forensics. I'm not trained in this sort of thing. I think I'd prefer to wait and see how Mulligan handles the situation.'

The senator gave Peter an almost imperceptible nod and the huge man climbed out of the Rolls. By this stage Guard

Mulligan was backed up against the burnt-out container and being threatened by the driver with the baseball bat. To his credit, he didn't seem cowed by these threats, but two against one, and one armed with a weapon ... Well, it offended the senator's sense of fair play.

'Guard Molloy, go with Peter ... Now! I assume you hope to retire on a full pension.'

Molloy almost tumbled out of the car.

The driver with the baseball bat had a sudden reality check when he saw Peter coming towards him. Peter extended his right hand and nodded at the bat. The driver hesitated, and Peter struck with the speed of a viper. His huge left fist came from nowhere and put the man on his back a full five feet from where he'd been standing. Peter picked up the baseball bat and looked at the other driver who had wet himself. He tucked the heavy end of the bat under his left armpit and with his right hand snapped the shaft. He turned to the prone man who, judging by the shape of his face, had a broken jaw, and threw the two bits of the bat at him. The heavy end caught the man in the crotch with a satisfying thud. Peter walked back to the Rolls and, settled in the driver's seat once again, looked in the rear-view mirror.

'Beautifully executed, Peter, as always. Your finesse improves with age!'

Ten minutes later, Guard Mulligan, having made copious notes, appeared at the senator's window and, without thinking, saluted him.

'As a direct result of the timely and greatly appreciated intervention of Mr ... eh, Mr ... Peter, I am happy to report that the suspects have co-operated fully in detailing the perpetrator of this breach of regulations, specifically in breach of a direct order given to the owner of the O'Farrell Commercial Vehicle Pa—'

'Thank you, Guard Mulligan. Your handling of the incident has been exemplary and will be commended to the commissioner in the fullness of time. However, time is something I'm rather short of just now. All I require at the moment is the name of the person who organised the removal of the vehicle to this yard.'

'Of course, sir. Sorry, sir. By coincidence, the name is the same as yours, sir … O'Gorman, Dominic O'Gorman. He owns this industrial estate and these low-loaders.'

'Indeed, that is a coincidence!' said the senator. 'Any other details you might consider relevant?'

'Not at this time, sir, but with Sergeant Reilly's permission, I shall make a full transcript of my report available to you at the earliest possible moment – no later than ten o'clock tomorrow morning.'

'Thank you again, Guard Mulligan. I will phone Sergeant Reilly and explain that you have made two arrests single-handedly and require his presence here immediately.' The senator closed his window. 'Bewleys Hotel please, Peter!'

And with that the Rolls purred off through the gate.

Chapter 12

Alex and Willy walked into the kitchen at No. 87 where they were greeted by the smell of ground coffee and freshly baked bread. Gran and Toots, both looking slightly shell-shocked, were sitting at the table. Willy kissed Toots on the cheek and sat down.

'Poor Mrs Slaney,' Gran said. 'The guards phoned her at half six this morning.'

Alex put a hand on her shoulder and gave it a comforting squeeze. 'Let's eat first. Then we can catch up,' he said.

After lunch Gran fetched Michael Slaney's briefcase and told Willy and Alex what she had told Toots earlier – that not long after Sean had been murdered, she and Father Tomelty had identified the handwriting in the letter, and that she knew who Alex's mother was.

'Please forgive me for keeping this secret from you, son, but it was done for the best of reasons.' Gran blew her nose. 'It's Vem O'Gorman – Vem Haughey as she is now.'

For a long time all that could be heard was the ticking of the clock out in the hall. Then Alex rose slowly, pushing his chair back, and began to pace the floor.

'Jesus, Gran! That's a bolt out of the blue! Are you sure? Why didn't you tell me before?'

'Yes, son, I'm sure. We had the handwriting checked by an expert, and it fits in with what I know was going on in your father's life at the time – and with what's happened since. Michael and Father Tomelty persuaded me to wait until you were at least twenty-one before I told you.'

The others held their breath. Alex walked to the tall

cupboard in the corner, calmly collected four small tumblers and the bottle of brandy and returned to the table. He set a tumbler in front of each person, pulled the cork from the bottle and poured a generous measure into each glass. He lifted his glass and, looking directly at Gran, raised it. The others lifted their glasses and waited.

'Mrs Casey … Sean Casey … Vem O'Gorman … Sláinte!' Alex said eventually.

'Sláinte!' they said in unison.

Alex slumped down into his seat. 'Jesus, Gran, you sure know how to shock! It'll take time for it to sink in. I've been so used to not knowing … And what should I do with that information? How does it affect things?'

Gran pulled a handkerchief from her apron pocket and dabbed at her eyes. 'There's more you need to know about the past,' she said.

Gran's words were like a slap in the face for Alex. He screwed up his eyes, dropped his chin and slowly shook his head side to side.

'It's to do with Michael,' Gran continued. 'You know the way he was murdered?'

'Who told you about that?' Alex barked and looked accusingly at Willy.

'Calm down, Alex. It was Norma,' Gran explained. 'The guard who phoned to tell you about Michael's death is Norma's husband's best friend.'

'What about Michael's murder? What do you all know that I don't know?' Now Toots was cross at being kept in the dark.

'He was tortured before he died,' Willy said. 'They think he died of a heart attack brought on by what was done to him.'

Toots let out a long slow breath. 'Poor Michael! What did he do to deserve that end?'

'When your mother left you at the house that night back in 1987 she was accompanied by a giant of a man, the most awful-looking man I've ever seen,' Gran continued. 'He never spoke, not one word, and had this terrible scar across his face from the top of his left ear to the right corner of his mouth, all the way across his face. It was horrible.'

'The same as Michael!' Alex and Willy said in unison.

Gran nodded. 'Once we knew who your mother was, we were able to find out all about them – the O'Gormans. The giant was Senator O'Gorman's driver – still is, from what Michael told me. Apparently he was maimed as a warning to others in the IRA not to talk to the Garda. No one knows exactly what happened or how the senator saved the big man's life, but he never leaves the senator's side. At Sean's wake this terrible well-dressed man arrived to talk to me and Michael. The big ugly driver was with him. We didn't know it at the time, but it must have been the senator. He told us he was Sean's business adviser and that he had helped him get the Excel Containers contract. He had papers we had to sign, and so we did – we just signed them, no questions asked.'

'He had no right to do that,' Alex shouted angrily. 'He took advantage of your grief. You probably signed away the business or something. I'm going to see him and have it out with him. My mother as well – she must have known what was going on.'

'We had to go along with what we judged to be the best for all of us at the time. This man was offering me help with rearing you and running Sean's business. We did the right thing at the time.' Gran looked defiantly at Alex.

'Of course you have to speak to your grandfather, Alex, and your mother, but it's best not to do it when you're angry,' Toots added.

Alex got up and stormed out through the back door. Toots got up to follow him.

'Leave him be, Toots,' Gran cautioned. 'Give him some space. This is difficult for him. Put on the kettle and we'll take a cuppa.'

As they waited for the kettle to boil, Willy looked at Gran. 'Was Michael Slaney also involved with the IRA?' he asked.

'Yes.'

'Did you know he was involved?'

She hesitated. 'Yes.'

'Was the business involved with the movement?'

'Willy, stop it!' yelled Toots as she poured boiling water into the teapot.

'It's all right, Toots. He needs to ask and you all need to know. In Sean's time, yes. Since then, I don't think so.'

'Could Michael have hidden things from you – business details, I mean?' Willy went on.

'Yes, God rest his soul.'

'Could Michael have hidden business details from Norma?'

Gran hesitated again. 'Yes, probably.'

'So Michael could have hidden business transactions from the senator?'

'I doubt it,' Gran said. 'The senator has a reputation as a very shrewd man. He was involved in the movement too, so, no, Michael couldn't have hidden things from him … well, not for long anyway.'

'What about the briefcase, Gran? We forgot all about it,' said Toots.

'Bless me, child, you're right. Go and get Alex. He needs to go through it!'

A few moments later, Alex came back in, still agitated but more in control of himself.

'Come on, big man, you're in charge now,' said Willy.

The words seemed to galvanise Alex. 'Okay, let's take a look,' he said.

Gran reached down for the briefcase and set it on the table in front of Alex. He emptied the contents onto the kitchen table.

'Mrs Slaney doesn't want the case back,' Gran said, shaking her head. 'Says it doesn't have any sentimental value for her. She's a right hard ticket.'

Alex closed the briefcase and handed it back to Gran. 'You keep it, Gran. It means more to you than to Mrs Slaney. You keep it for me.'

On the table in front of Alex were a number of spring-clip A4 files, two sealed envelopes and a small red notebook.

'Not much for twenty-odd years work,' Alex said, picking up one of the envelopes.

'But enough to die for.' Willy's hand shook as he reached for the red notebook. He was deathly pale and the others were now looking at him. 'It's identical – exactly the same as the one I found in my dad's room.' He opened it. 'It's another alphanumeric code.' He looked at Alex, then at Toots and Gran. 'Hollinger was right … it's a death warrant!'

Toots's ridiculous ringtone suddenly burst into life. She groped around in her bag for it.

'I really will change it,' she muttered, finally retrieving it. She stared at the screen and looked at Willy as she answered. 'Who's calling, please?'

She threw the phone down on the table as if it were hot and watched Willy. He'd taken his mobile out and set it on the table. Toots and Willy stared at the screen.

'What's up with you two?' Alex asked, half smiling.

Willy raised a finger to silence him, and a few seconds later Willy's phone rang. The screen indicated that it was a call from a private number. He stared at it for a moment, then pressed the end key to stop the call. It immediately rang again. This time he let it ring out until voicemail cut in. He went into the call log to check the details. Then he looked at the call log on Toots's phone.

'Have you only started receiving calls with no caller ID in the last week, say?' he asked Toots.

'Yes, I hardly ever get no-ID calls.'

'What's the big deal, you two?' Alex asked.

'In the last week or so, Toots and I have both been getting calls from a withheld number, and we've discovered that they ring one of us straight after the other.'

'So why didn't you answer your phone?'

'Somebody's tracking us. Because I didn't answer my phone, they can't tell where I am, they can only tell where my *phone* is.'

The office phone rang and they all jumped in their seats. Alex went to answer it.

'I've lived through the Troubles in the north and Sean's involvement with the IRA,' Gran said, 'and none of that worried me like this is worrying me. You're all so young. I'm scared for you all.'

'Bless you, Gran, we'll get through this. Don't worry.' Toots came round the table and gave Gran a big hug. 'What about a fresh pot of tea.'

Alex closed the office door and came back to the table. He didn't look best pleased.

'That was our friend James Hollinger. He and Inspector Sullivan will be here in five or ten minutes.' Alex shook his head. 'Bollocks! There are too many loose ends, too many unanswered questions.'

'Wait until plod and company arrive. I think I can throw light on some of our problems,' Willy said confidently. 'Let me sit at the end of the table with the window behind me. Alex, you sit on my left and Toots on my right. Gran, you sit at the end opposite me.'

Gran gave Willy a knowing smile. 'Well thought out, if I may say so,' she said, settling into the carver chair.

'I'm glad someone knows why we're playing musical chairs,' said Alex. 'I haven't got an effing clue.'

Willy booted up his laptop and connected it to his mobile and the iJack. He relaxed into the carver and took a mouthful of tea. 'Let me run this meeting, Alex. Even if they ask a question that you know the answer to, don't say anything. If I want you to answer or speak, I'll say so. Just trust me. These guys are going to arrive before I have the time to explain why. The same applies to you as well, Toots – no interruptions please.'

'You haven't told *me* what to do yet. Will I just knock them on the head if they get out of order?' Gran said with a mischievous glint in her eye.

'I want you to interrupt if you aren't clear about anything I explain. That will let me know if I'm getting too technical.

The others know about mobiles and computers, you don't, and I want my explanation to be in layman's language as far as possible.'

Alex rose from the table in response to a knock at the front door. He returned to the kitchen with Jim Hollinger and Inspector Sullivan and introduced them to everyone.

'Come and sit beside me,' Gran said, patting the empty chairs on either side of her.

Hollinger and Sullivan sat down. Sullivan took out his notebook and opened his mouth, but before he got the chance to speak, Willy butted in.

'Why did you have Guard Cosgrove follow me?' he asked calmly.

Sullivan, clearly taken aback, closed his mouth again. But not for long.

'First, there are a number of questions that we need to ask *you*,' he said, flicking open his notebook.

'Not until you've answered mine. Why was Guard Cosgrove following me?' Willy repeated.

'Mr McNabb, please do not stretch our patience any further!'

'I'll be happy not to once you've answered my question.'

Inspector Sullivan leapt from his chair. 'You impudent bloody northerner. Who the hell —'

Gran smacked the table with the flat of her hand. 'Inspector Sullivan!'

Silence descended while everyone stared at Gran.

Sullivan visibly pulled himself together. 'My apologies, Mrs Casey. Let's start again, shall we?'

'So why was I being followed, and why did you place a listening device in my room at the hotel?' Willy asked.

The second question brought a smile to Alex's face, but a look of horror to Gran's and Toots's.

'Under the European Convention on Human Rights you are required to obtain judicial authorisation to conduct covert surveillance,' Willy went on. 'May we see that authorisation please, Inspector Sullivan?'

Hollinger shook his head and looked at Sullivan, who shifted nervously in his seat.

Willy hadn't finished yet. 'Okay, so here's an easier question. Why are you tracking our mobile phones?' He pointed to the two phones on the table.

Sullivan rolled his eyes and stood up. 'I've had enough of this, Jim. You coming?'

He went to the back door and walked out, leaving it open. Hollinger gave the others a weak smile and followed Sullivan out.

'I enjoyed that,' said Gran gleefully.

Alex went out the kitchen door and looked down the drive before coming back in again. 'They're having a cigarette and a conference across the road, doubtless discussing their next move.'

'Okay, we don't have much time,' Willy said, opening the lid of his laptop. 'Let's recap what we know and don't know before those two buffoons come back.'

Chapter 13

The senator sat with his eyes closed in the back of the Rolls as they drove from Balbriggan to Bewleys Hotel. When he pulled up at the lights at Ballsbridge, Peter tapped the screen behind his head and watched in his rear-view mirror to see the senator open his eyes. He gave his boss a slight nod.

'I've been thinking, not sleeping, Peter,' the senator said. 'I've come to the conclusion, yet again, that I should have paid heed to your advice. I should have given the job to my daughter, *not* my son. He's an incapable halfwit, and now I'm going to have to do it all over again. How the hell am I going to keep this tidy? Money won't satisfy him, for he craves power, but doesn't understand how to use it. Let me have your thoughts before dinner, please. You know I value your opinion.'

The head porter was on hand as the Rolls pulled up under the awning at the front entrance of Bewleys.

'Good afternoon, Senator O'Gorman,' he said as he opened the passenger door. 'It's a pleasure to have you with us again.'

'Good afternoon, Brendan. How is your wife? Better, I trust. When I spoke to Sir Richard at Guy's Hospital the other day, he was quietly optimistic – said he expected a full recovery.'

'That's the information I have as well, Senator. A few weeks' convalescence and she'll be nagging the life out of me again. Thank you for everything you've done for her. Without your help she may well have died.'

'All I did was even the balance sheet, Brendan. It's fair to say that without your help some years ago I may well have died.'

Brendan Magee unconsciously put his hand up to a scar on his left temple, a scar inflicted by Sean Casey twenty-two years earlier. 'Shall I ask Simon to go up in ten minutes, sir?'

'Indeed, Brendan. Thank you. Peter!'

The senator walked into the hotel foyer where the duty manager was waiting at the open private lift that served the presidential suite. Peter, meanwhile, passed a fifty euro note to Brendan, collected the senator's overnight bag from the car, locked the Rolls and followed the senator to the lift. He would see the senator settled into his suite before returning to move the Rolls. He allowed no valets in the car, another throwback to the old days.

The duty manager nodded to the senator and stood aside to let him enter the lift accompanied by Peter. As always, they travelled up on their own. When they reached their floor, the senator sat outside in the lift lobby while Peter checked the suite. Satisfied, he beckoned the senator in, closed the door and sat down at the writing desk. A few minutes later he went into the bedroom where the senator was lying on the bed wrapped in a white dressing gown and handed him a sheet of hotel writing paper.

'Thank you, Peter. We'll talk after my massage.'

Peter collected the neatly folded clothes from the side chair and took them with him. Simon, the masseur, was waiting out in the lift lobby when Peter opened the door. The young man slid sideways into the suite, keeping as far away from the huge chauffeur as he could. Peter nodded at him and left the suite, taking the lift down to the lobby. When he exited, he locked the lift door and put the key in his pocket.

The receptionist recoiled a little as she took the senator's laundry from Peter. He gave her a fifty euro note, took the pen and pad that was offered and wrote down the time he wanted the fresh laundry to be delivered to their suite the next morning.

Brendan nodded to Peter from behind the porter's desk as the giant passed through the entrance lobby. Then he pulled his mobile phone out of his pocket. 'He's in the suite and the freak's parking the Rolls. Do it now!' he said in a loud whisper.

He had just returned the phone to his pocket when the ground disappeared from under him and his head was smashed through a glass panel beside the revolving doors. Then he was thrown to the ground and he heard the sickening sound of his own arm breaking. Lying on the floor in a pool of blood he watched, mesmerised, as Peter's foot came down on his genitals.

Peter took Brendan's mobile out of his pocket and walked back to the front desk. The receptionist leapt backwards as Peter reached over to grab the senator's laundry. He crossed the foyer to the private lift, the other guests gaping at him in horror. As Peter unlocked the lift door, the receptionist started to scream.

When the lift arrived at the top floor, Peter crashed in through the suite door, nearly taking it off its hinges. The senator, naked except for a modesty towel, sat up abruptly on the massage table. Simon let out a little squeal and jumped back. The senator sized up the situation immediately. He threw the towel away and quickly pulled on his crumpled clothes, ignoring the tie and waistcoat. Peter grabbed Simon by his tunic, hurled him into the bedroom, putting a finger to his lips to indicate silence, and closed the door. Then he went to the window that opened onto the fire escape and looked down the steel steps. Drawing back in, he closed the window but didn't lock it. He took the senator by the arm and led him to the bathroom, pulling the door over, leaving it open a crack. The senator spoke not one word.

They watched through the bathroom door as the bottom sash of the fire-escape window slowly slid up. All credit to the hotel maintenance team: there wasn't a sound from the pulleys and weights. Stooping to climb in, a black-clothed figure, his face concealed by a balaclava, looked around the room, a silenced pistol in his left hand following the direction of his eyes. Once clear of the window frame, he waved his companion in.

The first man indicated that he would take the bedroom while his companion checked the bathroom. The men parted and silently moved across the large room. As the gunman's fingers touched the bathroom door to push it open, Peter unexpectedly pulled it open and the gunman stumbled forward into Peter's open arms. Caught in a bear hug, his arms piniored to his sides, the gunman pulled the trigger and a bullet buried itself uselessly in the wall beside the door frame. Hearing the 'phut' of his partner's silenced shot, the first man spun round in time to loose one wild shot. Peter hurled his companion at him, and the two ended up in a heap, flattened to the floor by Peter's flying body. Peter stood up and straightened his uniform. The gunman Peter had thrown had been hit in the head by the wild shot from his partner's gun; the other was lying on his side under the corpse, his head at an odd angle.

The silence that followed was broken, first, by the wail of distant sirens, and then by the shrieks from Simon who had opened the bedroom door. Peter walked into the bedroom and retrieved the senator's overnight bag and personal effects. Simon collapsed in a dead faint. Stepping over the prone masseur, Peter handed the senator his mobile phone, pulled Brendan's phone out of his pocket and pointed to the last number the porter had called. He walked to the desk and wrote a brief note explaining what had happened downstairs and handed it to the senator.

'Thank you, Peter.' The senator read the note and registered the number on Brendan's phone. 'This is too bad, too bad indeed.'

He immediately called Mary Lennihan.

'Mary, would you ask the commissioner to give me a call. We have a small problem here at Bewleys Hotel and we need his help. Then cancel ... no, push my dinner reservation at Roly's back to eight thirty. Also, could you book a suite at The

Shelbourne. I may need two additional double rooms as well, and they must be on the same floor. Don't speak to anyone else before you call back to confirm, especially Dominic.'

He hung up and surveyed the room. 'Now, Peter, this is a bit of a mess, isn't it. I don't suppose either of these heroes has any identification on them?'

Peter shook his head but pointed at Simon who was sitting up and staring at the two bodies now divested of their balaclavas.

'Simon, young man, do you recognise either of these imbeciles? I feel sure they are colleagues of Brendan's – complete amateurs, no style!'

Simon looked at the senator, then Peter, and waved a limp hand towards the nearest body. 'That's Brendan's son-in-law, Packy Bolan, and the other one's his cousin, Tosser. They both porter here under Brendan.'

'Ah, the famous Bolans.' The senator shook his head. 'Brendan never could organise anything properly, and to use two of the hotel staff – tut, tut, very foolish. But I wonder who Brendan was working for?'

The hotel phone disturbed his deliberations. 'O'Gorman speaking … Ah, yes, commissioner. Thank you for calling me. There has been an attack on me. I'm afraid there is one corpse and a badly injured man in the room, and a well-beaten head porter in reception. Peter and I need to move out of here, but I'm a little concerned about the reception we'll get downstairs from your chaps. Can you get here to liberate us? We wouldn't like to have a run-in with your armed response team … Ten minutes? Thank you.'

As he replaced the room phone, his mobile rang.

'Mary … Yes, I've just spoken to him … The Shelbourne? Excellent. And Roly's Bistro? … Good. I've just had a thought – the private room at Roly's would be better if it's available … What? … When did he leave? Okay. Now, would you ask Vem to join me for dinner this evening at Roly's at eight thirty, and, Mary, make sure she knows it's not a request. Ask her to bring an overnight bag … Yes, thank you we're both fine. That's everything for the moment … Yes, please, keep the phone beside you all evening. Thank you, Mary.'

The senator put the phone in his pocket and sat back. 'Two questions, Peter – who was behind this attack? And why did Dominic pack a bag, clear his desk and leave the office about an hour after us? While we deliberate, I think a drink would be in order. Simon, would you care to join me?'

Poor Simon fainted again.

Chapter 14

Jim Hollinger and Inspector Sullivan were deep in conversation outside No. 87 when Sullivan's phone rang.

'Sullivan,' he answered abruptly. He listened for half a minute. 'Holy fuck, who did you send? … Sweet Jesus, tell him not to blink till I get there. He's done enough damage for one day.' Sullivan finished the call and gave Hollinger a look of total despair.

'There's been an incident at Bewleys Hotel,' he explained. 'One dead and at least two seriously injured. That was the desk sergeant. He had to send Cosgrove – the only man he had, God help us. How much worse can this day get?'

As if to answer his question, his phone rang again. Sullivan looked at the screen and groaned before taking the call.

'Good afternoon, Commissioner … Yes, sir … Yes, sir … Of course, sir …' He slipped the phone back into his pocket. 'He wants me personally at the Bewleys incident,' he told Hollinger. 'Something to do with his pal Senator O'Gorman. Wants me to make it all go away. In that case, I'd better go – prevent Guard Cosgrove turning it into a disaster.'

'That's okay. I'll stay here and try to find out who knows what. You take the car. I can ring in for a lift when I finish,' said Hollinger.

'Well, whatever you do, wipe the smirk off the face of that arrogant little fucker McNabb,' Sullivan said as he walked off.

* * *

Alex was in the office talking to Patsy Dan on the phone. When he came back into the kitchen, he had a smile on his face.

'I don't think I'm going to have any bother with my new traffic manager. He wants to swap two of the drivers round because he's unhappy about the mileage they're getting. And the two lads I took on from Molloy's pub are working their backsides off. They both want a shot at the licence!'

Willy glanced up from his laptop and nodded. He had Michael's little red notebook open and his fingers were dancing across the keyboard. Toots and Gran had cleared the table and put the kettle on again.

'Let's try and make sense out of it all,' said Willy. 'This little book is at the centre of our problems and—'

There was a knock on the back door and Hollinger opened it without waiting for a reply. 'Inspector Sullivan has been called away to a serious incident, so you're stuck with me, I'm afraid,' he said as he walked in and closed the door behind him.

'Why are you still here?' Willy asked, scowling.

Hollinger ignored him. 'We need to try to work together on this problem, Mr Casey, not see each other as enemies.'

'If you want our co-operation, you need to explain why you're tailing and tapping us,' Alex said.

'Someone has accessed – hacked into – bank accounts connected to the various money laundering operations we're investigating,' Hollinger explained, pulling out a chair and sitting down. 'We're trying to find a missing code book, the key to millions of pounds stashed away in the bank accounts. As Mr McNabb is a computer expert who lives in the geographical area from where the last hack was carried out, he came to our attention. And his involvement with your family made us all the more interested. Your business manager, Mr Slaney, had dealings with some rather dubious people, connected, we think, with the money laundering racket. His murder has forced us to reveal our hand. We think you can be a great help to us, Mr McNabb.' Hollinger turned to Willy and met his stare. 'We think you're probably Mouseman.'

Willy looked down at his laptop.

'Are you?' Hollinger didn't take his eyes off Willy.

Willy raised his head and looked around at everyone, his eyes finally settling on Hollinger. 'Yes,' he said quietly.

Toots gasped and opened her mouth to say something but was interrupted by Hollinger.

'In that case, my superior wants to meet you and talk to you about enlisting your services. He rates you as one of the best in the business and an asset we could use. He wants you to come to London straight away.'

'Not interested,' snapped Willy.

Hollinger drummed his fingers on the table and grimaced. 'Is Willy in trouble with the authorities?' Gran asked.

'He's in more trouble with the people who murdered Michael Slaney, Mrs Casey. He has something that they want. That's why we need to get him out of here immediately.'

Willy was looking at the little red book. He scooted it down the table to Hollinger. 'That's your key. That's what Michael died for.'

'Ahhhh, so that's what Mrs Slaney's intruders were looking for,' Hollinger said, flicking through the notebook.

'Her intruders?' Gran was alarmed.

'Yes, turned her house over when she was out earlier today,' Hollinger told Gran. 'Don't worry, Mrs Casey, she's fine – she's in protective custody now – but you can see how serious this all is.'

'So that's what it's all about – a stupid little book?' Toots blurted out.

'No, that's why Michael died,' Willy said, reaching into his computer bag and pulling out an identical little red book. 'This is what *our* troubles are about.'

He slid the second book down the table as well.

A wry smile spread across Hollinger's face. 'So you had it after all. I *knew* it! I take it you have an idea what this is worth to the men who're looking for it – several millions, we think.'

'Eighteen million, six hundred and seventy-three thousand, nine hundred and thirty-five pounds and ninety-nine pence at close of business on Friday,' Willy said as though he'd just recited a grocery bill.

Hollinger nodded and waggled the books in the air. 'I need to make a call and have a smoke,' he said, and he got up and went outside.

Willy gave everyone a weak smile. 'All I did was crack a code. I didn't take any of the money, honest.'

Alex started to laugh, and Gran patted Willy's hand. 'What a clever young man,' she said gleefully.

Toots glared at him. 'How could you not have told me?' she said.

'Do these thugs know you've cracked their code?' Alex asked.

'They know somebody has accessed the bank accounts and had a look around. They don't know who though – at least, I don't think they know.'

Hollinger came back in. He seemed shaken. 'I've spoken to my people in London. Stephen Reid, my boss, will be over in the morning to talk to you. He's very concerned about your safety – all of you. Willy, he's asked me to ask you to take a look at Mr Slaney's red book. He wants to know if you can crack it before he arrives. He—'

'Stop right there, Hollinger. You're making way too many assumptions,' Willy said. 'I haven't agreed to work with you yet. Can you give me some time to talk this over with Alex, Toots and Gran? After all, their lives are in danger now too.'

Hollinger's face hardened. 'We've arranged secure accommodation for you all for the next few days until we get to the bottom of this. You've opened a can of worms, Willy. You've accessed accounts that have lain dormant for more than twenty years, and accessed information that has direct links with the deaths of a number of my colleagues. You don't really have any option but to work with us – certainly not while good men and women risk their lives for your protection.' He looked straight at Willy, his face like thunder. 'Do I make myself clear?'

Willy was cleaning his glasses furiously and concentrating

on the task as if it was incredibly interesting.

'I think the idea of secure accommodation is a good one,' Gran said. 'But I'm staying put here. They took my Sean, God rest his soul, but I'll not hide from them, and that's final.'

'I agree with Gran,' Alex said. 'It's a good idea to be protected till the problem's resolved, but that applies to the four of us, Gran. Otherwise you'd be the obvious one for them to go after.'

Just then, Willy's laptop pinged.

'It's an email,' he said, and scratched around on the touchpad. He read something on the screen and then turned the laptop around to face the others.

'I think that's our minds made up for us,' he said. 'They're closing in.'

The email read:

MOUSEMAN: WE HAVE YOU

Chapter 15

Guard Cosgrove arrived at Bewleys Hotel to find paramedics attending to Brendan, the injured head porter, and the duty manager taking care of the receptionist who'd fainted. The lobby was full of gawpers and hangers-on. Cosgrove's first instinct was to do nothing; his second was to leave and return in five minutes when, hopefully, a more senior officer would have arrived; his third was to clear the lobby, which he did – everyone out except the wounded, the medics and staff. That some of the bystanders he shooed out through the revolving doors were probable witnesses did not occur to him, so keen was he to prove to Inspector Sullivan that he was capable of taking charge of a situation.

Fifteen minutes later Sullivan came through the doors with such force they continued to spin long after he reached the foyer. He stopped in the middle and surveyed the crime scene, taking in the paramedics with Brendan and the staff in a huddle behind the reception desk.

'Witnesses? Where are they?'

Cosgrove shrank within himself. Sullivan was about to devour the hapless guard when the duty manager spoke up.

'I saw it all – it was terrible. He just picked Brendan up and put his head through the window. Then he —'

'Thank you, sir. Hold on a moment. Are there any others?'

A number of people had followed Sullivan back in through the revolving doors and now clamoured for his attention, certain that their exaggerated version of events was the definitive one.

'Cosgrove, take all these good citizens into the lounge, get their details and statements ... and don't mess it up. Help will arrive shortly.'

The inspector turned to the duty manager, reaching for his cigarettes at the same time. 'Don't dare tell me it's a no-smoking area, okay. So, where are the other victims?'

'Kitchens. They —'

Sullivan held up his hand. 'Tell the sergeant here after I speak to him.'

Sergeant Foley had just arrived and was looking round the foyer. Sullivan gave him a quick update. Foley was an old-school pro who knew all about the pressures the inspector was under with the commissioner.

'You take charge here, Sergeant,' Sullivan said. 'I'll deal with any repercussions. Just keep a tight rein on Cosgrove – he's caused me enough grief already today. And there's another victim in the kitchens apparently. The paramedics are attending there too.'

As the inspector finished his briefing, his mobile rang.

When he answered it the exasperation was clear in his voice. 'Yes ... Sorry, Jim, this is a right royal fuck-up here ... Uh huh ... Uh huh.' As he continued to listen, he relaxed a little. 'It's about time we got a break. Where the hell are you going to put them? We've nowhere in the city ... Has that been approved on high? ... Well, if it's their suggestion, it comes out of their budget. It's certainly an easy place to secure ... Good. I'll finish up here shortly. I'll see you at The Shelbourne in half an hour or so.'

* * *

The two unmarked Garda cars, Alex and Gran in one and Willy and Toots in the other, made good time to the city centre. They turned into Kildare Street, then into an entry that led to the secure car park at the rear of The Shelbourne Hotel. The private entrance to the Royal Suite, as it was grandly named, was hidden from public view. The cars were security checked through two different steel security gates before they were allowed to enter the underground car park. To get into the hotel itself the group and their Garda escort had to pass through an airport-like metal detector, which caused Willy all sorts of problems, its alarm triggered by his gadgets.

The lift they entered gave an indication of the luxury they were to find in the suite itself. The four stepped into the middle of the main salon in complete awe – highly polished wood, deep-pile carpets, silk wallpaper, furniture that would be at home in a palace.

'Glad you came, Gran?' Alex said, breaking the spell.

'Humph! Must be hard to keep clean.'

Her response provoked a burst of laughter from everyone, including the two Garda officers.

'That's one for the visitor's book, Mrs Casey,' said the senior officer. 'Now, Mr Hollinger and Inspector Sullivan will be along shortly to explain how this is going to work. In the meantime, make yourselves at home. The main door to the suite is controlled from outside at the security desk. Call if you need anything before Mr Hollinger arrives. Otherwise, please wait until the inspector has arrived.'

The two officers got back into the lift.

The Royal Suite was a recent addition to The Shelbourne Hotel. It was built on the reinforced and structurally altered roof of the original hotel and its neighbour, the old IFI building. This office block was now the head office for the Newell Group, The Shelbourne's owners. The new structure could not be a conventional bricks-and-mortar build because of the loading it placed on the original building's foundations and walls. Yet it had to be totally secure because of the anticipated clientele, filthy-rich Russian oligarchs and top entertainers, among others. Calling it the Royal Suite was wishful thinking, but it impressed some of its less than aristocratic visitors.

The suite had been designed and assembled in Germany, then disassembled and shipped to Dublin where it was reassembled on the prepared roof by German engineers in just seven weeks. It was an engineering first for Krupt und Smerk, a company that anticipated a world market for their 'bomb-proof' concept – at least, so their marketing blurb claimed.

The interior design company, Original Thought, took ten weeks to complete the fit-out, and the complete project cost the Newell Group almost two million euros. It was costing the Irish government a discounted rate of seven thousand euros a week, pro rata, to accommodate the Royal Suite's latest guests, the Casey party.

The outer skin of the new structure was constructed from a composite material sandwich, the make-up of which was a closely guarded secret. It included zinc, aluminium, carbon fibre, Kevlar and twenty-four inches of high-density insulation. The roof was the same sandwich, but the external finish, in this instance, was copper which would weather down to complement the copper roofs on adjacent churches and the cathedral.

The floor-to-ceiling windows and terrace wall were of a new laminated glass panel, its components again known to only the most senior executives in Krupt und Smerk. However, they claimed it would stop an RPG and armour-piercing shells; field trials were ongoing and the results encouraging. Since the directors of the Newell Group did not envisage a circumstance where the glass would be tested to that level, they were happy to take the supplier's undertakings as to its 'fitness for purpose'. But all of this technical background was of no interest to the Royal Suite's present occupants.

'Okay, let's see what we have here,' said Alex when the police officers had left.

Ever practical, he started to walk around, the others following him in silence. The back of the main salon was taken up by the entrance lobby, a separate WC and small cloakroom. The front wall was glass, floor to ceiling, that looked out over a private roof terrace, itself surrounded by an eight-foot-high glass wall. The terrace afforded a magnificent view over St Stephen's Green, the roofs of surrounding buildings and the Wicklow Hills in the far distance.

Three doors opened off the salon. The first led to another drawing room with a view of tall buildings. It was furnished with two- and three-seater settees, occasional tables and a dining table and chairs. Filling one wall was a luxurious shelving unit that housed a plasma TV, sound system and bookshelves. A marble-surround fireplace with gas fire and a cocktail cabinet were on the opposite side of the room. A door off the right-hand wall led to a bedroom with en-suite facilities the like of which none of them had ever seen outside a magazine.

They returned to the main salon and Willy opened the second door. It led to an identical bedroom suite.

Alex went to the third door and opened it slowly, peeping through like a child until the others pushed it wide open from behind him. They fell into yet another plush drawing room, a match for the main salon, though smaller. They stood transfixed by the splendour of it.

Toots opened a door to what she presumed was a bedroom and shrieked with delight as she launched herself into the middle of the enormous four-poster bed that dominated the room.

'This is mine. I bags this room,' she yelled, tumbling about on the bed.

The others laughed at her childlike antics.

'Where's the bathroom? Where's the loo? It's bound to be gold-plated,' she said and bounced off the bed.

She walked the length of a row of floor-to-ceiling wardrobe doors, opening each one. The fourth proved not to lead to a wardrobe but to the en suite, gold-plated taps and all.

'So this is what royalty has to suffer. Dear help them.'

Gran's caustic comment was met with hoots of laughter.

'Look at the bath!' she went on. 'You could sail across it … and the shower! Alex, you could wash a lorry in there. I never saw the likes of it. What must this cost to live in for an hour, never mind a night?'

'Fortunately we aren't paying, Gran. Anyway, Toots has said she wants this room, so we mere mortals will never know what it's like to sleep where royalty has slept.'

'Ah well,' Gran said, 'I'll make do with one of the small rooms.'

'That's the spirit, Gran,' Alex said, grinning. 'We'll manage to put up with this luxury somehow.'

They all went back to the main salon where Willy had already set up his laptop and arranged his other gadgets on the desk.

'Let's have a beer and relax till our jailers arrive,' Willy suggested.

'Why is your gadget flashing like that?' Alex asked him.

'The monitor's telling me a number of things,' Willy explained. 'Firstly, there's a firewall that's preventing a breach of Wi-Fi security. Secondly, the suite is clear of listening devices. But it's the third thing that's the most interesting. The strength of the signal suggests that we're close to the control centre that has something to do with the red books. While we were waiting at Gran's, I scanned their contents into my laptop before I gave Hollinger the books.'

'Are you saying you've cracked the alpha-whatsit code in Michael's red book?'

'Alphanumeric code. Not yet. All I need is a couple of hours, but don't tell them that – not yet.' Willy still had a little niggle at the back of his mind – something Sullivan had said.

Dusk was falling when Toots came out of Gran's room.

'She's out cold … Ooooh could I have one of those, please?' She held her hand out for a bottle of beer. 'Then I'm going for a swim in my gold-plated bath.'

She laughed and was about to get up when they heard a faint mechanical click. The lobby door opened and Inspector Sullivan and Jim Hollinger came in, both looking exhausted.

'Your lives and my job are on the line, so you'll do as I say while you're in my protective custody,' Sullivan barked. 'Jim has told me where we are with these' – he pulled the two red books out of his pocket and threw them onto the desk beside Willy's laptop – 'and he gets what he wants in the morning, Willy. No more grandstanding from you or I'll throw you in Portlaoise and throw away the fucking keys, okay?'

With that he turned and walked out of the room leaving Alex, Toots and Willy in stunned silence.

Hollinger shook his head and sat down.

'We're under pressure from the Garda commissioner who thinks our priorities ought to lie elsewhere,' he said by way of explanation. 'Now, I need all you can give me by tomorrow morning, Willy. We've been told by our colleagues in America that a billion dollars is on the move in the next few weeks. It's going to destabilise the international money markets and bankrupt a Third World country.'

Willy remained silent, his face expressionless.

'In exchange for your help, you all get to stay in this rather magnificent suite. For your own safety, you can't leave here until this is over – I reckon forty-eight hours max. Room service is available twenty-four hours a day. You can get fresh air out on the terrace which is protected by one-way bulletproof glass. You can't be seen from outside, and the height of the glass was calculated to prevent a sniper from taking a potshot from any of the surrounding tower blocks. The door to the terrace is controlled using the buttons … over there.' He pointed to the side table to the right of the window.

His phone rang.

'On my way,' he said into it and stood up to leave.

'Before you go, Hollinger, can I use my gear here?' Willy asked. 'The internet connection seems to be blocked.'

'Of course you can use your gear. Why wouldn't you? The internet connection's out of my field of expertise, I'm afraid, but I'll text you a number in the next ten minutes, someone you can speak to about it. Anything else before I go?'

Hollinger took his leave of them, pulling his cigarettes out of his pocket before he even got to the lift lobby door.

Chapter 16

The Shelbourne Hotel was an establishment that smacked of old decency. It still offered full silver service afternoon tea in the Lord Mayor's parlour, boasted a traditional gent's barber shop and attended washrooms, and offered a traditional shoe-cleaning service to guests. It was a favourite watering hole for the horsey set during the RDS shows, and the county hunts still held their annual ball in its faded, but majestic, ballroom.

None of this was of any interest to Senator Eugene O'Gorman as he entered the hotel by the rear door from the off-street car park where a porter was waiting to greet him and escort him to his suite.

In the lift on the way up, George, always convivial and gossipy, gave a precis of the current gossip and informed them that the Royal Suite was currently occupied, although he had no idea by whom; there had been none of the usual pomp and ceremony that accompanied diplomatic or celebrity visitors to the hotel. As he was about to leave, however, a second fifty-euro note ensured that George would shortly discover the identity of the Royal Suite's occupants and share it with the senator, who seldom missed the opportunity to bump into the right people.

* * *

In the hotel's Saddle Bar, Jim Hollinger was nursing his second pint of Guinness and feeling sorry for himself. He had high cholesterol and his blood pressure was off the chart. His ex-wife, with whom he still kept in touch only because of their shared ownership of a holiday home he never used, continued to preach that he was overweight, drank too much and smoked like hell's chimney. Apart from that he was fine, if you ignored the fact that he averaged five hours' sleep a night, worked seven days a week and hadn't had a holiday in six years. But what was it all for? To be kowtowing to some self-centred, university-educated, fast-tracked Garda commissioner who he didn't even work for?

A mile away, in An Garda Síochána headquarters, Inspector Sullivan was in similarly despondent humour. He was waiting for a second round with the commissioner, this time at his own request. This meeting was to submit his resignation – at least that's what he planned to threaten.

* * *

At a private airstrip near Bray, Dominic O'Gorman had just taken off in a Bell LongRanger helicopter accompanied by four sinister-looking individuals in full blackout gear and armed with personal revolvers and Heckler & Koch assault rifles. One carried a full backpack, and the others each carried a coil of nylon rope over one shoulder. No one spoke to, or made eye contact with, Dominic.

* * *

At the Leopardstown Road junction on the N11 dual carriageway, Vem O'Gorman was using all the power of the Aston Martin and her not inconsiderable skill to frustrate the Garda traffic car that had clocked her at a hundred and eighteen miles per hour at the Milltown North slip road. She had the hood down, her hair was tied back with a stylish scarf and her designer sunglasses hid much of her face, but Guards Connolly and Flaherty knew exactly who the driver was. They also knew the prize if they could book 'The Flying Lady' – force-wide recognition and a place in the history books of Traffic Corps, not to mention the considerable cash pot that had accumulated over several years of chasing her. If they failed to book her, they had to pay a fine of twenty euros each into the pot.

'Bejesus, she can handle that car!' Connolly said, gunning after her in the force's Volvo V70 turbo.

* * *

Back in the Royal Suite, Gran was fast asleep, Toots was fantasising about the future as she soaped herself in the luxurious double bath and Alex was on the phone to Patsy Dan, discussing the next day's lorry schedule. Willy alone was not a happy man.

With his elbows on the table and his chin resting on his hands, he was studying the laptop and the iJack alternately. Neither of them agreed with the other: the laptop said there was an incoming email, yet the iJack said there was no signal available. Now and again Willy took his hand away from his chin to stab at the laptop keyboard, but he'd return to his meditative pose none the wiser. Finally, he sat back, stretched and yawned.

'This is bloody stupid,' he said to himself.

Picking up his mobile he searched for the text message that Hollinger had sent him and called the number in the text.

'Central Services Cleaning. How may we help you?'

'Hi, I'm looking for some technical help. Jim Hollinger gave me this number.'

There was a soft click. 'Who gave you our number?'

'Hollinger, Jim Hollinger.'

Just then the alarm on the iJack sounded. Willy immediately ended the call on his phone. He looked at the iJack screen for a moment, then turned his phone off altogether just as it was showing an incoming call. His hands flew over the keyboard of his laptop and he watched its screen and the iJack intently.

Both gave the same message: 'AlterNet Signalling in Operation.'

Willy leapt towards Alex, grabbed his phone, killed the call and turned it off completely. Then he ran into the master bedroom.

'Toots, where's your bloody phone?'

Toots giggled from the bathroom. 'You'll have to come in here to get it, you naught—'

Willy crashed through the door, ignoring Toots and her seductive pose in the bath, picked up her phone and turned it off.

'Out you get, Toots. We've got problems,' he said over his shoulder on his way back out the door.

* * *

Senator O'Gorman expressed his gratitude to George, the porter, in the customary way. The information he had gathered about the occupants of the Royal Suite was incomplete but sufficient: an elderly lady and a young man, both by the name of Casey, and another young man and young woman. How George elicited this information, the senator neither knew nor cared. The most interesting piece of information was that they were in protective custody, apparently assisting with enquiries not only for the Garda but for some English copper.

The senator opened his phone and pressed the button for Mary Lennihan. It was answered on the second ring.

'Mary, I need to speak to Vem immediately. Ask her to phone no matter what she's doing.'

As he finished the call, the hotel phone rang.

'Good evening, Senator, this is Susan in reception. Commissioner Shackleton has phoned to offer his apologies. He's running twenty minutes late and will join you at Roly's Bistro rather than come here first.'

The senator thanked her and hung up. He nodded to Peter who had just risen from the desk. 'That's good, Peter. That gives us a little more time. Now, what's this?' The senator reached out for Peter's note.

When he'd read it, he sighed. 'There are times when I wish I had put you in charge rather than Vem, good as she is. Yes, I agree. I think they're in trouble. So help them we shall.'

He was interrupted by his mobile ringing.

'Hello, Vem, where are you?'

'Giving two young guards a driving lesson on the N11.' Her raunchy laughter brought a smile to the senator's face. He had a big soft spot for Vem – always had, despite her early mistakes.

'Make sure you lose them before you get here. I'm at The Shelbourne, by the way. Come here, not Roly's. Don't garage the car. I think I may need you to make a special delivery. Pull in on the Stephen's Green side of the road opposite the hotel and call me when you get there.'

He closed his phone. 'Right, Peter, let's try to extract young Casey and his party before it's too late. Off you go!'

* * *

The Bell LongRanger helicopter carrying Dominic O'Gorman and the four armed thugs headed east after take-off, flying three hundred feet above the Irish Sea at Dublin Bay before swinging north-east in a lazy arc around the back of Howth Head and coming inland to make a pickup at a deserted stretch of coast just north of Balbriggan.

The landing site among the sand dunes was marked by the flashing headlights of a Range Rover. It had come south from Keady in County Armagh earlier that day, driven by an obese man who struggled to find room to turn the steering wheel. His passenger was a six-foot-two walking skeleton who had a skill that Dominic needed and was paying ten thousand euro for.

As the Bell landed, the skeletal passenger nodded to the driver, slipped out of the Range Rover and, ducking beneath the still-turning rotors while shielding his eyes from the maelstrom of sand and shale, walked with a peculiar hobbling gait to the open door of the helicopter. He climb in, assisted by one of the men in black. As soon as the door was secured, the Bell lifted off again.

Dominic and the new arrival shook hands. A black-clad

figure handed the backpack to the newcomer and sat down. The skinny man carefully extracted each of the items from the pack, his long, slender fingers seeming to caress them as he checked them and set them aside. Satisfied, he nodded to Dominic, and Dominic signalled to the man in black who knelt beside the bag and carefully repacked it, replacing the items in a specific order. Then he returned to his seat with the backpack and strapped himself in.

The pilot informed them that it would take seven minutes to reach their final destination.

* * *

'Bingo! They're at their fucking work again,' Willy shouted, staring at his laptop screen. He typed something on the keyboard then relaxed back into his seat. 'Let's see you pick the bones out of that, you bollocks!'

Alex came over to the desk as Toots appeared out of the bedroom.

'What the hell is going on?' he asked.

'We're being spied on and my equipment was being blocked. The phone number Hollinger gave me was compromised. Someone tried to tap my call. Basically, we can't trust anyone and we can't use our phones.'

The iJack pinged.

'Aaaah, now I see what's happening,' Willy said knowingly. 'Someone is using GPS and mobile phone traces to try and pinpoint our location. That suggests that it's not Sullivan or Hollinger who are spying on us – they know where we are. Someone is after those little red books and is most likely trying to get them before we pass them on to the guards.'

'If you're right, we're in more danger than Hollinger or Sullivan seem to think,' Alex said. 'We need to speak to them urgently. Is it safe to use a mobile to phone Hollinger? You have his number, don't you?'

'No, we can't use our phones, and I don't have Hollinger's

number – it shows up as "Private Number".'

'But surely we could use the hotel phone,' Toots said.

'For all we know it's tapped too, and the number would be easy to trace. No, it needs to be an untraceable number, like a pay-as-you-go mobile.'

Alex sprang up and rushed into Gran's bedroom. A few seconds later he emerged clutching a plain-looking mobile phone.

'I made Gran get this last year in case she had a fall or whatever when she's out,' Alex explained. 'It's very basic, but will it do?'

Willy took the phone. 'Perfect. What's the number for directory enquiries down here?'

'Look under D in the contacts list. It was one of the first numbers I put in it,' said Alex.

A rather sleepy and dishevelled Gran had emerged from her room, buried in an enormous bathrobe. 'What's all the fuss about?'

Toots went to her. 'Come and sit down and I'll explain.'

'Right, let's see who we can get hold of. I'll ask for both Sullivan and Hollinger.' Willy pressed the call button.

* * *

Inspector Sullivan had left the commissioner somewhat cheered; he still had his job. All sorts of promises had been made pending successful closure of the case. He had put his mobile on silent for the meeting and forgotten to put it back on again. Flashing mutely, it nestled in his coat pocket on the back seat of the car as he drove home, content that his charges were secure for the evening.

Jim Hollinger was on his fourth pint of the black stuff. He'd left the bar twice for a cigarette and once for a pee. He hadn't given his mobile number to anyone at Garda Headquarters.

Chapter 17

Peter left the senator's suite satisfied with the details of the improvised plan. Taking the staff staircase to the underground garage, he managed to avoid being seen by anyone – he was remarkably nimble on his size fourteen feet – and once he'd checked there were no staff or guests in the garage, he quickly crossed to the security door of the Royal Suite. He held the senator's business card up to the CCTV camera that was monitored at the security desk inside.

'I'm sorry, this is a restricted entrance and no one's allowed in,' the guard told Peter through the intercom.

Peter held up a sheet of hotel writing paper on which he had printed the message: 'Senator Eugene O'Gorman would like to meet the occupants of the Royal Suite. My chauffeur, who is mute, has my business card. Please take it to the suite.'

The guard read the message again, zoomed in on the business card and swept the garage with the camera to ensure there was no one else there. Everyone knew of the senator and his connections with An Garda Síochána.

'Okay, stand back and I'll open the door,' the guard said eventually.

The lock clicked, the steel door hissed open and automatically closed behind Peter. Guard Newland nodded to him. As the guard reached for the business card, Peter caught his uniform at the throat, lifted him over the desk and threw him against the security door. Guard Newland crumpled to the floor, unconscious and bleeding from a small head wound. Peter didn't even look round at him; he was sure he'd be out of action for the length of time required. He crossed the lobby, opened the inner door and started cautiously up the stairs, foregoing the lift. Seven flights later he arrived at the fire door leading to the Royal Suite. Peter knocked loudly on the door and watched the handle for any movement.

'What the hell! Who's that out there? No one's supposed to use those stairs,' shouted Guard McConaghy, a young man of twenty-one.

Peter knocked again, louder this time.

'Hold on! I'm coming,' McConaghey muttered. The person knocking had to have been cleared by the security desk downstairs, he reasoned.

As the door swung inwards, Peter yanked it quickly towards himself, causing McConaghy to stumble forward into Peter's arms. Peter then flung the poor unfortunate down the stairs, following him to make sure he was incapacitated. He needn't have bothered; the fall had broken Guard McConaghy's neck. Peter frowned momentarily at the unintended fatality, then sent one of a number of already prepared text messages on his phone: 'In the lift lobby'.

The senator replied: 'Wait!'

* * *

Vem swung off the Stillorgan Road on to the Anglesea Road to avoid a traffic jam ahead and at the Ballsbridge traffic lights slewed the Aston Martin to the left into Merrion Road, narrowly clearing the bull bars on a four-by-four that was crossing with the lights.

Guards Connolly and Flaherty, trying valiantly to catch 'The Flying Lady', had all but given up the chase. They radioed in to report their failure, and received the usual barracking for a missed booking and a reminder to add their fines to the pot.

Vem continued on towards the city centre, barely easing off even though the chase was over. Caught up in traffic, she was forced to travel around Trinity College and into Lower

Grafton Street. Instead of following the traffic left into Nassau Street, she smiled to herself and turned up into Grafton Street's pedestrian zone. Using the horn and an occasional rev of the V8 engine, she waved and laughed as the pedestrians and buskers scurried out of her way. At the top of the street she turned left into St Stephen's Green and found a space to park a few yards short of The Shelbourne Hotel on the opposite side of the road.

She reached across to the passenger side of the car and ruffled Charlie's head.

'Good, eh?' she said to him and climbed out of the car.

She lit a Sobranie cigarette and leaned against the bonnet of her prized Aston Martin. Charlie stretched and yawned, jumped over the passenger door and peed against the rear wheel of the car in front. He sniffed the air and came and sat at Vem's feet. She tickled his ears as passers-by admired the tableau – beautiful woman, beautiful car with hood down and handsome black-and-tan German shepherd.

Vem pulled out her phone and called the senator, wondering what mischief was afoot.

* * *

Inside the Royal Suite, Willy was disconnecting his gear and packing it away. He didn't want to risk being traced, so until he heard from Sullivan or Hollinger all devices were off.

Toots came over and put a hand on his shoulder.

'Please tell me this is going to work out all right,' she said. 'I'm scared.'

'It'll be fine,' Willy said, slipping his arm around her waist and giving her a squeeze. 'I tell you what, let's have a look at the room-service menu and see what's on offer.'

He wasn't hungry but he thought it would keep them all occupied until he could find out more about what was going on.

Just then Gran's mobile rang.

'About time,' he grumbled. 'Hello?'

As he listened, his face turned red and his expression hardened. After a few seconds he exploded.

'No disrespect to you, dear, but this is a fucking shambles. What do you mean you can't reach Sullivan, and why don't you have Hollinger's number? ... Who the fuck's in control in their absence?'

Willy listened for another few seconds, his face becoming more drawn.

'Stop right there. Get in touch with your effing commissioner and if he's not available, work your way down the list till you find someone who'll take responsibility for us. According to your Inspector Sullivan, it's life or death. I'd hate to see what you're like in an emergency.'

He hung up and flung the phone on the desk. 'They couldn't organise a piss-up in a brewery,' he exclaimed, cleaning his glasses furiously. 'I feel responsible for the trouble we seem to be in and I want to be in control of how the problem gets solved, not rely on some half-assed police force.'

Gran tutted and shook her head. 'Shouting at the poor girl on the end of the phone won't help,' she said.

Willy put his glasses back on and slumped into the nearest chair.

Suddenly Toots clicked her fingers. 'The guard on the door – why don't we ask him to contact someone? He must have a superior officer he can phone in case of trouble.'

'Good thinking, that girl,' Alex said, heading for the door. 'But there's no handle – it's locked from the outside.'

'Use the intercom ... on the left.'

Alex did as Willy suggested and waited ... half a minute, then tried again. He held his finger on the button for ages, but there was no reply.

'I don't like this,' he said. 'Surely someone's supposed to be on duty at all times. What do you reckon, Willy?'

'I reckon it's a size nine cock-up!'

* * *

As Vem waited for her father to answer her call, she became aware of the *whump whump whump* of a helicopter approaching from the west. She looked up just as the senator came on the line.

'I see you've upgraded your transport again, Eugene,' she said, watching the chopper come into sight over the green. 'Peter won't be able to drive this one.'

'What on earth are you blathering about? What's that dreadful noise? I can hardly hear you,' the senator shouted.

'It's a helicopter,' she said, laughing. 'I was only teasing you. Don't shout!'

The senator fell silent for a moment.

'Eugene? Are you still there?' She looked at the screen on her phone, then put it back to her ear.

'This is a prohibited area. Is it a Garda helicopter?' the senator said abruptly.

'Not unless they fly black ones with dark tinted windows. Hey, it's hovering over The Shelbourne ... the side door's just opened.'

'Be ready to move in a minute!' the senator snapped and ended the call.

* * *

In response to the buzzing intercom at the Royal Suite, Peter was preparing a text message for the senator when his phone rang.

'Open the door to the suite immediately and hand your phone to whoever is nearest,' the senator said sharply. 'Do it now!'

Peter hit the door-release button, the lock clicked and the door hissed open. He strode into the room, his arm outstretched clutching the phone, and nearly bumped into Alex.

Alex stepped back in horror and Toots screamed.

Gran shouted, 'You!'

Peter waggled his huge hand at Alex, the mobile looking

like a child's toy. When he saw Alex hesitate, he made a phone signal by putting his other hand to his ear.

'Take the phone, Alex,' Willy shouted, his voice almost drowned out by the racket coming from a helicopter nearby. He turned to the window and watched as the knotted ends of two ropes were lowered onto the terrace. 'Holy shit, we've got visitors.'

Alex put the phone to his ear, not taking his eyes off Peter. 'Hello?' he said.

'This is Senator O'Gorman. Listen to me carefully. Your lives are in grave danger from those people in the helicopter. Leave the suite immediately and get out of the building via the underground car park. Make your way across the main road at the front of the hotel where you'll see a lady with a green Aston Martin. She'll be waiting for you. Get in the car – she'll take you to safety … right? Just trust me. Now, give my phone back to Peter and get out of there!'

Alex was suddenly aware of Gran's and Toots's screams. He handed the phone to Peter and turned back to the room. Toots and Gran were clinging on to each other in the corner of the room while Willy just stood and gawped at the terrace. First, two pairs of combat boots, then bodies, appeared on the other side of the window. The first dropped a rucksack onto the terrace while the second reached to undo the top flap. Another two black shapes dropped from the sky, unshouldered assault rifles and disappeared to the left and right of the window.

'Run for the stairs!' Alex yelled, rushing across the room and lifting Gran off her feet. 'Willy, grab Toots. Come on! Follow me!'

Peter finished listening to the senator's instructions and pocketed his phone. He pulled Alex and Gran out through the door, then reached for Willy and Toots, nearly lifting them off the ground. He had just hit the button to close the door to the suite and waved them towards the stairs when there was a thunderous explosion from inside.

All the lights went out, leaving only the emergency light to illuminate the darkness with a blue ethereal glow; the suite door stopped closing, leaving a gap of about two feet. The ringing silence that followed was shattered by the rattle of automatic gunfire. The bullets ricocheted off the partly closed steel door into the masonry on the other side of the lobby.

Peter put his shoulder to the door and it began to close slowly, but a hand wrapped round the edge indicated that someone was pushing against him. Undeterred, Peter stepped back and threw his full weight hard against the door. This time it closed fully, cutting the fingers off at the second knuckles as cleanly as a surgeon's knife. Screams of agony were drowned out by the rattle of gunfire; no bullets came through, but the outer steel skin was punched out like the Wicklow Hills. Without electricity the door couldn't be locked, and sustained gunfire on one area of the door would eventually penetrate both skins, so Peter lay down on the floor to act as an enormous human doorstop. The last thing Peter saw was Gran's look of gratitude over Alex's shoulder as they disappeared down the stairs.

* * *

From her vantage point across the road from the hotel, Vem had watched the men descend from the helicopter, heard the explosion, then the gunfire. All about her was chaos as pedestrians ran for cover and motorists either braked or accelerated, reacting to the panic of the pedestrians and each other. One of the horses drawing a carriage around the green bolted and cut across a traffic island, overturning the carriage and throwing its occupants through a shop window. A drunk approaching Vem on the pavement stopped at the sound of the gunfire then collapsed onto the pavement screaming, 'I'm hit! I'm hit!'

Vem's phone rang and she answered it straight away.

'What the hell's going on, Eugene? Is this your doing?'

'Be quiet and listen. Four people you don't know are about

to come up Kildare Street from The Shelbourne garage – an elderly lady and three youngsters. Peter may or may not be with them. Get them into the car and out of the city. Make for the N4. One of –'

'I see them! One big young fellow carrying an old lady and another man in glasses and a girl.'

'Get them into that machine of yours and get the hell out of there,' the senator barked and hung up.

Vem frantically waved her arm in the air trying to get the attention of the foursome. The man in glasses nudged the girl and pointed at Vem. Just then, a double-decker bus pulled up beside her car, cutting off her view and escape route. Slowly the bus inched past, then had to stop: the car parked in front of Vem's had its tail sticking out, blocking the bus's path.

'Stay!' Vem commanded Charlie and she ran around the back of the bus. She collided with Toots who was being propelled forward by Willy as he struggled with his computer case and gadget bag. Vem took hold of Toots and heaved her into the back of the Aston Martin without opening the door.

Charlie greeted them by crouching, poised to leap into action, his hackles raised down his back and his teeth parted in a savage smile.

Alex followed Vem and set Gran into the back seat beside Toots.

'Thanks, Alex, love,' said Gran, sinking back into the plush leather seat.

Willy dropped his case and bag on the rear floor and climbed into the space left in the back seat.

Vem surveyed the chaos. The bus was stuck and hid them from view, so if the people in the helicopter were looking for them …

She ordered Alex into the front passenger seat, then ran around the car and punched the switch to close the roof. Scooting out of sight, she reappeared at the bus driver's door and hammered on it to get the driver's attention. He opened his window and they had a short conversation – not a very helpful one, judging by the gesture Vem gave him as she turned away. She ran back to the car, opened the passenger door and smiled at Alex.

'Prepare for company,' she said and turned to Charlie.

At her command, six and a half stone of German shepherd landed on Alex, its front paws on either side of his neck, its nose against Alex's.

'Fuck!' said Alex. He hated dogs.

* * *

In the Royal Suite, the leader cursed under his breath, pain shooting up his arm. The door was jammed by something. His colleagues had checked round the terrace; there was no other way in or out. The blast had only opened a gap of eighteen inches where the sliding glass balcony door overlapped the fixed pane; the suite was almost impregnable yet his targets had escaped.

The Scarecrow, as the bomb maker was known, approached him holding a small charge.

'Do you want me to open the door? It'll only take thirty seconds.'

'No, we're here too long already and I need medical attention.' He held up his injured hand, blood oozing from the towel wrapped around the cut ends of his fingers. 'Let's get out of here.'

Squeezing back out through the damaged window was more difficult than getting in, but they made it. The gunmen were already on their way back up on the ropes winched from the helicopter. The harnesses were lowered again and the Scarecrow helped the leader into his before strapping on his own. They were only halfway up when the chopper started to rise and turn, trailing them behind like streamers.

In the co-pilot seat Dominic was livid. 'Hold steady for a minute till the traffic stops. They must be down there somewhere. Move to the left of that bus so I can see the other side of it,' he ordered the pilot.

The helicopter drifted to the left, affording Dominic a view of the driver's side of the bus and the pavement area round the green. As he looked down from one hundred and fifty feet he saw something familiar, but he couldn't figure out what it was.

* * *

There were no pedestrians anywhere by this time and the traffic was completely snarled up. Horns were blaring and distant sirens echoed in the air without seeming to get any closer.

As Vem and her passengers sat in the Aston Martin, her phone rang.

'Hello, Eugene … Yes, they're all in the car and in one piece, but I can't move. The traffic's going nowhere. I can see Merrion Row's clear, but an effing bus has caged me in … I know it's urgent! What do you want me to do – fly?'

She cut the call and hit the steering wheel with the heel of her hand.

'Sit tight, everyone,' said Alex, opening the door. 'Move, doggie, please!'

Charlie smiled at him, his teeth a couple of inches from Alex's face, and the low rumble of a growl vibrated against Alex's chest.

'Get this bugger off me,' Alex said, trying to sound calm. 'If I can get out, I'll soon move the bus.'

Charlie tumbled out on Vem's command, standing on Alex in a delicate place as he did so. Half tumbling himself from the low car, Alex went to the bus, hauled the driver out and climbed in. He inched the bus backwards, leaving enough of a gap for Vem to pull out. When he returned to the car, Charlie was lying in the passenger footwell. Alex eyed him nervously.

'Put your feet in gently on either side of him,' Vem instructed. 'Whatever you do, don't stand on him. Let him wriggle into you to get comfortable.' She patted the dog as she spoke.

'What about me, do I get comfortable too?' Alex said and climbed in, carefully following her instructions. Once Alex was settled, Charlie dropped his head in his lap, licked his lips and scrubbed his chin in Alex's crotch.

'He likes you! Okay, it's time to go,' said Vem.

She put the car in gear and neatly eased the Aston Martin out between the parked car and the bus, then shot off down Merrion Row. At the junction of Baggot Street and Lower Pembroke Street she slewed the car right through a red light and hurtled down Pembroke Street, the V8 exhaust note growling back at them from the grand Georgian houses on either side.

* * *

Dominic, watching from above, suddenly realised why the sports car below seemed so familiar.

'The bitch! The interfering, fucking bitch! Follow that fucking car, and on your life don't lose it!'

The helicopter pilot pulled the stick back and kicked the rudder pedals. The machine rose and turned to follow the fast disappearing car.

'Any idea where they might be heading?' the pilot asked. 'This type of copter's not designed for close pursuit. Too cumbersome.'

'You're paid to fly the bloody thing, not to ask questions,' Dominic snapped. 'Just follow the car and shut up!'

The pilot looked round at him, distaste written all over his face. 'You'd want to mind how you talk to me. The only reason I'm here is out of respect for the senator.' He paused for a moment, checking the car's direction, then looked back at Dominic. 'He did authorise this flight, didn't he? Perhaps I should ask the office to call him.'

'Of course he did,' Dominic said, trying to sound conciliatory. 'There's a lot riding on this. We must intercept that car. I'll double your fee if we catch them, all right?'

The pilot nodded.

'I need a doctor urgently,' said a weak, hoarse voice in the back. It was the leader of the ambush team. He was holding up his fingerless hand, and despite the cloth wrapped tightly around it he was losing a lot of blood.

'You'll have to wait – the car's more important.' Dominic dismissively waved his hand behind him.

The Scarecrow, who had been tending the leader's wound, clicked on his microphone. 'I'd say ten minutes max and this guy's critical. He's about to lose consciousness. Anyway, I didn't sign on for a cross-country flight. I need to be back at the pickup site in ten minutes. Okay?'

Dominic twisted round in fury. 'Who the hell gives the orders around here? Certainly not you!' He pointed his finger at the Scarecrow. 'I'll decide when and where we land!'

* * *

Vem was working hard to cross the city. Traffic had backed up on every main arterial road around the city centre. Using her intimate knowledge of the minor streets, she travelled west in a zigzag pattern, unaware of the helicopter keeping tabs on them from above. Her mobile had rung twice but she ignored it.

Coming into Leixlip, she was forced to stop at a level crossing. Drumming her fingers impatiently on the steering wheel, she noticed three young lads with bicycles at the crossing barrier; they were staring up at the sky and chatting animatedly.

Vem lowered her window and the car filled with the *whump whump* of a helicopter. She looked up. 'Shit, it must have been following us. It's too big a coincidence that it's hovering above us, waiting. What can you do to lose a helicopter?'

'Go where it can't,' said Willy.

'And where might that be, Mr Clever Clogs?' Vem asked, looking at him in the rear-view mirror, one eyebrow raised.

'The airport – restricted airspace. We must be pretty close.'

'Good thinking! We could change vehicles there as well – hire something with a bit more space for us all.'

'Amen to that,' Alex mumbled as Charlie shifted his muzzle in his lap. 'I need to get this guy at arm's length for a while.'

'You don't know how honoured you are,' she said giving him a half-smile.

She put the car in gear just as the barrier was rising and accelerated through without waiting for the lights to change. As they headed further out of the suburbs, the congestion eased and Vem put her foot to the floor when she could. Her mobile rang again. This time she answered it, one hand on the wheel, the phone clamped to her ear.

'Hello? Sorry I couldn't speak earlier, Eugene, I was too busy driving.' She listened for a few minutes, glancing in the rear-view mirror as she did. 'The airport,' she eventually said. 'We're being followed by that helicopter. Clever Clogs here suggested we go where they can't … restricted airspace … okay. Listen, get Mary to phone some of the hire companies and book a Mercedes four-by-four or something like that. We're a bit squashed in here. Charlie's getting very familiar with someone's lap … Right, talk when we reach the airport. Bye, bye, bye, bye.' She flung the mobile onto the dashboard shelf.

'Airport nine kilometres,' Alex said, reading a signpost. 'We must be safe now.'

Ahead lay an old eight- or nine-storey red brick factory sprawled over two acres. The road cut between the two halves of the old buildings.

'The old Redland plant. Yeah, this is the start of the commercial area running to the airport,' Vem said and visibly relaxed.

* * *

A wave of despair had washed over the senator when Vem mentioned a helicopter. He had no doubt that Dominic was behind the aborted raid. What had he got himself involved in this time?

The senator knew it would help his friend, the commissioner, if he had some kind of eye-witness report of what had happened at The Shelbourne, so he asked Peter to prepare one. Peter's report was accurate – up to a point – and gave just enough detail to stop any further questions being asked. Peter had returned safely to the senator's suite after he'd rearranged the dead and injured Garda and sanitised the stairwell and lift lobby. The assumption would be that the perpetrators of the raid would be held responsible for it all. Guard Newland, having regained consciousness, had assured Peter he had no memory of the sequence of events, his amnesia fortified by the inexplicable disappearance of the CCTV tape from his desk.

The senator phoned Mary Lennihan and asked her to tell the commissioner that there was a change of plan – they would dine in his suite at The Shelbourne, not at Roly's. As the senator hung up he wished, not for the first time, that Peter had been his son, not that buffoon Dominic.

* * *

The pilot of the helicopter was watching the car and his radar. 'Shit, the crafty buggers! They're heading for the airport.' He adjusted the GSM on the control panel.

'That's good – plenty of open space.' Dominic grinned and slapped his thigh. 'Any of you any good from the air? Take a shot at the tyres if we get close.'

'It's *not* good,' the pilot said. 'The airport's surrounded by an exclusion zone. It's restricted airspace. Air traffic control is already asking us to identify ourselves. No unauthorised entry, and definitely no target practice! I'm not going into restricted airspace for anyone!'

Dominic sagged in his seat. 'Fuck that interfering bitch! Why's she helping them out anyway?'

'Can you fly as far as that big factory a mile or so ahead?'

The Scarecrow pointed out the front window between Dominic and the pilot. 'We could ambush them there, where the road cuts between the two big silos – get low in front of them and wham!'

The pilot glanced at the radar screen. 'It's very close to the restricted zone but worth a try. Chances are, when we go down close to the ground air traffic control will think we've landed and alert the Garda. How long do you need to get what you want from them, Dominic?'

'Oh, not long … not long at all. Go for it!'

* * *

The road to the Redland plant followed a long right-handed curve for nearly a mile before disappearing into the sprawling derelict site, reappearing on the far side to join a dual carriageway all the way to the airport.

Vem may have relaxed but she was still pushing the Aston along, hitting seventy where possible. Suddenly Alex shifted forward in his seat, much to Charlie's discomfort. The helicopter had swooped into view on their right and was flying straight towards the old factory.

'They know we have to stay on this road until the dual carriageway and they're trying to get in front of us,' he said. 'We've got no escape route.'

Vem dropped a gear and buried the accelerator. The Aston literally wagged its tail as it thumped them in the back and shot off. With the needle climbing towards one hundred and the big engine roaring, they caught up with a lorry in front. The turbo kicked in as Vem overtook it. Only then did she see another lorry approaching on the other side of the road. The drivers of the trucks stood on their brakes and pumped their air horns frantically. The Aston Martin slewed between them, the cacophony of noise buried by the howl of the V8, and seconds later emerged on the open road, narrowly missing both trucks. Vem eased back a little on the throttle when she caught a glimpse of Toots's face and Gran saying the rosary at record speed in the rear-view mirror. Even Charlie had shrunk down into the footwell. Only Alex was sitting upright, a manic grin on his face.

'Fuck, lady, you can handle this motor.'

But there was no time to bask in glory. Vem's work wasn't done just yet.

'Shit, what's the bastard trying to do?' she muttered as the helicopter suddenly appeared in front of them, hovering dangerously close to the tarmac. 'Hold tight, everyone, someone wants to play chicken!'

Vem kept her foot on the accelerator and didn't veer off course. She drove straight at the helicopter, her arms locked straight holding the steering wheel and her head down.

At the last moment the helicopter tilted to one side and started to lift, dirt and debris blown everywhere by the downdraught from the rotors. It wobbled noticeably as the Aston Martin hurtled below it, clearing its landing skids by only a couple of feet.

They were now speeding towards the airport on the Redland dual carriageway at a more respectable eighty miles an hour. Vem looked in the rear-view mirror and smiled at the back-seat occupants.

'I hope I didn't scare you all too much, but needs must when the divil calls. I don't think you guys are out of danger just yet, so I've organised a change of car. By the way, my name is Vem – Vem Haughey – and this is Charlie.'

Her announcement landed like a bomb in their midst. No one spoke. Alex was agitated, and not just because of the dog's head in his lap. This lady couldn't be his mother! No way! Vem didn't seem to know who they were, but this was not the time for family reunions. Alex absentmindedly scratched Charlie behind the ears, stealing sideways glances at this woman – his mother. Suddenly dozens of questions filled his head, questions that he longed to have the answers to.

* * *

As the helicopter lifted away from the Aston Martin, Dominic squealing like a baby, the rest of the crew relaxed back into their seats. The pilot shot Dominic a look of disgust.

The Scarecrow turned back to the injured man, who was almost comatose by this stage, and tended to his hand as best he could with the contents of an inadequate first-aid box.

'We'll call it a day,' said the pilot. 'I'll have you back at the pickup site in four minutes.'

The Scarecrow acknowledged the pilot with a curt nod and turned to the other three. 'Your boss needs urgent medical attention as soon as you land. You should call ahead for a private ambulance.'

'I'll take that decision when we land. It's none of your concern anyway,' Dominic said, trying to regain his composure and position of authority.

One of the men in the back reached forward and caught Dominic's right hand in a vice-like grip. Then he sliced across the palm of his hand just below the finger joints, deep enough to gash it open but not deep enough to sever the tendons. Dominic roared as he fought to release his hand.

'Bugger me, looks like your hand needs attention, Mr O'Gorman,' said the man. 'Maybe the pilot would be good enough to radio ahead for an ambulance now that we have two injured men in need of the best surgical attention Mr O'Gorman's money can buy.'

The pilot smiled wryly as he called the control room at the private airfield where they would land in three minutes.

Chapter 18

The Aston Martin turned into the airport complex and Vem slowly followed the signs for Car Hire. She pulled her phone out and rang Mary Lennihan. Mary told her that a Mercedes ML 420 would be ready for her at the Hertz desk and instructed her to drive on to Drumlosh House at Clonmacnoise for the night where the McShanes would take care of them.

The staff on the Hertz desk fell over themselves to be helpful. The senator's name carried weight everywhere, it seemed, a point not lost on the others, especially Alex. While they waited for the paperwork to be sorted, Willy and Alex wandered off to find some strong coffee.

'You've a lot to contend with right now, big man, but don't lose sight of where this all started,' Willy said as they returned with the coffees. 'It's just too much of a coincidence that your mother and her family came to our rescue today. What has all this got to do with the O'Gormans? And who the hell was in the helicopter?'

'I've no idea what's going on,' Alex said. 'I'm trying to keep an open mind, but I'm all over the place, what with meeting my mother for the first time. Do you think she knows who we are?'

'I'm not sure,' said Willy. 'She was having a good look round at us all when she was talking to her father on the phone earlier.'

'We're not really in a position to object to their plans, though. Let's play it by ear and stay alert,' Alex added in a whisper as they rejoined the group.

The journey from the airport to Drumlosh House was more comfortable. The Hertz people were a little cagey when they saw Charlie climbing into their nice, nearly new Mercedes, but Vem assured them he only tore people apart, not car upholstery. Nothing more was said on the subject and Charlie was happy to travel in the luggage space – for this journey anyway. Alex let Gran have the front seat this time to compensate for the cramped journey in the back of the Aston Martin, which gave him some time to think before he had to engage in any meaningful conversation with his mother.

The entrance to Drumlosh was through a grand Georgian drum gateway, complete with massive wrought-iron gates and castellated side pillars, and a long driveway cut through a nature reserve and wildlife sanctuary. Just before a single-lane stone bridge over the River Shannon was a beautifully restored toll cottage guarding another wrought-iron gate which made access to the hotel nigh on impossible for uninvited guests. Vem saluted the hefty gent who acknowledged them as he opened the gate. Obviously they were expected.

As they pulled up at the main entrance, a cheerful young lad came out to collect their luggage. His expression turned to one of horror when Charlie, rather than suitcases, appeared out of the boot. But Charlie had only one thing on his mind and made a beeline for the nearby plantation.

'Do they have kennels here?' Toots asked.

'They do, but he'll be sleeping in my room. He's better house-trained than me!' said Vem, laughing as she strode into the hotel foyer. 'Why don't we have a quick drink before … I was going to say before you change for dinner, but you've got no clothes. Let me see what I can do.'

She went off to find the owner, Clem McShane, a good friend of the O'Gorman family.

Twenty minutes later, Vem breezed into the bar. It was the first time the rest of them had the chance to get a good look at her. Toots guessed she was in her thirties, but Alex reminded her that as Vem was his mother she was more likely to be at least forty. She was slim and tall – almost the same height as Alex – and had lustrous black hair pulled loosely back in a ponytail. Her complexion was flawless, all the more impressive to Toots because the woman wore no make-up.

Vem bought everyone a round of drinks and Alex introduced himself and the others to her. She gave Gran and Alex a particularly warm greeting but none of them mentioned their family connection. Vem informed them they'd be kitted out in the latest sports outfits when the lady who ran the shop at the golf club arrived with the keys. Meanwhile, Willy, still concerned about their security, reminded Toots and Alex not to turn on their phones. Vem was curious about this request, but Willy deflected her question and changed the subject.

Half an hour later they had chosen fresh clothes from the golf shop and the porter took them up to their rooms, Charlie padding obediently at Vem's heels.

With Toots and Willy deposited at their suite, Alex and Vem helped Gran to get settled into her room. It was the best opportunity the three of them had had since they'd met to talk about the elephant in the room. Even though he was tired, Alex was bursting with questions and despite having waited twenty-two years for answers, he now felt like he couldn't wait another second.

'Okay, okay,' Vem said, holding her hands up and sitting down. 'Let's talk about this now. Do you mind, Mrs Casey, or would you rather get some sleep?'

'I'm as keen to hear what you have to say for yourself as Alex,' said Gran. 'There's plenty of time for sleep.'

Vem turned to Alex. 'What do you want to know?'

'Why did you leave me with my dad and walk away all those years ago?'

Vem flinched at his directness. 'Well, I was only nineteen at the time and under a lot of pressure from my father. He was furious that I'd had a baby outside of marriage. It wasn't the life he had planned for me. My mother died in childbirth and I never knew her. So I'm very much a product of my father's upbringing. He raised me to be a first-class country sportswoman, excelling in the traditional hunting, shooting, fishing. I'm an advanced driver too, as you've witnessed, and he sent me to a finishing school to learn the social graces. Then I attended Cork Catering College, which teaches to cordon-bleu standard. I spent my weekends sailing with the Ocean Sailing School in Kinsale. My academic education was completed with a two-year business course at the Trinity College School of Business Studies. This education schedule was laid down when I was just five years old – there was no room in it for an unwanted pregnancy, particularly when the father was seen to be an uneducated truck driver.'

'But how could you let your father do that? Were you not angry with him?' Alex asked.

'I know this is hard to hear, Alex, but I was grateful to him at the time. He handled the situation in the only way he knew how – as a business transaction. He made sure you were well cared for and I knew you were in good hands.' Vem smiled at Gran.

'And were you never curious about me?' Alex said, still peeved and hurt.

'Of course I was. My father kept me updated. I know you never wanted for anything.'

'Except a mother,' said Alex sulkily.

Gran shifted in her chair and Vem put a comforting hand on her arm. 'I know this is a lot to take in,' she said. 'Charlie needs his evening walk. The kitchen will be closing soon. Shall we meet for dinner in half an hour?'

She shot them a tentative smile and left the room with Charlie.

* * *

As soon as Willy closed the door of their room he took his laptop over to the desk and opened it. Toots rolled her eyes and sat down with the pile of sports clothes and began cutting the labels off.

She changed into a knee-length tartan skirt and V-necked sweater, looking every part the golfer, and ruffled Willy's hair. 'Will you be long?' she asked. 'I'm starving.'

'No, I'd say fifteen, maybe twenty minutes tops. You go on down and order for me – a sirloin and all the trimmings – I'll be down as soon as I can.' He put his head down and focused on the screen as Toots left the room.

A few minutes later he gave a gasp of surprise. There, in his email inbox, was a new message:

YOUR ABILITY TO FRUSTRATE US IS ADMIRABLE.
YOUR LEAD IS SHORT.

Willy couldn't help but admire his cyberspace stalker. He knew he was dealing with someone his equal. How were they able to send him these untraceable emails? He checked the iJack; it had nothing to report. He reviewed the precautions he'd taken and the events of the previous four hours. Everyone's mobiles had been turned off; only Gran's unregistered phone was active. The Shelbourne Hotel didn't know they'd left or their destination. No one other than—

'Fuck! Vem – the secretary on the phone – the senator. Fuck, fuck, fuck!'

He dressed hurriedly in his Greg Norman slacks and sweatshirt, admired himself briefly in the full-length mirror, pocketed the iJack and Gran's phone, and headed for the dining room in search of the others.

The group were seated in a secluded alcove off the main dining room. Willy marched straight up to Vem, ignoring the jokes about his attire, and demanded to see her mobile phone.

Vem was nonplussed at the abruptness of his request and refused in none too polite terms.

Alex intervened. 'Let him have it, Vem. He's our security expert. He'll have a good reason for asking.'

Vem reached into her bag and handed Willy her mobile.

Willy connected a lead from the iJack to Vem's phone and pressed a few buttons on his gadget. He stared at the screen for a few moments and sighed loudly before disconnecting the phone and handing it back to Vem.

'Apart from when you spoke to your father and the time you called Mary – isn't that her name? – have you made or received any other calls?'

Vem looked questioningly at Alex who gave her a slight shrug of the shoulders.

'No,' she said, 'but I did get a wrong number about twenty minutes ago when I was out with Charlie. Why?'

'Did you answer the call and speak to the caller, or did you answer and the line just went dead?'

'Answered and the line went dead. Why?'

'Sorry, one more. Did a number come up on the screen?'

'No, it said "Private Number". Why? What's going on?' Vem was starting to get a little rattled.

'Is that the first time you've had one of those calls … since you met us, I mean?' Willy asked.

'Yes.'

Willy groaned. 'I should've stopped you from using your phone – should've turned it off, like ours. Whoever was tracking us earlier knows where we are again. Somebody who knows Mrs Haughey and knows her phone number has put a trace on it. I'm certain.' He waved the iJack in the air. 'This detected the signal, and the missed call Mrs Haughey received confirms it – just the same as happened with our phones.'

Vem reached for Willy's hand. 'Please stop calling me Mrs Haughey. It's Vem. This trace you're talking about?'

Willy polished his glasses. 'The signal from mobile phones can be tracked quite easily as long as the phone is switched on. It's accurate to within fifty, sixty metres.'

'Bloody hell, I never knew that. But why would someone suddenly be tracking me?'

'They're not tracking you, they're tracking us. We discovered that while we were at The Shelbourne and turned our phones off. But they must know that you picked us up there and so they've been tracking your phone instead.'

'But hundreds of people know my number … Hold on, only two people knew I was at The Shelbourne earlier – Mary Lennihan and my father. But there's no way either of them would be tracking us. Apart from anything else, they don't need to – they were the ones who told me to come here.' Vem bristled, for she saw the change in Willy's body language. 'I trust both of those people with my life, one hundred per cent. I won't tolerate doubts or queries from anyone – one hundred per cent.'

'It couldn't be the senator,' Gran burst in. 'It was his man who rescued us at the hotel, something I'll be eternally grateful for.'

'Peter's a wonderful man, Mrs Casey,' Vem said, patting her hand.

'What alerted you, Willy?' Alex asked. 'What made you check for the signal again?'

'I got another email warning me that they were close.' He turned to Vem. 'You did a great job of beating the helicopter and then I screw up with the phone.' Willy shook his head.

'Yes, but it was you who told me how to beat the helicopter. So now tell us how we can throw them off the scent. How do we send them in another direction, give them false information?' Vem asked.

Willy suddenly smiled. 'Would you mind if you were separated from your phone for a day or so?'

'Not in the least. It's no use to me turned off anyway. Why, what do you want to do with it?'

'Send it on a journey back to Dublin, to The Shelbourne. Better still, let's send mine with it! They'll think we're heading back to Dublin.'

'Brilliant, Willy!' Alex gave him a slap on the back.

Willy turned his phone on again, took Vem's and put both phones on silent. Vem nipped out to reception to see if she could get a padded envelope. A uniformed taxi driver was just dropping off a fare and had brought his passengers' luggage into the foyer. Vem caught him just before he left.

'Would you be available to do a run to Dublin for me?' she asked.

'I am surely. I'm going back there now.' He produced a notebook. 'Where would you be going?'

'I'll not be travelling myself. I need you to deliver a package to The Shelbourne Hotel – to Senator O'Gorman.'

'Okay.' The taxi driver looked at her more closely now. 'Are you paying me now, or do I get it at the other end?'

'Ask the receptionist in The Shelbourne to call the senator. He'll make sure you're paid – there'll be a good tip in it for you.'

The driver raised an eyebrow and smiled. 'Have you the package ready?'

'Five minutes, okay?' Vem said and she went back into the dining room.

'Taxi's here now,' she said. 'I intercepted one that was delivering guests.'

Willy wrapped each phone in a napkin, put them in the envelope and sealed the flap.

'There you go. You'll need to speak to the senator and explain what we're … Here, what about asking him to send it on somewhere else – keep them running around for a while?'

'Okay, Mr Clever Clogs!'

Vem laughed and went back out to reception. She gave the package to the taxi driver and returned to the reception desk.

'Can you give me an outside line on the house phone over there please? And can I just check: when Mary Lennihan booked us in, she did say no names and no details to nosy enquirers, didn't she?'

'Yes, indeed, Mrs …' The receptionist caught herself on and gestured to the phone in the corner of the foyer.

Vem made her call to her father and then reported back to the others in the dining room.

'All squared up with the senator, and the package is on its way to Dublin. The receptionist knows to say nothing about us being here. Occasionally some of the papers phone to check if any notables are staying and send a photographer over. I think I'll walk out to the gatekeeper and give him a little inducement – keep him on our side.'

'Why not have something to eat first,' Alex said. 'Then I'll walk with you.'

'Good idea. Mind if I sit beside you, Clever Clogs?' Vem asked, laughing.

Willy blushed with pleasure and grinned sheepishly at Toots as Vem sat down beside him.

Chapter 19

The senator was watching CNN in his suite at The Shelbourne when the phone rang again. It was the commissioner. He was downstairs in reception, calling to see if the senator was coming down to the restaurant.

'If you don't mind, Wesley, I'd rather dine up here in the suite,' the senator told him. 'It's more private and we have a lot to discuss. I've taken the liberty of ordering for us both. It should be here in half an hour.'

Left with no say in the matter, the commissioner passed the message on to the receptionist and ordered two bottles of the '93 Châteauneuf-du-Pape to the senator's room – at least he would drink his favourite wine. Wesley Shackleton, Commissioner of An Garda Síochána and a past head of SDU, felt like a wee boy being called to the headmaster's office and he needed all the fortification he could get.

He took the lift to the senator's suite and, after he had freshened up, joined the senator in the lounge. They sat in huge armchairs on either side of the grand Adam-style fireplace, wine glasses in hand and the TV muted.

'I listened with great interest to your press statement about the incident at the hotel today, Wesley,' the senator said. 'You were more guarded than usual – not even a hint for the newshounds. Are you sure that was a good idea? They'll only start digging even harder.' The senator was doing a bit of digging of his own.

'Difficult situation, Eugene. I've got to be very careful,' said the commissioner. 'We're in the middle of something big and I don't want to rock the boat.'

'Yes, I understand that. This guy Hollinger the Brits foisted on you last year – any good? Trustworthy?'

The commissioner visibly flinched, obviously surprised at the extent of the senator's knowledge. 'Not relevant to this incident at all. Today was an attempted kidnap, nothing else.'

The senator took a sip of his drink and studied the commissioner for a moment.

'You're talking bullshit!' he snapped. 'Hollinger and Sullivan have been investigating young Casey and his pal in connection with Operation Bankroll, the money laundering investigation that Clinton instigated when he came to office. I know you people got involved at Blair's insistence. I've been monitoring the situation for years. The reason I invited you here tonight is so that we can pool information to our mutual benefit, not try to mislead each other.'

The commissioner blanched and shifted uncomfortably in his seat. A knock on the door saved him any further discomfort. Peter entered, followed by a waiter pushing a two-tier trolley laden with steaming salvers, huge china plates, silver cutlery, linen napkins and the commissioner's bottles of Châteauneuf-du-Pape.

'Excellent, Peter! Thank you,' said the senator, beaming from ear to ear.

He took his seat at the table and with a wave of his hand invited the commissioner to join him.

* * *

After the Scarecrow had been deposited at Balbriggan, the helicopter continued its journey to the private airfield near Wicklow. Dominic had wrapped his cut hand in his handkerchief and a chamois leather the pilot had given him. The injured leader was now unconscious and lying flat on the floor while the other men sat beside him to stop him being tossed about by the buffeted helicopter. They stared malevolently at the back of Dominic's head as if willing him to fall out.

At the airfield, a private ambulance was waiting to take the injured man to Blackrock Clinic. Dominic announced that he'd drive there himself. Although he was in considerable pain, he had important matters to attend to first.

In the privacy of his car, he turned on his mobile phone and pressed a button. An international ringtone sounded twice.

'Yes?' said a male voice on the other end.

'It's Dominic.'

'Well?'

'No.'

'Why not?'

'Unwelcome third-party involvement.'

'Who?'

'Eugene and Vem.'

'Your family, your problem. You've twenty-four hours.'

The line went dead.

Dominic was now in a cold sweat, shaking, a combination of shock from the wound and fear. Twenty-four hours! He made another call. It was diverted to voicemail.

'Hollinger. Leave a message.'

Dominic tried another number. This call was answered almost at once.

'Hello, Dominic. I hear you had the shit scared out of you and then you opened your gob when you should have been listening.' The rip of laughter from the voice turned into a hacking cough.

'Fuck off, smart-arse!' Dominic snarled. 'Send someone down here to drive me to Blackrock Clinic, then keep trying Hollinger. I need an update on the mobile traces urgently. They've disappeared.'

'So I heard. The Scarecrow tells me the woman has no fear – blew you away completely!'

'She'll have fear when I get a hold of her. She'll rue the day she toyed with me.'

'Yeah, yeah … Right, Barry'll be with you in five minutes. Is he covered for your car?'

'Yep. Tell him to hurry up. I think I'm going to pass out. Send a bottle of poteen with him.'

* * *

Relaxed after an excellent plate of beef and nearly two-thirds of the first bottle of Châteauneuf-du-Pape, the commissioner had regained some of his self-confidence.

'Perhaps, Eugene, you'd explain your interest in the Caseys. You seem inordinately well informed. Who's your source?'

'I lost a special notebook twenty-odd years ago and I'm now very close to getting it back.' The senator delicately dabbed the corners of his mouth with his napkin. 'However, I have now discovered that the notebook I lost all those years ago is in the very capable but inexperienced hands of one of the Casey party. The recently deceased Michael Slaney was in possession of a similar notebook, the key to illegal assets that technically belong to this person. Slaney developed a very expensive gambling habit, and in order to fund it he was involved in some private enterprise at the expense of his master, namely the same person who is trying to repossess my property. It was this person who, in questioning Slaney in an effort to regain possession of what they see as their property, pushed too hard and the poor man died before he could tell where the notebook was hidden. And so we come back to the Caseys. They now have the second notebook too, and I assume this person knows that.'

The revelation that the Caseys held both notebooks caused the commissioner to start, a reaction that did not go unnoticed by the senator.

'I'm trying to protect the Casey party until the young man can use the information in my notebook to access its hidden contents,' the senator continued. 'And I need you and all the assets at your disposal to help me in this endeavour. Now, a cigar, Wesley, while we attack the rest of this superb wine?'

'But you *still* haven't disclosed your source,' the

commissioner said, choosing a cigar from the box presented by Peter.

'Why, it's Inspector Chris Sullivan.'

The commissioner didn't seem surprised by this news. He puffed on his cigar for a few moments. 'And do you know who's behind all this?' he asked.

Senator O'Gorman looked at the Garda commissioner long and hard before he replied. 'Yes, unfortunately I do.'

* * *

Jim Hollinger phoned Dominic just as the surgeon at Blackrock Clinic started to repair his hand. The fact that Dominic had used the poteen to sterilise the wound and only taken one mouthful to steady himself impressed Dr Roberts. Dominic asked if there was somewhere private he could take the call, so the ward sister put a temporary dressing on the wound and directed him towards a room up the corridor.

Dominic slipped into the consultant's office and closed the door. 'Right, Jim, have you an update? We lost them?' he said.

'Yes, but I think we've found them again,' Hollinger said. 'At least, we found Mrs Haughey's phone and McNabb's. Both of them seem to be in the same location – a hotel is the nearest building on the map. They've moved east of that position now, suggesting they may be on their way back to Dublin. Miss Toomey's phone's still turned off.'

'So, what's the plan now?' Dominic asked, relieved to have a fix on them again.

'Just keep an eye on them. Hold on a minute … They're further east of their last position – definitely on the N4 heading for Dublin.'

'Okay. Now where's that hotel you think they were at?'

'Somewhere near Clonmacnoise.'

'Ahhh. Okay. Vem's pally with the McShane family who own the … something hotel near the ruins. That's where they'll—'

Dominic was interrupted by Dr Roberts who poked his

head round the door and pointed to his watch.

'Got to let sawbones finish on my hand,' he said to Hollinger. 'I'll phone you back in ten minutes.'

Twenty minutes later Dominic, sitting outside the surgery in his car, phoned Uel Fagan, his driver's boss.

'I need two men here in Blackrock with me and Barry. We've got a fix on our targets again. We'll wait at the Tower Inn on the main street till I hear where they finish the journey. Send some hardware, especially a long, sharp blade. Who have you near Clonmacnoise? They're at some hotel or other … Drumlosh Hotel, that's it! I need it checked out in case some of the group are still there. It needs to be somebody tidy – I don't want a war with Clem McShane.'

'My brother-in-law, Des O'Hanlon, is in Athlone, thirty minutes away from the Drumlosh,' Uel replied.

'Is he not still in for the job he did on McSweeney? That was barbaric!'

'Aye, but it got a result.'

'Certainly did – five years in Portlaoise! When did he get out?'

'Two weeks ago, on good behaviour, would you believe?'

The two men laughed.

'Okay, what'll he need?' asked Dominic.

'One thousand for himself and a mate, delivered tomorrow lunchtime latest. He's angry and broke.'

'He'd better be worth it. Send him over there now. Make sure no one's harmed. I want them removed somewhere secure. I'll do the rough stuff this time.'

Chapter 20

After their meal, Vem excused herself and rose from the table. 'Alex, give me five minutes, then we'll go for a walk. Meet me outside, okay?'

It was a clear, moonless night, with not so much as a breeze stirring the heavy, warm air. After a while Vem appeared, Charlie close by her side. She was carrying a broken double-barrelled shotgun under her arm and an ammunition belt over her shoulder.

'What the hell are you doing with that?' asked Alex.

'Clem told me they're losing a lot of young game to foxes, so I offered to be gamekeeper on our walk. Do you want one as well?'

'No, thanks. I'm not a big fan of guns.'

Vem shrugged and walked on. Charlie cavorted around her ankles, dashed ahead, then ran back to them again. He obviously loved being outdoors in the woodland.

'What age is he?' Alex asked, nodding towards the dog.

'Five going on one,' said Vem, laughing. 'Come on, Charlie, let's see if we can find a fox or two to chase!'

They set off along a rambling path that took them through the plantation. Vem seemed to know where she was going.

'I'm very fond of this place, Alex. It was here that Charlie pulled me back from the brink of self-destruction after my messy divorce.'

'How did he do that?'

'I was hiding from the world here and chasing the bottle.' Vem had slowed to a stroll. 'One evening five years ago, Clem asked me to take the dogs for a walk before dinner. He didn't have time himself that day before dark. The bitch, Sabine, had had a litter of five pups and he walked them in the planting every day. I said yes, and left for the planting with the bitch, her five wild pups and a full hip flask. An hour and a half later, just as it was getting dark, I returned with the bitch, four pups and an empty hip flask. Clem met me at the door. He just stood looking out at the planting not speaking, then said, "Charlie won't last the night on his own. The foxes will have him." He turned and went back into the house. I stood there for I don't know how long, racked with guilt, and wept for that pup, my lost mother, my son, my marriage … my life. After some minutes Clem came out and handed me this gun and belt. "Just in case he's injured and you need to finish him off", he said. I felt like shit, the lowest of the low. Clem never said another word – left me standing there buried in guilt and humiliation.'

Vem and Alex, deep in the plantation, had stopped walking.

'Slowly I set off for the planting, sick inside, with false hope sloshing about in the depths of my drunken mind,' Vem continued. 'Maybe the pup would know its own way home. Maybe it would come when it heard me blundering through the trees. Maybe, maybe, maybe … my head was full of maybes. I stopped here, in the middle of the planting, to pee and throw up, and then I sat down and leaned back against that tree there.'

Vem pointed to a magnificent beech, its crown disappearing into the night sky. As they stood there Charlie came bounding out of the undergrowth and jumped up at Vem, tail wagging, tongue slobbering, then sat down beside the base of the tree looking up at her.

'That's exactly what happened five years ago. I didn't find him – he found me, and I found myself.'

Vem turned away, the tears coursing down her face. Charlie jumped up, put his paws on her shoulders and licked her face.

'He did that the last time as well,' she said, laughing through her tears.

Alex put his arm around her shoulders.

'Can you forgive me, Alex, for not being around when you were growing up?' Vem asked.

Alex hugged her. 'Well, I understand why you weren't. We've a lot of time to make up.'

Charlie jumped up at them, trying to push between them.

'He wants in on the act as well!' Alex said, and set off with Charlie running round him, jumping up at his raised hand.

'It looks like I've found a son and lost a dog,' said Vem, smiling.

They walked on in silence, enjoying the balmy summer night and the heightened sounds and smells of the woodland. Ahead of them the lake spread out like a jewelled mirror, reflecting the overhanging trees at the water's edge and the twinkling stars above. Feeding trout cast ripples across the surface, and there was the occasional slap from a fish falling back after a jump.

'Willy and Toots should be taking this walk,' Alex commented.

'What about you? Any girlfriends?'

'No, not at the moment.'

Their conversation was interrupted by a low, throaty growl. Charlie had appeared out of nowhere and was testing the air, head erect, ears flicking to and fro, nostrils twitching.

'Could be deer or fox ... or his imagination.' Vem laughed quietly and closed the shotgun with a gentle clunk, two cartridges now in place and the gun cocked.

The breeze was coming off the lake, so the scent that Charlie had picked up came from the other side. Vem took a pair of small binoculars out of her gilet pocket and gave them to Alex.

'They're not night vision or very strong, but it's so bright you might be able to see what Charlie thinks he smells,' she whispered.

Alex adjusted the lens as he swept the far side of the lake, along which the driveway to the hotel ran. He stopped at the gatehouse.

'Take a look to the right of the gatehouse,' he said. 'It's neither deer nor fox.'

He held the glasses out to Vem. They both watched in silence, Charlie alert and tense by their sides.

'Jesus!' said Alex. 'From where I'm standing it looks like two people dragging something heavy towards the shed.'

'It's a body,' said Vem, peering through the binoculars. 'I can see the feet … and they've an arm each. What's going on?'

They fell silent again as they watched.

'Look, there's a van parked at the other side of the shed,' said Vem. 'There's a woman as well as two men. They've all gone into the gatehouse. Christ!'

'We've got two choices,' Alex said. 'Either we go back to the hotel to warn everyone, or we try to prevent them from reaching the hotel.'

'I say we go back to the hotel – strength in numbers. It always helps.'

'Yes, but we can intervene while they're all together. We can stop them – you, me, Charlie … and that.' Alex reached over and patted the shotgun.

'Okay, let's cut around the lake to the left and meet the driveway halfway between the gatehouse and the hotel,' Vem whispered.

She brought Charlie to heel and they set off at a gentle jog. They stopped just short of the driveway, the grassy bank up to the gravel surface offering them the ideal place to lie, hidden from view.

'They don't seem to be in any hurry,' Alex said into Vem's ear. 'Hold on, there's a car coming. Get down!'

They flattened themselves onto the bank, the dog knowing to lie down when Vem put her hand on his back. The headlights swept around the curve of the lake, lit up the driveway, washed over the shed and toll cottage, and stopped with their full beam on the majestic estate gateway. The driver gave the horn a sharp blast and the gatehouse door opened. A girl in her mid-twenties came out to the car.

'Hello, are you staying or eating?' Her voice carried clearly on the night air.

'Just visiting actually. Where's Willy John tonight? Out on the blatter?' The male driver laughed at his own joke.

'I'm not sure. I'm covering for him for a couple of hours. He didn't say he was expecting anyone this late.'

'Well, I'm here now. Are you going to open the gate or do I have to jump it?' the man said.

The girl turned to the control box and pressed a button. The car passed through the gates and she waved; then she gave it the fingers as the gates closed behind it. She disappeared back into the gatehouse and closed the door tightly behind her.

'She knew what to do, so she must have done it before,' Alex said. 'They'll have to make their move now. They can't rely on that smart alec in the car keeping his mouth shut about the new gatekeeper.'

Just then the gatehouse door opened again and two black-clad figures slipped out and round to the gable end, not far from Alex and Vem.

'Those two are blacked up,' said Vem. 'They're pros.'

Charlie growled quietly. He was flat on his belly, his hind legs under him, his chin on his forelegs, ready to launch on command.

'Shush,' Vem said to him under her breath. She studied the two assailants. 'The big man on the left has a sawn-off hanging from a shoulder strap. The thin one has a baseball bat, the tool of choice for thugs … Oh wait, they're on the move.'

They came out of the shadow of the gatehouse, silhouetted against the skyline. Vem pulled Alex lower down the bank.

'We'll let them pass and then I'll put Charlie on them,' she whispered. 'He'll take the one nearest to him. I'll take the other. You be ready to follow through after my first shot –

help the poor bugger Charlie catches. Shout the command LEAVE to get him off.'

Alex was impressed by Vem's calm confidence at a time when he was shaking with nerves. 'Okay,' he croaked.

'Relax, it'll all be over in a minute.' She turned to Alex and gave him a huge grin.

He suddenly realised she was enjoying this.

A minute later they heard the swish of feet through grass across the driveway from where they lay. Vem had hold of Charlie by the scruff, his every muscle straining to be released. Vem slowly raised her head until she could see the backs of the two shadowy figures. They were still too close for Charlie to get speed up for an attack. The big man was striding out, the sawn-off still swinging at his hip. His right hand could swing the gun up to fire in a split second. She'd better not miss!

Alex pulled himself up beside Vem. She was pointing the shotgun up the driveway at the two men, her hand on the stock, her finger over the triggers. Slowly, she eased her grip on Charlie. He started to rise up in response, his hind legs quivering with tension. The men took four more strides. Then Vem released Charlie.

'*Ionsai!*' Vem commanded.

Charlie erupted from half crouch to full speed in three strides. Vem rose and in one fluid movement lifted the shotgun to her shoulder.

'FREEZE!' she yelled.

The thin man with the baseball bat spun round just when six and a half stone of German shepherd was coming at him, and he caught Charlie with a sickening crack on the left shoulder. The blow knocked the dog slightly off target, which probably saved the man's life for Charlie's jaws locked onto the side of his head, not his throat. Man and dog rolled down the bank together, the man screaming wildly as his arms flailed about in mid-air. The more he struggled the more his face was ripped and his body raked by Charlie's claws.

The big man brought the sawn-off up and crouched low in one practised move. But Vem got her shot off first.

Alex flinched as he watched the sawn-off and the gunman's left arm and right hand explode. The power of the single shot spun him around, and as he fell on his face his bellowed curses drowned out his colleague's whimpers.

Alex scrambled up the bank where Charlie was lying on top of the man.

'LEAVE!' he yelled.

Charlie released his hold immediately, but didn't move. His left foreleg was turned back at an awkward angle under his shoulder.

The sound of a four-by-four accelerating from the hotel and a swathe of headlights added to the general confusion. The gunman was cursing and thrashing around on his back, blood squirting from his wounds.

'Leave Charlie to watch him,' Vem shouted to Alex. 'Come and hold this bastard till I stop his bleeding.'

The Range Rover stopped and doors slammed.

'Jesus Christ, Vem.' It was Clem. 'I thought it was foxes you were after.' He surveyed the scene, hands on hips.

'More like wolves, Clem. These bastards meant to do damage.'

Alex held the gunman as still as possible while Vem tore the man's shirt into strips to use as tourniquets.

'Anyone phone for an ambulance?' she shouted.

Another car pulled up behind Clem's and the driver got out. It was the man who had driven through the gates a few minutes earlier.

'Let me look at them please. I'm a doctor.' There were no jokes now.

He knelt down beside Charlie's man and looked at what was left of his face.

'Bloody hell, what a mess. Jean!' he called to his companion, 'bring my bag please ... and someone get this bloody dog off!'

'Charlie, HERE!' shouted Vem.

Charlie yelped as he raised himself on three legs and hopped over to Vem, his left foreleg swinging uselessly.

'Someone phone for a vet urgently!' Vem yelled, panic in her voice for the first time that night.

'I will if you tell me the number.'

Alex looked up to see an ashen-faced Willy standing over him.

'What are you doing here? Where's Gran and Toots?' Alex asked.

'We're here,' said Gran, leaning on Toots's arm. 'We wanted to know if you were both okay. You've been busy, haven't you?'

The sound of distant sirens cut through the night air.

'Thank God,' muttered the doctor.

Chapter 21

The Senator knew that once he told the commissioner the name of the individual behind this recent spate of criminal activity, it would quickly become public knowledge. An Garda Síochána leaked like a sieve, particularly the Department of the Commissioner – too many people wanted to play politics.

'If you tell me, perhaps I can help,' said the commissioner.

The senator hesitated for a moment, then said, 'It's Dominic … it's my son, Dominic.'

The silence that followed was disturbed only by the ticking of the antique ormolu carriage clock on the mantelpiece. The commissioner raised an eyebrow but said nothing.

The senator smiled at him. 'You may consider that little gem of information priceless. However, Dominic is merely a bit player. Someone else controls him – someone in your office.'

'That's a serious accusation to make, Eugene. I trust you can substantiate it,' the commissioner said calmly.

'No, and that's why we're here. You must uncover the cancer in your organisation yourself. I'll do all I can to assist.'

Just then, the senator's phone rang. He didn't recognise the caller's number. 'Good evening. Who is this please?'

'Er, you don't know me.'

The senator looked at the screen of his phone. The caller had a Northern Irish accent.

'Yes, what do you want?' the senator snapped.

'My name … eh, Mrs Haughey – Vem – asked me to ring you, sir.'

The caller had the senator's full attention now.

'My name is Willy McNabb. Vem asked me to tell you that there's been an incident at the Drumlosh Hotel. Charlie's been hurt, but we're all right. The two attackers are badly injured. The Garda's here and everything's secure now.'

'And is Vem okay?' the senator asked.

'Yes, sir, she's fine.'

'Who are the attackers?'

'We don't know, sir. An ambulance has taken them both to hospital. I guess the Garda will find out soon when they're fit for questioning.'

'Okay. Thank you for calling, William. I look forward to putting a face to the name tomorrow. Tell Vem I hope Charlie will be okay.'

He ended the call just as the hotel phone rang. It was Susan down at reception – a package had arrived for him. The senator told her Peter would be down to fetch it shortly and then he asked Peter to join him in the hallway for a private word.

Just as they left, the commissioner's phone rang.

* * *

The girl who had accompanied the two intruders to Drumlosh House had just given Uel Fagan the bad news.

'Dominic, you're in deep shit,' Uel said to him on the phone. 'It was a fucking set-up! Des has been shot to pieces, and his mate's torn to shreds by a fucking great dog. They were walking up to the hotel when all hell broke loose. The girl thinks there were three or four people waiting for them. When the boys hear of this, you're fucked, that is if they get to you before I do. You're one stupid bastard, and soon you'll be a dead bastard. You hear me?'

The line went dead.

Dominic looked up at Barry and his two mates who had been playing pool in the back bar of the Tower Inn. They were now blocking the door; Uel had obviously phoned them first. The tallest of the three opened his jacket just enough for

Dominic to see the flash of a knife. His smile was as thin and straight as the blade. Dominic glanced down at the phone lying in his injured hand. He tapped the screen and waited until he saw that his call had been answered. The he tucked the phone inside the bandage and started to speak before Jim Hollinger could answer.

'Barry, order a round. I'll pay. How long will it take Uel to get here? He knows we're at the Tower Inn in Blackrock, doesn't he? I want the chance to explain what went wrong at the Drumlosh. It was no set-up, honest to God.'

Knifeman leered at Dominic. 'We'll gladly drink your money while we wait, won't we, lads?'

The three of them laughed.

Meanwhile, Hollinger, his phone clamped to his ear, ran out to the foyer of The Shelbourne Hotel.

'I need a taxi to Blackrock. Now!'

George, the porter, stepped out of the door and gave his whistle a blast. A cruising taxi veered across the road and pulled up at the kerb. Hollinger stuffed a note into George's hand and climbed into the taxi.

'The Tower Inn at Blackrock. You'll get double the fare if you hurry,' he said to the driver.

He put the phone to his ear again. All he could hear was background noise, no speech, nothing distinctive. He needed to call for backup. Problem was, if he cut the call he might miss something important.

'How long to The Tower?' he asked.

'In this traffic, ten minutes, mate. It's a good time of the night to be in a hurry,' the driver said.

* * *

The senator returned from speaking to Peter just as the commissioner ended his phone call.

'Now, where were we? Ah yes, Dominic. I presume you've heard about the latest incident in this continuing saga, out at Drumlosh House?'

The commissioner nodded. 'Yes, that's what my call was about. I'm pleased everyone is fine. As long as reasonable force was used in the apprehension of the criminals, it's a satisfactory conclusion, I'd say. Inspector Jamison's in charge, but I've sent Sullivan over since there's a chance it's linked to the attack here.' He paused. 'Listen, Eugene, I'll try to help you with your endeavours provided I don't have to cross the line. But you need to give me what information you can before someone else gets killed.'

'Thank you, Wesley. I appreciate that. Okay, well, the young chap McNabb who's with the Caseys out at Drumlosh is a bit of a computer whizz. It seems he can reveal a good deal of information that you and your international colleagues want to get your hands on. More importantly, from my point of view, he can help me to reclaim my lost property. Sullivan has been keeping me informed, but someone must also be keeping the criminals informed and it has to be someone inside your organisation – they seem to know your next move before you've even decided on it. My understanding is that Sullivan and this chap Hollinger are the leads on this case. Is that right?'

'Broadly speaking, yes.'

'As for Hollinger – I asked you earlier if he was trustworthy. My information is that he is not. Indeed, I hear he may be a long-time member of the organisation that you and your international colleagues are trying to destroy.'

The commissioner was clearly taken aback. 'I'm sure your sources are impeccable, Eugene, but I have to take issue with your uncorroborated charge that one of my senior officers is corrupt. It also calls into question my own judgement. And how dare you use Sullivan as your own private police service.'

'Come now, Wesley. Sullivan and I go back a long way. We shared information on a drug seizure involving one of my vehicles years ago and we've continued to help each other out.'

'That's as may be, but it's a situation that cannot continue. I will not permit it.'

The commissioner had become quite red in the face. The senator wasn't sure whether it was down to the wine and warmth of the room or a warning that the poor man was losing his temper.

'Well, we still need to do something about Hollinger.' The senator paused as Peter came in and passed him one of his notes. He read the note, nodded at Peter and took out his phone.

'Excuse me, Wesley. I just need to make a quick call.'

He pressed a button and almost immediately started to talk.

'How did he get himself in this predicament, Mary?' He waved Peter's note in the air as if she could see it, then listened to her lengthy report. 'Who told you all this? ... Ah, of course ... Yes, do whatever you think appropriate to repay her good deed ... That's first class, thank you very much, Mary.' The senator ended the call.

'It seems that Dominic is at the Tower Inn in Blackrock,' he told the commissioner, 'the guest of some very angry men who are threatening mischief because of the botched raid on Drumlosh House. Could I suggest that you organise a rescue operation immediately. They may not be there much longer, and though he's a fool, I don't wish Dominic to come to any harm. Might I also suggest that your men detain Dominic in ... let's say, protective custody. Keep him out of the way for twenty-four hours. It'll give us time to get to the bottom of this mess!'

The commissioner stared at him for a few moments. Then without another word he called his office, issued the necessary orders and gave the senator a weary smile.

* * *

Dominic was in great need of the toilet, but Barry and his companions, now on their second pints courtesy of 'Mr

O'Gorman', were not inclined to let him move before Uel Fagan arrived. No one wanted to feel his wrath if Dominic somehow escaped.

Jim Hollinger's taxi arrived at the Tower Inn at the same time as a mud-splattered Toyota Land Cruiser pulled up onto the pavement outside the pub, disregarding the traffic bollards and white lines.

The taxi driver fumed about it as Hollinger took out his wallet.

'How much do I owe you?' Hollinger asked. 'Doubled, don't forget.' He kept an eye on the driver getting out of the Land Cruiser.

'Make it fifty, thanks.'

Hollinger passed over a note. 'If I give you another fifty, how long will you wait?'

The driver half turned to look at him. 'Half an hour. I'll wait in the car park over there. If you come out and I'm not there, I'll be in Capella's Coffee Shop twenty yards down the street on the left.'

Hollinger gave him two notes and got out. As the taxi made its way across the road to the car park, the driver of the Toyota, a big, coarse lump of a man, got out and stood talking to someone through its passenger window.

After a moment Hollinger followed him into the bar and cut the connection to Dominic's phone. He walked to the bar and waited to be served, immediately feeling he was under scrutiny from a group of men standing at the door to the snug. The Toyota driver spoke to them, then disappeared into the room, pulling the door behind him. The tallest of the group guarding the door looked at everyone in the bar, his gaze settling on Hollinger at the same time as the barman asked him what he wanted to drink.

'Could you give me directions to the railway station please?' Hollinger asked in a loud voice, hamming up his English accent. 'I'm to meet friends in a pub near the station and obviously this isn't it.'

The barman proved very accommodating, and Hollinger followed him to the front door, listened to the directions and crossed the road. While he was deciding on his next move, the sound of a fast-approaching car made the decision for him.

It also caught the attention of the young female passenger in the Toyota. She threw open the door and ran into the pub shouting 'Garda' at the top of her voice. Hollinger sat on a shop windowsill to watch proceedings, relieved to be outside, not in.

It was indeed an unmarked Garda car, though how the girl knew that was not clear to Hollinger. The passenger door and both rear doors opened before the car came to a halt and Emergency Response Garda in full combat dress jumped out. Two ran in through the front door of the pub and one ran down the street at the side of the pub, followed shortly by the driver. The fact that they didn't check out the building first told Hollinger they'd been tipped off.

He heard one shot, then nothing. A Garda van skidded to a halt behind the unmarked car and five uniformed guards spilled out onto the pavement. They huddled for a brief discussion, then three ran into the building and two down the side street.

Five minutes after it began, it was all over. The driver of the Toyota, along with the tall man and his two companions, came out of the Tower Inn in handcuffs and were shoved into the back of a paddy wagon that had just arrived. Dominic, not cuffed but firmly held by one arm, was led to the Garda van. The bar staff and customers came out to watch. Finally, the uniformed guards got into the van, leaving one in charge of the premises until forensics and the detectives arrived. The police vehicles and Emergency Response car pulled away and headed for the city.

Hollinger hadn't forgotten about the girl. She eventually appeared, pushing past the guard on the door, and climbed into the Toyota. Clever girl, he thought. She'd probably waited in the ladies. He walked back to the car park, got into the waiting taxi and instructed the driver to return to The Shelbourne.

* * *

When the procession of emergency vehicles had left Drumlosh House and Clem had taken Toots and Gran back to the hotel, Alex and Willy went to the gatehouse to help Willy John, the gatekeeper. The girl and van were long gone – no one had noticed them leave. Willy John had a bad cut on the side of his head but insisted he had suffered worse 'many a Saturday night'.

The fact that Alex had given a detailed account of the incident seemed not to entirely satisfy the sergeant and he wanted to detain Alex and Vem until the inspector arrived. But Vem demanded to travel with Charlie in the vet's car and the sergeant couldn't find it in his heart to stop her when he saw how distressed she was. In any case, he had the shotgun covered in Vem's fingerprints to prove she was the shooter, and she promised to return as soon as she knew that Charlie would be okay.

When the others were ensconced in the hotel bar, stiff drinks in front of them, Alex gave a more vivid description of the night's events than he had given the sergeant. Willy was fascinated by the fact that Vem had used the Gaelic word '*ionsaí*' to command Charlie to attack.

'The word "attack" is too simple. It could be used by mistake, even in conversation. I train my dogs with the Gaelic words for "attack" and "seize", et cetera, so it has to be a conscious decision to order the animal into action,' Clem explained.

'It was an awesome sight,' Alex said. 'Charlie was brilliant, as was Vem's shot at the gunman. She could have killed him, but she didn't.'

'She hit what she aimed for – the gun,' Clem said, 'and, of course, the hands holding it. Her ability is quite remarkable.'

The résumé of the evening's goings-on was interrupted by the arrival of the sergeant and Inspectors Jamison and Sullivan. Jamison immediately took charge in a relaxed manner, helped by the fact that he and Clem were old friends, and he asked Alex to recount again the confrontation with the two intruders. He seemed satisfied, but insisted that both Vem and Alex gave sworn statements at the Garda station in the morning, by which time they would also have the hospital's statements confirming the injuries sustained by the two individuals. Jamison didn't expect any further complications and he left with his sergeant.

Sullivan, however, remained.

'It's important that we move you again somewhere safe. I think you've grasped by now the kind of danger you're all in. You'll be all right here tonight. Inspector Jamison's sending a car and four guards to patrol the grounds. I imagine, Mr McShane, you'll put your own measures in place.'

'You better believe it! I'll be out and about all night with the dogs, so God help any intruders.'

'Can you tell us who was in the helicopter,' Gran asked, 'and why did it take Senator O'Gorman and his daughter to help us escape.'

'We've traced the helicopter, but not its passengers or pilot,' Sullivan said. 'The failed attack here was almost certainly a follow-on from the failed Shelbourne attack, but who orchestrated them' – he shook his head – 'we don't know at this stage.'

'And our narrow escape from The Shelbourne – where were you and Mr Hollinger?' Gran was determined not to let Sullivan off the hook.

'I was with the commissioner. I'm not sure where Hollinger went. I haven't seen or spoken to him since. In fairness, your safety is my responsibility, not his. He's on attachment to deal with the information that you, Mr McNabb, are supplying. Technically he's off duty-until the morning when he and his boss will be over to see you. Hopefully, you'll have something to tell them, Mr McNabb.'

Willy looked at the others a little sheepishly. 'I guess I'd better go to work then, hadn't I? Is there any chance of having some strong coffee brought up to the room, Mr McShane?'

'I'll fetch the coffee and keep you company after I've seen Gran to bed,' said Toots.

Gran took Toots's arm and gave Alex a kiss on the cheek. 'No more rough stuff tonight, young man,' she said. 'My nerves can't take much more!'

As Willy followed Toots, Gran and Clem out of the bar, Alex relaxed back into an overstuffed armchair and studied Sullivan.

'Tell me about Michael Slaney,' he said. 'Hollinger said you've been watching him for some time. I presume you know who murdered him. I need to know because, apart from running Casey Transport for the last twenty-odd years, he was a father figure to me – always there when I needed him. He's going to leave a big hole in our lives.'

Sullivan collected a bottle of whiskey Clem had left on the counter and took a chair across the table from Alex. He topped up both their glasses and settled back.

'Slaney first came to the department's notice three years ago. Hollinger's people asked us to put a surveillance team on a container that was coming into Dublin. While the container was in customs bond in Dublin docks, a small part of the load was removed. After Casey Transport lifted the container, it then spent a night in a secure truck park where the missing part of the load was replaced – or so it appeared. The contents were cigarettes en route for Africa. The container took a circuitous route that allowed it to be filled out with Irish whiskey and other bonded goods held in the customs warehouse at Dun Laoghaire before shipping to its final destination. The person who checked the vehicle and container into the secure truck park was Slaney, not the driver. At the time, no one thought anything of it. However, over the next six months the same thing happened on another three occasions and alarm bells started to ring.'

Sullivan took a sip of his drink as he thought through his story – Alex deserved to escape the worst details about his friend's behaviour.

'On the third occasion, the customs officer on the take in the Dublin bond was identified and persuaded to co-operate with the Garda,' Sullivan went on. 'I can't tell you much more – official secrets and all that – other than that we had reason to believe that Michael Slaney was number two in the operation, in this country at least. That's why we believe he had the red notebook in his possession. But it doesn't explain why he was murdered. My theory is that he was skimming to fund his gambling habit – we know that he owed close to a million to some very heavy people – and that he was killed by his own people because they discovered he was stealing from them. I'm hoping Mr McNabb will be able to throw some light on this.'

'I can't believe we're talking about the same person,' Alex said. He'd shrunk back into the armchair and was ashen-faced. 'The man who picked me up when I fell, who taught me everything he knew about the haulage business, who persuaded me to go to university. This can't be the same man who guided Gran for over twenty years in the business and never took a holiday. No, I can't believe it.'

Sullivan took a sip of his whiskey.

'I wish I could tell you different, but I can't. The lorry being burnt out on Friday night, and his murder the next day supports our theory. We would have arrested him if he was still alive. Some of what I can't tell you is about to break.'

Alex looked at Sullivan, an air of defeat about him. 'Michael resigned from Casey Transport the morning before he was murdered. We had a difference of opinion about something. Now that I think about it, he said a strange thing that morning as he was leaving. "Whatever happens now, just remember, I did it for Sean," he said. Then he told Toots it was over, whatever that meant. He was in tears when he left.'

Sullivan stared into his glass and said nothing. After a few minutes, Alex stood up and walked out of the bar, leaving his drink sitting untouched on the table.

Chapter 22

Security activity round The Shelbourne had eased and Hollinger's taxi was able to stop near the front entrance. Garda were discreetly checking visitors in and out, careful not to exacerbate the situation. It was the height of the tourist season after all. Hollinger returned to the bar and had just perched on a high stool when his mobile rang. Confirming the barman's 'Same again, sir?' with a nod, he answered the call. The voice on the other end was glacial, deadpan.

'Dominic's been arrested. It's up to you now. I gave him twenty-four hours four hours ago. That leaves twenty for you.'

'No, it's not possible! They have the book and I won't get it back till the morning. I need to wait for Sullivan to bring me to the group in the morning to avoid raising any suspicion. Also, the senator's sniffing about. I need to keep an eye on him too. I need more time.'

'How much more?'

'Forty-eight hours – if there are no more cock-ups. Fagan's girlfriend wasn't lifted with the others and I don't know how much she knows, do you?'

The voice was silent for a moment. 'How do you know about that?'

'I was watching from across the road.'

'Why didn't you phone?'

'No number. Dominic was your contact, not me. I hope for your sake he keeps his mouth shut.'

'Forty-eight hours … less the four already wasted.'

The line went dead.

Hollinger breathed a sigh of relief and ordered a double instead. He needed to speak to Dominic. Time was short and he needed manpower. When he met the Casey clan with Sullivan in the morning, he'd need backup. Sullivan would not willingly part with whatever information they gathered, so it would have to look like third-party intervention to keep Hollinger in the clear. He'd also have to sideline Stephen Reid, his boss from London – at least until Dominic's men had the red books and the relevant information.

Hollinger knocked back his whiskey and decided to go to his hotel. On his way over he called Sullivan.

'Tomorrow morning – when and where? I presume the Caseys are in another "safe location" like The Shelbourne.' He gave a hollow laugh.

'Yes, they're in a safe location in the midlands,' Sullivan said, 'but I'll move them in the morning. I'd say we'll sit down with them about lunchtime, location to be confirmed.'

Hollinger cursed under his breath. Lunchtime – more time lost! But there was nothing he could do about it. As he finished the call, it struck him that Sullivan had been coy about the group's present location. Was he just being careful on the phone or did he no longer trust Hollinger?

When he got to his room he made a second call.

'Dominic's been arrested and his people are panicking. It's down to me now, they say, and they want the goods within the next forty-four hours. I've told them I can do it but I need help. With Dominic out of action, I don't have the manpower.'

'What do you need from me, bearing in mind it's very short notice?' asked Stephen Reid.

Hollinger had already mentally prepared his wish list. 'A sniper and a snatch squad of four, a four-by-four and driver, handguns and an Uzi or similar. I also need a helicopter to shadow me and be ready for a quick extraction. And last but not least, I need the second payment in the Cayman account before we start in the morning.'

'I'll say this for you, Jim, you were never short of balls.

Okay, a sniper and snatch squad – how long does it take to drive from Belfast? Say four hours all told to allow for preparation and arming. They should be with you by six in the morning. The four-by-four and the guns can travel in convoy with the squad, so they should also be with you by six. Helicopter – it'll be on standby from eight in the morning. That's the best I can do for you.'

'The hardware needs to be in position when I need it – and the money. There are too many corpses already and too many people who can point the finger at me. I don't trust anyone, least of all you, Stephen.'

The laughter down the phone was mirthless. 'I should take offence but I won't. I understand the strain of being undercover in the front line. We'll make the transfer at nine tomorrow morning. Now, *you* listen to *my* shopping list.' The momentary silence on the phone was heavy with menace. 'Two little red notebooks, Mouseman and his equipment unharmed, the old girl dead in front of her family, young Casey and the girl hurt but alive. That way, we'll have their undivided attention. If there are any others present, use your discretion.'

Hollinger shuddered.

'So, we both understand each other?' Stephen Reid went on, a new ominous threat in the tone of his voice. 'Failure in this mission is not an option. If you fail, you'll be dealt with severely.'

When he hung up, Hollinger felt physically sick. Sleep was out of the question. He opened the minibar.

* * *

At Garda District Headquarters Dominic was in a fury, fuelled partly by fear and partly by anger, fear that time was running out and anger for being 'held for his own protection'. He detected his father's hand in the latter. He needed to talk to Hollinger. On his arrival at the station he'd had to surrender his mobile phone and other personal effects, and although these had been returned an hour later, there was no signal in the building. His request for a landline was 'being organised'.

The room Dominic occupied resembled a hotel bedroom – it was comfortably furnished with an en-suite facility – without a window or a handle on the inside of the door. It was normally used for the detention of celebrities, diplomatic passport holders or other VIPs.

Eventually a senior officer came to see him. Detective Inspector Monaghan was large, affable and nobody's fool.

'Mr O'Gorman, I've been handed your case by the commissioner no less,' he began. 'First of all, have you been treated properly? Is there anything you need?'

'I don't consider being locked up here as being treated properly,' Dominic snarled. 'This matter will not be over when I leave this building. I suggest you complete whatever formalities you're here for and release me instantly.'

'You'd do well to show a bit more respect, Mr O'Gorman. We can deal with your case here, or two floors down where the hardmen are.' The DI spoke to him as if he was addressing a nine-year-old. 'Now, you're not under arrest. You're here for your own protection and so we can ascertain what was going on in the back room of the Tower Inn. You were found in the company of some rather nasty people. What I need to understand is this: were you there of your own free will, and if so, why? And if not of your own free will, are you going to press charges for kidnap?'

Dominic's heart sank; he could see the no-win situation he was in. While he considered his options, a young Garda officer put his head round the door.

'DI, there's a call for you. It's the commissioner. It relates to Blackrock and Clonmacnoise. There's been a development.'

Monaghan rose, smiled at Dominic and excused himself. Outside the closed door he patted the officer on the shoulder.

'You should be on the stage, lad. Your talent's wasted here. That'll give Mr O'Gorman something to think about. Take him a cup of our best coffee in ten minutes and tell him I've been called away. Okay?'

Monaghan walked off with a quiet chuckle.

* * *

Vem arrived back at Drumlosh full of good news about Charlie only to find a very despondent Inspector Sullivan sitting on his own in the lounge.

'Where is everyone? Have they all gone to bed?' she asked, still on a high from the events of the evening and the encouraging news about Charlie.

Sullivan gave Vem an update, telling her all about Michael Slaney's involvement and how much it had upset Alex. Just as he finished, Alex came back in.

'Inspector Sullivan's just told me all about Michael. I'm so sorry, so very sorry,' Vem said.

Alex shrugged. 'He deserved better, whatever his faults. What about Charlie? Will he protect us again?'

'You better believe it! It'll take more than a poke in the eye to stop him. His left front leg is cracked and dislocated. The vet says he'll mend completely with plenty of rest and lots of TLC. I take it you heard, Inspector. Charlie was the man – the dog – of the moment. Without him it all could have turned out very differently.'

'So Alex told me. Quite a performance, I believe.'

'Coffee, anyone?' said Toots arriving with a percolator and cups on a tray laden with sandwiches. 'Oh hello, Vem! What about Charlie? Is he okay?'

After a few minutes Willy shuffled in, tired but looking very pleased with himself. He made a beeline for the coffee.

Then Clem arrived with three fully grown German shepherds at his heels.

'Bloody hell,' exclaimed Alex and went towards the dogs. Charlie had won him over. 'They're gorgeous.'

On an almost invisible hand gesture from Clem the dogs approached Alex, wagging their tails. He patted their heads in turn.

'Saul, Matt and Juno,' Clem said proudly. 'Right, I'm locking up now. What would you like to do, Inspector? We can offer you a room if you want.'

'That's a generous offer, which at this time of the morning I'm going to accept,' said Sullivan. 'Thank you.'

'Good. I'll lock the front door now. Please don't go out before seven without telling me. You'll get me by pressing ten on the house phone. Sal'll show you your room in a minute, Inspector. I'll say goodnight. See you all in a few hours.' Clem disappeared with a wave.

A few moments later, Sal appeared at the door. 'Hello, Vem! Hello, everyone. By the way, I'm Clem's wife. He introduces his dogs before he introduces his wife. Inspector Sullivan, I'll show you to your room and get you a change of clothes.'

The others drank coffee and ate sandwiches until Inspector Sullivan returned, looking more relaxed without his jacket and tie. Once he had settled with a plate of sandwiches and some coffee, Willy began.

'Right, I've just spent some time working on the little red notebook that Michael Slaney had.' He flicked through the pages as he spoke. 'The alphanumeric code was similar to the red notebook I have – a little more sophisticated but the same principle. However, the information in the book is incomplete. After a lot of digging around I decided to hack into the Irish Government Customs and Excise database.' Willy gave Sullivan a sideways glance. 'That's where I hit the jackpot. The numbers in this book are excise certificate numbers. A certificate is issued to each consignment of goods when it leaves a bonded warehouse for an overseas destination – at least, that's what the blurb says.'

'So what information does the certificate contain?' Sullivan asked.

'Date, destination, what the goods are. It'll even tell you the name of the truck driver who signed the consignment out of the warehouse. It tells you everything relevant to the container.'

Sullivan rose from his chair and gave Willy a slap on the back. 'Great work, Mr McNabb. Right, I've some calls to make – no time to waste.' He wished everyone goodnight and left the room.

Alex turned to Toots, Willy and Vem. 'Should we go to bed and start early in the morning?'

'I really need to sleep, big man,' Willy said. 'Even if only for three or four hours. But I need to tell you all something while Sullivan isn't here. I haven't told you everything.'

'Why? What's going on?'

'I still don't trust the inspector,' Willy said. 'Look how quickly he disappeared when I told him I'd broken the code. It was Sullivan and Hollinger who insisted we move somewhere safe, and the next thing we know there's a helicopter pursuing us. Meanwhile someone is tracing our phones. I'm not saying it's Sullivan, but there's a weak link somewhere.'

'What do you mean you haven't told us everything?' Vem asked.

'The information I've given Sullivan is worthless on its own. The excise certificates can't be accessed without a password. Minotec, an American security company, designed the password programme now in place for all Irish duty-free exports. Once a consignment has been allocated a certificate, the originator creates a password to protect the details of that consignment. No one, other than the originator of the certificates, knows the password. The list of certificate numbers that I've obtained from the red notebook doesn't give one vital piece of information – the container number to which each certificate refers. There are literally thousands of customs-cleared and sealed containers all round the world at any time, but only the originators of the ones using the Minotec system can match the contents and the container number.'

Willy yawned loudly before going on. 'If you want to hijack a load of booze, say, you need either the password or inside information. Equally, if you want to hide something in a cleared and sealed container, you need the password to keep track of it.'

'You're definitely on to something, Willy,' said Alex. 'Sullivan told me that on the four occasions they knew about, our loads had been opened in the bonded warehouse after they had been cleared and sealed. Yet they were resealed before we lifted them, and then they were opened and closed again while in transit, just like Patsy Dan's, although the others weren't set on fire. Customs confirmed that some of the load had been removed in the warehouse and later replaced with something similar to clear the visual inspection at the point of delivery.'

'I'd say something had been put into the container, packed to look like the rest of the consignment,' Vem said. 'Presumably the time delay between the two openings of the container was at least twenty-four hours, enough time for professionals to pack their goods to exactly match the rest of the consignment. If you followed one of the altered consignments, I'll bet the same sequence is repeated prior to delivery – the container is opened, the contraband removed and the original goods returned. That way no one ever knows the illegal goods have been moved from one country to another.'

'What was it Hollinger said we were caught up in?' asked Toots. 'Money laundering? And what was Patsy Dan's load … cigarettes? It's probably quite easy to make a bundle of notes look like packs of cigarettes.'

'According to Sullivan, the Garda have been able to track the most recent goods removed,' said Alex. 'The bent excise officer agreed to co-operate. But Sullivan wouldn't tell me any more than that. Presumably they can track the removed goods to their destination, so they can work out who's involved and, possibly, what's being concealed in the consignment.'

He was pacing now as he thought out loud.

'What are the chances of you identifying one of the

doctored consignments and tracing it, Willy? And what about the stolen goods? Can you follow them to their destination?'

'Given a few hours, yes. But not tonight. I need sleep first.'

'Yes, you're right.' Alex smiled. 'Let's try to get some sleep and meet for breakfast at … seven thirty?'

* * *

The senator and the commissioner had finished their brandies in a more jovial atmosphere, and the commissioner was waiting for his driver to pick him up and take him home. Just before he left the senator's suite, his mobile rang. He looked at the screen and indicated the master bedroom door. The senator nodded, and the commissioner answered his call just as he closed the bedroom door.

'Good news, I hope?' he said. As he listened, his smile broadened. 'That is indeed good news, Sullivan. Is he finished or is there more? … Fine. Have you told Hollinger yet? … No, good. Let's keep this to ourselves till we meet in the morning. I'll be there by nine at the latest.'

The commissioner could hardly hide his smile as he opened the bedroom door and returned to the drawing room.

'I must thank you for your hospitality, Eugene,' he said, making his way to the suite door. 'We'll continue our discussions another time. Goodnight.'

When the commissioner had gone, Peter appeared from the second bedroom.

'The commissioner seemed happy with his phone call – left in what one might describe as indecent haste. Anyway, enough for one day, Peter. Wake me at six thirty, please. Goodnight.'

* * *

DI Monaghan returned to the holding room thirty-five minutes after he'd left Dominic O'Gorman. The passage of time had done little for Dominic's nerves or temper, and the vending machine coffee he'd been brought hadn't helped. He had rehearsed his spiel a half-dozen times, but one look at the DI's face told him things were not looking good.

Monaghan set a manila folder on the table and turned to the young Garda officer on the door.

'Son, go and get yourself a cup of coffee and don't come back for ten minutes. On your way out, step into the control room and turn off the video and recorder for this suite.'

The colour drained from Dominic's face.

Monaghan slipped off his jacket, folded it over the back of the settee and methodically rolled up his sleeves. He sat down on a chair at the table opposite Dominic. Dominic was the first to break the silence.

'DI Monaghan—'

'Don't speak. Just listen.' The soft lilt in Monaghan's voice was more threatening than if he had screamed at him. 'Just listen. Uel Fagan says, and I quote' – he opened the folder and read the top sheet – '"You're in deep shit. You're fucked. You're a double-dealing son of a bastard."' He closed the folder and stared at Dominic.

Dominic dropped his eyes and kept quiet.

Monaghan continued. 'His brother-in-law, Des O'Hanlon, is going to lose his left arm at the elbow and three fingers on his right hand. His pal is going to lose his left eye, ear and cheek. Want to have a look?'

The DI opened the folder again and carefully laid out six colour photographs, explicit images of nasty injuries. 'You can see the shattered bones in Des's hands and arm.' He traced the damaged bones with his index finger. 'I'm amazed they can save the right hand. There's not much of it left – just mush. But this … now this is a work of art!'

He pushed two photographs of what appeared to be a man's face towards Dominic. Dominic jumped up, knocking his seat over, and ran into the en suite where he retched into the toilet. When he returned, the DI was chasing the photographs around the table like playing cards.

'As I was saying, Mr O'Gorman, Uel Fagan is not best pleased with you. He's told me a wonderful story, a story he's sure will get you remanded in custody where he says "all sorts can happen". I've no idea what he's referring to but he seems to think you'll understand. Said something about a snitch called Feeney. Was he hurt while in custody or something?'

The door opened and the young guard looked in.

'Perfect timing,' said the DI, waving him in. 'Mr O'Gorman here is going to tell us a story about Clonmacnoise, the Tower Inn in Blackrock and, best of all, a helicopter raid on The Shelbourne Hotel where one of our men was severely injured and another killed.'

Monaghan stood up.

Dominic jumped up too. 'Nooooo!' he yelled.

Monaghan turned to his right then suddenly spun back round, swinging his fist like a ball on a chain. It hit Dominic high on the chest, just below the oesophagus, and lifted him off his feet. He landed half into the bathroom, his head crashing open the door.

The DI turned to the horrified young guard. 'Oh dear. A glass of water for Mr O'Gorman. He appears to have fainted, doesn't he, son?' he said quietly.

'Indeed, sir,' the guard said and left the room.

DI Monaghan sat down at the table and chased the photographs round and round while Dominic got his breath back. When the guard returned with the water, Monaghan stood up and began to roll down his sleeves again.

'Show Mr O'Gorman how to work the bed settee,' he said. 'I'm told it's very comfortable. And in the morning there'll be no solicitors, no recordings, no witnesses and no other options. I ask and you answer, or, to quote your friend Fagan, you're fucked!'

Monaghan lifted his jacket and walked out the door.

* * *

Hollinger left the bar after his nightcap. He'd just been speaking to the guy tracking McNabb's and the woman's phones. Apparently they were at Abbeyleix, about seventy miles south of Dublin, on the N8, the main road to Cork. Yet Sullivan said the Caseys were in a hotel in the midlands and staying the night. Something was wrong. Either the group had split, which was a possibility, or the phones were a red herring, also a possibility. There was, of course, another option – Sullivan could be lying.

On his way to the lift he opened his phone and scrolled down to the phone company's number. His call was answered immediately.

'Keep tracking the two as agreed, but put a trace on another number as well. I'll text it through now.'

He scrolled down to Inspector Sullivan's number and texted it through to his contact.

Twenty minutes later Hollinger flung his phone on to the bed in anger. He'd just been told that McNabb's and the woman's phones were still en route to Cork, but that Sullivan's, was untraceable, as were all Garda phones. Bloody An Garda Síochána! He'd no idea where McNabb and his information was or how to find him.

Chapter 23

Willy awoke feeling muzzy-headed and knackered. Beside him Toots was gently snoring, a soft seductive sound that was at odds with the persistent beeping of his iJack. He slipped quietly out of bed and had a quick shower, then settled at the desk and turned on his laptop, connecting Gran's pay-as-you-go and the iJack.

He used the iJack to check for any listening devices, wiretaps and the like, then opened the temporary email account he had set up at the internet café in Ballsbridge – its IP address would appear as the point of origin of any email traffic he generated while in the south of Ireland. The result was good and bad. There had been five attempts to trace his email address, which was worrying, but all they would have been able to find out was the IP address assigned by the café's internet service provider. No taunting emails, which intrigued him – it was as if the game-playing was over and the finale underway. Willy thought about identifying the source of the attempted traces but decided he didn't have the time to spare. Instead, he got to work on the little red book.

He hacked the Excise Department's mainframe and opened the master list of validation certificates. He picked out the last half-dozen certificates allocated to containers lifted by Casey Transport and started the lengthy process of comparing the individual loads' consignment details to Patsy Dan's load. He was trying to find a similar load to investigate its movements and destination. On the fifth one he got a match. Now he was able to hack into the originator's system and identify the designated password as well as the contents of container EX/173926/40. Willy cursed his own stupidity and put it down to tiredness. He should have gone straight to Excel Containers' list – they were Casey's main client and Patsy Dan's load consignor.

* * *

Downstairs in the lounge, Vem was sitting talking to Sal when Alex appeared at seven fifteen.

Vem gave Alex a hug. 'You look rested.'

'Optical illusion, I can assure you,' he said.

Gran was next to appear, then Toots and Willy. As they all made their way to the dining room, they met Chris Sullivan coming down the stairs.

'Have I missed another meeting, or am I just paranoid?' he said.

Alex sensed it was time to clear the air.

'Willy, why don't we get a quick breath? Join us, Chris?' He and Willy headed for the front door and Sullivan hesitated for a moment, then followed.

'I know that look in Alex's eye. There's going to be some clear talking out there, you wait and see,' said Gran, settling herself at the dining table with Vem and Toots.

'Inspector Sullivan and Eugene – the senator – go back a long way,' Vem said. 'For years, Sullivan has been the person on the inside who's been keeping us posted about developments that affected our interests. A good job too, for all our sakes.'

Vem went on to tell Gran about the discussion the previous evening and the senator's part in their rescue.

Toots's mind drifted off to something that was troubling her, something Willy had intimated to her before they came down for breakfast. The attempted raid at Drumlosh the previous night was amateurish compared with the raid on the Royal Suite at The Shelbourne. Was it a reconnaissance job that had gone wrong? When and where would their attackers strike next? Willy had said he was uncomfortable about the absence of taunting emails. Toots hoped she was wrong, but she had a sense of foreboding about the next few hours.

Outside, Alex laid it out for Sullivan.

'I've analysed the last twenty-four hours in a dozen different ways and come to the same conclusion, Chris. Either you, Jim Hollinger or someone both of you report to is keeping the bad guys informed of our whereabouts. They knew we were in The Shelbourne's Royal Suite, they have the means to track mobile phone signals, they knew we were here last night. Where were you and Hollinger during the attack at The Shelbourne? We were like sitting ducks. Someone is feeding information to them. If it's not you, then who?'

Alex's tone took both Willy and Sullivan by surprise.

'I can't answer for Jim but I can for myself,' said Sullivan. 'I didn't know where you were until I heard of the attack here from the commissioner himself. How he knew you were here I don't know, but it's a question you can ask him yourself at nine o'clock this morning – he's coming here to meet you. I was told you were being moved to The Shelbourne by Jim while I was dealing with the incident at Bewleys Hotel. I only knew about it when you were virtually on your way.' He glared at Alex. 'As for the attack there, we had taken all reasonable precautions to protect you. We just never anticipated an airborne one. And, here, last night? I didn't know where you were until after the incident had taken place.'

Alex stopped walking and looked Sullivan in the eye. 'Good. Let's get some breakfast. We'll talk more, and better, on a full stomach.'

They turned back to the hotel, Willy trailing behind the others digesting the implications of what Sullivan had said.

There was an air of expectation round the breakfast table, but Alex, Willy and Sullivan sat down without a word.

Sal brought tea and coffee and set them on the table. When she returned with the cooked breakfasts, she leaned down to Vem.

'The senator was on the phone. I explained that you'd just started breakfast. He asks that you call him when you're finished. Okay?'

'Thanks, Sal. I'll call him now. Alex, will you join me? I imagine I'll need your input.'

* * *

Dominic hadn't slept; he'd heard or seen each of the Garda security checks through the night. The pain in his chest and the fear that washed over him periodically seemed to consume his overactive mind, and by six he had persuaded himself he was going to die. Ironically, acceptance of that fact helped him to drift into a fitful sleep.

'Good morning, Dominic. Slept in, have we?'

The soft voice in his ear had a distant, dreamlike quality. Then suddenly Dominic's world turned upside down. The bed beneath him was suddenly on top of him and he tumbled onto the floor.

'This is our five-star alarm call. Wait till you try the economy one tomorrow morning.' DI Monaghan's low voice was hard and cold.

Dominic struggled out from under the mattress and crawled into a corner where he balled up and began to whimper like a child.

'Guard McConaghy had a one-year-old,' Monaghan continued. 'He's probably whimpering too because he's looking for his daddy, a daddy that won't return, thanks to you. You're probably counting on *your* daddy, the infamous senator, to help you – yes? Well, I can tell you, your daddy isn't coming either. So, remember the rules? I ask, you answer. I'm going to send in some breakfast in a few minutes. Eat. Get this room and yourself straightened up. I'll be back in twenty minutes.'

The door closed as silently as it had opened. Dominic sat on in his corner, rocking to and fro, his shoulders lifting now and then as he tried to control the urge to sob.

* * *

Jim Hollinger didn't sleep well either, though for different reasons. He couldn't get his mind off the fact that he'd lost his quarry, albeit temporarily. The ex-Provo leader of his newly formed heavy mob had called him just after six to confirm that they were at the agreed rendezvous and waiting for orders. Stephen Reid would be landing at Dublin airport in the next hour, and would immediately request an update. Sullivan was Hollinger's only hope; he had to persuade him to divulge the group's whereabouts. Safe in the midlands, he had said. But the trace on the mobiles had them static in or around Kent Station in Cork. He decided to call Sullivan.

* * *

Mary Lennihan had called the senator at seven forty-five as usual. She had been with the senator for more years than either of them cared to remember and was a remarkable woman. Business colleagues considered her the 'general manager' of the O'Gorman empire; she called herself the boss's secretary. In truth, she was indispensable to the senator and to the business.

After a summary of the previous day's business, Mary updated the senator on Dominic's predicament. Sullivan had been a valuable source of information for Eugene, but Mary had the ear of Bridget Shannon, the administrative manager for the whole of An Garda Síochána. She knew *everything* that happened in the force. To ignore or underestimate Bridget was to invite disaster, even if you were 'that clown the commissioner', as she called him.

Mary had learned of Dominic's involvement in the disastrous 'heli-flop', as it was being referred to by senior Garda, when the helicopter hire company called her for an order confirmation prior to take-off. When she heard about the attack on The Shelbourne, she had immediately phoned Bridget to advise her of Dominic's possible involvement. Later, Bridget had phoned Mary to let her know about

Dominic's extraction from the back room of the Tower Inn and his present predicament in a Garda cell.

'DI Monaghan is in charge of the investigation into The Shelbourne incident,' Mary told the senator. 'He's questioning Dominic personally. Rumour has it that Dominic received a "Monaghan" last night, whatever that might be, and the expectation is that he will co-operate fully this morning. Some low life called Uel Fagan, on the promise of a suspended sentence, is being very helpful about his part in organising the raid on Drumlosh House. It would seem he was acting on Dominic's instructions.'

Mary paused to allow the senator to digest the seriousness of his son's situation.

'The difficulty we now face is the death of young Guard McConaghy. The mood among the Garda is anger. There's an expectation that you'll try to ride to Dominic's rescue. That'll be met with uproar and possibly some high-level resignations. You're damned if you do, and he's damned if you don't.'

'I'm sure you have a suggestion, Mary. Indeed, I fear I know what it will be. Might we get away with a request for solitary confinement, do you think? Some degree of protection for him? Dominic wouldn't last a week in prison – too many enemies on the inside and the outside. Can you sound out your source?'

'Eugene ...'

The senator knew what was coming: Mary only called him by his first name when she was about to contradict him.

'... I seldom disagree with your judgement on important issues, but I must on this occasion. In my opinion, Dominic is beyond the pale. He must take responsibility for his own actions at last. If he co-operates and delivers the information the Garda need, then he has a chance of protection. If you intervene on his behalf, you'll have both the Garda and Dominic's enemies against him – and perhaps you.'

'Call me back in ten minutes please, Mary.'

The line went dead.

* * *

Hollinger phoned Sullivan and left a message on his voicemail: 'Jim here. I need to speak to you as a matter of urgency. Reid will be landing soon and we need to arrange when and where we're meeting you and the Caseys. Call me, would you?'

He was now totally convinced he was being kept in the dark deliberately. Someone suspected he was involved in this sorry mess. Not Sullivan – that would be a stretch. It had to be the senator; his tentacles reached everywhere. Hollinger called The Shelbourne.

'Good morning. Could you tell me if Senator O'Gorman's still there? I was with him last night and I need a quick word.'

'Yes, he's still here. Shall I put you through?'

'No, thanks. I'm not far away. I'll call round.'

Hollinger groaned at his dishevelled appearance in the mirror, ran from the room and took the stairs two at a time. Ten minutes later, as he walked into The Shelbourne, a Rolls-Royce was pulling away from the kerb, its hazard lights flashing.

He acknowledged the porter's greeting and crossed the reception area to the desk.

'Good morning, my name is Hollinger. I'm here to see Senator O'Gorman. Can you call his room and —'

'I'm sorry, sir, the senator has just this minute checked out. Are you the gentleman who phoned ten minutes ago? I told the senator, but he was already —'

Hollinger was on the pavement in four strides, but there was no sign of the Rolls. He started back in the direction of his hotel, rehearsing the next few hours in his mind. A shower, change of clothes, a quick bite of breakfast and then off to meet Stephen Reid. He wasn't looking forward to that at all. As he crossed Merrion Road, his phone rang. Number withheld.

'Hello?'

'Good morning, Jim. Sullivan here. Just returning your call.

Now, time and place for our meeting later. Time's no problem – two o'clock. Place … I'll phone you again in an hour when that's finally agreed. Sorry I can't be more help at the moment, but the venue is out of my control.'

'That's bullshit, Chris,' Hollinger snapped. 'Quit giving me the runaround. The deal is that Stephen Reid and I talk to the McNabb kid and have sight of his material today. How the hell do I even know what general direction to head in if you won't tell me where we're meeting?'

'As soon as the commissioner arrives, I'll ask him to confirm the location and I'll phone you straight away. That's the best I can do.'

Hollinger sighed loudly. 'Right, I'll wait until I hear from you.'

He decided to call Garda Command and Control. Pat Brannigan answered.

'Hollinger here. How're you doing, Pat?'

'Better than that poor young bugger at The Shelbourne yesterday. God's curse on that bastard O'Gorman.'

'Yeah, it's bad. I'd just left when the balloon went up. Actually, it's about that I'm calling. I'm supposed to meet Chris Sullivan and the commissioner at … what the hell's the name of that hotel? I can't get either of them on their mobiles. I need to phone, tell them I'm running late … traffic's hellish.'

'The commissioner's just left, so he's going to be late as well. Hold on, Jim … Here you go – Drumlosh Hotel.' Pat read out the landline number for hotel.

Hollinger smiled to himself. How easy it was to get information! Next, he searched the internet for Drumlosh House and got the address and directions. Then he spoke to Joe, the leader of his new squad, and gave him the details.

'We'll meet at Moate, about twelve miles east of Clonmacnoise. Say eleven thirty?'

By the time Hollinger arrived at his own hotel to get changed, he had a spring in his step.

* * *

From the landline in the office behind reception, Vem dialled the senator's number.

'Eugene, you're on speaker.'

'Morning, Vem. You are to be congratulated on your efforts last night, but I'm glad you're in one piece. And Charlie – I understand he played a major role. How are you all this morning?'

There was a softness in her father's voice that she didn't hear very often.

'We're fine, thank you. Alex and I just happened to be in the right place at the right time, but we're not in the clear yet. We still need all the help you can offer.'

'Are you on your own, Vem?'

She nodded at Alex to answer.

'Good morning, Senator, I'm Alex Casey,' he said. 'We haven't had the pleasure yet, but may I take this opportunity on behalf of us all to thank you for your timely intervention yesterday at The Shelbourne. I'm fairly sure we owe our lives to you – and to Vem's driving.'

'Thank you, Alexander. I look forward to meeting you later today.' The senator cleared his throat. 'Vem, I had a lengthy dinner last night with Commissioner Shackleton. You will be disappointed to hear that Dominic is up to his neck in this whole disaster. In fact, it appears he was in the helicopter that chased you yesterday.'

Vem's eyes widened and she raised a hand to her mouth.

'I am certain he is not the brains behind the operation,' the senator went on. 'He hasn't the organisational skills, but neither the commissioner nor I have any idea who is.'

Alex was amazed at how unemotional the senator sounded, naming his own son a conspirator.

'The weak links, from your point of view, are Inspector Sullivan and this Englishman, Hollinger. I've known Sullivan for twenty years. He has been my eyes and ears in the Garda for the last ten. I'm still inclined to trust Sullivan in spite of a disagreement yesterday to do with an unrelated matter. How do you feel about him, Alexander? After all, you have been closely involved with him since this started.'

'As it happens, I had a talk with the inspector before breakfast,' Alex said. 'I put it to him that the leak in our lines of communication had to be down to either himself or Hollinger. He defended his position reasonably well. I'm now inclined to lay the blame at Hollinger's feet.'

'I see we think the same way, Alexander. I'm impressed,' said the senator. 'Now Dominic – he and the man Fagan who organised the fracas at your hotel are in custody. If we assume that Dominic and Hollinger were working together, then Hollinger is now isolated without any troops. I'm guessing he doesn't know where you are at the moment.'

'Do you know if Dominic has been charged or where they're holding him? Can we see him?' Vem asked.

'No, he hasn't been charged. He's at Garda Central – in a holding room, not a cell. As to seeing him, no – not yet. DI Monaghan is in charge of the investigation into The Shelbourne incident and is personally questioning Dominic. He will not enjoy his time with Monaghan. The DI has a reputation for softening the hardest of hardmen, a label that definitely doesn't fit Dominic.' There seemed to be a trace of disappointment in the senator's voice. 'I had a long chat with Mary and she's of the opinion that I shouldn't interfere. Feelings are running too high in the Garda with the death of Guard McConaghy.'

Vem and Alex exchanged horrified looks.

'At The Shelbourne?' asked Vem. 'Are you saying that Dominic was involved?'

'Yes, a young guard was killed, but no, Dominic was not involved in his death. I will give you all the details later when we meet. My suggestion is that you go to cousin James's house at Bearna. Apparently James's daughter and a friend are in the cottage, but you can stay in the Old House. They usually hire it out for weddings but it's not booked for the next two weeks, so it's ideal until the dust settles. I have strong contacts from the old days with some gentlemen who will guarantee your safety during your stay. What do you think?'

Despite herself, Vem laughed. 'Safe I can believe. Gentlemen I sincerely doubt.'

'Agreed then. Good! I am leaving Dublin now. Peter and I have a call to make on the way and we will join you for dinner. Seamus O'Byrne will be in charge of the security detail at Bearna. He'll be expecting you – just you and the others. Alexander, what you tell Sullivan, and indeed the commissioner, is up to you. If they are to follow you to Bearna, you need to let Seamus know vehicle details, et cetera. Sorry, hold on … Ah, very thoughtful. Peter has given me a note. "Please ask Miss Vem how is my friend Charlie?"'

'Tell Peter thank you. Charlie's in very capable hands and isn't too badly hurt. I'll have him home in two weeks and Peter's welcome to call and see him then.'

Vem returned the phone to the cradle and noticed Alex's quizzical look.

'Peter is mute,' she explained. 'He always writes notes when he has something to say. But him and Charlie are close – they seem to communicate by ESP. It's uncanny. He can get Charlie to do things I can't! And talking of special relationships – Seamus O'Byrne, your father Sean and Tommy Toomey, Toots's dad, were the tightest group in the IRA. They were inseparable for years. You must talk to Seamus. He, of all men, can tell you about your dad. I thought he'd emigrated. Haven't heard his name mentioned in years.'

They returned to the dining room to find Willy, Toots and Gran still at the table. Sullivan was outside having a smoke.

'Okay,' said Alex. 'First of all, a young guard was killed during the raid at The Shelbourne. We don't know who by, but it raises the stakes. For our safety, the senator is organising our transport to a new location. No one must know its whereabouts. I'll tell you about that in a moment. Second, Willy your iJack thingy was flashing in the office –'

'Shit!' Willy pushed his chair back so hard it fell over, and was gone.

Alex followed him to the office.

'What's wrong?'

'Another email. "I lost you last night ... but I've found you again," it says. No you haven't, you bollocks, you're still on a fishing trip!'

'I hope you're right,' said Alex.

'You know what? I don't think these emails have anything to do with the red books. I think it's the authorities trying to trace Mouseman. The email sent to your computer was to do with Michael Slaney and the burnt-out truck. These ones are opportunistic.'

'I'd love to believe you, but it's a bit of a coincidence. What about the phones?'

'The phones are a different thing. They're being used to track us, no doubt about it. But these emails? They're too random, too vague. And anyway, why say "We're getting closer" and the like? Why take the risk of spooking us? No, I'm convinced they're not related.'

'Okay, well I'll take your word for it. Right, I need to fill you in on some details from our chat with the senator because we have a couple of critical decisions to make.'

As they rejoined the others, Vem caught Alex's eye. She indicated Sullivan with an almost imperceptible nod.

'Chris was saying that Jim Hollinger was on the phone earlier,' she said.

'Jim's boss is due over from England this morning,' Sullivan said. 'He wants to meet you, Willy, and discuss the red books. And a job.'

Willy shrugged. 'I haven't done any more on the books. I told you what they contain, Chris. I'll need more time, and some peace.'

'So what do I tell him then?' The frustration was clear in Sullivan's voice.

'As far as I'm concerned, Jim Hollinger's out of the loop,'

Alex said. 'Willy, do you agree?'

'Absolutely. I'll do what I can with the books for the people who need to know … and I'll decide who those people are.'

The hardness in Willy's voice took them all by surprise. He threw down his napkin and shoved his chair back. 'Excuse me, please. I'll be in the office. C'mon Toots!'

Chapter 24

Detective Inspector Monaghan moved quietly for a big man. Six foot three, shoulders of an ox, slim waist and the legs of an athlete. Gaelic football had been his passion, but the need to earn a living to support his widowed mother and five siblings had put paid to any thoughts of being a professional footballer – that, and the fact that he had not been good enough. He carried his fifteen and a half stone with pride, he dressed well and he'd broken many hearts until one Kathleen Maginness entered his life. A short courtship, a quick wedding and Pader Monaghan was a happy man. He loved his job – was considered a bit of a loose cannon by some – but he got results, and conventional wisdom said he would reach the top in the next few years. Though not obviously ambitious, he wasn't about to let a little shit like Dominic O'Gorman spoil his record.

'Good morning again, Dominic. I see you haven't finished your breakfast. Not up to your usual five-star standards? I do apologise. Unfortunately economy-class meals are even worse, and you can never be sure what's in them – a mouthful of spit, a shot of piss, maybe a sprinkling of powdered glass … But that's academic really, isn't it, because you're going to be the model of co-operation today.'

The DI lifted the food tray and threw it at Dominic.

'How careless of me. You can see why I became a detective and not a waiter.'

Dominic cleaned the food scraps off his clothes and gathered the plates and cutlery together on the tray. He set it all on the end of the settee. DI Monaghan watched with a slight smile.

'Good man! Tidy room, tidy mind. We're going to get along just fine. Now, let's recap our agenda for today: the gathering at the Tower Inn, the incident at Drumlosh House and, finally, the tragic fiasco at The Shelbourne. You're going to tell me all about them. I ask, you answer. That's the easy bit. The difficult question comes first.'

Monaghan walked once round the room and stopped beside Dominic, his large left hand resting on Dominic's shoulder.

'Who's behind all this criminality? Who's the brain? It certainly isn't you. Maybe you did it for the glory, to prove to the boys you were as good as them. Every criminal group has its bond of honour, and for members to break it is certain and painful death. Where you sit in that scheme of things I neither know nor care.'

Monaghan stepped away from Dominic, pulled out a chair and sat down facing him.

'There's another kind of honour among the criminal classes. It's called vengeance. You do ill to one and the others will even the score. So, Dominic, you're between a rock and a hard place – I'm the rock and Portlaoise is the hard place. I've no doubt the people you work for will now try to kill you. But if you answer my question truthfully, depending on the information you provide and our success in catching those people, we'll try to protect you – try, mind.'

Dominic sat motionless throughout this monologue, a glazed look in his eyes, fear imprinted on his face.

'If you lie to me or I'm not satisfied with your answers, I'll throw you to your own for them to deal with you as they see fit. I'm not peddling fear, I'm dispensing truth.' Monaghan stood up. Dominic involuntarily flinched and Monaghan smiled. 'I have to leave you for a couple of hours. One of the guards will bring you pen and paper. Use the time wisely. You don't know what I know – so I'll know if you're not telling the truth.'

As he opened the door, he turned back to Dominic. 'Tell

the truth and you might see your next birthday. Give me lies and you won't see next week.'

* * *

Peter made good time to Balbriggan and drove straight to the front door of the Garda station. The senator stepped out of the Rolls and went in. The duty guard took a few moments to look up, but instantly recognised him from his previous visit.

'I'm very sorry to keep you waiting, sir. I'll get Sergeant—'

'Relax, young man. If you are busy, then I must wait. I am here to see Guards Mulligan and Molloy if they are available. In the meantime, I will speak to Sergeant Reilly.'

The young guard scuttled off and within a few minutes Sergeant Reilly arrived, closely followed by the others.

'Good morning, senator. If you would like to follow me to my office, I have the reports you want and will be happy to go through them with you.'

Fifteen minutes later, the senator was back in the Rolls.

'Peter, one last diversion before Galway. Garda Headquarters.'

They took the M1 for Dublin. Traffic was light, and thirty-five minutes had them two miles from Garda Headquarters. The senator lowered the privacy screen.

'Pull over when you can, Peter, I need to make a call that may change our destination.'

The senator punched a button on his phone. 'Mary, I have decided to take your advice and let Dominic take his chances. However, I would like to have a brief conversation with DI Monaghan, face-to-face, about a related matter. I'm about two miles from Garda Headquarters, but it may be diplomatic if I don't go there under the circumstances. Please phone the DI and ask where would be convenient to meet as soon as possible.'

Two minutes later, the senator's phone rang.

'Hello Mary … Yes, I know where it is … We will go there directly. Thank you.' He hung up and caught Peter's eye in the rear-view mirror. 'The North Star Hotel, Amiens Street.'

The senator closed the privacy screen and returned to Guard Molloy's excellent forensic report.

* * *

Stephen Reid had not flown to Dublin on 'company business' or, indeed, with the knowledge of any of his colleagues; a couple of days on the River Tay was the entry in his diary. He travelled club class as usual and went straight to the business lounge on landing. This would guarantee a degree of privacy and seemed the ideal vantage point from which to supervise operations.

Reid had an impressive background. Winchester and Oxford led to the Foreign Office, then MI5, MI6 and, latterly, the shadowy Special Services set up by Margaret Thatcher after the Brighton bombing. Their original brief, to deal specifically with the growing sophistication of the IRA, had been extended after the Good Friday Agreement to encompass any and all terrorist-linked criminality. But his unhindered progress towards the top job had been unceremoniously derailed two years previously when an acrimonious divorce, following a sordid and spectacularly public affair with one of his colleagues, put paid to his promotion prospects. Never one to miss an opportunity, he had turned adversity to advantage by ingratiating himself with the criminals he had previously prosecuted while keeping a low profile in the department and continuing to have access to classified information. Now he blended quietly into the background, his presence ignored, his misdemeanours forgotten.

He got a cup of coffee and a croissant, selected a table overlooking the runways and called Hollinger.

'Good morning, Jim. Tailwind, we're in early. I have some calls to make before I leave the airport, then I think we should meet before you see McNabb and his pals. There's a complication that we need to discuss. Where are you now?'

Hollinger told him he was at his hotel in Dublin. 'But I suggest we meet at Leixlip or thereabouts, Stephen. It's on the way to Drumlosh House where the Casey group are staying, and it saves you coming into the city. Traffic's bad.'

'Good thinking. When I'm near Leixlip, I'll call you again. You go on and pick somewhere that offers a bit of privacy and good coffee.'

Hollinger was puzzled. This was a different Stephen Reid from yesterday – too relaxed, as though it was a social meeting they were arranging. Why meet in some place that makes good coffee to discuss a complication to a multimillion-pound illegal operation? Something was wrong. He opened his laptop and, using three different eleven-digit passwords, checked his bank account. The money was there. One million pounds sterling.

During the next twenty minutes, Hollinger divided the money over four different accounts in four different countries. Satisfied, he closed the laptop, packed his case and checked out of the hotel. He walked up the street to a newsagent's, bought *The Irish Times*, paid with a five-euro note so he had some change for a payphone, and hailed a taxi.

'Airport, please, and twenty extra to get me there quickly.'

Hollinger paid no attention to the nondescript individual who passed him as he climbed into the taxi and took out a mobile phone as the taxi pulled away.

'Mr Reid, he's in a taxi and we'll follow, but he isn't heading in the direction of Leixlip. He said the airport.'

'Thank you. Don't lose him, and keep me posted.'

Reid ended the call and made another.

'Joe, it's as I suspected – he's heading for the airport. Are you there yet?'

'Just pulled into the short-stay. We'll be in place, don't worry.'

Hollinger arrived in the departures hall an hour after his conversation with Stephen Reid. During that time he had analysed the situation he now found himself in. He'd developed an affinity for Willy and the rest of the Casey group that prevented him from participating in their murder, no matter how tenuous his link with the actual act. The phone conversation with Reid had made him nervous about his own chances of surviving the next few hours. The new guy, Joe, had been too cocky on the phone. On balance, he was happy with his decision: his money was in place and a swift exit offered the best solution to his predicament.

Hollinger checked the flights on the departures screen. The one to Amsterdam in thirty-five minutes opened the door to Europe. He went to the Aer Lingus desk and treated himself to a business-class seat. The flight was departing in ten minutes, just time to visit the toilets on the way down to Gate 17.

* * *

Commissioner Shackleton was a man who aspired to greatness. He considered what others might call luxuries to be necessities. His five series BMW and uniformed driver, his Savile Row suits and his James Taylor & Son handmade shoes were all suggestive of a man who had arrived. He was on the A-list for all the best social occasions, rubbed shoulders with visiting royalty and heads of state, counted the president and the Taoiseach among his golfing partners and had film and pop stars round for drinks. What he lacked – and what he envied Senator O'Gorman – was real influence. When the senator spoke, others listened. When Wesley Shackleton spoke, others asked the senator if what the commissioner had said was correct. Even in operational matters, when his senior officers consulted him it seemed to be more out of courtesy than necessity. So despite all the trappings, Wesley Shackleton was an embittered and deeply unhappy man.

The commissioner's driver pulled up at the gatehouse on the driveway to Drumlosh House and sounded his horn. A Garda officer in combat fatigues appeared from behind the shed at the side. Choosing to ignore the uniformed driver, the guard addressed his remarks towards the rear of the car.

'May I see some identification please?'

'Guard, do you know who you're talking to?'

'I do, sir. I'm sorry, sir, but Inspector Jamison was clear in his instructions. No ID, no entry.'

'This is bloody ridiculous!' The commissioner reluctantly produced his ID card. 'You'll hear more about this.'

'Yes, sir.' He turned to the driver. 'And yours, please?'

Satisfied, the guard opened the gate and delivered a sharp salute as the car passed.

Inspector Sullivan had been outside having a cigarette and recognised the car as it swept up the drive. He went in search of his jacket.

'We've got company,' Alex said over his shoulder as he stood at the dining room window. 'Sullivan just dumped his fag and looks agitated. It's the commissioner, I presume. I want a quick word with Willy and Toots. We'll be back later.'

Alex, Willy and Toots left quickly before the commissioner arrived.

A few minutes later, Inspector Sullivan led the commissioner into the dining room and made the introductions.

Vem stood up. 'Nice to meet you again, commissioner. The Blazers' Hunt Ball, I think, last January?'

'You've a good memory, Mrs Haughey.' He turned to Gran and gave her a polite nod. 'Mrs Casey, my pleasure.'

Sullivan looked round the room. 'The others, they're still here I hope?'

Vem took charge – she could sense Gran's coldness towards the commissioner. 'They'll be back in a few minutes. They know you're here. Please join us – tea and coffee will be along shortly.'

* * *

Willy, Toots and Alex were ensconced in the office. Willy took the lead.

'I still don't trust Sullivan. His defence of himself yesterday was plausible, but not watertight. If we believe his story, then Hollinger is the suspect, and if he's the suspect, Sullivan's too close to him to be clean. The commissioner's an unknown quantity to us. His judgement's suspect if one or other of his lead men in this investigation is bent. On that basis, I vote we tell them no more – certainly not until we meet the senator. I think we can trust him. He saved our skins yesterday ... And Vem is one fine lady. There's no way she'd be party to any shady dealings that endangered her newly found son. You saw her in operation last night, Alex – the lioness protecting her cub.'

'I agree with you about Sullivan and Hollinger,' said Alex. 'Let's contain the information among ourselves. I also propose that we don't disclose our next address to anyone. At this point in time, me, Vem, the senator, his secretary Mary Lennihan, the senator's cousin James, and the gentlemen' – Alex made quote marks in the air – 'who will be our protectors at the new location are the only people who know where we're going. The *gentlemen* that the senator refers to are in fact some of his comrades in arms from the old days. Apparently they would die for him, so if we trust him we trust them.'

'These *gentlemen* – do they have names?' Toots asked.

'Yes, Seamus O'Byrne for one—'

She jumped up and clapped her hands in obvious delight. 'Seamus O'Byrne, your father and my father were the tightest group in the movement. They were inseparable for years. You ask Seamus. He, of all men, can tell you about your dad. Wow, this has made my day. Wait till you meet him, Willy – he's brilliant!'

Willy and Alex grinned at each other.

'That settles it,' said Willy. 'That's a good enough pedigree for me.'

'Three out of three – a unanimous decision, motion carried,' declared Alex. 'Let's go back to the others.'

* * *

Toots led the two boys into the dining room. Conversation round the table was stinted and Vem's smile told them how glad she was to see them back. Inspector Sullivan and the commissioner stood up, and Sullivan made the introductions. As they arranged themselves around one table; Sal and Therese arrived with tea, coffee and scones.

The tension round the table was palpable; no one seemed to know where to start. Gran surprised them all.

'Where were the guards yesterday when we needed looking after?' she asked tersely. 'Why did it fall to a private citizen to organise our rescue?'

The commissioner looked to Sullivan for help.

'I've already asked Inspector Sullivan,' Gran went on, 'so I'm hoping you'll give me a satisfactory answer, for he didn't.'

'Now, Mrs Casey, I—'

The commissioner silenced Sullivan with a wave.

'Mrs Casey, I was informed by Inspector Sullivan of the security arrangements put in place for your protection. Obviously, we were caught out by the use of a helicopter in the attack. However, I can advise you that we now have the leader of that attack in custody and he is being interviewed as we speak. You may feel our arrangements were not up to the mark, but I would suggest that the speed and success of our response to an unanticipated attack proves that we have your well-being uppermost in our plans.'

Sullivan's phone rang. 'Excuse me, I need to take this,' he said, putting the phone to his ear.

'Sullivan ... What? ... Jesus Christ! ... Where? ... The commissioner's with me ... we're on our way ... I'd say half an hour.' He turned to the others. 'Jim Hollinger's just been found murdered in the gents' toilets at the airport. Another Slaney-style butchery job by the sounds of it.'

There was stunned silence round the table.

Sullivan got on the phone again. The commissioner, too, pulled out his phone. Willy held Toots's hand, and Alex and Gran just sat and stared at each other across the table.

Vem excused herself, muttering something about needing to phone Eugene, and she ran off to the office.

When she returned to the dining room, tension and sorrow hung in the air. The commissioner looked at her with relief.

'Thank God you're back. Maybe you can talk some sense into these young fools. I need the information they have to prevent any more bloodshed – indeed, to ensure your own safety.'

'Young they may be but fools they are not.' Vem looked sternly at Sullivan. 'Did you say you were leaving, Inspector Sullivan?'

The commissioner opened his mouth to protest but Sullivan took his arm.

'You're right, Mrs Haughey. We need to move. Phone me later and let me know you're all safe – I don't need to know where.' He almost pushed the commissioner out of the room.

'Arrogant prick!' Vem said, sitting down. 'Do you know what I remember about the commissioner from the Blazers' Ball? He groped me on the dance floor, then propositioned me at the bar. I hope he carried the marks for a long time afterwards.'

* * *

The senator and Detective Inspector Monaghan met in the cocktail lounge of the North Star on Amiens Street. At that hour of the day it was known for its coffee and scones rather than its Dublin City Margarita. When the senator arrived, Monaghan was already seated in a corner booth that guaranteed a reasonable level of privacy. He rose and extended his hand.

'Good morning, Senator. It's been a while since last we crossed swords. What an unbounded pleasure to meet you again.'

'You are a poor liar, Monaghan. Men from your county all are. Only old goats like me know that your charm is your deadliest weapon.'

'Touché, Senator.' Monaghan chuckled. 'I've already ordered, what'll you have?'

'Black coffee and a small jug of cream, thank you. How is Dominic bearing up under the Monaghan onslaught? Well, I trust?'

The DI grinned. 'At this moment I hope he's writing his confession.'

The senator gave him a thin-lipped smile. 'I am going to give you some information that your colleagues in Balbriggan provided me with – relax, it's all above board. Some of it you are going to have to take on trust.' He handed the DI the forensic report.

Monaghan scanned the first page. 'I'm not sure I see the relevance of this to The Shelbourne incident.'

'You will, believe me. But first – and this is off the record – I know who killed Guard McConaghy. On my oath, I can tell you it was not Dominic. He never left the helicopter, and he did not cause any other person to kill McConaghy either.'

Monaghan was struck by the sincerity in the senator's voice. The man was known for many dubious things but lying was not one of them.

'That's a big statement and it requires big trust. I'm afraid I need more.'

'Ever the poker player. That is why I gave you the report. It can tie a seemingly petty incident in Balbriggan to the brutal murder of Michael Slaney, and it can tie both those events to the helicopter attack on The Shelbourne and the attempted murder of myself. It is all in how you read the forensic information and the situation report' – he set Guard Mulligan's report down on the table – 'and whether or not you believe what I'm going to tell you.'

The senator spoke without pause for several minutes. DI Monaghan listened with increasing incredulity, then anger. Assuming it was accurate, this could go to the very fabric of government. But who was working for whom? Who was leaking information? Who could he trust?

'Why tell me, Senator?'

'Because you're above suspicion.'

Suddenly the men's phones rang almost simultaneously. The senator listened for a moment, then held the phone to his chest and glanced at Monaghan. He had hung up and was frowning at the floor.

'Hollinger?'

Monaghan nodded, already reaching for his coat. 'Your sources are just too good, Senator, but that's a matter for another day. I must go.'

'Before you do, I have a request. Please protect Dominic. He is now at the top of a very ruthless organisation's hit list, I'm quite sure. I will be using all my resources to protect young Casey and his pals, but I cannot help Dominic where he is.'

'Believe me, I'll treat Dominic as any other suspect in my custody. He's no use to me dead.' Monaghan slid out of the booth and walked off, his phone clamped to his ear.

The senator signalled for another coffee and continued with his call.

'Right, Mary, get Johnny Todd at the boatyard to call me, and Seamus O'Byrne too. Then ask Sylvia at Wicklow Helihire to have a six-seater on standby for a pickup near Clonmacnoise in a couple of hours. With floats if possible. Phone me as soon as you have it all arranged.'

The senator then phoned Peter and asked him to pick him up. The next phone call was to Drumlosh. It was Vem who answered.

'I've been trying to call you for ages,' she said.

'I presume you've heard about Hollinger. What's happening at Drumlosh?'

'Sullivan and the commissioner are about to leave. Eugene, I'm worried about the journey to Bearna – in fact, I'm worried about after we get there. These people seem to know everything.'

'Yes, I know. I'm worried too. Mary's working on it. I'll

phone you as soon as arrangements are in place, but Vem, in the meantime be vigilant, and tell no one anything until I speak to you again.'

Ten minutes later, Peter arrived at the North Star and handed the senator a note: 'They followed us from The Shelbourne. Careless! If we head north ...' As he read on, the senator started to laugh. 'You're a cunning devil, Peter. That's going to give Guard Mulligan something to get his teeth into. I must tell Wesley the next time we speak – make sure he promotes that lad. Can you do this without wrecking the Rolls?'

Peter nodded.

Everyone underestimated Peter, but the senator knew what a remarkably clever man he was. At the time of his disfigurement, he had been a senior lecturer in the Language School at University College Cork, fluent in French and Gaelic. Only one of the perpetrators of his attack was still alive, that person's identity a mystery that the senator and Peter had been trying to unravel for more than twenty years. Now that two other people – Slaney and Hollinger – had recently been disfigured and killed using that signature MO, Peter's blood was up and was more focused than ever on settling the score with his attacker.

Sitting in the back seat of the Rolls, the senator answered his phone.

'All organised, Mary?'

Mary gave him the details and reminded him to call Vem.

The coast road to Balbriggan was all twists and turns, and the tail they had picked up at The Shelbourne was forced to stay closer than was wise. About three and a half miles short of Balbriggan, the road took a sweeping turn to the left and a lane branched off sharply to the right, running down to a cliff edge about thirty feet from the road. It was a favourite spot for fly-tippers.

In the short straight leading up to the bend, Peter accelerated. He raised his left hand in warning and the senator braced himself. Peter braked hard just past the apex of the corner. The pursuit car, which had also accelerated, encountered the now stationary Rolls in the middle of the road around the bend and took the only evasive action it could. Braking hard, it swerved off down the lane on the right. It was travelling sideways when it disappeared over the cliff edge.

Peter drove on, and the senator called Mary Lennihan.

'Phone Guard Mulligan at Balbriggan Garda Station please. Tell him a car with two occupants has gone off the coast road at a bad bend three or four miles south of the town ... What? ... Yes, I'll call Vem now.' He glanced at Peter and rolled his eyes.

* * *

After a long conversation with the senator, Vem returned to the dining room. Clem followed her in.

'The senator and Clem have organised our escape from here, hopefully undetected.' Vem nodded to Clem. 'Will you explain?'

Clem grinned. 'This takes me back to my army days,' he said, clearly enjoying himself. 'We're going to take you out of here in the back of my old four-by-four Land Rover. There's an old monastic site on the east side of the Shannon above Clonmacnoise where you'll board a small cruiser. Johnny Todd will take you up the river about six miles to Long Island. At the back of the island you'll transfer to a helicopter. From there it's a short hop to Bearna.'

The group stared at him.

'Is this for real or are we extras in a James Bond movie?' Willy said eventually. 'I can't believe anybody would go to these lengths to save our skins – or could arrange it so quickly. Awesome!'

'But where does this leave you and Sal? Those guys aren't going to be too happy with you for aiding and abetting our escape?' Alex said.

'Once we're at Bearna we'll tell the bad guys where we are. It's all but impregnable,' Vem said. 'That makes us the bait and keeps everyone else safe. Willy, when you've taken all you can out of Michael Slaney's book, we'll give it to the villains to keep them off our backs. But prior to that we'll give a copy of its contents to Detective Inspector Monaghan so the Garda will have a head start. He's in charge of the investigation into The Shelbourne incident and now Hollinger's death. The senator reckons he's one of the few senior Garda officers who has the integrity to deal with the information and make things happen. The senator's meeting us at Bearna this evening and can fill in any details I've missed.'

'Vem, there's another problem,' Gran said grumpily. 'I can't swim.'

Everyone smiled. Vem patted Gran's hand kindly, trying not to laugh.

'It doesn't matter, Gran. You'll be wearing a life jacket. It's perfectly safe.'

Gran settled back in her chair, a little more relaxed now she had been reassured.

Chapter 25

Stephen Reid looked around the airport lounge. He shared it with two business types who were deep in conversation, a strikingly attractive Eurasian woman who would have had more of his attention under other circumstances and the Polish barista who had brought his coffee. He was waiting for Joe to call him back to tell him the job was done. Earlier, Joe had spotted Hollinger in the airport and Stephen had instructed him to get Hollinger's bank details and the red book before dispatching him. The last he'd heard was that Joe had followed Hollinger into the gents.

Stephen stood up and stretched. He just got back to his table with a copy of the *Financial Times* when his phone rang.

'That was quick. Where are you?'

The voice that answered sounded like death itself. Cold, lifeless, evil. Stephen's hand began to shake. He spilt coffee in his lap but didn't react.

'Your man executed Slaney and he's just executed Hollinger,' said the voice. 'Now I have no one on the ground ... except you.'

Stephen must have looked as though he was having a heart attack. The barista rushed around the counter to offer assistance but Stephen waved him away.

'Sean Casey's mother and his bastard have my book and that little group are playing silly buggers. I need my book ... *you* need to get it for me. Don't try to hide from me. I'll know when you have it.' There was a pause. 'She was beautiful, wasn't she? Seems to have gone now.' The line went dead.

Stephen scanned the room, shaking with fear. The

Eurasian woman had indeed gone. The barista was at his side again.

'Are you sure you're all right, sir?'

'I'm fine. Just had some terrible news – a family bereavement. Perhaps a glass of brandy?'

His phone rang again.

'Had to get out in a hurry,' said Joe. 'Security man came in. I have the laptop but no bank details. A lot of the stuff seems to be encrypted. Bad news about the red book too – no sign. What now?'

This time Stephen Reid did have a heart attack. He was dead before his phone hit the floor.

Joe heard the clatter down the line. He waited for Reid to pick it up. There was a distant shout, then more voices. Joe heard the entire goings-on – the shouts for a doctor, the Garda. Finally, an authoritative voice came on the line.

'Hello, is there someone there?'

Joe cut the call.

Inside and outside the terminal building, mayhem broke out. Hollinger's body had been found, along with the body of the security guard who'd interrupted his torture. Outside the arrivals exit, Joe and his mate, Wally, pushed a couple aside to jump into their taxi.

'Out of here, *now*, before it's closed off.'

The driver looked in his rear-view mirror and quickly decided not to argue. 'Where to?'

'The Coachman Inn on the Belfast Road.'

Joe and Wally didn't say another word during the two-minute drive. When the taxi stopped at the pub they climbed out and Joe gave the driver twenty euros.

The two men walked in the main entrance of the pub, through the public bar, through the carvery, out the side entrance and across the car park to their car.

The taxi driver drove back to the airport to find the main access road blocked by the Garda and a queue of vehicles building rapidly. He asked what the security alert was all about, and when a guard told him there had been a double murder the taxi driver explained about his two passengers.

By the time he had given a statement to the senior Garda officer, Joe and Wally were speeding out the M50 towards the tolls. They joined the queue at one of the pay lanes rather than use an Autopass lane. They were the last but one car through before the red lights came on and the barrier stayed closed.

Joe kept an eye out for Garda cars as Wally drove at high speed, weaving back and forth across the lanes. They left the M50 at the M4 junction and were still on the roundabout when a squad car screamed round to close off the exit from which they had just emerged.

'Now where?' asked Wally.

'Take the M4,' said Joe. 'Go like hell till we put some distance between ourselves and Dublin.'

He relaxed a little and tried to unravel the mess created by the latest developments. He didn't know what to do with the information he'd gleaned from Hollinger – more importantly, how to turn it into money. He'd just lost his paymaster.

'We're near the Drumlosh place, Joe. What now?' Wally asked half an hour later.

'We'll go on in and rough them up a bit – make them more co-operative. All in one piece though. No bodies … yet.'

* * *

Clem had organised the exodus from Drumlosh with military precision. His Land Rover was parked in the kitchen courtyard, an area invisible from outside the building.

Toots took charge of Gran who, for all her craic and bravado, was more than a little nervous. Not only could she not swim, as she kept telling everyone, but she'd never been in an aircraft of any description. Ever the pragmatist, Willy saw an opportunity to test his iJack on the water and in the air. Alex and Vem were just content to be in each other's company and seemed unfazed by the prospect of a dramatic departure. Willy John had gone back to the gatehouse after a hearty breakfast, none the worse for his adventure the night before.

Clem delivered his human cargo to the old jetty at the monastic site where Johnny Todd was waiting with his cruiser. Although it was the height of the summer season, the river was quiet, with few other boats in sight. Johnny's passengers settled themselves reluctantly in the cabin. It would have been pleasant to stay out in the open, but security trumped pleasure. Johnny cast off and made good time upriver to Long Island, keeping close to the shore. Half an hour later, they rounded the end of the island and passed through a reed bed, marked by a sign saying 'No entry for boats – shallow water', and motored to a helicopter tied to a hazard buoy in the middle of the backwater. There was an air of silent expectation as Johnny gently brought the cruiser to rest against one of the helicopter floats.

'It doesn't look that big when you're beside it. Do you think we'll all fit in?' Gran said nervously.

'Is this your first flight in a helicopter ma'am?' the chopper pilot asked.

'First time my feet have left the ground full stop. It looks awful funny when you're up close.'

'Front seat definitely for you, ma'am. Age and experience first!'

As everyone took their places, Phil Larsen introduced himself, explained safety procedures, fitted them with life jackets and headsets, then showed them how to fasten and release their seat belts and open the doors in an emergency. Willy would not be allowed to play with his toys, much to his disappointment.

* * *

When Clem returned to Drumlosh House, he stopped at the gatehouse.

'I'm going to override the gate control and use the master control in the hotel,' he told Willy John. 'I'm going up the tower for a couple of hours. I'm half-expecting unwelcome visitors, so I might as well give myself the advantage.'

The clock tower rose from the centre of the hall roof. It gave a three hundred and sixty degree view of the estate and the adjoining golf course and nature reserve.

Willy John smiled. 'Would you be taking the Persuader up with you by any chance, just to reinforce the advantage?'

'The Persuader' was an American Barrett M82A1 sniper rifle, accurate up to a thousand metres in Clem's hands, and used to great effect to scare the hell out of would-be poachers and trespassers. Garda Inspector Jamison tolerated its use so long as no one was hurt; his crime figures benefited and the tinkers gave the area a wide berth.

'Yes, she's coming up with me. Will you come back to the hall with me, WJ?'

'I'll stay here, boss, if it's all the same to you. Get my feet up and catch up on my reading.'

'All right, but remember – if anyone arrives and doesn't take no for an answer, no heroics. Stay outside where I can see you, and don't get in my line of sight.'

Clem climbed into the Land Rover and motored back to the hotel, leaving Willy John to close and lock the gate behind him.

An hour later, Willy John heard a car at the gate. He picked up the two-way radio and pressed the send button. Clem, watching from his eyrie in the clock tower, could listen in to the conversation at the gate without Willy John doing anything that attracted attention.

'I'd say you were right about trouble, boss. I don't like the look of this pair,' Willy John said before going out to the car.

He approached the driver's side. 'Sorry, fellas, the hotel's closed.'

A man climbed unhurriedly out of the passenger side and, coming round the front of the car, raised a snub-nosed Colt 45 and pointed it at Willy John's chest.

'Open the fucking gate or I'll open you, you fucking asshole.'

'Take it easy ... take it easy. I'm going to walk to that control box, so don't do anything silly,' Willy John said.

He backed away from the car towards the box on the right-hand pillar, the man following. Willy John transferred the radio to his left hand and reached for the open button. He pressed it and nothing happened.

'It must be controlled from the hotel at the moment. I can't override it.'

The gunman stepped closer and raised the Colt to the side of Willy John's head.

'Use that fucking radio and tell whoever answers it to open the fucking gate now or, so help me God, you'll never open another gate.'

Willy John stepped back a pace and lifted the radio to his mouth.

'Clem?'

At the same time as the report from Clem's rifle reverberated down the drive, the remains of the Colt and bloody pieces of the man's hand smashed into the windscreen of the car. The gunman was on his knees, whimpering like an injured animal and holding his wrist just above the mangled mess that had been his hand.

Willy John, quick for his size and age, dived towards the driver's window, snatched the ignition keys and threw them over his shoulder, then reached back in and caught the driver by the throat, forcing his head back against the headrest.

'Get out and help your mate before he bleeds to death,' Willy John barked.

He released his grip on the driver's throat and took a Walther PPK out of the man's frozen hand. The driver stepped out of the car. Under Willy John's guidance, he propped the gunman up against the bumper of the car and used his belt as a tourniquet high up on the injured arm. Willy John turned as he heard the Land Rover door slam.

Clem was carrying a pump action seven-shot twelve-bore rather than the Persuader. He looked down at the gunman.

'It's amazing what they can do with prosthetics nowadays. Open the gate, WJ, the override is off now.'

'Women and a couple of young bucks I was told ... Fuck me!' the gunman muttered.

The driver, whom Willy John had pinioned against the gate with one hand, shook his head gently as though coming out of a trance.

'You're in big trouble,' he said to Clem. 'He's Joe's wee brother. Joe promised his dying ma he'd care for him, and look what you've done.'

They were interrupted by the beep of Willy John's radio. Sal's voice came through. 'There's a four-by-four turned in at speed.'

Clem took Willy John's radio. 'Thanks, Sal. Call Jamison's men. Tell them to close the drive now. And call an ambulance. Stay there, everybody!'

Clem ran past the car and into the space between the shed and the cottage, pumping a cartridge into the breech of his shotgun. A moment later a black Range Rover skidded to a halt behind the car. The driver threw open his door and got out, waving a Glock semi-automatic towards Willy John who was shielding himself with the driver of the car.

Clem stepped into the driveway behind the Range Rover and fired into the air.

'Don't move,' he shouted. 'Set your weapon down and tell your passenger to do the same.' He crouched down on one knee, taking aim at the driver of the Range Rover.

The man lowered his Glock slowly to the ground as he half turned towards Clem.

'It's a twelve-gauge pump, Joe, and it's pointed at me,' the driver shouted in to his passenger.

'That's right, Joe,' Clem shouted. 'So throw your weapon out before you get out.' Clem heard the click of the door catch and fired high again. 'Mind like a sieve, Joe. I said throw your weapon out first.'

A snub-nosed Colt came flying out of the driver's side and

217

landed on the ground beside the Glock. Willy John pushed his human shield aside and stepped forward to collect the weapons as Clem swung the shotgun to point at the opening passenger door.

'Very slowly, Joe. Hands first, up high.'

As Joe's hands, then legs, came into view Clem stepped forward and rammed the barrel of the shotgun into the man's gross belly, pushing him off balance against the car door. Willy John, carrying the Walther, the Colt and the Glock, waved the new arrival over to the gate beside the other driver.

'Now, Joe, I'm going to step back and let you throw your other weapon on the ground, or you lose a hand like your little brother,' said Clem.

Joe slowly fished a small Derringer pistol out of his jacket breast pocket and dropped it at his feet.

Clem kept talking. 'For your information, lads, your quarry has moved on to the west coast, so all this effort – and your brother's suffering – has been a total waste of time.'

Willy John took his cue. 'Have they gone to Bearna, boss?'

'Shut up, WJ. These guys don't need to know that!'

'Sorry, boss.'

The wail of sirens drowned out any further talk.

* * *

'I've been instructed to take you to Bearna via the scenic route,' Phil Larsen said into his microphone.

Flying at four hundred and fifty feet, he gave his passengers a running commentary as they passed over Shannon Harbour, Portumna and the twin towns of Killaloe and Ballina at the southern end of Lough Derg, then low over the wild and beautiful landscape of The Burren and on to Lisdoonvarna and Galway Bay.

'I hope you don't mind a slight detour,' said Phil.

He followed the Cliffs of Moher to Hags Head and, as he turned due west, he pointed over the vast expanse of ocean. 'Next stop, Newfoundland.'

His enthusiasm was so infectious that for a few minutes his passengers forgot their troubles and soaked up the experience, leaning over each other to get the best views.

Turning north-east, Phil took in the Aran Islands – Inishmore, Inishaan, Inisheer – then Galway Bay for a second time and, finally, the city of Galway itself, before pointing the helicopter north towards Bearna, the small coastal town that was their destination.

He reduced his airspeed as they neared the coast; a stone jetty and a row of fishermen's cottages came into view about three-quarters of a mile west of the town.

'There's the Old House,' said Phil, pointing.

Across the road from the jetty, on top of a low hill, was a moated and castellated manor house surrounded by an impressive stone wall.

After they landed, they thanked Phil profusely, much to his embarrassment. Gran, the last to climb down, was grinning from ear to ear.

* * *

Detective Inspector Monaghan retired to his office giving explicit instructions that he was not to be disturbed. Dominic's statement, detailing his involvement in The Shelbourne fiasco, tallied with some of the information the senator had given. He failed, however, to divulge the most important fact, namely, the identity of his paymaster. Monaghan and the senator both knew that Dominic was not the boss, only the hired help.

The incident and forensic reports about the load tampering and subsequent truck fire at Balbriggan meant nothing on their own; the fire appeared to be a one-off incident. However, when considered in conjunction with the death of Michael Slaney, the man responsible for the load tampering, and the pursuit of the group which included Alex Casey, owner of the burnt truck and employer of Slaney, it all seemed to have a wider significance.

But now Hollinger had been murdered. He and Inspector

Sullivan had been investigating an international money laundering operation linked to drug smuggling in Europe and the UK. Somehow – by accident, according to the senator – young Casey and his pal, a computer whizz, had been caught up in that investigation.

Was Dominic's boss, Slaney's murderer and Hollinger's murderer one and the same person? Presumably it was the same person who was pursuing young Casey and his pals. And how had the Casey group been able to stay just ahead of their pursuers? Surely it was down to good planning as well as luck, and good planning required experience and money. Senator Eugene O'Gorman had the money and the experience to mastermind the group's escapes. He had the ear of the commissioner, and it was no secret that Inspector Sullivan was his eyes and ears in the force. So were the pursuit and the narrow escapes just a very cleverly orchestrated series of events to make Alex Casey and his pals dependent on, and beholden to, the senator?

DI Monaghan rose from his desk, collected his files and left the office.

'Find Senator O'Gorman and tell him to phone me as a matter of urgency,' he said to the duty officer as he passed the front desk. 'Then call Inspector Sullivan and ask him to do the same. Tell them I need to meet them – together or separately.'

Monaghan opened the door of the holding room quietly and slapped the files down on the table. Dominic, who had been dozing on the settee, jumped and struggled to his feet, disorientated.

'Come and sit at the table, Mr O'Gorman,' Monaghan said, pulling out a chair for him. 'Your confession has as many holes as a colander. Another two men have died since we last talked. You might have been able to save their lives if you'd spoken up. Does the name Hollinger mean anything to you?'

Dominic reared back from the table, his eyes wide, his expression manic. Then he collapsed into himself, dropped his head into his hands and jabbered incoherently.

'The manner of his death was similar to Slaney's,' Monaghan went on.

Dominic raised his head, abject terror showing in his eyes. 'You couldn't protect me now, Monaghan, even if you had a mind to. Slaney was the first link, Hollinger the second. I'm the third. They'll get to me somehow.'

The certainty with which Dominic talked about his own demise and the lifeless expression that now replaced the fear unsettled Monaghan.

'Who are *they*? If I knew, then I might have a chance of protecting you. Otherwise, you're right – they probably *will* get to you.'

'That's the problem. I don't know who *they* are. I don't know where they are either. I don't even know how to contact them. I'm given a word to text to a five-digit number and they call back. After the call they text me a new number and word. I last did it yesterday, after The Shelbourne problems. Usually when I send the text they phone back almost immediately, but yesterday they didn't … sorry, I need the loo.'

Dominic left the table and went to the bathroom. But when he didn't return after a couple of minutes, Monaghan knocked on the bathroom door. There wasn't a sound, so the DI knocked again, then opened door.

'Sssshit,' he said under his breath.

Dominic was sitting on the toilet lid, fully clothed, rocking gently back and forth, hugging himself. His eyes were blank, his face expressionless.

'He's away with the fecking fairies.'

Monaghan lifted his documents and opened the suite door.

'Get the bloody medics,' he said to the first guard he saw. 'And don't tell anyone, especially his family.'

Monaghan's phone rang. It was Chris Sullivan.

'You want to meet?' Sullivan said. 'Why don't you come and join the circus at the airport? We're finding dead bodies all over the place.'

Chapter 26

From the helipad at Bearna, Vem led the way towards a path enclosed by seven-foot-high laurel hedges, immaculately trimmed, with occasional pieces of sculpture recessed into the foliage. They rounded a corner and climbed a flight of stone steps with elaborately carved balustrades. It brought them up to a gravelled turning circle in front of the Old House.

A figure stood at the top of the double steps that swept down from the front door. Gran and Toots stopped in their tracks.

'If that's not a sight to bring joy to the heart and a tear to the eye, I don't know what is – Seamus O'Byrne.' Gran said the name slowly, as if savouring the sound. '*Now* I feel safe.'

'Uncle Seamus!' Toots cried as she launched herself at him.

'God, girl, wouldn't your father be proud of you!' He wrapped his arms round her and lifted her off her feet. 'I've seen photos of you over the years but my God, what a heartbreaker you've turned into.'

Seamus kept one arm round her as they walked towards Gran.

'Mrs Casey, may I say that you're also a sight for sore eyes. What a long overdue pleasure.' He bent down to embrace Gran. Then he stepped back and his steely grey eyes fell on Alex.

'If only I could turn the clock back, your father would be standing here, not me. I've never forgiven myself for not being at his side when he needed me.' He shook his head. 'I may not have been able to change the course of that evening, but Sean Casey didn't deserve to die alone.'

Alex stepped forward and, with locked right hands, the men embraced each other. Then Alex introduced him to Willy and Vem. Seamus was civil to Willy, but with Vem there was genuine delight.

'I've heard such a lot about you from your father, Vem. I've been warned not to challenge you to race cars or to shoot.'

Vem took Willy by the arm and walked towards the front door.

'C'mon, let's give them time to catch up,' she said. 'Anyway, I'm starving.'

They were greeted in the main hall by an elegantly attired, rather effeminate-looking man.

'You're very welcome back, Miss Vem. How well you look in spite of your journey,' he said. He turned his attention to Willy, sidling close to him. 'And who might *you* be?' He extended a limp hand.

'Behave yourself, Pierre,' Vem said, laughing. 'This is William McNabb, from Northern Ireland. He's Toots's boyfriend and a real computer ace. Willy, this is Pierre Angelinni, the manager at the Old House.'

As Willy shook his hand, Pierre fluttered his eyelashes ever so slightly.

'A pleasure, William. You're very welcome here. Feel free to fiddle with my gizmos anytime.' Willy didn't know where to look. 'Seriously, William, I recently installed a webcam and the blasted thing has a mind of its own. Perhaps you could have a look for me.'

'Not a bother, Pierre. Can we do it later? Just now, I think we could all do with something to eat.'

'Of course. A light luncheon and suitable refreshment is laid out in the dining room. Follow me!'

Toots, Alex and Gran joined Willy and Vem a few minutes later. Seamus had some business to attend to and said he would be back later.

'Best not lose sight of the reason we're here,' Alex said when they finished eating. 'What more have you to do before we can get rid of the cursed books, Willy? And when can we start to use our phones again – well, mine anyway? Yours is still in Cork.'

'You can use your phone now if you like. We *want* them to know where we are now, isn't that the plan? The books? Give me three or four hours and I'll transfer all the information onto a flash drive.'

'I'll speak to the senator and find out what his schedule is,' said Vem. 'He should be on his way.'

* * *

At the gatehouse at Drumlosh, Sergeant Mulcahy and two of the guards who'd spent the night patrolling the estate's boundaries pulled in behind the ambulance. Tired and dishevelled, the men were disappointed not to have been involved in this recent incident.

Clem walked the sergeant a little way up the drive, out of earshot. 'What are you going to do with this lot? You're short on manpower, aren't you?'

'You could say. Jamison's at a wedding. Told me not to disturb him unless it was life or death.'

'Well, I have a suggestion,' said Clem. 'Arrest the two drivers. One was aiding and abetting, the other one was waving a gun. Get that Joe fella's particulars and let him go. Charge him with unlawful possession or something. I'll give you whatever statement you want. Jamison will understand. He knows what's going on here.'

Mulcahy was doubtful, but he was aware how well Clem and the inspector knew each other. The two rogue drivers were cuffed together in the rear seat of the squad car, and two guards set off with them under orders not to un-cuff them until they were inside the cells.

Joe was cautioned and ordered to attend the station in the morning at ten o'clock. He allowed himself a little smile as he drove away from Drumlosh. He wouldn't be attending any Garda station in the morning. Bloody fools!

* * *

The senator had been dozing in the car for an hour and was pleasantly surprised to see that Peter was turning into the drive of Drumlosh House when he woke. As they would be passing on their way to Bearna, the senator had suggested they call for some lunch and an update on the day's events.

Clem came out to meet him as he stepped out of the Rolls.

'Senator, you're welcome. Come and join us. Good day, Peter. An uneventful drive I hope?'

Peter nodded and followed them in.

Over lunch, the senator and Clem compared notes and assessed the situation.

'This Joe fellow – is he the head man?' the senator asked.

'No, definitely not. Not officer material. I'd say he reports to someone else. He's a fat slug. Northern accent, his demeanour deferential but not subservient. Also, he was too relaxed. He'd missed the prize but didn't seem to be bothered. That's my reading of him.'

The senator nodded. 'I'd also value your input on how you would try to take the Old House if you wanted to break in. A soldier's perspective.'

'Funny, I was thinking about that earlier. An interesting objective, for sure. A frontal attack on the main gates to draw the majority of the guards, sustained for ten, twelve minutes, say. At the same time a snatch squad via the north-west corner. It's the most inaccessible part, but probably where the security is weakest. Once inside the walls, the service bridge over the moat leading to the stores would give quick, covered access to the kitchen and pantries.'

'And how would you try to *protect* the Old House?'

'Light. Flood the place with light. Two snipers on the roof with clearance to shoot on sight. Ground troops between the house and the moat. And, of course, the bridge up.'

'Okay. Thank you, Clem. Would you mind giving Seamus O'Byrne a call later and having a chat with him? Two heads and all that. He's a good man, and he will listen – not too proud to take advice. Now, I'll settle the account for Vem's group last night. Then Peter and I had best be on our way.'

* * *

DI Monaghan parked his car and walked the last quarter mile to the airport, such was the chaos at the main entrance. Inside was just as bad. The departure area had been sealed off, and those remaining inside were waiting to be interviewed as possible witnesses. Passengers arriving for flights were besieging the airport staff, and tempers were flaring all round. God help us when there's a major terrorist incident if this is the best we can do, thought Monaghan.

Chris Sullivan spotted him and broke away from the forensics team.

'Thanks for coming, Pader. There's no way I'm going to be out of here in the near future. *His* presence isn't helping either!' Sullivan nodded towards the commissioner who was giving an impromptu interview to RTÉ. 'Bloody man. Any opportunity to advance himself. Anyway, come with me.'

Monaghan followed Sullivan along the row of check-in desks, up the escalator and into the departure area. Two uniformed guards stood at the door to the business lounge.

'Is this your incident room, or is there more trouble in here?' Monaghan asked.

The guards on the door nodded them through and Sullivan walked over to a corner that had been screened-off. Monaghan looked round the screen and saw a body slumped in one of the club chairs.

'This is how he was found by the staff. He'd just taken a phone call. Medic says massive heart attack. Died instantly. We were downstairs attending to the Hollinger scene, so the manager came and got us.'

Sullivan pulled a British passport out of his own pocket.

'Well, at least you've been able to ID him,' said Monaghan. 'So what's the problem? Straightforward natural causes, surely?'

'Aye, natural causes all right. It's the ID that's the problem.'
Sullivan opened the passport and handed it to Monaghan.
'Meet Stephen Reid, Jim Hollinger's boss.'

* * *

Joe had been less than honest with Reid when he spoke to him
before he'd collapsed. Hollinger had been very forthcoming
about the whereabouts of the book. If security hadn't arrived
when it did, he would also have given up his bank codes.
Hollinger's heart had been stronger than Slaney's but his pain
threshold far lower.

Joe struggled out of the Range Rover and made his way
towards Biddy Quinns. It was a shoddy-looking riverside pub
in the centre of Athlone, the sort that tourists photographed,
stepped into, then hastily withdrew from under the baleful
glare of Biddy herself. Should a stranger dare enter, all
conversation would stop. If their courage took them to the bar
and they ordered a drink, Biddy would look them up and
down, remove the clay pipe from her toothless mouth and
direct a gob of brown spit into the turf fire. If the visitor's
nerve and stomach still held, she would come round from
behind the bar in her filthy bare feet, open the door and tell
them to fuck off. If they stood their ground, as Joe did the first
time he visited, Biddy would nod her approval and allow
them to stay, but only for one drink.

Why any tourist would *want* to stay longer was anyone's
guess. Why Joe stayed on his first visit, and returned half a
dozen times over the next two years was a closely guarded
secret.

Joe went through the door of the pub. Biddy nodded to
him, reached into her filthy bodice and produced a key on a
chain. Joe squeezed round behind the bar as Biddy inserted
the key and unlocked a door. The door swung open with a
metallic clunk revealing a gloomy passage. Joe stepped in and
the door immediately closed behind him. In near darkness he
followed the dank-smelling passage down a gentle gradient

that turned suddenly to the right where he was then confronted by a seamless metal door, no lock, no handle. He waited perhaps thirty seconds before the door swung open, the sudden brightness temporarily blinding him after the gloom.

'Come in, Joseph. How nice of you to call.'

The voice was soulless, disembodied, cruel. It emanated from a large Perspex oxygen tent on the other side of the room, a hermetically sealed pliofilm tomb that the incumbent would never leave. Sustenance, both nutrients and drugs, was administered intravenously; waste material removed by tube.

The occupant was only visible via the wall-mounted plasma screen behind the bed. He could best be described as a skin-covered skeleton under a sheet, a human shell. Francis Xavier Fitzpatrick, millionaire playboy, drug baron and money launderer, gunrunner and the Irish underworld's number one fixer, had been reduced to his present state by alcohol, drugs and, finally, AIDS. Although his body was painfully and slowly being destroyed by disease, his mind remained as clear and active as ever.

'What news of my code book?' The question rattled from the speakers mounted on the plasma screen.

'It's still in the possession of the young fella, McNabb, and he's now apparently holed up in some O'Gorman property near Galway.'

'Ah, the Old House at Bearna. I know it well. I tried to buy it myself from the Hueys, but they didn't consider me a suitable owner for a part of their family heritage. Mind you, I doubt the O'Gorman money was any cleaner than mine.'

The rattling sound from the speakers that was laughter sent waves of revulsion through Joe.

'What sort of petty-minded people am I now surrounded by? First Slaney double-crosses me, then Dominic O'Gorman, the useless fool, gets himself caught. Hollinger tries to do a runner, and now Reid and his dicky fucking heart! Not one of them could deliver. What a useless bunch of losers.'

The oxygen tent shook as a paroxysm of coughing took hold of Fitzpatrick. After a few minutes it ceased, the silence broken only by the low hum of the equipment that kept the man alive.

'And what about you, Joseph, are you going to do any better? You came highly recommended a couple of years ago and have performed satisfactorily up to now. But this is the big one. My code book can reveal the whereabouts of millions of dollars and tons of heroin and cocaine. Senator O'Gorman's been looking for his book for twenty years. Think what it must be worth. Compound interest, Joseph, compound interest over twenty years. Will you let me down the same as the others?'

Joe knew better than to answer these rhetorical questions. He watched a stream of pale yellow liquid pass through one of the tubes and tried not to gag.

'Get the book for me,' Fitzpatrick suddenly barked. 'Let me see it. Let me show them that I control the money laundering side for Europe and South America before it's too late. I could flood the market and put the Colombian cartels out of business. I could close Afghanistan down. That's the prize you let slip past you at Drumlosh House, Joseph.'

The rasping voice faded to silence for a moment. 'That was your first and only fuck-up. You won't get another chance.'

* * *

The senator left Drumlosh content that, with Clem's military input and Seamus O'Byrne's natural cunning, the Old House would be a safe haven for Vem and the others – and for himself: he was getting old, yet he still had so much to do. Vem, Mrs Casey and Alex needed the truth about their heritage, but explaining it to them was a daunting prospect, not because it was shady or in any way dubious, quite the opposite. No, it was the dramatic effect it would have on them for the rest of their lives. Dominic, perhaps, was beyond help. He had made his choice and it was a poor one. He had been caught and should take the punishment. But it would feel like unfinished business to the senator, a book left open. And Peter, faithful Peter. What was to become of him? Where would he find a niche to suit his particular talents? The record needed to be set straight regarding the recent deaths he had caused. The senator's history lesson was going to require very delicate handling indeed.

His ruminations were interrupted by the phone ringing. It was Vem wanting to know when he would be arriving. He smiled to himself. That girl would be his brightest legacy. After he had spoken to her, he phoned Mary Lennihan.

'The papers – are they all in order?' he asked. 'Have the solicitors approved them?'

'Yes, indeed, Senator, though they're somewhat reluctant. They feel it puts too much control in the hands of one person. It's also given the insurance people a headache.'

'What a lot of old women! I've run the whole outfit for fifty years, so where's the problem?'

'Just flagging up their concerns, Senator.'

'Covering their own backs, more like. Anyway, what time are you coming over tomorrow?'

'Early afternoon as agreed. Helihire are booked for one o'clock.'

'Right. Well, I'll see you then.'

'Before you go, Eugene …'

The senator braced himself for the bad news he knew was coming.

'My contact at Garda HQ phoned ten minutes ago. It's Dominic. He's regressed again, worse than the last time. The doctor wants to section him, but Monaghan is keeping that quiet for the moment.'

The senator was silent for a long time.

'It would appear that I have made the right decision after all,' he said eventually, 'despite the concerns of solicitors and insurance brokers. Thank you, Mary. I will speak to DI Monaghan shortly.'

* * *

As they left the airport lounge, Inspector Sullivan and Detective Inspector Monaghan met the commissioner.

'Well, that went quite well,' the commissioner said, looking pleased with himself. 'Keep the press on your side. You never know when they'll come in useful. Now, what's the story here? Natural causes apparently. Obviously nothing to do with downstairs.'

'Not that simple, I'm afraid, sir,' said Sullivan. 'The body in there is a Mr Stephen Reid. He was Jim Hollinger's boss. Arrived this morning for a meeting with Jim, myself and McNabb, the computer expert.'

'Oh dear. That's very unfortunate, Chris. Will you handle the meeting yourself or' – the commissioner flapped his hands – 'do you want someone else to sit in with you … Pader here, for instance?'

Monaghan, watching and listening intently, raised an eyebrow.

Sullivan took a deep breath. 'Commissioner, of the four due at the meeting today, only two of us remain alive. Both of us must now be considered top of the killer's hit list. A homicidal maniac is out there looking for McNabb and me, his objective to torture information out of us, then murder us. With respect, sir, *very unfortunate* doesn't really cover it.'

Both Monaghan's eyebrows shot up.

'Another thing,' Sullivan went on. 'There's a leak in the lines of communication somewhere above me, and the hole's the size of a fucking bucket!'

Monaghan's jaw dropped.

Sullivan turned away before the commissioner could respond, but had only taken half a dozen paces when he stopped and turned back. 'And I resign, effective immediately.' With that, he strode off down the stairs.

Monaghan spotted the TV crew assembling at the business lounge door; he had a severe allergy to cameras.

'I'll go and talk to him for a bit, settle him down,' he said and took off after Sullivan without waiting for the commissioner's response.

*   *   *

In a spotless toilet off Fitzpatrick's room in Biddy Quinns, Joe washed his hands twice and sluiced cold water over his face, rubbing wet hands around the back of his neck. Relieved, cleansed and cooled he felt ready to continue with the 'interview'.

'So glad you washed your hands thoroughly, Joseph. I can't be too careful with germs.'

So, a camera in the fucking bathroom …

'Let us proceed with the business in hand. You've told me who has my book. Have you anything more to tell me?'

'No, I don't think so, other than to discuss my requirements for its retrieval.'

'Oh dear, surely you haven't forgotten Mr Hollinger's laptop. Don't tell me I've misjudged you?'

Joe held his composure but his stomach constricted as though he'd been kicked. His brow beaded with sweat.

'Not at all. I intend to get McNabb to work on it – find out what secrets it holds – then I'll pass the laptop and its information over to you.'

'Good answer, Joseph. You just saved yourself a quick dip. Do you see that other door there, the one beside the bathroom? Open it.'

Joe turned the handle and pushed. As the door swung into the gloom beyond, a revolting, nauseating smell hit him with the force of a fist and he stepped back involuntarily. There was nothing through the door that he could see. No floor, no walls, just the darkness and the stench.

'I'm lucky,' said Fitzpatrick. 'I can't smell what you find so offensive – one of the few advantages of living in this bubble. Let me tell you what's out there. If you step – or are *assisted* – through that door, you will fall twelve feet into the water. There are no steps or handholds, the walls are smooth as glass. So your only option is to go with the flow. It's where the river goes underground via the castle beside us, before it joins the Shannon a mile or so away. The tunnel is blocked at the other end by a cast-iron grid. No one can see or hear anything from the outside – at least, no one has ever come back to tell me otherwise.'

The death laugh started again, followed by bouts of coughing. Joe looked around for a chair. He needed to sit down.

'Now you understand the price of poor performance,' Fitzpatrick went on. 'Slaney understood well enough when they took him to Lock Number Two. All I'm doing is following a pattern established when that bastard Sean Casey murdered my brother Patrick. Now, Joseph, tell me what you need.'

* * *

'I think it's time Gran and I had a talk,' Vem said to Alex. 'I'm not trying to exclude you, but we've some issues that need to be put to bed.'

'I'm all for that, Vem, and I'm sure Alex would much rather do *man* things with Seamus, than *woman* things with us,' said Gran. She was looking forward to discussing Sean and Vem's relationship – how they met, how long they had known each other – all the usual mother things, plus a whole lot more.

Seamus welcomed the opportunity to show off his plans and a chance to get to know the son of one of his best friends.

'Let's walk down to the road, Alex,' Seamus said. 'That way I can explain the strengths and weaknesses of the Old House as a fortress.'

As they set off, Gran and Vem watched them from the sitting room on the first floor. Seen from the back, they could have been father and son; both had that confident swing in their step that only comes with self-belief. The two women smiled to themselves for different reasons, but they were united in their love for Alex.

Unusually for a house of the period, the driveway ran straight up from the county road to the front door, a distance of eight hundred and ninety-six yards. Over that distance the drive rose one hundred and thirty-seven feet, a steep but not uncomfortable rise for a horse-drawn carriage. The explanation for the position of the Old House lay behind and on either side of the five acres of garden, moat and coach house – a flooded quarry.

It had been built in 1866 on the site of the quarry winding sheds and breaking yard, and the driveway laid on the old scree run where the blocks of Connemara marble had been 'slyped' down to the old jetty across the road. The quarry was U-shaped, the base of the U wrapping the back of the house with the legs running two hundred yards down each side towards the road. The Marquis of Moycullen, for whom the house had been built, had ordered that a moat be constructed to join the side legs of the flooded quarry.

'Looking at the house from here, Alex, you can see what Moycullen had in mind when he picked the site. From the house, commanding views over Galway Bay and the land to either side. From here, an impregnable manor house with natural defences on three sides. A twenty-five-foot-high quarry face rising out of maybe fifty feet of water, topped with a twelve-foot wall – that's the back and two hundred yards down each side well protected. As you see, the wall then carries on down the two sides and round the front of the site. Inside that, and a short walk from the house, we have this – a thirty-foot wide, fifteen-foot deep moat complete with drawbridge and sheer sides. Now you can understand why the senator was keen to get you here until this trouble you're having is sorted out.'

Alex turned on the bridge and looked up at the Old House. He was impressed. The reasons for such a grand, yet comfortable, home were understandable; the cost must have been prohibitive. They walked on down to the entrance and, again, Alex stopped and looked back.

'There was money about in those days, Seamus. Money and style.'

'Aye, and there's money about these days as well, and here comes some of it now. Stand in, or the Peter boy'll drive over the top of you.'

The Rolls-Royce glided to a halt just inside the entrance and the rear window quietly dropped to reveal the occupant.

'Good day to you, Senator,' Seamus said, smiling. 'Let me introduce you to the son of one of my best friends. This is Alex Casey, son of Sean Casey.'

Alex took the senator's extended hand.

'Good day to you, Alexander. What a pleasure to meet my grandson! Drive on, Peter.'

The poignancy of the moment was not lost on the senator. Twenty-two years ago a similar stop in a mean street in the docklands of Dublin had been the starting point for this handsome young man's life.

Seamus's mouth fell open in surprise. 'Wait, wait, wait. So Vem … Vem is your mother?' he said to Alex. 'Sean and Vem … well, I'll be dammed!'

'I only found out two days ago myself. I still can't get used to it,' said Alex.

The pair started out to walk the boundary, making notes on an Ordnance Survey map as they went, comfortable in each other's company. They headed west along the wall from the castellated archway, unaware of the black Range Rover parked half a mile back on the road towards Bearna.

* * *

Vem and Gran were deep in conversation when the senator walked into the drawing room.

'Good afternoon, ladies. Do you mind if I disturb you?'

Vem jumped up and greeted him with a hug and a kiss on the cheek.

'Eugene, let me introduce you to Mrs Enda Casey.'

The senator walked over to Gran who had risen slowly. He

held her hand, his eyes never leaving her face.

'Mrs Casey, it is an honour and a privilege to make your acquaintance again. I hope the circumstances of this meeting are not as painful as our last, and that the results may be even more beneficial.'

Gran gave him a little nod.

'I owe you an apology for the burden I placed on you twenty-two years ago,' he continued. 'When I explain the circumstances that forced me to take the action I did, I hope you will agree it was necessary and correct for all concerned, not least Alexander. I met him outside with Seamus O'Byrne. He is a fine-looking young man, and a credit to you, Mrs Casey.'

Gran still didn't say anything, nor did the senator's eyes leave her face.

'Now, please excuse me for taking Vem from your company for half an hour. There are business matters that must be dealt with before the end of the day.'

'Senator O'Gorman, we've much to talk about. Do your business with Vem but when you're done, there are scores to settle and accounts to be squared.'

* * *

When Pierre had shown Toots and Willy to their room, they had kissed long and hard. But after a few minutes of kissing and hugging, Willy reluctantly broke their embrace.

'Sorry, Toots – work before pleasure. I must extract all the information I can out of Michael's book. Keep me company, but keep your distance,' he said, laughing at Toots's attempted pout. 'I'm serious, so you can cut that out, okay?'

For the next hour and a half not one word passed between them. Willy spoke plenty to himself, cursed occasionally and finally stood up, stretched and went to the bathroom. When he returned, he inserted a flash drive into the laptop and transferred all the files from the hard drive to it. Then he plugged in a second flash drive and repeated the process.

Finally, he destroyed the specially created partition on the laptop, leaving no trace of his workings.

He gave one flash drive to Toots, instructing her to give it to the senator when he arrived. The other one he hid, keeping the hiding place to himself. When he was done, they went to find Alex. Willy wanted to test his theory about the code on the Casey Transport files.

Chapter 27

Joe listed his requirements and explained his plan of attack, justifying the amount of hardware he needed and the number of men.

In his heyday, during the Troubles, he had a reputation on both sides of the sectarian divide as one of the top strategists. It was his attention to detail and his ability to pre-empt the other side's movements that had put him at the top of Fitzpatrick's list for this operation. Had it not been for his unique talents, his failure to mention Hollinger's laptop without being prompted would have been enough to send him for a swim in the tunnel.

'It sounds like you're preparing for World War Three,' rasped Fitzpatrick. 'That's good. My expectations are high, very high.'

The coughing started again but didn't subside this time. A door behind the tent opened and a male nurse entered. He walked to the console which carried the monitor and a battery of dials and switches, adjusted a number of valves on lines leading into the tent and then left without saying a word.

'He's trying to keep me alive. I have, at best, three months, so the outcome of your operation is critical and I *must* live to see the results. Years of work. Failure is not an option. I told Hollinger how Slaney only sang for seven minutes before his heart gave out. I then explained that he would sing for seven hundred minutes if he failed – circumstances, unfortunately, prevented that. You, my friend, will sing for as long as it takes me to die if you fail. And to ensure you stay with us, we'll use a drug that'll prevent your heart from letting you down.

Believe me, your mind is incapable of comprehending how hellish those two or three months will be. So, I repeat – failure is not an option.'

Joe left after another paroxysm of coughing brought the nurse in again. This time the nurse looked at Joe and shook his head, a gesture that gave Joe a moment's pause.

* * *

DI Monaghan caught up with Inspector Sullivan at the bottom of the stairs leading to the check-in concourse and grabbed him by the arm.

'Chris, you and I need to talk urgently. The problem at An Garda Síochána is much bigger than you know and if we don't do something about it, it's going to bring us all down.'

'I've had a bellyful of that self-serving prick Shackleton. I've had enough. I don't care any more. I'm out.'

'Fine, but I'm not, so I need your help before you quit. Please?'

Sullivan said nothing for a moment. He looked around the concourse. 'Give me a few minutes, then we can get a coffee. I'll do what I can to help you but I'm not changing my mind – I'm quitting.'

Sullivan spent a few moments with each of the officers and medics involved in the operation of recording and removing the bodies. Monaghan was impressed with his thoroughness and his sensitivity – he gave several minutes to a young guard who was fresh from college and had just seen his first corpses. Satisfied that everything was under control, Sullivan told the plain-clothes sergeant to phone him if he had any concerns – he would only be five minutes away. Then he and Monaghan bought sandwiches and coffee and found a quiet corner of the food hall.

'No bullshit, Pader. I've just lost a colleague I worked closely with for many months.' Sullivan glanced around and lowered his voice. 'So, what have we got? A seemingly insignificant truck robbery and fire, the murder of Michael

Slaney, the fiasco at The Shelbourne, the arrest of Dominic O'Gorman, the cock-up at Drumlosh House and the deaths of Hollinger and Reid.' Sullivan counted out the incidents on his fingers. 'I smell corruption and incompetence at the expense of the innocent. So tell me, why the hell would I want to be a part of all that? What is there in that dunghill worth saving?'

'You said it yourself, Chris – the innocent. The Caseys, young Siobhan Toomey, the McNabb fella – they need our help and protection. You know all of them better than me. But they don't trust you at the moment, and I can't blame them – everything you've done to keep them safe has backfired. *You* know An Garda Síochána is leaking like a sieve, but they don't. You need to prove to them that you're on their side. You won't achieve anything by resigning. Would you reconsider?'

Sullivan gave him a weak smile. Monaghan knew he'd hit the target – Sullivan was too good an officer to walk away.

'You're a persuasive bugger, Pader,' said Sullivan.

* * *

Willy and Toots looked into the drawing room to see Gran sitting on her own, staring out the bay window.

'All alone, Gran?'

'Sitting on your own doesn't mean you *are* alone, Toots. This journey, and the people we've encountered, has opened doors in my memory I closed many years ago. It has brought me back some fine company. My Enda, your dad Tommy, and Seamus here, one of the best friends we ever had.'

'You're an inspiration to us, Gran. Isn't that right, Willy?'

'Absolutely! I've decided I'm going to adopt you as my gran, so there.'

Gran smiled at the compliment.

'Now, do you happen to know where Alex is?' Willy asked. 'I need his help for a few minutes.'

'I saw him and Seamus walking up the wall twenty minutes ago.'

'Thanks. Right, I'll see you later,' Willy said, then disappeared.

'I like him, Toots, though he always seems to be in a hurry.'

'Not always, Gran,' Toots replied cryptically, a mischievous grin spreading over her face. 'Not always.'

* * *

The senator was standing at the French windows in the presidential suite, so called because De Valera was said to have slept there. It gave onto a small balcony with views over the gardens to Galway Bay and The Burren in the far distance. Vem was sitting at the desk, on the phone to Mary who was listing the documents that she would be bringing for signature the next day. She interrupted only once – to have a point clarified; otherwise she sat in awe as the true extent of the senator's assets was revealed to her.

Mary finished by quoting the current stock market value of the holdings and outlining the structure of O'Gorman Holdings from the proposed date of signature. Vem hung up, leaned back in her chair and sat motionless for a while. The senator didn't intrude on her thoughts; he knew the extent of the information she was trying to absorb and the life-changing effect it was going to have on her.

Vem turned in her chair and looked at her father, standing erect, the black malacca cane in his right hand. Not bad for seventy-five, she thought.

'How on earth did you fit it all in, Eugene? Why did you never have a hobby?'

'I did. I had two – making money and, from November 1987, fighting evil.'

* * *

Willy caught up with Alex and Seamus as they followed the path running alongside the back wall. He told Alex he needed five minutes of his time.

'We're almost done,' said Alex. 'Can we talk after?'

Willy was happy to trail along. He was fascinated to hear Seamus explain matter-of-factly how an intruder at a certain point might be pushed back into the quarry, or shot as he cleared the wall. Seamus was thorough in his analysis of potential problem areas and fanatical about detail, and Alex seemed to be enjoying learning from a master. They could be discussing a clay pigeon shoot for all the emotion they showed, Willy thought.

At the corner formed by the north and east walls, a viewing platform had been built that gave an uninterrupted view of the surrounding countryside. They climbed the steps and leaned on the wall. Away to the west they got a glimpse of the Atlantic, to the north, Lough Corrib in the distance, and to the east, Bearna, with Galway behind.

After they left the viewing platform and, protected from view, Seamus pulled a small radio from his jacket.

'Number Two, Number Three, come in please.'

'Number Three, over.'

'Number Two here, over.'

'There's a black Range Rover nine hundred yards east of the site on the shore road. Investigate please.'

'On our way.'

Alex and Willy were startled; they hadn't noticed anything.

'Best to check it out,' said Seamus.

'Makes it all kind of real,' said Willy.

'It's real all right, son. We're dealing with very bad people.'

Willy looked about him. 'When do the rest of your men arrive?' he asked. 'I assume there'll be more than you inside and those two you've just spoken to?'

Seamus smiled. 'There are eleven of us in total, and we're all here. They arrived at three o'clock this morning, and everyone was in position before daybreak.' He had a playful grin on his face. 'Remember when you had a pee a couple of hundred yards back there, Willy? Well, watch ...'

Seamus brought the radio up to his mouth. 'Number Nine, over. Give us a wave.'

As they looked back along the wall, an arm appeared out of the scrubby ground and gave them a thumbs up and then the fingers before disappearing again.

Seamus chuckled. 'He's letting you know that you just missed him when you had a pee there earlier, Willy.'

'Come in Number One.'

The voice from the radio suddenly had Seamus's full attention. 'One.'

'Snoopers confirmed and contained. Do you want them in?'

'Negative, on my way. There in five.'

Seamus left the two lads staring after him.

'I'll not tell Toots you exposed yourself to that fella,' Alex said and ducked as Willy took a swipe at him. 'Makes you wonder where all the others are, doesn't it?'

'It'll be a while before I take a pee outside again,' said Willy. 'Right, can we go in so I can test my theory, Alex? I need you to let me into Casey Transport's files.'

* * *

Seamus drove along to the Range Rover whose occupants were now sitting in its rear seats. Before he got out of his vehicle, he looked up and down the road, removed his sunglasses, pulled on a cotton balaclava and replaced the sunglasses. He stepped down from his four-by-four and climbed into the driver's seat of the Range Rover. He started the engine and drove it towards the old jetty, parking the vehicle facing out to sea. One of his men was sitting in the front passenger seat; the other was in the luggage well behind the rear seats. Both were wearing balaclavas and dark glasses and holding pistols.

'What have we here, Number Two?' Seamus asked.

The man beside him didn't speak, just handed him a 1:5000 section of Ordnance Survey map clearly showing the Old House with its perimeter wall and the surrounding area up to about a mile from the house. On it were notations and crosses which matched the places where Seamus and Alex had stopped as they walked the perimeter.

'Very interesting, and very amateurish, wouldn't you say?'

Number Two nodded. Seamus turned round so he could look directly at the young man and woman in the back seat. Neither of them had said a word, and both looked scared to death.

'Both of you – strip,' ordered Seamus.

The young man, a good-looking, well-groomed lad, turned to his companion.

'Don't do anything. I'll handle this.'

He turned back towards Seamus just in time to meet the fist that hit him on the nose with a sickening crunch of cartilage and bone. His head flew back. Number Three, sitting behind the back seats, caught him by the ears and held tight. Tears, snot and blood covered the young lad's face, his cry of pain fading to a whimper.

'I forgot to say, don't speak until you're spoken to. Now, miss, take your clothes off … quickly, or I'll have to help.'

The girl, who had short auburn hair and fine features, closed her eyes and, with difficulty, undressed to her bra and pants. She reached behind to undo her bra but Seamus stopped her.

'Let's see how we get on before you go any further. Now, help him undress – shoes, socks, pants and underpants. Leave the shirt – it's mopping up the blood and goo nicely.'

Seamus waited while she helped her boyfriend to remove his clothes, all while he was being held by the ears.

'Okay, we'll start again.'

Number Three released his grip on the young man's ears.

'I don't want to hurt either of you, so when I ask a question, you answer. Truthfully, okay? Oh, I almost forgot …' Seamus nodded to Number Three. 'Introduce these good people to your friend.'

There was a metallic click, and the masked man reached out between the captives and waggled the six-inch double-sided blade of his flick knife for their inspection.

'Now, first things first. Who sent you?' asked Seamus.

The girl looked at the young man, then at Seamus. 'We don't know,' she said. 'It was all arranged by phone and email. We never met him, and he never used a name. He said the Range Rover would be delivered to an agreed rendezvous with five hundred euro in an envelope – that's it there on the dash – and another five hundred would be left when we return the Range Rover and our surveillance notes. That's all. Honestly!'

Seamus shook his head. 'I'm disappointed in you.'

He nodded to his colleague in the back, and the girl cried out and reached for her right shoulder. He'd cut the shoulder strap of her bra and sliced into her flesh. Tears sprang from her eyes as blood oozed between her fingers.

'The next cut will leave a scar. I want the truth,' Seamus said.

'I'm telling the truth. Honestly. That's all I know. Please don't mark me. Danny, do something, I'm scared!' Sobs racked the girl and the tears streamed down her cheeks.

'Yes, Danny, do something, before I feed you your manhood,' Seamus said, peering over the seat back. 'Small and all as it is, it could still choke you.'

'Jen's told the truth. Look, this guy phoned me and –'

'What guy? I need a name.'

Seamus nodded. There was a flash of the blade, and Danny now sported a shallow cut on his left arm from shoulder to elbow. He howled like a stuck pig.

'The next wrong answer you'll be eating it,' Seamus reminded him.

'Okay, okay. He's a friend of my dad's – a guy called Uel Fagan. Yesterday morning this guy phoned, said Uel Fagan had recommended me and asked could I do a quick recce job. Then he said about the car and the money, just as Jen says. That's the truth, honest.'

As he spoke, Jen turned to look at him with disgust.

'You're a right wee shite, Danny Craig, an unmitigated shit. You never told me all that. You said there would be no risk, just watch the comings and goings for a few hours.' She turned to Seamus. 'Mister, can I please go? This has nothing to do with me.' She looked at Danny again, her eyes narrowed and her face drawn with anger. 'You stay away from me you ... you ... fucker!'

Seamus burst out laughing. 'Aye, away you go, love. I think you've been punished enough having to spend time with this gobshite.'

'Jen, please don't—'

Seamus delivered another blow, to Danny's mouth this time.

'I told you – don't speak until you're spoken to.' He gave him a backhanded slap across the cheek. 'That's for telling that nice young girl lies, and to remind you to stay away from her, like she asked.'

Five minutes later, and with very little extra persuasion, Seamus had all he was going to get. They threw Danny into the sea to wash off the blood and snot, then told him to get dressed.

'Take the Range Rover and your blood money and get the hell out of here. If I ever see you again, cross the street. And since you don't know who I am or what I look like, that's a lot of streets to cross.'

As the Range Rover disappeared at high speed, Seamus walked back to his four-by-four.

Number Two and Number Three had already resumed their posts and were nowhere to be seen.

* * *

Alex and Willy had closed themselves in Willy's bedroom, and Willy had his laptop open.

'Right, give me the company's URL and the admin passwords,' he said.

'Caseytransport l-t-d, all one word, dot i-e ... and the

password is SEANYBOYPLUS2, all caps. Gran wanted to call me Seany when I was a baby. Fortunately everyone else called me Alex.'

Willy laughed as his fingers flew over the keyboard.

'Okay, that's us. Now, how has this been set up? Ah ... that's fine, good! Now ...'

It only took Willy two or three minutes to get to where he wanted in the system.

'Right, Patsy Dan's load that was opened at Balbriggan was a part load of cigarettes. Patsy was to deliver it to a bonded warehouse in Cork where all or most of the cigarettes were to be replaced by Cork Gin for shipping to Kuwait ... Tut, tut. And Kuwait a dry country. The Excise Validation Certificate lists the originator as "The Lanes Group, Export Division" and the recipient as "Shalim Import/Export Kuwait". We know the container number from your paperwork, but to test my list of codes I've pretended we don't know.'

Willy hit Enter with a flourish.

'Bingo, there it is. The same container number as on Patsy Dan's manifest.'

'Okay, Einstein, let's try another one. I'll pick one of last month's loads, but I won't tell you the container number.' Alex reached across and scrolled down the shipping list and picked a validation number. 'Try this one.'

Willy pecked away at the keyboard for a minute, referring to his list and the book.

'Container number XL 40V173/6, loaded in Warehouse Three, Belfast,' he said tentatively. 'A mixed load of cigarettes from Gallaher and whiskey from Bushmills bound for Pennsylvania Wholesale Ltd in the US. What does the manifest say?'

'That's the right number. No details of the contents, of course, but originator and destination are correct too. It looks like you've cracked it, Willy. Well done! Now what?'

'Now we give this cursed book back to whoever owns it

and get a copy of its contents to the Garda. And good bloody riddance. I don't know what to do with the first book though. I don't know who it belongs to. If we give it to the wrong people, we'll be running for ever. Maybe we should ask the senator.'

'Good idea,' said Alex. 'You go and find him while I give Patsy Dan a call to see how he's coping back at base.'

* * *

After a lengthy chat with Willy about the red books, the senator called Mary Lennihan.

'Will you find DI Monaghan and ask him to phone me please? Also, ask Commissioner Shackleton if he could see me at four o'clock tomorrow. It's important, and I really have to insist. Tell him it's relevant to the ongoing situation we are all caught up in. And one other thing, Mary. Could you rearrange your schedule and be here for twelve o'clock tomorrow, not one? Sorry to mess you about … Good, thank you.'

Monaghan returned the call almost immediately. 'How can I help you, Senator?'

'May I have an update on Dominic please,' the senator said.

'Your son's a central figure in an ongoing Garda investigation, the details of which I can't discuss with you.'

'DI Monaghan, I'm not the least bit interested in the details of your investigation. I am, however, interested in the physical and mental well-being of my son.'

'Senator, my apologies. I assumed that with our leaks you already knew.' The sarcasm was not lost on the Senator. 'He is indeed unwell. All I can say at this moment is that Dominic has … regressed. He's in expert hands, and I'll take whatever instruction I am given by the doctor.'

'Thank you for your frankness, Detective Inspector. As long as he's being looked after properly – that's the main thing. Now to another matter. I expect to have in my possession in the near future the book that has caused so much grief. I will also have an explanation of its contents and a copy. To whom do you suggest I direct the information?'

'Inspector Sullivan. It's his investigation, and I've no doubt he's the best person to handle it. And the original, Senator – what do you propose to do with it?'

'Return it to its owner, some hours after Inspector Sullivan receives his copy.'

'With respect, Senator, I think Inspector Sullivan should make that decision. That book has caused the deaths of too many innocent people. Its value in leading us to the perpetrators is enormous.'

'I appreciate that, Detective Inspector, but its value to the future safety of young Casey and the others is even greater. If the book is returned, the villains will have no reason to pursue the youngsters any longer. William McNabb has unravelled its mysteries, so he can explain to Sullivan how best to understand the information in it. There will be a sufficient time delay before I hand the book over to the criminal gang.'

Monaghan fell silent for a moment. 'Do you know who the owner is?'

The senator had been expecting that question but still wasn't sure how to answer it.

'I am now absolutely certain of the person's identity. Proving it is another matter, and for that reason I am not prepared to divulge any details at this point. I have been pursuing him and his people for more years than I care to remember. Their end will be in a manner and place of my choosing. One thing I can tell you though – this will all be over in the next twenty-four hours and the glory will be yours and Sullivan's for the taking. Tell Inspector Sullivan to expect a call from William McNabb this evening … and please keep me informed about Dominic.'

The senator hung up without waiting for a reply.

Chapter 28

Joe left Biddy Quinns dazed and shaken. As he opened the door of his Range Rover, he looked over to the River Shannon and the weir below the castle. How many poor sods had finished in that tunnel? How much longer could that living corpse Fitzpatrick dispense death and damnation from his spectral Perspex tent.

He looked at his watch and cursed. He had a lot to do and not much time to do it in. As he worked through the traffic to get out onto the Galway Road, a question kept niggling at the back of his mind. Who was Fitzpatrick's eyes and ears? The quality of information he was in possession of demanded an engaged and able-bodied person with the authority to make things happen. Whoever it was had only spoken to Joe once – to confirm the authenticity of text messages he would receive in relation to the work he was to do. All Joe's instructions had been by text and all payments by bank transfer. The texts had been signed FXF, but he doubted they came from Fitzpatrick himself.

Joe's phone rang.

'There's a gypsy camp two miles out of Galway on the R336 – the coast road to Bearna. Your boys are there and expect you in one hour. Try not to be late. Also, we have a car near the Old House. I can confirm that all their players are there now and have minimum protection – current estimate two, maybe three, guns – so your operation should be straightforward, given the men and firepower you've requested. You need to start immediately.'

As he listened, Joe tried to identify the voice.

'I will repeat the instruction I gave to Hollinger before his untimely death – the old woman dead in front of the others, Casey and the girl hurt but alive. Use your discretion with the others. By that time McNabb will be keen to give you a kidney, never mind the book, his laptop and any other information he may have gathered. Finally, there is another similar book. Make sure you bring it as well.' A long pause played havoc with Joe's nerves. 'I'll know when the operation is over. I will be in contact. Please don't do anything foolish – Biddy Quinns is never far away.'

The line went dead.

The long blast of a horn caused Joe to swerve back onto his own side of the road, narrowly missing an oncoming lorry. As soon as he could, he pulled off into a gateway and tried to gather himself.

The caller had to be Fitzpatrick's man. It was definitely the same voice as the one that had contacted him about the text messages.

* * *

Seamus was parking his four-by-four outside the Old House when Peter suddenly appeared. For a man of his size he was remarkably good at making himself invisible when it suited him. He remembered the big, sad face with affection from his youth. No one took on Peter O'Donnell, either physically or verbally. He had a prodigious intellect to match his massive frame, and had always been happy to debate any subject. He was universally respected as a man of honour with a sense of fair play. It just made what happened to him all the more appalling, especially as he was innocent of the crime the bastards accused him of.

'Where were you hiding just now, shorty? I could have run over you,' said Seamus, smiling.

Peter gave him a bone-crushing bear hug. Then he stepped back, gave a half-salute and pointed to the second floor of the house.

'Boss wants me? Okay, Peter. Thanks. By the way, I may need you down at the gate later, assuming you remember how to use a twelve-bore.' Seamus reached into the back seat of the four-by-four. 'Here's a radio.'

Peter nodded and gave Seamus a parting pat on the back that nearly knocked him off his feet.

Back in the house, as Seamus knocked on the senator's door, he couldn't help but think of the times in the past when he had reported to him for instructions. The senator was renowned for his lateral thinking, and many an operation had been successful because of it. His ability to exploit the strength of those he commanded and expose the weaknesses of his enemies had earned him the respect of all who soldiered under him.

'Come in, Seamus, come in. It's good to get the chance for a proper chat.'

'How are you keeping, Senator? It's been a while. And Dominic. What's this I hear about him running with that scumbag Fagan?'

'Ah, Seamus, some men won't be told. However, all that is for later. There is work to do now. Thank you for responding to my cry for help at such short notice. My friends and family are in great danger.'

'Especially your grandson.'

The senator smiled. 'Indeed. How is he handling all this? Is he saying much?'

'Not really. He's got his head screwed on. Asked all the right questions as we walked the boundary.'

'Good, and what was that all about down on the jetty? I noticed you let a young lady go. Getting soft in your old age?'

'An innocent, caught up with a useless prick hired by Fagan to spy on you and your guests.'

'That's interesting. Uel Fagan was picked up at the same time as Dominic. When was the young man hired?'

'He said Fagan had recommended him to some guy who phoned him yesterday morning. Danny Craig is the young

lad's name – probably local. Said his father was a friend of
Fagan's. Might be worth checking.'

'Good work, Seamus. Had he gleaned anything of interest?
Would he have been able to make a head count?'

Seamus pulled the map from his pocket. 'The map's
amateurish, and he won't have a head count because we were
here before dawn. By the way, there are two young girls in
one of the fishermen's cottages right by the jetty, so—'

'Ah yes. My cousin James's daughter and her friend.
Would you mind calling by, inviting them up for dinner?
Don't alarm them. I'll explain things when they get here.
Other than that, we are in your very capable hands!'

'It's a pleasure, Senator. Let's hope it passes easy.'

'Oh, I doubt that, Seamus. I doubt that very much.'

* * *

Toots knocked on the senator's door and waited. She felt like
a schoolgirl going to the headmaster's office.

'Ah, Siobhan, come in. Come in and join me. Get yourself
something to drink, and sit down and tell me all about this
young man of yours. And yourself … what have you been
doing since I last saw you … I don't know how many years
ago? I knew your father. Fine man. A man to be proud of, no
matter what you hear to the contrary.'

The senator, if Toots had but known, was as nervous as she
was, although in his case, because of memories he could never
divulge.

'Thank you. What should I call you? Senator or what?'

'I would be pleased if you would call me Eugene, and I
shall call you Siobhan, as I just have. I am old-fashioned about
names.'

His smile was genuine and put Toots at ease. She quickly
précised her early days at home and at school, and told him
about her mother and sisters and, finally, about university
and meeting Willy. For some reason she felt at ease talking to
Eugene, and was soon telling him all about the phone traces,

the emails, the meetings with Sullivan and Hollinger, the attacks and their escapes. Indeed, she filled in some gaps for the senator that helped confirm his suspicions about who was behind their troubles. He had told Monaghan he was one hundred per cent sure of the identity of the chief villain. Now he was one hundred and ten per cent sure. When she was ready to leave, she produced the flash drive.

'Willy said I was to give this to you. It's to do with the book. He'll tell you about it. I can't.'

The senator chuckled. 'Yes, I was chatting to him earlier about this. I presume he felt the less you knew the less harm could come to you if things did not work out as we hope.'

'That's what he said – or something like it.'

The house phone rang.

'Excuse me, Siobhan. Let me take this,' the senator said, picking up the receiver. 'Hello? … Yes, I did invite them, Pierre … I apologise for not telling you sooner. Please ask them to come up. Siobhan is with me and she can take care of them. Thank you, Pierre.'

There was a glint of amusement in the senator's eyes. 'Pierre gets very uptight when he's not the first to know about anything that affects his domain.'

'He's a right character. What is he – French?' Siobhan asked.

The senator chortled. 'French, my foot! Get him drunk and all you get is pure north Dublin. Took the name and the accent to get on in hospitality, and good luck to him. He has done a first-class job here since cousin James hired him. Anyway, there are two girls about your age staying in one of the cottages across the road, and I thought they would be safer here tonight. I asked Seamus to bring them up.'

There was a knock on the door and it slowly opened.

Toots's hand flew to her mouth and a look of delight spread over her face. 'Oh my God. Bearna. Of course!'

Liz O'Gorman and Kate Rutherford came in, then stopped, amazement registering on their faces when they saw Toots.

Liz stepped back and stood on Kate's foot. Kate yelped and pushed Liz, who grabbed Kate for support, and the two landed in an undignified heap in the doorway. Neither had spoken a word.

Laughing, Toots crossed the room and helped the girls up, hugging them each in turn.

'That has to be the best entrance ever,' she said.

'What the hell are you doing here?' said Kate. 'And who are you – her new man?'

The senator shook with laughter. 'Thank you for the compliment, young lady. Sadly no. I am Senator O'Gorman, Elizabeth's ... second cousin once removed? I think that would be correct, but uncle seems better. Lovely to see you, Elizabeth – it's been many years. And who, pray, are you?'

'This is Kate Rutherford, a friend of ours, Eugene,' Toots said.

Kate offered her hand. 'A pleasure to meet you, sir.' She gave him a half curtsy.

'Ladies, before you bombard Siobhan with your questions, allow me to welcome you to dinner and invite you to spend the night. The reason I asked you up here, apart from adding immeasurably to the already high quality of the dinner guests, is for your own security. I am expecting a little trouble tonight and thought it wise to bring you inside the stockade, as it were. Try not to be alarmed. Siobhan will explain. Now, much as I enjoy being surrounded by elegant young ladies, I need to ask you to adjourn to the drawing room or wherever you decide. Just make sure you stay inside the house, now we are in the gloaming of the day.'

When the girls had left his room, the senator rang Peter's number.

'Peter, as soon as you can please.'

* * *

Joe turned his Range Rover off the county road onto a potholed track that led straight to the back of the encampment known locally as Tinker Town, formerly a lay-by, now a four-acre gypsy site and growing.

Two other Range Rovers and two Toyota Land Cruisers were parked beside the biggest, shiniest aluminium towing caravan Joe had ever seen. As he pulled up in front of the caravan, the top half of the door swung open and a young woman leaned out on the lower half, nestling a sawn-off shotgun in the crook of her arm. Her dark, almond-shaped eyes, swarthy complexion and long black hair reminded Joe of a photograph he had seen years ago advertising holidays in Eastern Europe. Her untamed beauty and the view offered by the tight, low-cut tee shirt, gave Joe goosebumps and a stirring in his loins underneath all the rolls of fat.

As he manoeuvred his bulk out of the Range Rover, the woman made no effort to hide her disgust at the sight of him. Joe followed her into the caravan.

Inside, to his right, were a number of closed doors which he took to be bedrooms and a bathroom. In front of him was a compact but practical kitchen, and to his left was the main sitting and dining area. Occupying one side and the end of the banquette around a table were five men in their mid-twenties or early thirties. All had the same swarthy good looks as the girl, who had now disappeared. No one spoke. One of the men pointed to an empty space to the right of the table, and Joe squeezed in as best he could, then studied each of the men individually.

He was determined to impose his authority. Drawing on years of experience, he tried to hide his discomfort and fear by examining each man's face in turn. His stares were met with complete disinterest. They each held his gaze until he moved on to the next face.

Then one of the bedroom doors opened. Joe turned to look and was immediately fascinated. The girl had her back to him and was pulling a narrow wheelchair out of the room. In the kitchen area, she turned the chair and Joe recoiled involuntarily when he saw the creature sitting in it. The man's face had the same swarthy skin as the others, but there the similarity ended. He had the fiercest yellow-green eyes Joe had ever seen – like an eagle's, wide and unblinking. His face was etched with deep wrinkles, and just visible below a nicotine-stained white moustache was a cruel, ugly mouth. A majestic mane of long, white hair flowing down to his shoulders failed to hide the most disturbing feature of all ... he had no ears.

Joe couldn't take his eyes off the place where the ears should have been, not even when the wheelchair bumped against the table leg. It was only then that he looked down and realised there were neither feet nor legs, just stumps. Two huge hands came up and gripped the edge of the table. None of the fingers had nails, and Joe began to feel sick. He heard the tap running and a glass being filled. The girl placed the glass of water in front of the maimed hands. The right hand pushed it towards Joe.

'Drink!' the man demanded. Even his voice sounded deformed.

'The Russians did this to my father,' said the girl with a degree of tenderness in her voice that surprised Joe more than her words. 'He led a group of Chechen freedom fighters for six years until he was betrayed by his own brother for one thousand US dollars. The Russians tortured him for four months, using drugs to prevent his heart giving out. My brothers and cousins and I' – she indicated the five men at the table – 'rescued him and took him to a field hospital set up by UN peacekeepers. They did their best for him and we took it from there. We caught his torturers and skinned them alive. We are still looking for the one who betrayed him. We missed him by this much' – she indicated a tiny gap with her thumb and finger – 'and he fled to England, then ended up in Ireland. To pay for this pursuit, we do what we do best to earn money. We kill.' She said this in a matter-of-fact way, as if she was talking about doing a household chore.

This lot after Biddy Quinns! Joe felt trapped. How had he

let himself be closeted with this pack of sadists?

'I am Khazbiika. My brothers are Abdiel, Musa and Sulim.' The girl waved a hand at the three men opposite Joe. 'My cousins are Bashir and Hashid. My father is Ajay. We also have other men. We cost fourteen thousand euros and you will pay now, please. Then we will start.'

Joe died – in his mind, at least. Everyone around the table was watching him expectantly. But the old man was the worst – Joe felt as if he could see inside him, that his flared nostrils could smell his fear.

'I … I … I didn't … I don't know anything about money.'

Khazbiika pulled an evil-looking skinning knife from somewhere on the frame of the wheelchair.

'You come looking for us and tell us you know nothing about money?' She moved so fast Joe didn't see what she did, but he felt the blood spring from the slice she had cut into his left cheek.

'Christ, what are you doing? What the fuck is this, you … you fucking bitch?'

None of the men moved. Joe fumbled for his handkerchief to stem the bleeding and Khazbiika slashed again, this time across the back of his hand.

'For Christ's sake, fuck off, you –'

His shouts were interrupted by the ringing of a mobile phone. No one moved to answer it. It just kept ringing and ringing. Then Joe realised it was his own. Struggling to move out from behind the table, he retrieved the phone from his trouser pocket.

'Hello!' he shouted, the fear and pain clear in his voice. Blood was dripping from his hand and running under his shirt collar.

'Ah Joe, I gather from your tone of voice that you're with my friends, the Chechens.' It was Fitzpatrick's mystery man. 'I trust they have made you welcome?'

'What the fuck is going on here, whoever you are? I've been set up. Cut, abused, threatened, plus a demand for a fucking king's ransom that I know fuck all about. I'm out of this whole fucking mess, you hear? I'm out!'

As Joe leaned his hand on the table to push himself past the wheelchair, an excruciating pain shot up his arm. He screamed in agony and looked down to see his hand bent back until the fingertips nearly touched his arm, crushed in one of Ajay's huge hands. Joe collapsed back onto the banquette, tears spilling down his fat cheeks making the cut sting. Ajay's cruel mouth was twisted in a maniacal smile that revealed a ghastly row of steel teeth.

'Joe ... Joe?'

He heard the voice in the distance and looked for his phone. The girl picked it up off the floor and smiled as she gave it to him.

'Yes!' Joe yelled into the phone, fear and panic pumping through him.

'That's better. Of course you don't have to pay my friends. You will make sure the senator pays them when you have taken the Old House and its occupants. You'll keep the senator alive long enough to do that. And when you deliver what I have asked you for, I'll see *you* get paid. It's all a matter of commerce, don't you see? Everyone gets paid when everyone gets what they want – all right? Now, put the gorgeous Khazbiika on the phone please.'

Joe gladly handed the phone to the girl and sank into himself.

Khazbiika's brothers and cousins looked at Joe as one and smiled, their perfect white teeth gleaming against their dark Eastern European complexions. They looked like a group of apprentice vampires waiting their turn to bite.

Khazbiika carried on a conversation on the phone in a language that Joe didn't recognise. When she finished, she spent the next few minutes in discussion with her family. Joe couldn't understand a word. Finally, she smiled and produced a first-aid kit from the cupboard beside her.

'Let me fix your cuts.' She said it as though she'd had no

part in inflicting them. 'Then we tell you what is planned for later. Your friend on the phone, he is very kind man. Says you are one of the best. We will be safe with you.'

Joe swore inwardly. *Them* safe with *him*? His only concern was how he could extricate himself from this quagmire.

He winced as Khazbiika applied a salve to his face.

Chapter 29

Seamus was sitting on a bollard at the end of the old jetty, smoking his pipe and looking far off into the distance. Willy walked down the drive behind him, fiddling with the settings on the iJack. Suddenly, Seamus turned and waved.

'You must have eyes in the back of your head, Seamus. How did you know I was there?' Willy asked.

'You clicked your machine there and you might as well have shouted. That's one of the secrets of good surveillance – hearing some sound that shouldn't be there. The other is to learn to look without staring. Keep your eyes relaxed and use your peripheral vision. Anyway, what brings you down here?'

'I want to ask you about your two-way radio frequency. This machine of mine might be of some use to you later on.'

'Tell me about it and I'll tell you if it's of any use,' Seamus said, his eyes narrowing.

Willy explained what the iJack did and how it had been used in the last two days to great effect. 'But there's more to it than that,' he said. 'One of the things that interested us when we were developing it was whether we could pinpoint the exact position of a two-way radio – one that doesn't have inbuilt GPS.'

'You're saying that if this works, you'd be able to point to where, say, my men are at this moment?' The disbelief was plain in Seamus's voice.

'If they use their radio, yes. Can we give it a try?'

'Okay, are you ready?'

Willy nodded.

Seamus clicked on his radio. 'Number Six, this is One. See anything?'

'This is Six. Nothing.'

Willy smiled and pumped the air with his fist. 'The signal registered okay, but the message was too short to give me a location. Try it again.'

This time Seamus watched over Willy's shoulder.

'Number Ten. This is One. Come in.'

'Ten in!'

'Anything, Ten?'

Willy was tracking left and right.

'Nothing One. All clear.'

'Say again Ten.'

'All clear.'

Willy pointed to the east wall. 'Is he over there?'

Seamus smacked his arm down. 'Don't point! Someone else might be watching and you've just identified a position.'

'Right, sorry about that. Can we go again?'

They worked three more calls, and Willy identified the location of all of them.

'I think you might be on to something there, son. This could be very useful. Only problem is, we don't know the distance, just the direction. Am I right?'

'Yes. If we had two iJacks, we could triangulate, but sadly we don't. Still, I imagine you can make assumptions once you know the direction.'

'It's certainly worth a try. Good work! Thank you.'

As Willy and Seamus walked back up the drive, Willy scanned the airwaves, the iJack pointing ahead of him towards the house.

'Wow, there's something there!'

He stopped and watched the readout as the scanner did its work. Seamus looked on with interest.

'No, it's gone, probably nothing.'

They walked on.

'Wait, there it is again, straight ahead of us. Hold on.'

The scanner locked on and they heard a babble of voices.

'Bloody hell, it's a foreign language!' Willy cranked up the volume so they both could hear it clearly. 'Sounds Eastern European. Polish? Lithuanian?' Willy turned left and right. 'It's coming from the house, or in a direct line behind it. What's behind the quarry?'

Seamus nodded in the direction of the house. 'Those hills there run up from the far side of the quarry. They're not very high, but give a great view out over the bay.'

They stood a minute longer, but the signal had gone.

'Very strange,' said Seamus. 'That bothers me – someone using a VHF radio on the hill.' Seamus took out his own radio. 'Number Six, this is One. Come in.'

'Six here.'

'Move to the back corner of the roof and check the hillside behind the house from the quarry to the summit.'

'Understood, One. Over.'

Willy and Seamus set off up the drive again.

* * *

At the airport, Sullivan went to the toilet area to check on progress. The scenes-of-crime team had all but finished, the bodies had been removed and witness interviews were in hand. He took the escalator back up to the second floor and walked to the business lounge. Monaghan was there talking to the forensics officer in charge, holding a clear evidence bag in one hand and signing a paper with the other.

'Don't worry, Chris, I'm not tampering with the evidence,' Monaghan said. 'Can I have a quick word?'

Without waiting for an answer, he strode off towards the airport's administration block. Sullivan followed him through a Staff Only door. Monaghan walked up to the reception desk and showed his ID.

'Would you have a private office available right now?' he asked.

The receptionist indicated for them to follow her down a

corridor. Then she opened the door to a small room and left.

'Right, Pader, what's this all about?' Sullivan asked, sitting down.

'This is Hollinger's phone,' Monaghan said. 'I asked forensics if they had Reid's as well but it's already been sent to HQ. Dominic O'Gorman told me he got in touch with his boss by texting a code word to a five-digit number. He also said that Jim Hollinger was contacted by these people, so perhaps the same system was used with him. I want to look for single words and five-digit numbers on the messages log in here.' He waggled Hollinger's phone. 'Is that okay with you? I don't have time to wait for forensics.'

Sullivan nodded.

Working the keys through the thin plastic of the evidence bag, Monaghan turned on the phone and scrolled through the texts.

'Probably all sorts of good stuff here … here we are – the word "Tara" sent to eight six three six five. That has to be one.' Monaghan wrote it down in his notepad. He scrolled to the end of the log then turned Hollinger's phone off.

Meanwhile, Sullivan had taken out his phone, opened the text message app and entered the word and number.

'Don't try that yet, Chris. I need to bring you up to date about the book first.' Monaghan went on to tell Sullivan that the senator planned to return the code book to its owner and explained why.

'But where does that leave our investigation? If we had the book and were able to make contact using this number, we could set up a drop and catch at least some of them.'

'Aye, but you'll have difficulty persuading the senator to give us the book before he's good and ready. He's being very coy. He thinks he knows who the owner is and he's hatching a plan of his own.'

Sullivan nodded slowly.

'We'll be given details of the books contents well before the owner gets it. McNabb will tell you how to interpret that information. That might be a good time to try sending the Tara text. You may get a call in response. The senator seems to think we may recognise the voice. If someone does call you, find me and don't tell another soul before you and I get together.'

'This is crap, Pader. Who does the senator think it is?'

'He wouldn't tell me. I'm as much in the dark as you are.'

Sullivan nodded. 'I look forward to identifying this mystery man. He has a lot to answer for.'

* * *

Seamus left Willy at the front door.

'I'm going to the viewing platform, just to take a look down into the moat and satisfy myself about something.'

Just as Willy went into the house, two chambermaids came out of the dining room, chatting to each other in the some foreign language or other. He swiftly turned and hurried back out the front door. He found Seamus in the garage pulling a walking stick and a builder's hard hat out of the back of his four-by-four.

'Seamus, the chambermaids in the Big House – they're speaking the same language we just heard on the radio.'

'Jesus! We'll need to check that out. But first, I need to have a look at the flooded quarry. Number Six has located a sniper on the far side of it.'

When they reached the viewing platform, Seamus tapped Willy on the shoulder.

'Keep your head down,' he said. 'The gunman probably won't be fussy who he takes a potshot at.'

Seamus donned the hard hat and stood up so his head and shoulders showed briefly above the wall. Then he ducked down, took the hat off and put it on the end of the walking stick and poked it above the wall.

The impact of the bullet carried the hat twenty feet down the garden. Willy instinctively dropped to the floor as he heard a second crack from above and behind. It echoed from the hill on the other side of the quarry.

When Willy looked up again Seamus was sitting with his back against the wall, holding a Zippo in one hand and his pipe in the other. He grinned at Willy as he puffed away.

His radio crackled. 'Come in One, this is Six.'

'Go ahead, Six.'

'Straight down the pipe! He has a companion. I have a bead on him too. He's moving back very cautiously, and he has a rifle – similar piece. Dragunov I think.'

'Take him out, Six.'

The radio went dead and Seamus held up his hand warning Willy to stay silent. Ten seconds later there was another sharp crack. This time, Willy could tell it came from the roof of the Old House.

'Jesus Christ!' Willy whispered. Seamus raised his hand again.

The radio crackled. 'Come in, One.'

'Go ahead, Six.'

'Both shooters down. Hill's clear. Check the lake below you, though. I can only see from the middle to the far shore. Something's causing a ripple.'

'Good work. Keep your position.' Seamus let his hand drop.

'Straight down the pipe – what does that mean?' Willy asked.

'The gunman was lying on his belly, so the bullet entered his head and exited his arse.'

Willy grimaced.

Seamus stood up slowly and peered over the wall down into the flooded quarry. He slid back down to the viewing platform.

'The silly sods have started too soon.' He lifted his radio. 'All alert. All alert. Hostiles in the quarry. I'll deal. Six and Seven, keep a visual on the road. Two, Three, Four and Five, be ready to turn any friendly traffic. Eight, Nine and Ten, watch the front. Peter, secure the house, then get the radio to the senator and ask him to call in.'

Willy was huddled into the corner of the platform as far as

he could get, scared and fascinated in equal measure.

'Are we safe or should I run for the house?' he asked. In truth, he didn't think his legs would carry him if Seamus told him to run.

'We're safe at the moment. It'll be darker in a few more minutes, then we'll move. In the meantime, wait here for me.'

Seamus jumped down from the viewing platform and ran off. He reappeared a minute or so later with an old army satchel and took out four hand grenades, putting two in each of his side pockets. Then he levered himself onto the three-foot-wide wall and crawled along on his belly, occasionally looking down into the quarry.

About fifty yards along from the viewing platform, he stopped, got up on to his hunkers and took one of the grenades out of his pocket. He pulled the pin, counted two, three, four and lobbed the grenade out about twenty feet. As it fell, he took out another and repeated the sequence, then pulled back from the edge and lay flat along the wall.

The two grenades exploded with a deafening bang that echoed round and round the quarry.

Seamus looked cautiously over the edge. Even in the gathering gloom he could see that the grenades had done their job. Little remained of the inflatable or the two men who had been in it. Shreds of material, a wooden paddle and a plastic bucket were floating in the water. Then a life jacket containing only a torso and two arms bobbed to the surface.

He made his way back to the viewing platform and slid down beside Willy.

'I'm getting too old for this,' he said, rubbing his hand over his face.

His radio crackled into life again.

* * *

In the caravan two miles away, Joe, worried by the lack of radio response from the Chechens deployed at the Old House, dispatched Hashid to find out what had happened and prepare to create a diversion when Joe ordered him to. He was finally managing to assert some authority – fourteen thousand euros was a considerable incentive to these people. It was just as well, given the consequences of failure outlined for him so graphically at Biddy Quinns.

For the moment he had to continue preparing for an attack and decided their best chance was to make use of the last of the daylight. He discussed tactics, through Khazbiika, with the remaining men who claimed little or no English. But he was also trying to devise a plan of his own to separate himself from the Chechens.

'I need to be on site. Khazbiika, you come with me to interpret,' Joe said. 'Tell your father and brothers to wait for my command, then attack as planned.'

Khazbiika translated and a heated discussion followed.

'My father is not happy,' she reported. 'He says we wait until Hashid returns, then we move.'

'Hashid's orders are not to come back. He is to create a diversion when I give the order. Is that not what he was told?'

Khazbiika looked uncomfortable. Her father rattled off a few quick words, pushed back from the table and turned the chair on its wheels. Khazbiika followed him.

'What the hell's going on? Where the fuck are you both going?'

Joe struggled to get out from behind the table, but Abdiel motioned for him to sit down again.

'You fucking sit down!' Joe yelled. 'You bunch of assholes may already have lost three or four men and time's running out. We can still succeed if we get a move on. Call your bloody cousin and tell him to do what I told him to do, otherwise you can kiss fourteen thousand euro goodbye.'

He pushed himself clear of the table but Abdiel caught his arm. Joe shoved Abdiel back into the seat and threw all his weight on top of him, pushing his left forearm into the man's throat and raising his right fist.

'Enough!' Ajay roared. 'Fight the enemy, not each other.'

His ugly face was a mask of fury.

Joe pulled himself up off Abdiel and turned to face Ajay and Khazbiika.

'So you speak English after all.'

'Father goes to get ready,' said Khazbiika. 'I need to help him. You wait!'

'I'll wait in the car,' Joe said, 'but be quick, we need to move. And for the last time, somebody call Hashid and tell him to do what he was fucking told.'

He pushed past Khazbiika and Ajay and squeezed out through the door. Abdiel followed, but made no move to stop him.

Once settled in the Range Rover, Joe slipped a packet of cigarillos out from the door pocket and made great show of opening it and looking into it. Although it contained two, he crushed it as though empty, leaned across and opened the glove box. He reached in and withdrew a fresh packet, then sat up again and made much of opening it, selecting a cheroot and reaching down for the lighter. As he drew his hand back with the lighter he scooped the Walther PPK he'd pulled out of the glove box onto his lap. Joe lit his cigar, inhaled deeply and felt the nicotine kick in. Abdiel appeared to relax a little. Joe shifted his position in the seat to get comfortable and slipped the Walther between his enormous thighs, safely out of sight.

After some ten minutes, Khazbiika appeared at the van door with the collapsed wheelchair. She handed it down to Abdiel and stepped aside. Ajay appeared, shuffling across the floor on his buttocks and his knuckles. Abdiel opened the chair and positioned it to the side of the caravan door. Then he put a hand under each of Ajay's armpits and lifted him out of the van and into the chair. Joe tried not to stare. Bizarrely, he felt a moment of sympathy for the man.

Khazbiika kissed her father on both cheeks and climbed in beside Joe.

'We spoke to Hashid,' she said. 'He is in position. Both our gunmen are dead. He said there must be shooter on roof of house. He also see a broken body in water. It has no head. We fight bastards! He waits for your command.'

As Joe reversed away from the caravan he saw Ajay being pushed up a ramp into the back of one of the Land Cruisers. It was only then Joe noticed that the windscreen was missing, and protruding through the opening was the barrel of an M20 machine gun.

How in hell will Ajay hold it, Joe wondered, realising at the same time that it would be pointed at him as he drove in front of the Toyota, an unexpected complication to his own escape plan.

He turned out of the gypsy encampment and took the coast road west. He had just two miles to engineer his getaway.

* * *

Dominic O'Gorman had been mildly sedated and put to bed in the holding room, much to the annoyance of the duty doctor who wanted to hospitalise him. He would be reporting this breach of procedure to the highest authority at the earliest opportunity, he said, and left strict instructions that no one was to try to question Dominic.

Monaghan walked into the reception area and asked the guard on duty if O'Gorman was still in the same room.

'He is, sir. The doctor's not a bit happy about it.'

'Tell the doc I'd like to see him. And bring me a coffee … and a muffin or something.'

He opened the door of the holding room and went over to the bed settee.

'Well, Mr O'Gorman, and how are we?' he said, looking down at the prisoner.

Dominic's eyelids fluttered but his eyes stayed closed; his lips were pulled tight across his teeth as though he was trying to stop something nasty being put into his mouth. Good-looking in an old-fashioned way, Dominic had once graced the gossip columns of the glossy magazines with a succession of beautiful women on his arm, heralded as the most eligible bachelor in Ireland. Now in his late forties, Dominic was not weathering well at all. His thinning, sandy hair, pudgy face and red, veiny nose bore testimony to too many years of hard living, excessive drinking and probably a smattering of drugs.

Monaghan lifted Dominic's mobile from the table and opened the message log. He scrolled down the texts looking for the same type of number and word combination he'd found on Hollinger's phone.

Suddenly the door swung open and banged violently against the doorstop.

'DI Monaghan, I left—'

Monaghan put a finger to his lips and pointed to Dominic on the settee.

'Sit down, doc,' he whispered.

The duty guard set a cup of coffee and doughnut down on the table. The DI took a bite of the doughnut and swallowed it down with a mouthful of coffee.

'Now, doctor, how is the patient? Is he still in cuckoo land and, if so, when will he return to the real world?'

The doctor shot Monaghan a look of disgust. 'If I could move him somewhere with proper facilities, he would have a much better chance of a quick recovery. As to the timing – days, weeks, who knows? Certainly not hours.'

'Okay. But he's fine here for now, yes? His life's in imminent danger and I have a responsibility to protect him, even though good men have died as a result of his activities.' Monaghan enjoyed another mouthful of doughnut. 'So when you've made arrangements for his transfer to a *secure* medical facility, you can have him.'

Chapter 30

After briefing the senator by radio, Seamus led Willy off the viewing platform and along the back wall to the kitchen walkway.

One moment Willy was opening the kitchen door, the next he felt an almighty kick in the small of his back that hurled him through the open door. Then he heard the report and knew he'd been shot. He tried to pull himself up, but a spasm of pain cannoned through his body and he sank down into a pool of darkness.

When Seamus heard the gunshot, he dropped to the ground outside the back door.

'All stations report. Six, go again if you get visual.' The radio rattled as his men called in one by one, all negative. A minute later, there was the muffled crack of a single shot from the rooftop of the house.

'One, this is Six. Gun on the hill down but not out.'

'Understood, Six. Mark his position. I want him out. All stations level red. Repeat, level red.' Seamus crawled into the kitchen and closed the door.

The kitchen rapidly filled with people and noise. Toots, hearing the gunfire, came racing and, when she saw Willy lying on the floor, flung herself down beside him, a keening sound coming from her throat. Gran, Alex and Peter arrived not long after her.

Mrs O'Doherty, the housekeeper, immediately took charge, instructing the two chambermaids to cut some bath towels and tea towels into strips and fetch her a basin of tepid water. She pulled the back of Willy's shirt out of his trousers and ripped it up the middle, then examined the puncture wound, less than half an inch in diameter, in his right side. Willy screamed and thrashed in pain. Toots held his head and spoke quietly to him.

'We need to turn you over, Mr McNabb, and it's going to hurt, okay?' Mrs O'Doherty said. 'Miss Toomey, if you would keep his left arm above his head, and Mrs Casey, you take his legs.'

Mrs O'Doherty pushed Willy over, rolling him on to his back. Willy howled, the tears streaming down his face. The housekeeper pulled the bloody shirt away from the exit wound and made a clucking noise. The chambermaids set a bowl of water and strips of material down beside her.

'Find Pierre and ask him for the first-aid kit,' she instructed the chambermaids. 'He's probably hiding in the office.'

Toots was now cradling Willy's head in her lap, gently stroking his cheeks, talking and smiling encouragingly to him. His eyes were open and he tried to smile back, but the pain won and he could only grimace instead. Mrs O'Doherty cleaned the wound, gently but firmly probing all round it.

'Straight through and not too much damage,' she pronounced. 'No main arteries and no bones broken. What do you think, Mrs Casey?'

'I think you've done this before!' Gran gave Mrs O'Doherty a knowing look. 'Hopefully no internal bleeding, thanks be to God.'

One of the chambermaids set the first-aid box beside Mrs O'Doherty, who extracted a pill bottle and shook out a couple of painkillers.

'Bring a glass of water, girl.'

While Toots gave Willy the painkillers, the two older women, with practised hands, set about dressing and bandaging the wound. The painkillers acted almost instantly and Willy soon visibly relaxed.

'We need to move him to a bed or settee – somewhere more comfortable than the floor,' said Mrs O'Doherty. 'The men'll need to deal with the scum outside before we can phone for an ambulance and get him to hospital.'

Pierre came in from the hall carrying a mountain-rescue stretcher. 'I thought this might be of use,' he said, all traces of his French accent gone.

'Good thinking, Mr Angelinni. Fellas, give us a lift would you?' she said to no one in particular.

Seamus and Peter slipped their hands under Willy and got him onto the stretcher. Willy tried his best not to shout but the pain was too great. Once Mrs O'Doherty had checked to see if the wound was still bleeding, Alex and Peter each took an end of the stretcher and carried Willy into the drawing room, passing the senator on the way.

'I must leave you all to it,' said Seamus. 'I'm keeping the outside security lights off. We're using night-vision goggles and gunsights. It's a perfect night for them but artificial light renders them useless, so minimum lighting and shutters everywhere, please. And don't stand in front of the windows. Senator, I could use Peter if that's okay with you?'

'Absolutely, Seamus … Right, everyone, I think we should adjourn to the drawing room. Pierre, perhaps you could organise some food for us all. I've a feeling it's going to be a long night.'

Outside, Seamus pointed to his four-by-four. 'Peter, you drive. We're going to put one or two of those fuckers out of their misery.'

* * *

As Joe entered a right-hand bend a mile down the road from the gypsy camp, he slipped his hand off the wheel and pulled the pistol out from between his legs. Khazbiika saw the move and whipped out a stiletto knife from somewhere. She struck at Joe. The blade glanced off his forearm and buried itself in the layers of fat below his ribcage.

Joe pulled the trigger at the same moment the blade pierce his gut. The bullet killed Khazbiika outright, entering her chest. Joe struggled to control the car, dropping the pistol and seizing the wheel with his right hand while using his left to keep Khazbiika in an upright position lest Ajay and Abdiel in the vehicle behind saw her slump forward.

Joe's plan, only half formed, was to turn onto the jetty leaving the Chechens exposed on the main road outside the gates to the house. The radio, now lying on the floor where Khazbiika's dead hand had dropped it, exploded with a jabber of words, none of which he understood. There was a silence, then a single word which he recognised all too well.

'Khazbiika!'

At the gates, Seamus and Peter were parking when their radio crackled.

'One, this is Four. Range Rover and Land Cruiser ex the gypo camp on their way out towards you.'

'Understood, Four. Let them pass, then you and Five follow them.'

Joe started to swing right at the bend before the jetty. Immediately there was the staccato rattle of machine-gun fire from the Land Cruiser behind; the bullets ripped into the left rear corner of the Range Rover. The vehicle bucked erratically, first right, then left as Joe overcorrected. As the road straightened out and the Land Cruiser came into line behind the Range Rover, Ajay unleashed another burst of automatic fire. This time he took out the front passenger side door window, narrowly missing Khazbiika's lifeless head.

'Two and Three, come in. We've got company!' Seamus said into his radio. He selected an Uzi for himself and handed Peter the double-barrelled twelve-bore. 'You take the Land Cruiser and its driver. I'll sort out the other guy.'

At the last possible moment, Joe swung the wheel to the left and slewed the Range Rover onto the jetty, braking hard and forcing Ajay's Land Cruiser to stop out on the road. The machine gun was now pointing ineffectually past the tail of the Range Rover, unable to swing around far enough to the left to hit its target.

Peter stepped out from behind the gate pillar, the twelve-bore at his hip, and pulled one trigger. The Land Cruiser lost its driver's side door while Abdiel died in a hail of glass, metal and shot. Peter aimed lower and pulled the second trigger. The front tyre shredded and the Land Cruiser settled down on the twisted rim. He broke the gun, reloaded and indicated that he would deal with the Range Rover.

Shaking, Joe was just easing the door of the Range Rover open when it was suddenly wrenched off and Peter pulled him out. A huge fist crashed into the side of his head, knocking him back into the vehicle. Joe slid down into a deep black hole of unconsciousness.

Meanwhile, Seamus opened the rear door of the Land Cruiser and stuck the Uzi into Ajay's side.

'Get out and lie down!' he yelled.

Ajay turned his head slowly. Only then did Seamus see a piece of door frame embedded in the man's eye socket, blood streaming down the right side of his face. Seamus yanked the rug from the man's knees, expecting to see a hidden weapon.

'Fuck!'

He took a step backwards. The creature – for that was surely what he was – slowly started to raise his right hand. Seamus squeezed the trigger and released a single shot. The torso slumped sideways onto the dead driver. Seamus turned from the Land Cruiser and spat a mouthful of bile onto the road.

Peter took the pistol out of Joe's hand and noticed the knife sticking out of his gut. When he wrenched it out only a weep of blood appeared, the wound sealed by rolls of fat. He turned and gave Seamus a thumbs up, broke the twelve-bore and waited for further instructions. Two heavily armed men appeared from the shore and consulted with Seamus. Radios crackled on all sides.

'One, this is Six. I have three armed males approaching the east side of the quarry on foot. Three-quarters of a mile, moving cautiously.'

The radio that Khazbiika had dropped to the floor of the Range Rover came to life, as did one in the Land Cruiser. There was a babble of foreign language, a pause, then more. After a longer pause, they clicked off.

'Seven, this is One. Join Six … Six, are they still coming?'

'Yes, still heading for the east corner of the quarry.'

'Six and Seven, when you can, disable all three. Do not kill.'

Seamus turned to the two men nearest him. 'Secure the three of them after they're disabled. Take Four and Five. Understood?'

The men loped off up the road in the direction of their incoming colleagues.

Seamus and Peter stood awaiting news from the other men. For a moment all they could hear was the laboured, raspy breathing of the fat man and the quiet lapping of the water against the jetty.

A few minutes later, a double crack came from the roof of the house, the two reports almost simultaneous. They were followed immediately by a third single crack. Seamus's radio burst into life.

'One, this is Seven. Second and third men leg-shot. Leader is arm-shot and on the run towards the quarry. Trying for cover.'

'Drop the leader!'

The words had hardly left Seamus's mouth when there was another crack from the roof.

A few seconds later: 'One, this is Six. Leader down but not out.'

'Well done! Seven, get back on station. Six, observe and talk ground team in to targets. Two and the rest of you, exercise care. You are level red. When that group is secure, there's an armed and wounded gunman on the north side of the quarry. Six can talk you to the area, but exercise care. When you've all the wounded together, I'll send transport. Then operation clean-up – no traces for the hillwalkers tomorrow.'

'Senator, this is One.' Seamus waited.

'Yes, One,' the senator eventually responded. 'Can you update us please?'

'Area will be secure in thirty minutes. We have no casualties and one injured prisoner so far. Enemy have three dead and three injured – we're on to them now. Peter and I will clear the road, then return to base. Tell everyone to stay in the house.'

'Understood, One. Thank you.'

Seamus and Peter used the four-by-four to pull the destroyed Land Cruiser off the road and in behind the wall. Peter then reversed the damaged Range Rover up from the jetty and parked it beside the Land Cruiser. They lifted the dead woman's body out of the Range Rover and placed her in the back of the Land Cruiser with the other two bodies.

Seamus and Peter were meticulous in clearing the roadway of any fragments left from the exchange before turning their attention to the fat man. By this time he was semi-conscious and in great pain, though there was little blood from the wound. Straining under the weight, they loaded the injured man into the back of the SUV, his howls of pain meeting with nothing but irritation and impatience.

Seamus pocketed the two radios the Chechens had been using and asked Peter to drive again. He called Six for an update as they bumped up the drive, the fat man moaning in the back.

'The group of three have been disarmed and cuffed, field dressings applied,' Six reported. 'Two and Five are searching behind quarry for injured sniper. I'm covering but have seen nothing. Light's getting difficult.'

'Okay. All stations, maximum vigilance. It's not over yet. One out.'

Peter parked at the garage and looked to Seamus for instructions.

'When the boys call in, Peter, will you drive out and collect the wounded that can't walk? But before that, you can help me with this lard bucket.' He turned to the injured man. 'Do. You. Speak. English?' he said loudly.

'Of course I fucking do,' the man snapped back.

'What's your name, smart-arse?'

The man's eyes narrowed. 'Joe.'

'Right, Joe, here's the situation. Senator O'Gorman is inside and has a lot of questions for you. Answer his questions truthfully and Peter will drop you at Galway General. Refuse to answer or tell lies, and we'll put you back in the Range Rover and drive it out onto the sand at low tide. You'll be able to watch the tide come in with your hands tied to the steering wheel. The choice is yours, Joe ... wet or dry?'

The sound of a distant shot interrupted their chat.

'That's not one of ours!' Seamus grabbed a pair of night-vision binoculars, jumped out of the SUV and ran to the viewing platform. Peering cautiously over the wall he scanned the far side of the quarry and waited for a radioed update.

'One, this is Five. Two's down but not out. I don't have visual. What about—'

The crack of the Barrett sniper rifle from the roof of the house echoed round the quarry, followed by a long silence.

'One, this is Six. Shooter down and out. Definitely out, at two o'clock and three hundred metres above shoreline. Five, Two is north-north-east of your position, two hundred metres. Clump of gorse at base of stone wall running north-south. He's not responding to radio.'

Seamus stood up and scanned the landscape in the direction Six had indicated. He could see Five running towards the stone wall. Seamus jumped off the platform and ran back to the SUV. He pulled open the rear door, hauled Joe out onto the ground and aimed a kick at his wound. Joe howled and writhed in agony. Seamus caught Joe's shoulders and held him on his back, kneeling on the gut wound, his face a few inches from Joe's.

'One of your fucking mates has shot my brother and it's

made me very angry. So you'd better tell the senator the truth and hope my brother's okay or you're going to be eating your dick – assuming I can find it down there.'

Seamus grabbed Joe's belly round the wound and squeezed. 'That's before you watch the tide come in. Understood?'

Seamus stood up and kicked Joe again for good measure.

'Peter, take this bastard into the workshop at the back of the garage. Tie him to a leg of the bench – it's screwed to the floor – and close his right hand in the vice. That'll hold him until the senator comes out for a chat with him. But on no account is this bag of shit to be released until I get back.'

While Seamus jumped into the SUV, nearly driving over Joe in his haste to get to his brother, Peter did as he'd been instructed. Joe writhed and smashed about like a bull, in spite of the gut wound, but as the vice tightened he became very compliant. Peter gave the vice another little twist and left to fetch the senator from the house.

When Peter entered the drawing room, he handed the senator a note asking him to come to the garage.

'Thank you, Peter. Alexander, will you accompany Peter and me to the garage, please?'

Vem was about to protest, but the senator raised his hand.

'I need his help, Vem, and that's an end to it.'

They made their way to the garage, but Peter hesitated outside the workshop door. It was ajar and he knew he'd shut it tight. He pulled it wide and stepped in.

Joe was slumped forward on his knees, prevented from falling to the floor by his hand in the vice. The black handle of a stiletto knife protruded from his chest. The expression on his face was one of pure terror. A deep cut ran from above the left ear to the right corner of his mouth. Peter stepped forward, lifted Joe's head up by the hair and pulled open the torn mouth. The tongue was missing. Alex turned away and bent double, retching noisily. Even the senator, a veteran, was speechless. Peter released Joe from the bench and laid him gently on his back.

The sound of hurried footsteps outside broke the silence. Alex ran out of the workshop, through the garage and into the yard. The two chambermaids were running down the drive. The senator appeared beside him and took the radio out of his pocket.

'This is O'Gorman. There are two girls running down the driveway of the house. Stop them immediately. Don't kill them.'

Halfway down the east wall, a figure rose out of the undergrowth, pointed an automatic weapon and fired a short burst. A line of gravel and dust danced in front of the two girls. One girl jumped the spray of dust and stones and kept running, the other one slowed and hesitated. As the first girl neared the gate, the gunman fired a single shot. She pirouetted forward, almost somersaulting, before crashing onto her back, screaming and cursing, her left leg twisted at a crazy angle. The second girl slithered to a stop beside her and crouched down to help her up. The gunman fired another short warning burst and the two girls collapsed in a pile, yelling what sounded like abuse.

Nine walked over to the girls and hit each on the jaw with his clenched fist. Then he walked back to the east wall without saying a word.

'Alexander, Peter, may I suggest you collect the two young ladies and tie them up in the workshop either side of Joe. I need to return to the house to make a couple of phone calls. Then I'll join you in questioning them. Alex, take the radio, please, and explain to Seamus what is happening.'

Alex and Peter set off down the drive while the senator returned to the house.

* * *

'One, this is Alex.

'One. Yes?'

'The senator asked me to give you an up – '

'I need medical assistance, not a fucking update. My

brother's bleeding to death here.'

'The senator's called for medical assistance, Seamus. I'll explain the urgency to him.'

Alex turned to Peter. 'I need to speak to the senator. Are you okay on your own here for a bit?'

Peter pointed to where Nine was hidden in the undergrowth, then at himself, and gave Alex the thumbs up.

Alex ran back to the house, colliding with the senator at the kitchen door. He explained the need for immediate help.

The senator took hold of his arm and led him outside. 'Listen!'

In the distance Alex heard the *whump whump* of a helicopter.

'That's the air ambulance coming. Look, you can see its lights over Bearna. Radio Seamus and tell him to signal the pilot. He'll know what to do.'

Alex called Seamus and watched as the chopper hovered near Seamus and his group, bathing them in light. The helicopter came to rest near Seamus and let the medics off, then lifted again and hovered a little distance from them.

The senator pointed down the drive. Peter and Nine were carrying the two girls up towards them. They walked to the garage door and Peter set the injured girl down carefully; Nine simply dropped his. As he turned to go, he spat on the ground beside the girls. He caught Alex and the senator watching him.

'I heard the poor bastard in there!' he said, nodding towards the workshop. 'I don't know what they did to him, but if you hadn't called when you did I'd have cut the bitches in half before they got out the gate.' He walked off towards his spot on the east wall.

Alex shook his head and turned back towards the house. Events were getting on top of him.

The helicopter landed again briefly and then took off. Seamus radioed to confirm that his brother had been taken to hospital and that one of the medics was staying to check on the other wounded. Two ambulances were on their way, as was the Garda.

The senator put a hand on Alex's shoulder. 'I know that the last few days have been traumatic. Unfortunately, it's not over yet. We still have to strike a deal with the people who own the book in order to bring them to justice. You have a major role to play in making that happen. I know we have only just met, but I need you to trust me. You've just witnessed the lengths to which they will go. So a great deal depends on us working together.'

The senator patted Alex on the back and walked away as the wail of distant sirens filled the air.

A cloud of dust followed Seamus as he raced up the drive in the SUV and slewed to a halt outside the garage. Peter had tied the two girls up in the workshop and was standing at the door beside the senator.

Seamus jumped out of the vehicle and made to push past them. The senator took his arm firmly.

'Five minutes, Seamus, but no more blood.'

The senator walked towards the house as Peter closed the workshop door behind him and Seamus.

Down the driveway, Nine heard a girl scream and grinned to himself. An eye for an eye.

Chapter 31

The senator walked into the drawing room, where everyone had gathered, relying more heavily than usual on his malacca cane. Vem rose to meet him, her concern clear on her face. The senator refused her offer of help, took a seat beside the fireplace and asked Pierre to organise drinks for everyone. He looked across to where Toots was sitting on the floor beside Willy.

'Siobhan, how is your patient?'

'I'm doing fine, Senator,' said Willy himself. 'I've no intention of missing the finale.'

'Good man, William. I thought you were sedated. Doctor Rafferty, a medical friend from Galway General, is on his way to take a look – then hospital for you. And how are you bearing up, Mrs Casey?'

'Nothing wrong that a night's sleep won't cure, Senator. What about yourself? You look worn out.'

'I am, dear lady, indeed I am. Ah Pierre, your timing is perfect.' Senator O'Gorman took his brandy and studied his companions as Pierre served the others their drinks.

He pulled a cigar case from his inside pocket and extracted a Cuban Montecristo. 'I hope no one minds.' He rolled and sniffed the cigar appreciatively before lighting it. 'One of my last vices …'

Just then, Alex was followed into the room by a gangly, stooped man in his sixties wearing a linen suit that looked as though he had slept in it, half-moon glasses hanging on the end of his beak-like nose.

'Eugene, I told you years ago to stop that disgusting habit before it kills you,' the man said.

The senator smiled. 'This is Doctor Rafferty, everyone. Good of you to come so quickly. That's our patient over there.' The senator nodded to where Willy was lying on the stretcher.

While the doctor examined Willy, Seamus and Peter appeared; the senator asked Seamus for a quick word and they stepped out into the hall. Alex collapsed into a two-seater settee where Kate quickly joined him, a move that didn't go unnoticed by Gran and Vem.

When the senator returned, the doctor gave his prognosis.

'The patient will live, though he refuses to go to hospital until tomorrow. Whoever tended to the patient's wounds did an excellent job – someone with experience, I'd say. Right, I must return to the hospital now. You've given us quite a busy night ahead. Good to see you, Eugene. Maybe it'll be under better circumstances next time.'

When the door closed behind the doctor, the room fell silent. Everyone turned towards the senator expectantly.

'Seamus has the exterior under control, the Garda are on the gate and the injured Chechens, as we now know they are, have been taken to hospital,' the senator began. 'By early morning, the less fortunate members of that group will have been removed and we will be back to some kind of normality. The first thing we need to do now is get all relevant information to Inspector Sullivan. William, I need to ask you to explain to Sullivan what you found and how best to use that information. Do you feel up to that?'

'Absolutely, Senator, but the inspector may not want to listen.'

'He will listen, William, I can assure you. There is more riding on that information than I can tell you at the moment. A courier will be here in fifteen or twenty minutes to collect the flash drive. Perhaps if we were to move you to the office to talk to Sullivan?'

'That would be good, and if I could sit rather than lie, that would be even better.'

Alex and Peter carried Willy into the office, with Toots and

Mrs O'Doherty in close attendance. Kate and Liz, sensing they were intruding on private business, went to bed. Alex looked puzzled when he returned to find Kate gone.

'I don't want to say too much until William has finished his telephone conversation with Inspector Sullivan,' the senator said. 'Just to clarify Sullivan's position – his efforts to help you were well intentioned. Unfortunately someone above him in An Garda Síochána was leaking details of your movements to the criminals.'

'Do you know who this git is, Senator?' asked Alex. 'Will they have access to the information on the flash drive?'

'Yes and no, Alexander. Yes, Detective Inspector Monaghan and I are fairly certain we know who the guilty person is. And, no, that person will not have access to the information until you give the book to him tomorrow afternoon.

'What? Why would we give valuable information to someone who's tried to kill us for it several times?' said Alex.

'Simple, Alexander. We need to catch them red-handed. I've considered all the options, and this is the only option guaranteed to draw that person out. I would do it myself except they wouldn't agree to a meeting with me. You, on the other hand, are only known to them as one of the people who has the book. It would be expected that you, or perhaps William, would deliver it in an attempt to sue for peace. But there's another reason why it has to be you. You are my grandson, and I expect you to do it for me – for the family and the business.' There was an air of finality in his tone.

'That's unfair, Eugene,' said Vem. 'How can you put Alex in a dangerous situation that has nothing to do with him?'

'You know why I've asked Alexander to make the handover, Vem, and he will know why too shortly. Please be patient until William returns. Then I'll explain all.' The senator suddenly looked his age.

Peter came in and handed him a note.

'Good, the courier is here,' he said. 'Please excuse me for a few minutes while I brief him and see how William is getting on.' As he rose, he smiled at Vem. 'I'm glad to see that fire in your belly, girl. Just be patient though.'

Vem turned to Alex. 'With the senator and Peter organising the handover, nothing will be left to chance. That's something.'

When the senator returned, the increasing strain was etched on his face.

'Alexander, will you give Peter a hand to bring William back please?' He sat down and, pushing the cigar aside, took a drink of his brandy.

Once Willy was settled back in the room – on the settee this time – the senator invited him to bring everyone up to speed and asked Peter to bring Seamus in in thirty minutes.'

'Inspector Sullivan is going to visit me in hospital to talk about the flash drive,' Willy said. 'He says it's safer than talking on the phone. He also said he would get in touch with you, Senator, via Mary Lennihan, as he doesn't have your mobile number.'

The senator nodded.

Willy continued: 'As I understand it, Hollinger and Stephen Reid had a system using five-digit numbers to text code words to their boss. Sullivan's going to use Hollinger's phone to see if he gets a response from the bad guys using that system. However, Sullivan's main concerns are the two books. He's not happy about what you plan to do with the original book, Senator. He thinks he should at least be consulted before you dispose of it. As for the book I found at home, which from my point of view started this whole bloody thing off, he thinks there's more to it than he's been told. He wants to know what's happening with it – have I analysed it, et cetera. Oh yes, Alex – Guard Mulligan from Balbriggan has been trying to get in touch with you. He says it's urgent – to do with the truck fire.'

'Yes, so Patsy Dan told me when I spoke to him earlier,' Alex said. 'It's as we suspected – the forensic tests on the container found traces of methyl … benzo something or other, better known as crack cocaine, on the cigarette packaging.' Alex threw a glance at the senator who was nodding to himself.

'Just as Peter and I suspected,' the senator said. 'Drugs in and dirty money out. Very clever.'

'That's it really,' Willy said. 'I didn't tell Sullivan where we are, though I assume he knows by now. The locals will surely have reported the Battle of Bearna to Garda HQ.'

'Actually, no, William. I've called in a few favours to make sure it's kept quiet for twenty-four hours. We need to give Alexander time to carry out the final act that will close the whole operation down. He'll explain to you later, William.'

Pierre had come into the room and was holding a cordless phone. 'Mary Lennihan has passed this number on to Inspector Sullivan. He's on the line now, sir.'

The senator took the phone. 'Good evening, Inspector. So did you get a response from Hollinger's phone? … Excellent. And did you recognise the person who called? … You're sure? … Now that *is* surprising … No, I'll speak to you in the morning. We may need to rethink the final act.'

The expression on the senator's face as he handed the phone back to Pierre was a combination of disappointment and frustration. He frowned and rubbed his chin.

'It would appear I have made a mistake in my judgement of Sullivan. Alexander, go and find Peter and Seamus please. Ask Seamus to bring any mobile phones or radios the villains were carrying. We need to check them for contact details. Vem, ask Mary to get DI Monaghan to call me urgently, and to make sure he is on his own when he does. She can give him the number for the house here. Then ask her to contact the courier company and tell their rider to pull in and await fresh instructions. Now, William, I need to know what you told Sullivan, and his replies, word for word. Please try to recall as much as possible.'

Willy grinned as he struggled with his pocket. 'I can do

better than that. It's all here.' He held up the iJack. 'I recorded the call.'

'I congratulate you on your perceptiveness, William. May I listen to the call please?'

* * *

Monaghan was inwardly fuming. Ten minutes earlier, Sullivan had phoned to tell him he had spoken to Willy and had agreed the collection of the flash drive. He also told him that he had sent the contact word via text message on Hollinger's phone and had received a call in response; Sullivan hadn't recognised the voice. What had made Monaghan mad was the fact that Sullivan had done all this in the commissioner's office, with the commissioner present, not on his own as they had agreed. Now the commissioner had brought Monaghan in for this meeting.

'Damn the senator. What in hell has got into him?' Sullivan's voice was strained. 'All this cloak-and-dagger stuff is clouding the issue. His refusal to tell me where they are – it's ridiculous.' He turned to Monaghan. 'What about his son? Can we use him to get to –'

Monaghan's phone rang. Monaghan looked at the screen, pressed the cancel button and answered Sullivan.

'No. Dominic is now under medical care. He's incapable of talking coherently. Anyway, Chris, we agreed to let the senator do things his way. Why the change of mind?' Monaghan couldn't keep the irritation out of his voice.

'Perhaps I can answer that, Pader.'

The oiliness of the commissioner's voice made Monaghan's skin crawl.

'I've some leave due and for health reasons I intend to take it now – doctor's orders and all that. I've appointed Chris as deputy chief commissioner with immediate effect and he's taking over from me. We've decided to bring this investigation under the control of this office, which accounts for the enquiry's change of direction. It's urgent that we find the senator and his pals. There's been too much bloodshed already.'

Monaghan was astounded. For a second he didn't move. Then he rose from his chair. 'I need to return this call. I'll be right back.'

'No, don't bother, Pader. There are a number of cases I need to review with Chris before I leave. So can we meet here again tomorrow morning, say … eight o'clock?'

Monaghan was furious by the time he got to his own office. He slammed the door so hard the partition walls shook the length of his floor. No one would be knocking on his door for a while. He returned the call from Mary Lennihan. She gave him the phone number for the senator, but before they finished the call Monaghan explained that he needed her to deal with something urgently.

'I need you to arrange to have Dominic removed from here as soon as possible to a suitable medical facility where I can have access to him later. It's up to you where he goes, but the address – and his identity – must be kept secret, especially from the commissioner's office. It needs to be done now. Let me know as soon as you can who'll collect Dominic – presumably it'll be a private ambulance. He must be moved by eight tomorrow morning at the latest when the shift in the station changes.'

Mary Lennihan, not known for fussing or flapping, saw no reason to do so now and discreetly set about organising Dominic's transfer.

* * *

The senator had just finished listening to the iJack recording of Willy's conversation with Sullivan when the house phone rang. It was DI Monaghan. The senator put him on speakerphone and played him the recording of Sullivan's call with Willy. Everyone listened in silence.

'Sullivan's lack of interest in the detail on the flash drive alarms me, Pader,' the senator said when it came to an end.

'That, and his increased interest in William's red book. Something's changed. And now he tells me he didn't recognise the voice that responded to the coded text.'

'Well, let me alarm you some more with my account of the meeting with him and the commissioner. I wish I'd had William's foresight and recorded it.'

DI Monaghan related the details of the meeting as it had happened. There were gasps round the room when he told them about Sullivan's sudden promotion; Willy and Alex were especially surprised. The DI then told them about the plans he had made with Mary Lennihan to remove Dominic from his present accommodation.

'Thank you for being so considerate,' said the senator. 'There was indeed a risk Dominic could have been used as a pawn at the very least, so it's a good idea to move him. Now, we need to be careful what we do next. The courier with the flash drive will have been stopped by Mary, awaiting instructions. Where do you want me to direct him?'

There was silence for a few moments.

'Hugh Cranleigh of Cranleigh Groves Solicitors,' said Monaghan. 'Hugh is a good friend of mine. I'll phone him and tell him it'll be delivered … When, do you think?'

The senator looked at his watch. 'About one in the morning, I'm afraid. He lives on Shrewsbury Avenue, doesn't he, big Georgian house on the corner?'

'Number seven.'

'Right, Pader, I need some time to rethink my strategy. I'm even more convinced I'm right about the identity of our mystery man, but I'd better not say any more just yet. This Sullivan thing has thrown me a bit. I'll call you at eight o'clock in the morning.' He hung up

'Was that call recorded, William?' the senator asked.

'Not intentionally, but yes. I can wipe it if you like.'

'No, that's fine. The more we record at the moment the better. It seems we have been the victims of a highly organised and professionally executed sting.'

'Who is DI Monaghan?' Alex had asked the question they all wanted the answer to. 'We've never met him, have we?'

'Ah, yes, you are quite right to ask, particularly in light of my mistake over Sullivan. DI Monaghan is in charge of the investigation into the attacks on you in The Shelbourne and at Drumlosh House. He also dealt with the arrest of Dominic and an unsavoury character called Uel Fagan. It was Fagan who orchestrated the attack on Drumlosh and sent the two young people in the car who were attempting to spy on us here. Monaghan's handling of the incident involving Dominic, in particular, and a subsequent meeting he and I had, persuaded me he is a man I can trust.'

'We can't be right all the time,' said Gran. 'Clever people who set out to deceive win sometimes, hurtful as that may be. In light of what you *have* got right, Senator, I for one feel perfectly safe in your hands.'

'I'm humbled, Mrs Casey. Thank you. However, just to err on the side of caution I might have a word with Cranleigh – ask him not to release the flash drive to the authorities without calling me first.'

'You don't need to worry about the security of the flash drive,' said Willy. 'It's password-protected and the contents encrypted. Force of habit, I suppose. If anyone wants in, they'll need me.'

The senator gave a little chuckle. 'Excellent, William. Well done.'

'I think we've something here, Senator,' said Seamus. He and Peter had been quietly working away at the Chechens' mobile phones and two-way radios. 'This is their leader's mobile phone, and there's a recent text message. I'm going to fetch one of the girls in to translate – she's been *very* co-operative so far.'

'May I see it, Seamus,' Willy adjusted his position on the settee. 'Can you get my laptop, Toots?'

Peter handed the senator a second mobile along with a note.

The senator read the note. 'Thank you, Peter, that's just what we needed. Alexander, this is a text message that Joe had saved as a draft. Presumably he was to send this when he had possession of the flash drive and the job was finished. When we send it, you will take the call – if they call back – and arrange a meeting. But let's find out what this other message is about first.'

Willy had connected his laptop to the Chechen leader's mobile. He tutted and muttered as he tapped away on the keyboard, the others looking on expectantly.

'The language is Chechen, isn't that right?' Willy said. 'Here we go …' He hit one last key, then sat back with a satisfied smile on his face. 'At least now we'll know if the girl tells us the truth.' But the smile disappeared as he read the message, and his face paled.

Seamus brought the dishevelled and cowed-looking girl into the room.

'Her name's Naazneen,' he said. 'She's their leader's daughter-in-law, married to one of the injured fighters.' He pushed the girl down into a chair and looked her straight in the face. 'What you did to Joe, I'll do to you if you tell any lies. Do you understand?' The girl nodded. Seamus thrust the phone into her face. 'Translate this message and no fucking about.'

The girl sniffed and rubbed her eyes, then read the message aloud.

'Joe, the man I am sending to you will explain the target. Make good use of his expertise. When he has assembled all the equipment, kill him. Burn the building with all inside. There must be NO SURVIVORS! Text the word "algone" to 81872 on completion. I will respond.'

The girl looked round the room and burst into tears. 'I did not know all were to die. Please, I did not know!'

'Histrionics – just as bad as lies.' Seamus slapped her hard across the face.

There were gasps from the others.

Seamus tapped a few buttons on the phone. 'That text was sent on Sunday at five o'clock. They were well warned and had plenty of time to prepare.' He turned to the girl. 'Where are the two regular maids from here? How did you get the job in their place?'

'The girls are tied in our caravan. They are not hurt. Ajay arrange us this work with man at camp – Francie. Dirty man. Always feel my bottom when he go past.'

Seamus struggled not to smile. He knew Francie Nolan of old; what she said about him was all too plausible.

He pulled Naazneen out of the chair and pushed her out the door in front of him. 'Back shortly,' he said to the others. 'I'll arrange for the girls to be released.'

Willy disconnected his laptop. 'She was telling the truth about the text message.' He shifted uncomfortably and groaned.

'Senator, I wonder if Willy could be taken up to bed,' Toots said. 'He's exhausted and in a lot of pain.'

'Of course, Siobhan. I must apologise, William, for keeping you so long. You have been an immense help.'

After Willy had wished everyone a goodnight, Peter and Alex carried him to his room, with Toots and Gran in attendance.

* * *

By the time Peter and Alex had returned to the drawing room, Pierre had appeared with trays of sandwiches, biscuits and two thermoses of tea or coffee. The senator had a few puffs on his cigar before settling himself.

'Right, first things first. We need to use the leader's mobile and see if we get any response. If the attack had been successful, he would be contacting his boss about now. When he calls, you need to answer, Alex. Explain that you have the book and want to arrange a meeting tomorrow afternoon. Tell him it must be at a place of your choosing and no one else is to be with him – no heavies. Make no specific arrangements on that first call – we'll get them to call back, make them sweat a little. Peter and I have selected a location, suitable for a number of reasons, but I won't go into detail until after you have spoken to them for the first time, lest in the tension of the moment you accidentally let something slip.'

The senator could see Alex stiffen.

'Please don't take that the wrong way, Alexander – I trust you implicitly. However, you are going into a situation of which you have no previous experience, against the most cunning individual you will ever meet. I would be concerned making this call myself. So, what you don't know you can't give away.'

Alex nodded.

'When the phone rings,' the senator went on, 'introduce yourself and ask who you are speaking to. They'll be surprised to hear your voice and not the Chechen's. If there is no reply inside ten seconds, hang up. Believe me, they'll ring back. You must try to speak to the man in charge, not one of his hirelings. How you handle that is entirely up to you. Once you know you are talking to the right man, tell him you have his book and he is to phone you at ten o'clock tomorrow morning on this same number. At that time you will tell him when and where the meeting is to take place – then hang up. If he tries to phone back, don't answer. Indeed, if he phones any time before ten tomorrow morning, don't answer. Oh, and we need to record this conversation, Alexander. Can you work William's machine?'

'I think so. I've looked over his shoulder often enough.'

The senator could read the tension in Vem's face. 'He will have cover, don't worry,' he said to her. 'Peter and I have been through the plan from every angle.'

Seamus leaned forward. 'Who's providing cover, Senator? I would be reluctant to move either of my guys off the roof until this is over.'

'I'll do it,' Vem said without hesitation. 'In fact, I insist on doing it.'

Eugene was taken aback. He had seldom seen her so animated.

'I'm a ten out of ten shot at eight hundred metres. I can conceal and lie for hours. And I'm Alex's mother … so that's final!'

The senator and Seamus exchanged looks and shrugged.

'Okay, the iJack is all set to go,' said Alex. 'Shall I do this now?'

The senator nodded.

Alex placed the phone and iJack on the coffee table between them. He keyed the word 'OBERON' in the message pane and sent it to 36251.

'I suppose we just wait now. No way of knowing how long —'

The phone rang and Alex jumped. Then he leaned forward and, after putting the phone on speaker, pressed Answer.

A rasping, evil-sounding voice rattled out of the phone. 'Good evening, Ajay. What's the situation?'

'Good evening. My name is Alexander Casey. To whom am I speaking?'

There was silence for a full ten seconds. Then, 'Alexander, I don't think we've had the pleasure. My name is Fitzpatrick … Francis Xavier Fitzpatrick. That name will mean nothing to you, I suspect. But I wager there are those in your company who will be … unsettled to hear it.' The death rattle that doubled for laughter led to a bout of coughing.

Alex ended the call.

Silence, broken only by the ticking of the mantle clock, filled the room. Suddenly, the senator rose from his chair like a young man and rushed across to Peter who was silently rocking back and forth, his fists clenching and unclenching, his breath coming in short gasps. The scar on his face was livid, his temples pulsating. The senator slapped his face hard. Peter staggered back from the sudden rush of blood and oxygen through his body. It was the second time in their years together that the senator had witnessed the effect on Peter – a kind of catatonic shock – of some triggered memory too painful to bear. This time the trigger seemed to be the voice of Francis Xavier Fitzpatrick.

As they tried to gather themselves, the phone rang again. This time Alex let it ring several times before answering.

'Good evening, Senator,' said the harsh, gravelly voice. 'I'm quite sure you're listening. And, hello, Peter. I'm sure you're there too ...' The man started to cough again.

Alex cut in. 'Mr Fitzpatrick, I have a book I think you want. I'm willing to meet you tomorrow, at a place and time of my choosing, to exchange it for a guarantee of safety for myself and my friends. Call me on this number at ten o'clock tomorrow morning and I'll give you the details. Got that?' Alex cut the call, tension etched on his young face.

The phone rang again a minute later but this time Alex let it ring out. Then he took the phone and iJack over to a wall socket and plugged them in to charge them. He put a hand on Peter's shoulder by way of reassurance. Peter nodded and left the room.

'I'm sorry I had to hit him,' the senator said. 'We thought we'd killed Fitzpatrick a long time ago and that only one of Peter's torturers remained alive. Poor Peter! That was a hell of a shock for him.'

'Perhaps we should concentrate on the job in hand, Eugene,' Vem said. 'Alex handled the call very well. Now we need to complete tomorrow's arrangements.'

'You're right, Vem, of course. Seamus, would you mind bringing Peter back into the room. He needs to be involved in this.'

* * *

The phone line between Athlone and Dublin was red hot by the time Francis Xavier Fitzpatrick had finished shouting at his accomplice on the other end. His bouts of coughing were so severe that the male nurse attending him actually threatened to disconnect the phone, a threat that under normal circumstances would have cost the nurse his life.

The knowledge that they had lost the Chechens and, more importantly, the initiative, angered Fitzpatrick beyond measure. To be told what he had to do by the bastard Casey was poison to him. The opportunity to mount another attack on the Old House at Bearna, even if they could gather and brief a squad, had gone. They had lost the element of surprise.

Knowing the senator as he did, the choice of venue for the handover would be almost impossible to turn to their advantage, particularly given the short notice they would receive. Fitzpatrick reluctantly came to the same conclusion as his accomplice: accept the terms for the handover, turn it to their advantage if possible, and mount some sort of attack on the Old House at the same time. Gaining possession of the red book was the primary objective, of course, but the destruction of the O'Gorman empire would be the cherry on top.

* * *

Seamus found Peter sitting on the north wall behind the garage, looking down into the quarry. He was dishevelled and his face bloody where he had been scratching at his scar.

'Alex really needs your help right now, Peter. If he's to get the better of that evil bastard Fitzpatrick, your knowledge and experience will be invaluable. Go and clean yourself up and come back to the room. The senator wants you to help finalise the plans for tomorrow.'

Seamus turned back to the house, praying that the next sound he heard wouldn't be a hollow splash.

'I have the ability and I have the motivation,' Vem was saying to Alex just as Seamus entered the drawing room. 'To my way of thinking, that gives me the right.'

'You win,' said Alex and sighed. 'So where is the handover to take place, Senator? Can you tell me now?'

'Yes, Peter and I settled on Mullaghmore Point. It's about fifteen miles north of Sligo.'

Seamus nodded but said nothing.

'It probably means nothing to you or Vem, but I see Seamus understands the historical significance of the place. One of its main attractions is that there is only one road to the place. The point itself is elevated but overlooked by a small hill half a mile back. That's where your cover will be hidden, Alex. It's a secure vantage point. The only house in the vicinity is right out on the headland and it is currently unoccupied. We propose that the handover takes place at four o'clock in the afternoon. The forecast is for a bright, sunny afternoon and at that time of day the person you are meeting will have the sun in their eyes. Tourists will not be a problem – coaches can't use the road – yet it *is* a public place, offering that extra degree of security.'

Just then, Peter came back into the room. Seamus nodded to him.

'Will I be on my own – other than my cover?' Alex glanced nervously at his mother.

'No, you will have the best possible companion with you. Won't he, Peter?'

Peter remained impassive.

'Peter will drive you there and stay with you the whole time. Don't worry – he will come prepared. If at any time you feel threatened, you will alert your cover and Peter using prearranged signals. Peter will be your eyes and ears while you make the handover. He will see any danger signs long before you do. Watch carefully … Peter, hands up, behind your head.'

As Peter raised his hands, there was a flash of steel followed by the thud of a knife as it embedded itself in the wooden fire surround next to the senator. They all looked at the fireplace, then back at Peter – he had a Glock 13 in his hand.

Even Seamus was impressed. 'Jesus, remind me never to pick an argument with you, Peter.'

Alex got up and pulled the knife out of the wood with some difficulty.

'The bloody thing was an inch into solid mahogany,' he said, looking at Peter. 'Christ!'

'The best possible companion, Alexander.' The senator was smiling, obviously enjoying the theatricals.

'I can conceal two of my men near the car park as backup for Peter and Vem,' said Seamus. 'But my main concern is keeping the house protected. Fitzpatrick won't be able to mount another attack tonight unless he has an army close by. He might try to pull something off at the house tomorrow while the handover takes place. I'll leave the two snipers on the roof. That still leaves four on the ground in here.'

There were nods of agreement from the others.

'Do I carry any sort of weapon?' Alex asked, even though he felt sure he knew what the answer would be.

'Definitely not,' said Seamus. Without experience it would be a liability. You'd be cut down before you got your hand in your pocket.'

'Right, that's settled then,' said Vem. 'Seamus, what about a bit of target practice? I don't mind doing it in the dark provided the rifle has a night-sight?'

The pair disappeared, and Alex stood up as though to follow them.

'Alexander, will you stay here please? I need to explain why it is you who has to do the handover. Peter, could you bring me a brandy and then leave us please?'

Peter set the brandy down beside the senator and closed the drawing room door behind him as he left. The senator took a sip.

'There's so much to tell, Alexander, yet so little time. Even your mother doesn't know it all yet. The detail will keep until the morning when Mary Lennihan is here. Mary has worked with me for thirty years and understands the running of O'Gorman Enterprises far better than I. She is one in a million and, thankfully, has agreed to stay on for a year after I handover the reins. That is why she is coming here tomorrow – to meet her new boss, one Alexander Sebastian Casey.'

Alex's jaw dropped and he stared at the senator. 'You mean me?' He tapped his own chest. 'Me?'

'Yes.'

Alex fell back in his seat. 'I don't understand. How could I become the head of your business? That doesn't make sense.'

'No, Alexander, what doesn't make sense is that I retired some months ago and put Dominic in charge, not Vem. Mary told me at the time that Dominic was the wrong person, and I'm going to have to grovel tomorrow when she arrives.'

'But why me? Why not Vem? What has happened to Dominic anyway?'

'Dominic has had a nervous breakdown. I have only three months to sort this all out. Vem will be acting managing director for the next year until you are ready.'

'What do you mean you only have three months to sort it out? Are you going to live abroad or something?'

The senator smiled. 'If only, Alexander. I have prostrate cancer. It was in remission until recently. Dr Rafferty, whom you met earlier, recently confirmed it is back with a vengeance. He thinks three months is optimistic, but I have always been an optimist. I'm booked into a clinic in Switzerland that specialises in assisted suicide, to give the treatment its vulgar tabloid name. I have lived my life as I chose, and I shall end it as I choose. My ashes will be returned for you, my grandson and heir, to do with whatsoever you think is appropriate. I have no foolish or romantic requests on that score.'

Alex stood up and started to pace the room. The senator watched him with a tolerant smile. Finally Alex stopped in the middle of the room.

'I'm sorry to hear about your illness, Senator – Grandfather. I'm not sure what to say! Thank you, for a start, but –'

'Don't thank me, Alexander – not until you understand the implications of what I have given you. Some might consider it a poisoned chalice, others an incredible opportunity. You must make your own decision. Either way, you will be at the helm of a business with a turnover in excess of three hundred million euro and assets worth eighty million.'

Bewildered and overwhelmed, Alex collapsed into the nearest chair.

Chapter 32

Vem and Seamus came into the drawing room as the senator and Alex were shaking hands.

'Is this what I think it is?' Vem asked.

The senator nodded. 'So did Vem pass muster, Seamus?'

'Three to Vem and two and a half to me, though I would say three.' Seamus smiled.

'He's a chauvinist,' said Vem, laughing. 'Doesn't know when to admit defeat.'

'The important thing is – I would go out with Vem as my cover without hesitation,' said Seamus. 'Anyone who can use that old Mauser of mine for the first time and shoot so well in the dark ... I'm happy!'

'I had no doubts,' said Alex. 'I saw her in action at Drumlosh. Listen, Vem, I know it's late, but could we have a chat, just to help me sort things out in my head?'

'Certainly, come on. Let's get some fresh air. Are we okay to go outside, Seamus?'

'No problem. Just stay inside the grounds.'

'I will say goodnight and see you early in the morning. We can talk more then.' The senator patted Alex on the shoulder and kissed Vem on the cheek.

Seamus said goodnight to them all, pulled out his radio and walked out towards the kitchen.

Alex and Vem stood at the open front door admiring the gardens and the distant ocean bathed in moonlight. Vem took Alex's arm and led him down the steps, the two of them chatting away, heads close together.

* * *

Willy, unable to sleep because of the throbbing pain from his wound, called softly to Toots. She wakened with a start.

'What's wrong? Are you all right?' She fumbled for the bedside light.

'I just can't sleep. I'd love a cup of tea, though, and could you bring me the iJack and phone. I might as well try to be productive if I have to be awake.'

Alex and Vem, just back from their walk, were still deep in conversation when Toots came into the kitchen.

'How's the patient, Toots?' Alex asked.

'Wants a cup of tea and his toys. Can't sleep,' she said grumpily. 'Do you know where his iJack is? And that phone?'

'They're recharging in the drawing room. I'll bring them up and give him the news,' Alex said and was out of the kitchen before Toots could speak.

'What news?' Toots asked Vem.

'Make Willy his tea and Alex can fill you in. I'm off to bed. It's been quite a day.'

'You're going to have to rewind,' said Toots when she arrived up with Willy's tea. Alex was sitting in a chair beside the bed.

Willy filled her in on the news that Alex was to take over as boss at O'Gorman Enterprises.

'What do we call you – Your Highness?' asked Toots.

'Enough of that,' said Alex. He went on to tell them about the phone call with Fitzpatrick and the arrangements for the handover.

'Fair play to you, big man. Anything I can do to help?'

'I don't think so, Willy. Peter and the senator seem to be on top of it.'

'What about the call with Fitzpatrick that you recorded? Let's listen to it in case there's anything I can add.' Willy said.

Alex fetched the laptop, which Willy connected to the iJack.

'Let's see if I can get a fix on the caller's location. I'll just hack into the main mobile networks – see what I can find. Also, I can set you up with a wire for the handover tomorrow. We would be listening here. Seamus could have his men and Vem on the radio and alert them if anything was wrong.'

'That would be brilliant, Willy – for my confidence, if nothing else. The whole thing's terrifying. I'd feel you were with me.'

Willy pulled a tiny mic and transmitter wire out of his bag. 'We can tape it to your chest. Then we'll be able to hear you – and them, so long as they're not too far away.'

'You're a genius, Willy!'

There was a ping from Willy's laptop.

'Now we'll see if … Yesss.' Willy punched the air. 'The call was made from an unlisted mobile somewhere near a place called Biddy Quinns in Athlone.'

'That information will make Peter very happy,' said Alex. 'Right, I'll give you two some peace and go and tell him.'

Alex found Peter sitting with Seamus outside the garage. He hunkered down in front of them.

'I understand the name of the owner of that wretched voice we heard is of some significance to you, Peter. Well, Willy has managed to trace the location Fitzpatrick's call came from,' he said.

Peter shot forward and took hold of Alex's arm, despair on his face.

'He traced it to a place called Biddy Quinns –'

Peter released his hold on Alex and crashed his right fist into the cup of his left hand. He jumped to his feet and emitted a strange kind of throaty roar like a caged animal. The name Biddy Quinns meant a whole lot to him, a painful lot. Shaking, he tried to write on his pad but his hands were out of control; perspiration poured off his face.

Seamus stood up and put a hand on Peter's shoulder. 'Relax, old son, relax. The time has come at long last for you to get your revenge, but it needs to be well thought out. Let's you and me discuss strategy.'

Seamus turned to Alex. 'Great news, Alex. Thank Willy in case we miss him in the morning. Will you excuse us now, please?'

Peter brushed Seamus aside and hugged Alex till the breath almost left him. Then he shook his hand till his arm hurt. If he could have smiled, it would have spread from ear to ear.

Alex left the two old warriors to discuss tactics, wondering how the senator would react when he heard the news in the morning.

* * *

Seamus and Peter were sitting on the viewing platform when the radio crackled into life.

'One, this is Seven. We have a single male approaching by foot on the road, about four hundred yards.'

Seamus stood up and found the man with his night-vision binoculars.

'Seven – no action. Leave it to the guards on the gate, but keep a bead on him.' Seamus sat down again. 'We'll see what Galway's finest do, Peter.'

The two guards at the gateway heard the pedestrian before they saw him. He was singing at the top of his voice and sounded a bit the worse for wear. As he neared the entrance, one of the guards stepped out into the road. The man jumped back in fright and surprise, staggered to the left, then steadied himself.

'Mother of God, but you scared me, officer. I never seen you till just now when I saw you.' He was slurring his words.

'You're out very late, sir,' said the guard.

'Ach, sure didn't me and my friends have words in the town. They fucked off and left me to hoof it.'

'Have you far to go?'

'Naw, just a wee bit more up this road – I think it's this road anyway.'

'Well, be careful now. Don't be falling into the sea.'

'I'll be grand, I'll be grand. I'll bid you goodnight, officer,' said the man and staggered off into the darkness.

The guard watched him go. He could murder a pint himself.

From the platform behind the house, Seamus and Peter had watched the encounter. When the man set off again, Seamus lifted his radio.

'Six, this is One. Unidentified male your side now. The guards seemed satisfied. I'm not.'

'Six here. Keeping an eye.'

Peter passed a note to Seamus when he sat down.

'I agree,' Seamus said. 'What are the chances? Let's wait and see what Six tells us.'

Seamus pulled his pipe and tobacco pouch from his pocket, then filled and lit his pipe. After a couple of puffs the radio crackled.

'Six again. He's disappeared. The road dips and swings inland about two hundred yards past the corner, reappears in fifty yards. No sign.'

'Is there any cover on the land side he could use to get up behind the house?' Seamus was rising as he spoke.

'Affirmative. Good stone wall runs north to meet east–west stone wall on the north side of the quarry. No gates and all standing, so good cover all the way.'

'Six, stay on the wall. Five, come in.'

'One, this is Five.'

'Five, did you get all that?'

'Affirmative.'

'Follow and watch. Do not engage.'

'Understood.'

'Now, we'll just wait, Peter.' Seamus relit his pipe and settled into the corner.

Three minutes later the radio crackled again.

'One, this is Five. It seems your man needed a crap. He's on his way. Should be visible to Six now.'

'One, this is Six. Phantom crapper in sight and striding on.

Appears much relieved.' Seamus could hear the laughter in his voice.

'All stations, this is One. As you were. Now we're all relieved.'

* * *

The morning dawned bright and clear, just as the forecast had predicted. Toots was in the kitchen at seven thirty fetching a pot of coffee. She was going to need a lot of it – Willy had hardly slept, due to a combination of pain and excitement. Gran was in their room changing Willy's dressings. Liz and Kate had gone to collect a change of clothes from the cottage. The two real chambermaids had appeared, somewhat ruefully, apparently none the worse for their period of captivity. The two guards on the gate were due to be relieved at eight. They would come up for breakfast before returning to Galway. Mrs O'Doherty was making breakfast and Pierre was fussing around making sure everyone had what they needed while they waited.

All appeared to be in order, except that the Rolls-Royce was missing, as were Peter and Seamus.

Alex had been woken by Peter just before six and, along with Vem, summoned to the senator's suite. Fitzpatrick's location, as identified by Willy from the call to the Chechen's phone, had not surprised the senator. Biddy Quinns was a known republican meeting place – had been for three generations. However, the fact that Francis Xavier Fitzpatrick was still alive troubled the senator greatly. Having listened to Seamus's and Peter's proposal to deal with him, the senator felt he should inform Alex and Vem of the decision he had taken.

Coffee and fruit juice had been delivered and the senator was in good spirits. 'Seamus and Peter have gone to Athlone,' he explained. 'Peter is quite determined to put an end to Fitzpatrick once and for all. Twenty-four years ago, he was the beast that cut out Peter's tongue and inflicted his other wounds.'

'For pity's sake ...' said Vem.

'He was aided by three others. Two were dispatched within a year of Peter's recovery, if that is what you can call his present state. He has persistently refused any remedial surgery, convinced he carries the mark of the devil for his past sins. You see, Peter was convicted of murdering the man who raped his then fiancée. She never got over the rape, and his conviction pushed her over the edge. The poor girl committed suicide the day he went to prison.

'Peter was never a particularly religious man, but in prison he found *his* God. His faith gave him the will to survive and a thirst for vengeance. On his release, he found it almost impossible to get employment. We were hiring for the haulage business at that time and Michael Slaney, one of Peter's few loyal friends, asked me to give Peter a job. That was the start of his career as my chauffeur.

'Six months later, Fitzpatrick and his cronies engineered a situation expressly to get Peter into trouble again. Their reason? The rapist he had killed was a cousin of Fitzpatrick's. The Garda arrested Peter on trumped-up charges and I bailed him out. But Fitzpatrick was so enraged he went after him. They drugged Peter and took him to Biddy Quinns. That's where the torture took place.'

'Dear God, what an appalling story,' said Vem. 'What that poor man has suffered – is still suffering. How does he cope?'

'With God's help ... that is what he will tell you. God, and the opportunity he has had working with me to deal with some very unsavoury customers – to right some awful wrongs. So that is why he and Seamus are away to Athlone. It also explains why he is going with you, Alexander, to meet our Mr Big. If I am right, the man you will meet at the handover today is the fourth member of the group.'

'Bloody hell! But why me?'

'Because in another few hours you will be the chief executive of O'Gorman Enterprises. As such, you will be charged with carrying on the work I have started. That will free me up to deal with the consequences in the unlikely event that anything should go wrong. You will understand this better when you meet the man I expect will turn up.

'What will Peter do if your suspicions are correct?'

'He will kill the man – that's what he'll do.'

Alex stared at the senator, so alive and energised that he wondered if he had imagined being told the night before about his illness. How could this man only have three months to live?

The senator appeared to read his mind. 'Yes, Alexander, Vem knows about my illness. So does Mary Lennihan. But no one else does, and that is how it must remain.'

Alex looked from Vem to the senator. 'I need breakfast,' he said suddenly. 'Can we talk again after that?'

'Perfect,' the senator replied. 'I have a telephone call I need to make. Vem, will you stay, please. The call is to do with Dominic and I'd like your opinion.'

Alex gave them both a big smile as he left the room.

'I'm very proud of that young man,' said the senator.

Vem smiled; she was proud of him too.

The senator called DI Monaghan.

'You're very punctual, Senator,' said Monaghan when he picked up.

'Good morning, Pader. I have my daughter with me and the telephone is on speaker so she can listen to the discussion. Now, what is the position with Dominic?'

'It's likely we'll ask to have him sectioned under the Mental Health Act – for his own protection if nothing else. However, much may depend on the outcome of today's events.'

'I agree. Let's see how that goes. Have you had any contact with the commissioner or Inspector Sullivan?'

'No.'

'That surprises me. They both think the flash drive was delivered last night to Garda HQ. Are they not looking for it?'

'Neither of them are here yet.'

'What are you going to tell them if they ask where it is?'

'The whereabouts of the drive is their problem, not mine. It's best I don't know any more about what you're up to than I already know, Senator.'

'I take your point, Pader. Perhaps you would phone tomorrow when you have a clearer idea about Dominic's, and your own, position. Goodbye.'

Eugene smiled thinly and looked at Vem. 'What did you make of that?'

'Sensible man. He doesn't want to be seen to have colluded with you, or vice versa.'

'I agree. Now, let's go down for breakfast.'

After they'd eaten, Alex asked Kate and Liz to spend some time with Gran while he, Vem and the senator met with Willy.

'So what are Peter and Seamus proposing to do, Senator?' Alex asked once they were settled in Willy's room.

'After you have made the call to Fitzpatrick, giving him the time and place of the handover, Willy will confirm that the calls are still coming from Biddy Quinns. Peter will then deal with Fitzpatrick. Seamus will handle anyone else.'

'Okay,' said Alex. 'And what about the handover this afternoon. Willy, are you sure the wire will work?'

'Absolutely, big man. Let us demonstrate.' He nodded at Toots.

She left the room and after a few moments, Willy flicked a switch on the iJack.

'Hello, Pierre, could we have coffee for five in our room please?' they heard Toots say.

'Certainly, Miss Toomey. I'll be up with it in a jiffy.'

A minute later Toots came back into the bedroom.

'Well? Did it work? Can you see the phone?'

'I can't, I must admit. I'm impressed,' said Alex.

'As long as the other person is within three or four metres, we should be able to pick up everything that's said. I did some more tinkering after a little trial Seamus and I carried out yesterday in the grounds. If Vem, Seamus and Seamus's men are using radios at the handover today, I can patch the mobile phone through to the radios at the same time, as long as the line is open. So if Alex has a problem, he can tell them and they can react immediately. He won't be on his own out there.'

'Thank you, William,' said the senator. 'Alexander, does that ease your worries?'

'It does indeed. Great job, Willy.'

There was a knock on the door and Pierre came in bearing coffee for everyone.

As Vem cleared the table for the tray, the Chechen's mobile rang. Alex looked at his watch.

'He's five minutes early. We'll let it ring.'

The senator nodded his approval.

At exactly ten o'clock the mobile rang again. Alex let it ring for a while before answering.

'This is Alex Casey. Let me explain the arrangements for this afternoon, Fitzpatrick.'

'I'm not interested in your arrangements, Casey,' the odious voice cut in. 'I'll tell—'

Alex ended the call. He looked at the senator nervously.

'That was the right thing to do, Alex. Don't let him control the call.'

The phone rang again. Eventually Alex picked up.

'You'll call me from the reception of the Downhill House Hotel in Ballina at two o'clock,' said Alex. 'No cheating – I'll call back to confirm you're at that location. Then I'll give you the time and place for our meeting. Is that clear?'

Alex took the paroxysm of coughing as confirmation and ended the call.

'That wasn't what we agreed,' the senator said to Alex, looking puzzled.

'I want to keep them on the wrong foot as long as possible,' Alex explained. 'Giving them the details at the last minute will leave them just enough time to make the rendezvous, but no time to reconnoitre.'

'Excellent.' The senator gave an I-told-you-so look to Vem.

Willy was tapping away at the keyboard of the laptop. 'I'll have the location for you in a couple of minutes, Alex.' He fell back onto the pillows, his face showing signs of the pain. 'When am I due another painkiller, Toots?'

'Now. Then I'm going to phone Dr Rafferty – it's time you were in hospital.'

The laptop pinged and Willy lifted his head to look at the screen. 'Same place. Biddy Quinns in Athlone.'

Alex phoned Seamus to tell him.

'Well done, boys,' said the senator when they were done. 'You're definitely showing an old dog new tricks!'

Chapter 33

The Eircom van, parked across the road from Biddy Quinns with its little white tent and guardrail round the pavement, offered good cover, although there weren't many people about at that time of the morning. Peter was seated on a stool inside the tent, overalls straining to cover his bulk. A woolly beanie, a set of ear defenders and glasses masked his face from the casual observer. Seamus sat in the open van door, fiddling with a laptop and generally looking busy. From that position he had a clear line of sight to the pub.

They watched a car pull up at the pub. It dropped off a well-dressed man wearing sunglasses and a slouch hat who went into the building by the side door. Neither Peter nor Seamus recognised him or the driver of the car. Half an hour later the man came out again and walked towards the town centre. Peter frowned at a distant memory.

A short time later, Seamus's mobile rang. He listened, thanked Alex and cut the call. He nodded at Peter. In full Eircom uniform, clipboard in hand and headset hanging round his neck, Seamus crossed the square and knocked on the side door to Biddy Quinns. He took a step back and waited, knowing he was being observed via CCTV. An intercom beside the door buzzed and a heavily accented voice asked him to identify himself. Seamus said he was a telephone engineer and held an ID card up to the camera, his thumb over the picture.

'I only need in to check the junction box. There was a report of an intermittent fault on the phones in the castle. I just need to eliminate the pub line.'

After a minute's delay the door was opened by the male nurse, who waved him in. As Seamus stepped into the hallway, he dropped his clipboard, scattering pens and paper into the hallway. While Seamus picked them up, Peter left the tent and strode purposefully across the square to join Seamus in the hallway. The nurse seemed a bit surprised, but shrugged and led the two men to the wall cupboard where the phone line came into the building. Peter passed Seamus in two strides, spun the nurse round and delivered a perfectly placed uppercut. He caught the crumpling body and laid him on the floor. Seamus taped up the man's mouth and used cable ties to bind his arms and legs. He left him for safekeeping in a corner between the wall and a heavy metal desk and, pulling a sawn-off shotgun out from his overalls, took up position covering the outside door and the door to the sickroom. Peter walked through and scanned the brightly lit, pristine room and had a quick look around. In the centre of the room was a Perspex bubble containing the living corpse of Francis Xavier Fitzpatrick and a bank of beeping, blinking machines.

'What's happening, Theo?' the corpse rasped.

Peter glanced at the monitor on the wall. As soon as he saw Fitzpatrick's face he smashed the Perspex cover over the trolley bed where the living corpse lay. He wrenched tubes from the body and kicked bleeping machinery out of his way. Then he stepped in close so that Fitzpatrick could see him. The sheet covering the skeletal form seemed to flatten, as though the body beneath it was deflating. The hideous face contorted in horror. Peter clamped his hand over Fitzpatrick's mouth, muffling his screams, and watched the man's feeble attempts to fight for his life. Then he lifted him by the throat and carried him with one hand, tubes trailing behind, fluids dribbling across the floor, to the door he remembered so well. The parchment-covered skeleton was weightless to him. He opened the door, held the writhing form over the void, then dropped him into the freezing waters of the Shannon.

Peter reached for the light switch and looked down at Fitzpatrick's pathetic efforts to stay afloat. Then he unzipped his trousers and pissed onto the upturned, choking face, the final indignity that he too had suffered twenty-four years previously. When he was done, he turned out the light and quietly closed the door.

Back in the pub, he picked up the comatose nurse, and Seamus lobbed an incendiary grenade into the chamber and closed the airtight door. The muffled *crump* of the explosion followed them out of the building. The few pedestrians in the square looked on with curiosity, but showed no interest in interfering with the enormous Eircom engineer carrying a limp body over his shoulder. Peter climbed into the back of the van and laid the nurse on the floor. Seamus eased in behind the steering wheel and drove up the hill. In his rear-view mirror he saw the first trace of smoke drifting into the air from Biddy Quinns. He smiled, lifted his pipe from the dashboard and placed it between his teeth.

* * *

The sound of the helicopter arriving galvanised everyone. As the rotors came to a stop, Vem and Alex walked down the path to the landing pad to meet Mary Lennihan.

Phil Larsen helped her down the ladder. Her face was wreathed in smiles, and when she saw Vem she burst into girlish giggles.

'I don't know why I've waited so long to go up in one of these things. It was astonishing.'

'You'll be getting Phil to take you to do the grocery run from now on,' Vem said.

Mary looked past Vem at Alex, who had held back, waiting to be introduced. Her eyes travelled quickly from head to toe.

'Alexander Sebastian Casey! You're the spitting image of your father.' She stepped forward and extended her hand. 'I've been so looking forward to meeting you. All I've heard is Alexander this and Alexander that. You've a lot to live up to.'

'I could say the same about you, Mary. From what I hear, the senator would be lost without you.'

Mary smiled at the compliment. Standing five foot ten inches in court shoes, she was still a trim size fourteen, and with a head of thick white hair, fine aquiline features and penetrating grey-green eyes, she exuded self-confidence. She released her hand and linked his arm.

'Now, tell me all that's been happening here. Where's the senator? We've a lot to get through this morning, as you can see.' She indicated the two bulging document cases sitting on the ground beside her overnight bag. The pair walked off, leaving Vem and Phil to carry her bags up to the house.

When Mary and Alex walked into the drawing room, the senator rose stiffly to greet them.

'Good morning, Mary. I see you two have met. Before we have coffee, would you mind calling the commissioner? I need to confirm our four o'clock meeting this afternoon. Alexander, I received a message from Seamus just now. One down, one to go. He and Peter are on their way back. They should be here by half twelve, in plenty of time for your little trip.'

He reached for the mobile phone Mary was holding out to him. 'Ah, good morning, Wesley. And how are you this fine day?'

He listened for a moment, then held the phone away from him, looking at it as if it had bitten him. 'Mary, would you? It's his recorded message.'

Mary took the offending instrument and spoke into it. 'Commissioner, this is Mary Lennihan for Senator O'Gorman. Please call back at your earliest convenience regarding your meeting this afternoon. Thank you.'

Gran arrived with Kate and Liz.

'Mrs Casey, this is—' said the senator.

'Mary Lennihan. I know. How nice to meet you at last – to put a face to the voice.'

The two ladies shook hands, then spontaneously embraced, the others looking on in some surprise.

The senator took Mary by the arm. 'I detect a subterfuge?' he asked.

'Indeed, Senator, but that is a story for another day, as you would say.'

Alex introduced Kate and Liz.

'Liz I have met briefly before,' said Mary. 'Good to see you, dear.'

Pierre and the maids set out coffee and tea on the dining room table, then discreetly withdrew. Mary's phone rang. She answered it, then passed it to the senator, mouthing 'commissioner' to him.

'Good morning, Wesley. This is you I hope and not some machine.'

The senator's expression barely changed as he listened to the commissioner.

'I have to say I'm disappointed, Wesley. Things of importance need to be discussed … As you will.'

He handed the phone back to Mary who ended the call.

'Things are moving faster than I expected,' the senator said. 'Alexander, Vem, we need to have a quick chat before Mary begins proceedings.'

Bewildered, Alex and Vem stood up and followed the senator out to the front terrace.

'Seamus said that someone visited Fitzpatrick before they went in,' the senator said to them. 'Neither he nor Peter recognised that person. However, the description fits the individual I suspect is the mastermind behind the whole operation. My conversation with the commissioner just now proves I'm being distanced from the final episode of this wretched business. That suits me, and also makes up my mind about a matter that's been troubling me. I am now certain that more than one person will turn up at the handover, so you must both be very alert. They may separate and try to draw your attention in two directions at once. Alex, at no time must you block Vem's line of sight. Do not underestimate your opponents. These are ruthless people.

Once they have the red book, you will be an irrelevance. Now, Alex, walk me through the actual handover step by step.'

Alex glanced at Vem. 'We will arrive at Mullaghmore at least an hour ahead of them, so I'll find a good place in the car park to hide the book. When I see them arrive, I'll take up my place and do my best to make sure they stand where we want them to. As soon as I've said my piece, I'll instruct them to call my mobile five minutes after I leave, which is when I'll tell them where the book is hidden.'

'I like that, Alex, especially hiding the book – if they go for that, of course. We'll run it past Peter and Seamus when they return. How do you feel about it Vem?'

'Fine, as long as I have a clear line of sight.'

'Let's see what Seamus says. Right, time to go in and talk to Mary. We've a lot to go through before you leave.'

When the trio returned to the drawing room Mary and Mrs Casey were deep in conversation. Kate and Liz had gone upstairs to see Willy and Toots; Pierre and the maids had cleared the table.

'Alexander, it is important that William and Siobhan are at this meeting. Would you organise a lift down for William? I'm sure Pierre will be happy to help. Ask Elizabeth to join us as well. Katherine is welcome to sit in if she wishes.'

The senator took his place at the head of table and Mary disengaged herself from Gran and sat beside him. She opened one of the document cases and extracted a slim folder, placing it in front of the senator. He started to read it as Mary took three other similar folders out of the case, along with a thick spiral binder. She opened the binder and sat back in her chair, completely relaxed.

When the senator had read the entire document, he closed the folder and set it back on the table.

'Excellent, I feel better already. I think a glass of champagne will be in order in half an hour or so, Vem. Would you tell Pierre the '79, please?'

Kate and Liz came in, not sure what was happening. The

senator made the introductions. 'Come and sit down, girls. There are no secrets about what Mary is going to explain.'

Alex arrived with Willy, the invalid's left arm draped across Alex's shoulders. Toots fussed along behind. Willy gave everyone a good morning as Alex set him gently onto a chair, the expression of pain on his face belying the cheery tone of his voice.

'My apologies for bringing you downstairs, William. Mary, this is William McNabb, our only casualty to date, and Siobhan Toomey, the late Thomas Toomey's daughter.'

Mary greeted them both warmly.

'It's as well to be down,' said Willy. 'The ambulance will be here in ten or fifteen minutes.'

'Then, Mary, if you would perhaps deal with Ennis Digital and Electronics first.'

Mary adjusted her half-moon glasses and looked round the group before turning her attention to the open ring binder in front of her.

'In this' – Mary patted the ring binder – 'is a statement of the affairs of Eugene O'Gorman, details of all his holdings and bank accounts in Ireland and abroad, and also his last will and testament, co-executors named as Mary Amelia Lennihan, Victoria Elizabeth Mary Haughey, née O'Gorman, and Alexander Sebastian Casey, his principal heir.'

She had everyone's full attention.

'This binder has been prepared by the senator and myself in conjunction with O'Gorman Enterprises' legal and financial advisers. It has been signed off by independent auditors. It has been verified by the state board of revenue, customs and excise and by the Ministry of Internal Affairs. In other words, it is financially accurate and legally binding on all parties involved, absent any legal challenge before the expiry of a seven-day waiver, which gives the signatories time to avail themselves of independent legal and financial advice. Copies are in the folders in front of you. At the senator's request, I will deal, in principle, with the portions relevant to those present and will start with you, William Alfred McNabb.'

'Me? I don't even—'

Mary held up her hand, selected a tab and open the binder.

'The senator, in appreciation of your technological efforts to help and protect Mrs Casey, Alexander Casey and Siobhan Toomey during this difficult period, and in recognition of your outstanding IT abilities and scrupulous honesty, gives you the interest accrued on his offshore bank accounts.' She looked over her glasses at Willy. 'That is, the accounts that are detailed in the little red book you found in your home some years ago. Those accounts – the capital and accrued interest – pertain to a business established some twenty-five years ago. The senator felt it was prudent, at that time, to keep details of the business hidden – offshore, to all intents. Your father, Alfred Spencer McNabb, was the administrator of that business. When he was unfortunately killed, the account details were buried with him – until you discovered the book, that is.'

Willy, bemused, opened his mouth to speak, but Mary stopped him with a frown.

'We – that is, O'Gorman Enterprises – monitored the accounts for years but could not access them without the appropriate codes. Your success at hacking into the accounts six years ago intrigued us, and we have tried ever since to trace you without success, until you declared yourself to be Mouseman a few days ago. So congratulations, Mr McNabb. You did a great job of avoiding detection … By the way, we were never as clos to tracking you down as our emails suggested.'

'So it was you who sent those emails!' Willy said. He shook his head and beamed at everyone round the table, clearly proud of his detective work at uncovering the accounts.

'However, there is a binding undertaking attached to the gift,' Mary went on. 'The interest must be used, at least in part, to buy a forty-nine per cent holding in Ennis Digital and

Electronic Limited, one of Europe's leading innovative electronics development companies with a prestigious client list. It is at present a wholly owned O'Gorman subsidiary, but forty-nine per cent of its stock will be made available for you to purchase to foster your abilities and secure your future potential. That forty-nine per cent shareholding will cost around seventeen million euro, leaving you a handsome balance out of the accrued interest in the red book accounts. The original capital must be paid to the senator prior to him reassigning all his other holdings.'

'From the look on your face, William, I don't think you have grasped the full import of what Mary has just told you,' said the senator who had been watching Willy closely. 'All will become clear in time.'

There was a knock on the door and Pierre came in carrying champagne.

'The ambulance has arrived for William,' he said, 'so I assumed a quick glass might be in order.'

The senator was relaxed as the glasses were filled and a toast was drunk to Willy's speedy recovery and to the future of Ennis Digital. Armed with his copy of the agreement and with Toots in close attendance, Willy was lifted onto a stretcher. As he disappeared through the door, he looked over his shoulder at Alex.

'Good luck, big man.'

When they had all settled again, the senator looked at Mary. 'Next, I think we should explain briefly about the joint venture with cousin James, as Elizabeth is present.'

Mary turned to the appropriate page in the ring binder.

'As you know, Elizabeth, the senator and your father, James, have a joint venture, Ireland's Heritage Hotels, of which this, the Old House, is one. The senator is handing his shareholding over to James in the short term. The shares in IHH, like those of Ennis Digital, cannot be traded on the open market and, in the event of financial or personal problems, must be offered back to O'Gorman Enterprises at an independent market valuation. I stress this point because of your position as the eldest in your family, and because of your father's health. The condition attached to this share transfer is that the voting rights rest with you, but are subject to the advice of O'Callaghan and Stewart, the company's auditors, until you graduate. After your graduation, you take full control of the holding. In the interim, all dividends and related profits will be placed in trust for you until your graduation.'

Liz looked shell-shocked. A normally voluble and excitable young lady, she showed uncharacteristic self-control when she went to the senator and gave him a hug and a prim kiss on the cheek, the tears welling up in her eyes.

'Thank you, Uncle Eugene. I'm very grateful.'

'Say no more, Elizabeth. It will all be fine.' The senator patted her shoulder fondly, keenly aware of the battle James was fighting with alcohol, and how it was adversely affecting his whole family.

'Come on out for a breath of air, Liz,' said Kate, seeing how overwhelmed her friend was by this unexpected turn of events.

The two girls excused themselves, Kate giving Alex a little smile on the way out. Alex blushed; the senator noticed all this with keen pleasure.

'Mary, I gave Alexander a brief rundown yesterday of the arrangements concerning him. In light of the handover meeting this afternoon, I propose we finish our discussions when he returns this evening. The contents of that large folder in front of Mary represent the past for me, and the future for you, Alexander. I wish you every success and as much pleasure adding to it as I had creating it. You will return to Trinity and complete your degree alongside your work at Casey Transport and O'Gorman Enterprises. It will be a demanding schedule. Vem will be acting CEO until your graduation. Mary has agreed to stay on for at least a year. You would be wise to persuade her to stay longer. O'Callaghan and Stewart, our auditors, will work for you, as for Elizabeth. Use them as your sounding board, hide nothing from them and, until you know better, take their advice. What do you think, Mary? Can we adjourn the rest of the business until later?'

'Absolutely. As long as I have the signed documents back with the solicitors before close of business tomorrow, everything will go ahead as planned.'

The senator turned to Gran. 'I hope that you in no way feel I have usurped your position at the head of the Casey family. That is not my intention. However, personal circumstances, as well as our present problems, have precipitated what I must do. You see, I have a very short time to live, perhaps only three months. It had been my intention to resolve our family relationship, to get everything into the open, when Alexander had graduated. However, I do not have the luxury of time. That is why Alexander is being thrown in at the deep end, so to speak.'

'I trusted you when you came to Sean's wake,' said Gran. 'I have no reason not to trust you now. If you feel Alex is up to the responsibilities you're placing on him, then I'm sure you're right. As for your personal circumstances, three months is long enough for any man to make his peace with God.'

The senator gave her a gracious nod in acknowledgement of the gentle advice he had received.

'Thank you, dear lady. Perhaps we can take a walk later so we may talk some more.'

Mary gathered the folders and the ring binder and returned them to the document cases. 'I'll ask Pierre to keep these in the safe until later,' she said. 'Mrs Casey, shall we join Liz and Kate for some fresh air?'

The two ladies left Vem and Alex with the senator. He looked from one to the other, nodding slowly.

'To go through the list of holdings was going to take too long. It will keep until later. I expect Peter and Seamus back any moment now, so we'd best concentrate our energies on the handover this afternoon. Now, if you will excuse me for a few minutes.'

The senator rose with difficulty and, leaning heavily on the malacca cane, left the drawing room.

Alex walked across the room, opened the French windows and stepped out onto the terrace. Vem followed him.

'I can't get my head around the events of the last few days, Vem. It's too much. How am I supposed to take over and run a multimillion euro business? Even with you and Mary to help it's impossible. I've another year at university. I have Casey Transport. That's enough. As for Willy, what does he know of business? The whole thing's a nightmare.'

Vem reached across and took his hand.

'Be patient, Alex. Wait until you hear all the details. Your role, initially, will be symbolic until you get to grips with each aspect of the whole enterprise. There's no need to worry about it now. Mary and I will be with you all the way.'

'I wonder how Charlie is,' Alex said. 'He'd have been good company this afternoon.'

'The vet says he's doing well, and I'll have him back next week. But you know what? I'm glad he's not fit for active service just yet.'

Alex gave Vem a hug. 'Come on, Ma. Let's go get these bastards.'

Chapter 34

Seamus and Peter made good time back to the Old House. On the way, they released the male nurse who seemed to be only too happy to be away from Biddy Quinns. Mrs O'Doherty insisted on making them bacon and egg butties, despite their protestations that they needed to see the senator.

In the drawing room, the senator rejoined Alex and Vem and waited for Seamus and Peter to finish their breakfast. Their idle conversation was broken by the ringtone of the Chechen's mobile.

Alex's heart skipped a beat as he pulled it out of his pocket. He gave the senator an enquiring look, selected speakerphone and answered the call.

'Don't hang up, Casey.' A cold, hard voice echoed round the room. 'We have something you value. Listen.'

There was a pause, then: 'Alex, this is Willy. They've taken Toots.' He sounded groggy yet panicked.

The line went dead.

In three strides the senator was at the French windows shouting for Mary. Then he crossed the room to the door and called Peter and Seamus. He sat down again, took out his phone and passed it to Vem.

'I want to speak to Dr Rafferty.'

Seamus and Peter rushed into the room followed by Mary, Gran, Liz and Kate.

'Siobhan has been kidnapped,' the senator announced. He raised a hand to stop the anticipated flood of questions. 'Get Monaghan, Mary, then the commissioner. Seamus, take a couple of your men and get to the hospital. I'll speak to

Rafferty and make sure William is placed in a private room in the meantime. Put your men on the door with instructions that no one other than Dr Rafferty and a nurse gets into the room.'

Vem handed the senator his phone.

'Rafferty, where are you? ... Well, send security to his room immediately. Someone has abducted the girl ... I know. Make sure William's safe. Seamus O'Byrne is on his way with two of his men. William will need a private secure room after his operation.'

The senator set his phone down, then took another from Mary's outstretched hand.

'Pader, we have a situation. Someone has abducted Siobhan Toomey from the hospital in Galway. She was there with William McNabb who was shot yesterday. How did they know they were there? ... Could you to talk to your colleagues in Galway? I suspect that's where the leak is. While you're on the line, I need to know what's happening about the flash drive. Someone's life depends on it.'

'It's with Cranleigh, the solicitor,' said Monaghan. 'He's confirmed its arrival. Nobody's asked me about it – neither the commissioner nor Sullivan are here. If somebody expresses an interest in it, I'll speak to you before I tell them its whereabouts.'

'Thank you, Detective Inspector. Please keep in touch.'

'No reply from either of the commissioner's phones,' Mary said. 'I've left a message on both. I'll give Clem McShane a call. After Peter's visit to Athlone this morning, there may be some local repercussions and Clem knows the area well.'

The senator turned to address the room. 'Now listen, everyone. I'm fairly sure I know who is behind all this. When Siobhan's captors ring back, I will deal with it. Peter, the handover goes ahead as planned, so you get ready to move. Alexander, as this is the phone the kidnappers called, I need to hold on to it. Use your own or borrow one from Pierre and set up William's equipment.'

'How can the handover go ahead as planned? What about Toots?' Vem asked.

'Siobhan will be back here safe and sound by then. Provided William is out of their reach, we still hold the trump cards – the flash drive and the red books.'

'But if Peter, Vem and I leave for the handover, and Seamus and a couple of his men are away at the hospital, it leaves you rather vulnerable here,' Alex said.

'They'll not attack here now, Alexander. The abduction of Siobhan is an opportunistic move born of desperation. What we have is of huge value to the kidnappers and that's all they care about. I know that sounds callous, but that is the reality of the situation.'

This last comment caused a few raised eyebrows but, surprisingly, it was Gran who spoke out.

'The senator's right. This needs to be handled in a calm, practical way. Panic will get us nowhere.'

'I'll go and check over Willy's equipment,' Alex said. 'Then I'm ready to go. I need to show somebody how to monitor the iJack, so –'

Kate jumped to her feet. 'I've done a fair bit of radio and TV work on the production side. I could help.'

'Great,' said Alex. 'Come with me and I'll give you a demo.'

Right on cue, the Chechen's phone began to ring again. The senator made no move to answer it – just cocked his head and waited. After a minute it stopped ringing.

Gran gave him an approving nod. 'Treat 'em mean and keep 'em keen. Fair play to you, Senator. I don't think I'd have the nerve to do that. What about trying to persuade them to bring Toots here – draw them into a trap, with Clem, perhaps, to close the door?'

'A woman after my own heart, Mrs Casey,' said the senator. 'But how to persuade them. I am certainly not going to answer that phone until I hear that William is safe.'

Just then, the Chechen's phone rang again. The senator ignored it. Instead, he turned to Vem.

'Why not discuss your predetermined signals for the handover with Peter. He knows the location better than most. We have no idea how this will play out now, but we can be sure of one thing – they will not go easy. I don't think Alexander should hide the red book. He needs to have it to show them. They may want to check it to confirm its integrity. And they will certainly have backup of some sort. I don't want another shoot-out like last night. Or heroics, especially from Alexander. He is a young man with a lot to prove.'

'Don't worry, Eugene – I'll take good care of our boy.'

The senator's own phone rang. Mary listened, then pressed a button.

'Seamus, you're on speaker.'

'Seamus, is William safe and secure?' the senator asked.

'Yes, he's in theatre now. The Garda detention suite is earmarked for his post-op care. No one will get near him who shouldn't.'

'Okay, Seamus. Thanks. That allows us to move forward. Your men know the score?'

'Yes, boss. The doc knows the boys, and they know the nurse in charge of Willy's aftercare.'

The conversation was interrupted by the ringing of the Chechen's phone.

'The abductors are on the other phone, Seamus. Stay on the line and listen,' the senator said. 'Mary, answer that and put it on speaker please.'

Mary accepted the call and set the phone on the table.

'Casey, don't fuck about with me again,' the brash voice shouted into the room. 'When I call, you answer.'

'This is Senator O'Gorman. You will talk to me from now on, and I do not approve of foul language.'

There was a moment's silence, then the voice came back.

'Fuck your airs and graces, just listen. The—'

'You will listen to me. The young lady, Miss Toomey, will not be harmed by you or any of your colleagues. You will let me speak to her on the phone. Only when I've spoken to her and am reassured that she's being treated well can we begin to discuss the handover of the book. Your superior knows I am a man of my word. So let me give him my word on this. He will never see the book if Miss Toomey is harmed in any way. It will be handed straight to the authorities. Alexander Casey has already made arrangements for the handover. That still stands, but only on the release of Miss Toomey.'

The senator nodded to Mary who ended the call.

The senator spoke into the other phone. 'What do you think, Seamus? Do you know who it is?'

'No, but Uel Fagan probably does – his dirty marks are all over this. Is he still in police custody?'

'As far as I know. I will ask Mary to contact DI Monaghan and arrange for you to talk to Fagan. In the meantime, what about searching the gypsy camp where the Chechens stayed. And that young buck who was spying on us here – did he not say his father knew Fagan? I'll leave it with you. Keep me posted, Seamus.'

The senator ended the call just as Mary held her phone out to him.

'Clem for you. I've filled him in so far.'

'Well, Clement, any thoughts?'

'Uel Fagan controls the muscle in the area, so anybody recruited at short notice would be his. He has a fixer called Kevin Reilly, used to hang around Biddy Quinns a lot. I'll see if I can track him down. He'd be running things while Fagan's inside. He and his mates will definitely know what's going on. I'll call you when I have anything.'

'Thank you, Clement. I may need you here later. I'll let you know.'

The senator handed the phone back to Mary.

'I need a few minutes to gather myself. Perhaps a little brandy, Mary, when I come back.' He stood up and walked out of the room, using the malacca cane to steady himself.

Mary shook her head. 'It's too much for him. He needs a rest. I'll be back in a minute.'

* * *

Alex and Vem followed Peter out to the Rolls, Vem carrying the case containing Seamus's sniper rifle. When he had repacked the rifle the previous night, Seamus had also shown Vem the AR15 assault rifle that neatly fitted in the other side of the gun case.

'This is the best scattergun in the business – kicks like a mule and sprays .38 rounds all over the place. If you find yourself in a tight corner, keep it on semi-auto. Use it from the hip and enjoy the show.'

Alex was more concerned with how he could communicate with Peter and Vem. He and Peter sat in the front seats trying to work out hand signals that would seem quite natural close up, but be clear from a distance. He also checked the phone connection and the link-up with the radios that Vem and the backup team would have. Kate had grasped the set-up with the iJack quickly. She had also made it clear to Alex that she wanted to see him when he came back, and had given him more than a peck on the cheek before he left.

Vem left Alex and Peter to it while she returned to the house.

Back in the drawing room, the senator suggested that Kate, monitoring the recording equipment, commandeer the corner with the writing desk and landline extension. Vem reappeared to take her leave.

'A quick word before you go,' the senator said.

Father and daughter had a brief conversation out of earshot. As Vem headed for the door, she wiped a tear from her cheek with the ball of her hand. She turned at the door.

'See you all later. Kate, keep us posted about Toots please.'

'Will do, and please bring Alex back safe.'

Vem walked out to the Rolls.

'Are we ready, boys?' she said, trying to make light of their mission, but the information the senator had just given her, and a particular instruction, were weighing heavily. 'Alex, in the back with me. You can tell me what signals you and Peter have agreed.'

Peter, dressed in his bottle-green chauffeur's uniform and peaked hat, started the engine and they drove off.

* * *

After a fifteen-minute catnap, the senator rejoined the others in the drawing room where Pierre had set out plates of sandwiches and a thermos each of tea and coffee.

The senator's mobile rang. Mary picked it up. 'Certainly, Seamus,' she said and passed the phone to the senator.

'We're at the gypsy camp,' said Seamus. 'They've packed up – hardly anyone left here. One old crone told me the site was cursed and they'd never be back. Someone's put the frighteners on them, but long before Miss Toomey was taken. Something else is going down that we don't know about.'

'Perhaps I have miscalculated, Seamus, and they are going to have another pop at us here after all. Come back here now. We need to review the situation.'

The senator looked around him, more troubled than he cared to admit. He was unnaturally anxious. Everyone was too spread out.

'Katherine, ask Alexander to call me. Mary, what about Monaghan? Has he arranged for Seamus to talk to Fagan?'

'Fagan's refusing to talk to anyone other than his solicitor. The DI has asked the solicitor to visit the jail to try to persuade Fagan to talk, but he isn't hopeful.'

'What's especially troubling you, Senator,' Gran asked.

The senator relayed the conversation with Seamus and explained his own fears. He was missing Peter badly; it was usually him he confided in.

'I don't believe anything other than their own superstition scared them off,' Gran said. 'The old woman was correct – that amount of death associated with a gypsy site is considered a curse. The fact that the Chechens lived in their midst and brought about their own destruction is the worst omen imaginable for the Roma. Only their own superstitions would make them move out, not some threats from an outsider.'

The senator's phone rang again. This time he answered it himself.

'Clem here. Can't find Kevin Reilly or any of his mates. They haven't showed at any of their regular haunts this morning. There's a lot of fear among the hardmen after the fire at Biddy Quinns. There's talk about a turf war … Eastern European mafia et cetera.'

'Peter will be delighted to hear that.' The senator chuckled. 'There's nothing like a bit of dissension among the ranks. Can you come here with whatever company you can drum up, Clement? I fear we may have a situation developing here again, so all hands will be welcome.'

'On my way, Senator, though it's only myself and Sal. See you shortly.'

Mary was in conversation on her phone. 'Hold on, Detective Inspector, the senator's free now.' She passed her phone to the senator in a move smoothed by decades of working together.

'Your suspicions about a leak were probably correct, Senator,' said Monaghan. 'But I'm fairly certain it was just canteen gossip – nothing malicious. Someone must have overheard a conversation about Toots and Willy going to the hospital. One of my colleagues will be calling with you shortly to offer his assistance and further protection if necessary. As for Fagan, he's flat out refused to give any information. Sorry I can't do more on that front.'

Frowning, the senator sat back into his chair when they ended the call. He would be glad when it was all over. He was too old for this caper now.

The Chechen's mobile rang, making them all start. The senator took a deep breath and looked at the others.

He put it on speaker and answered.

'What about Miss Toomey?' the senator asked.

'All in good time, Eugene, all in good time,' said a cultured voice.

The senator looked at Mary and cut the call, much to the surprise of the others.

'You and Mary recognised that voice, didn't you?' said Gran.

Before he could reply, the Chechen's phone rang again.

'Senator?'

Toots's voice echoed round the drawing room before being drowned out by a spontaneous cheer from everyone.

'I'm all right,' she said. 'They haven't harmed me in any way.'

There was silence again.

'Eugene, your young companion is unharmed and at this moment alive. However —'

'My instructions to your man were absolutely clear. Miss Toomey must be returned to me – here – before we talk about anything else. That is still the position.'

'I'm sorry, Eugene, that's impossible. You see, I'm on my way to the four o'clock rendezvous. I've stopped for a light lunch in the Downhill House Hotel in Ballina, as instructed.'

The senator paused before he replied.

'You will call me at two sharp, as was originally arranged, and I will return the call to the hotel to confirm your presence and Miss Toomey's well-being. Then you will tell me how you plan to return her, unharmed.'

The senator hung up, then immediately demanded to speak to Clem.

Mary was ahead of him and already had Clem on the phone. She handed it to the senator.

'Clement, where are you? ... Can you make for Ballina with all haste please. You need to be at the Downhill House Hotel as soon as you can to verify Miss Toomey's well-being and freedom. I have just spoken to her abductor ... Good man, I knew I could rely on you. Many thanks!'

No sooner had he finished that call than his own phone rang. It was Dr Rafferty, reporting that Willy was out of surgery and in a secure suite.

'He's very lucky,' the doctor said. 'There'll be no permanent damage, though it will hurt for a while. I'm keeping him mildly sedated until I hear about his lady friend, I don't want him getting too agitated. It wouldn't help his recovery at all.'

'I have just spoken to Siobhan,' the senator explained. 'She is alive and unharmed, and I am confident we will have her back in our care in a couple of hours. Perhaps that will give William some reassurance. Your help is much appreciated, Rafferty. We'll talk again soon.'

The senator looked exhausted. Even the unflappable Mary was concerned. Gran got up and crossed the room to him, holding out her hand.

'Up and out, Senator. You need a breath of fresh air. Mary and Kate will mind the phones.'

'You have a determined look in your eye, Mrs Casey. I doubt I could refuse even if I wanted to.' The senator stood up and took Gran's arm.

As Gran and the senator strolled round the fountain and lily pond in the middle of the turning circle, Seamus hurtled up the driveway, a cloud of dust following his old four-by-four. He skidded to a halt in front of the garages and stepped down, flapping his arms to disperse the dust cloud that enveloped him.

'Nothing subtle about your return, Seamus,' joked the senator, 'but good to see you again. Let me update you on the situation before you check our security, though I think any trouble here is unlikely now.'

Eugene excused Seamus and himself, and Gran returned to the house while the two old comrades discussed the position.

* * *

After his short walk with Gran and his chat with Seamus, the senator was feeling more upbeat. Security at the Old House was back to an acceptable level now that Seamus had returned, and Clem on his way to get Toots.

The Chechen's mobile rang at exactly two o'clock. Mary placed the phone on the coffee table and put it on speaker. The senator waited a moment.

'Are you at Downhill House Hotel?' he asked.

The voice that replied was not the well-spoken voice of the previous call; it was the harsh voice from the earlier calls.

'When you phone the hotel reception, ask for Jed,' it said.

The line clicked off leaving an anxious silence hanging in the drawing room.

The senator nodded to Mary and she punched in the number she had written on her pad earlier.

'Good afternoon, Downhill House Hotel. Pat speaking. How may I help you?'

'May I speak to Jed, please?' Mary said.

'May I have a room number please, and a surname ... Sorry, hold on one moment please.' All they could hear was muffled speech. Pat came back on the line. 'I'm putting you through now, caller.'

There was a rattle as someone fumbled with the phone. Then: 'Senator, things have changed. You've to tell me where the boss is to be at four. I'll keep the pretty wee girl with me until I hear from the boss that he's got whatever it is he's to collect. And he says you're not to hang up again or I'll hurt the girl.'

'If the girl is hurt in any way, you'll have me to answer to, Kevin Reilly.' There was silence on the other end of the phone. Eugene knew his long shot had hit the mark. 'What happened at Biddy Quinns shows you that we don't fool about. If the girl is safe, you are safe.'

'I'll phone back in a minute,' Reilly said and ended the call.

The senator was feeling the strain. 'I really miss Peter at times like this.' He spoke so low it was almost as if he was speaking to himself.

Several minutes passed before the phone rang again. Mary pressed the speaker button.

'Speak, Kevin,' the senator said.

'The boss says I'm to do whatever I want with the girl after he gets what he wants. So, what's she worth, Senator?'

'Your life, Kevin ... your life.' His voice was quiet and

chilling. He looked up at the others and put a finger to his lips.

'Ten grand, Senator. She's got to be worth ten grand.'

The senator waited a few seconds before responding. 'One hair, Kevin – damage one hair on that girl's head and you will eat your eyeballs. You will survive for many hours under my care and you will remember that one hair with your dying breath. That's my promise, Kevin.'

Liz looked at her Uncle Eugene in horror. He was usually such a kind-natured old gentleman.

'Your life, Kevin, your life for one hair.'

They could hear Reilly's erratic breathing down the phone.

'I'll call back,' Reilly said and cut the call again.

The senator crashed his fist on to the table, the mobile bouncing to the floor. 'Damn and fucking blast!' he said, spittle flying everywhere.

He rose from the table. 'Mary, phone Peter!' He stomped across the room and out the French windows to the terrace. 'Seamus!' he roared. 'Now, please!'

He came back into the drawing room and sat down as Seamus came in from the garden.

'Seamus, I have a problem with our friend Kevin. He's asked for ten thousand euro in exchange for Siobhan. I tried to scare him but I may have overestimated the strength of our negotiating position—'

'I have Peter on the phone,' Mary said.

The senator took the phone, told Peter about the conversations with Kevin Reilly and explained his approach.

'Your thoughts to Alex, please, and have him call me back.'

Seamus returned from reception with a road map of Ireland. He spread it out on the coffee table in front of the senator.

'Where was he when you spoke to him, boss?'

'Ballina – the Downhill Hotel.'

'Okay. If he's not going to release Miss Toomey until after the handover, he'll run for home. He'll stick to the main roads where possible – Swinford, Charlestown – and turn off at

Tulsk for Roscommon, then Athlone.'

Mary interrupted again. 'Alex on your phone, and I've Sal on mine, holding for Clem if you need him.'

'Excellent, Mary. Alex, what does Peter think?'

'He reckons Kevin Reilly will go home before he tries to negotiate with you over Toots's release. He's sure Fagan will be pulling strings from afar – won't miss the opportunity to earn some money. He also says, and I quote, Reilly's a bad bugger. He'll hurt Toots if he's cornered.' Seamus was nodding his head in agreement. 'Peter suggests we turn and head for Athlone. We could cut Reilly off at Tulsk.'

'Okay, stay on the line, Alexander. Clement, did you hear that?'

'Loud and clear, Senator,' said Clem. 'But listen, I'm in Swinford now.'

'First class. Alexander, did you hear that? Clement is closer, so you carry on. The handover goes ahead as planned. I'll keep you informed. Thank you again, and call me when you reach Mullaghmore.' He ended the call to Alex. 'Seamus, what do you think?'

'Clem's your man, sir. He knows the bastard we're dealing with!'

'Clement, is that a fair comment?'

'Absolutely, Senator. I've just turned and I'm heading back out of Swinford towards Charlestown. There's a village three or four miles out – Cuilmore – narrow main street and an awkward corner in the centre. That's where I'll get him. I know him to see and I'm pretty sure he'll be driving a Toyota Land Cruiser, Uel Fagan's preferred mode of transport. He'll be easy to spot.'

'Remember, Siobhan will almost certainly be in the vehicle.'

'Understood, Senator.'

Eugene collapsed back into his seat. He looked exhausted. Pierre came in with more coffee to help keep everyone on their toes.

'I've just called the hospital,' said Mary. 'William's fine – still sedated, otherwise safe and secure. Dr Rafferty would like to see you, Senator, when this is over. He's concerned about your stress levels.'

'Typical doctor,' the senator muttered and went towards the French windows, waving to Seamus to follow.

But before they reached the terrace, the Chechen's ringtone cut through the air like a knife. Mary answered it.

'If you hold, I'll ask the senator to come to the phone,' she said.

'Ever the efficient assistant, Mary.' It was the cultured voice again. 'But you can take a message this time. My man tells me Eugene's being awkward, melodramatic – "Your life for a hair." Well, here's one for Eugene: "A book returned or a life forfeit." Pass it on, Mary.'

The line went dead.

'Mrs Casey, say a prayer for us please,' the senator said, his voice without emotion.

He followed Seamus on to the terrace and closed the French windows behind them.

* * *

Peter pulled the Rolls into a lay-by, turned to face Vem and Alex and pointed at his watch. Alex called the senator's number.

'We're about half a mile from the turn-off for Mullaghmore, Senator. I'll just put the phone on speaker, okay?'

'Peter, our opponents are about half an hour behind you, maybe less. Have you time to set up as you planned?'

Peter nodded. Alex replied, 'Yes.'

'Are you absolutely certain your plan is as safe as possible? Siobhan is still at risk. I don't want to put anyone else in danger.'

Peter nodded again. Alex replied, 'Yes.'

'And are we agreed that you won't hide the book, that you just give it to them?'

Peter looked at Alex and shrugged. 'Yes,' said Alex. 'What's happening with Toots?'

'We are in negotiations. All will be well. You deal with your problem and it will all turn out okay. Good luck … and stay safe!'

Peter started up the Rolls again and took the turn-off for Mullaghmore. About two hundred yards in, the single track road swung to the left, the ground rising on the right to the hilltop that would be Vem's vantage point. Peter stopped and got out; the others followed. He pointed to the hedgerow that followed the rising ground, then at Vem, and then indicated, using his index and middle fingers, that she should walk.

'Do I follow the hedge to the clump of gorse up there?' Vem pointed to the top of the hill.

Peter nodded, shielded his eyes with the flat of his hand and looked from side to side, indicating that she would have an all-round view.

Vem followed Peter to the boot and withdrew the Mauser. Peter pulled a groundsheet out of the boot and wrapped Vem's rifle in it, knotting both ends. He handed Vem back a shapeless bundle that certainly didn't look like a rifle.

'Thank you, Peter.' She stood on her toes and gave him a kiss on the cheek. 'Alex, no heroics, mind.' She embraced him and set off up the field.

Meanwhile, Peter was lifting two 'Road Closed' signs and a bundle of tools out of the boot. There were half a dozen full sandbags as well. He set the signs out in the middle of the track, the sandbags piled round them; two split open and spilt out on the road.

'Good idea, Peter,' Alex said. 'It'll force them to come on foot.'

At the end of the lane, Peter drove the Rolls into the car park and pulled into the back corner, the last part of the car park visible from the road. There was one other car, but no sign of the occupants.

Peter and Alex walked to the shelter in the opposite corner

of the car park and Peter pointed to the top of the hill. Alex just caught sight of Vem settling herself down, tucking into the side of the gorse clump, disappearing from sight.

Peter walked around the shelter. Turning to face the corner in the road leading down to the car park, he showed Alex how he would move round the back and far side of the shelter to keep it between himself and the roadway.

'Okay, time to take our positions,' Alex said into his mic. 'I'll go and wait in the car.' He took the little red book out of his pocket and handed it to Peter; Peter gave him the keys of the Rolls.

'Thank you, Peter. Okay, let's get these bastards.'

The two men shook hands.

Alex turned away and walked back to the Rolls, gleaming in the afternoon sun. He slipped in behind the wheel, leaving the door open, and waited.

Chapter 35

Clem parked his Range Rover outside Delaney's Public House in the centre of Cuilmore, twenty or thirty yards before the tight bend he'd mentioned to the senator.

'Sal, would you recognise Kevin Reilly again? Remember he was with those hoodlums who tried to gatecrash Jeanne Rankin's birthday party last year – the mouthy one, sticky-out ears and always wears sunglasses?'

Sal nodded. 'How could I forget Willy John frog-marching him down the drive and the catcalls of his mates. God help Toots in the hands of that creepy git! I'd recognise him for sure.'

'He'll probably be driving a Toyota Land Cruiser. You take over driving our car. As soon as Reilly comes into sight back there' – Clem pointed back the way they'd come – 'phone me. I'll be just around the corner. I'm going to get a bottle of beer in Delaney's and play the drunk, cross the street in front of him. You try to pass the Toyota while I have it stopped – cut in in front of it, block him in. Hopefully he won't recognise me until you have him jammed in. Then we'll play it by ear.'

'But you need to be careful. If he twigs, he'll drive over you. He's bad enough for it.'

'Right, I'm away to the pub. Open the hidey-hole and give me the Colt before I go.'

He took the pistol, kissed Sal, then disappeared into the bar and reappeared a minute later with an open bottle of Guinness.

Sal watched as he tipped the bottle to her and staggered backwards, sweeping his arm in a great arc skywards. She smiled at the play-acting, knowing that it hid stretched nerves and a measure of fear. He was well used to it from his days in the paras, but he always insisted that the day he felt no fear before a mission was the day he could die. He staggered down the street, every bit the mid-afternoon drunk.

Clem crossed the street unsteadily and sat on the edge of an old horse trough now used as a planter, taking an occasional swig from the bottle. His presence elicited disapproving glances from the good ladies of Cuilmore, but envious smiles from some of the thirsty drivers caught in the slow-moving traffic. A short time later his phone chirped.

'Reilly's just coming into the village,' said Sal. 'At least, a Toyota Land Cruiser came round the corner like a bat out of hell and had to slam on the brakes to avoid the traffic … Yes, it's definitely Reilly. He's just put the driver's window down and is gesticulating wildly at a Vauxhall Cavalier in front of him – it's trying to reverse into a parking space … No, the other driver's given up and is moving on. You'll see a red Vauxhall first. Reilly's right behind. I'll keep the line open.'

Clem heard Sal start the Range Rover just as the Vauxhall came round the corner. It was closely followed by the Toyota. Getting between the two vehicles was going to be near impossible, for Reilly was almost touching the Vauxhall's rear bumper.

Clem was about to leap out into the road when a blast on the horn of a petrol tanker coming the opposite direction made him jump back beside the trough. While he was hidden from the Toyota by the tanker, Clem raised his phone.

'Where are you, Sal?'

'Two behind the Toyota. I'm stuck until the tanker passes and the silly bitch in front turns right.'

Clem stepped to the right and walked around the back of the stationary tanker. The driver of the Vauxhall had now stopped and was waiting for a motorcycle to pull out of a space. Kevin Reilly's hand was stuck on the horn of the Toyota and passers-by had stopped to watch the carry on.

Clem squeezed in between the Vauxhall and the tanker, and when he reached the Toyota he leaned an elbow on the lowered driver's window and thrust the bottle of Guinness into Reilly's face.

'Give us a fag and I'll let you have a swig,' Clem said while discreetly pulling a Colt pistol out of his coat pocket.

'Fuck off, you drunken shit! … Hold on, I know you.'

Reilly reached for a Glock 13 that was lying on the passenger's seat. At the same time, the Vauxhall in front suddenly pulled into the now vacant parking space. Reilly had his Glock by the barrel and swung it round towards Clem. But it hit the bottle of Guinness which exploded, showering them both with glass and foaming beer. As Reilly struggled to control the four-by-four, Clem grabbed the nearest thing to hand: Kevin Reilly's seat belt. His full weight hung on the belt, tightening it on Reilly and pinning his right arm to his side. Reilly dropped the Glock, grabbed the steering wheel with his left hand and swung the Toyota to the right. Squeezed against the tanker, Clem grabbed the Toyota's roof rack, but his right leg caught on the tanker's rear bumper and snapped with an audible crack. Clem cried out, dropping the Colt pistol, but he held on to the Toyota, his left foot on its running board, the broken right limb hanging limp.

Reilly, realising that his passenger was struggling to hang on, broke into raucous, evil laughter. Now clear of the traffic jam, he took off up the street out of the town and looked ahead for a suitably protruding object to scrape Clem off the side of the Toyota, all the while swinging across the road to try to loosen Clem's grip.

'That'll teach you and your fucking wife to laugh me out in front of my men. When I knock you off, I'm going to reverse over you. I want to hear you fucking pop!'

Sal witnessed the whole incident. As soon as the tanker passed her she pulled out in front of the car that was turning right, mounted the kerb, scattering pedestrians, drove behind a telegraph pole and back onto the road. She saw the Colt pistol lying in the middle of the road, slammed on the brakes, jumped out to retrieve it, got back into the Range Rover and floored the accelerator. The Toyota was turning a slight right-hand bend and she could see Clem struggle to hang on to the erratic vehicle. Reilly was trying hard to shake him off. So intent was he in trying to dislodge Clem that he failed to see the Range Rover rapidly overhauling him.

'I have you now, you fucker!' Reilly shouted gleefully.

Ahead, on the other side of the road, the gate to a field was half-open, sticking out on to the road.

Reilly crossed over and lined up on the gate. Clem let go and threw himself backwards into the ditch just as Sal drove up the inside of the Toyota, pushing it towards the ditch. Reilly stood on the brakes. The Toyota hooked the gate on its the bull bars, the vehicle swinging into the ditch, while Sal slammed the Range Rover into its side, sending a shower of sparks into the air. The two vehicles crashed to a halt, noses deep in the ditch. Sal took a few seconds to gather herself, then clambered out of the car through the passenger door.

Reilly had hit his head on the steering wheel. When Clem had jumped, the seat belt loosened and didn't hold Reilly in his seat. Now his nose was broken and his forehead deeply gashed by the rear-view mirror. He was aware of movement to his left and moaning from behind.

Wiping blood out of his eyes, he struggled to release the seat belt and find the Glock. The angle of the Toyota – nose down into the ditch – meant he was lying forward against the seat belt, tightening it. Pushing back on the steering wheel, he released the belt and reached into the footwell where he could see the Glock. He straightened up and pulled on the door catch before realising the door was jammed by the field gate. He saw Sal climb out of the Range Rover and shout something to Clem, who called back. That gave Reilly the time to reach behind the front seat, grab a handful of Toots's hair and pull her up, screaming, in between the front seats. What he didn't see was Sal throwing the Colt to Clem.

Sal could see Toots in the back seat of the Toyota and gingerly picked her way round to the driver's side. Reilly wrenched Toots's head up by her hair and forced the muzzle of the Glock into her left ear. Toots screamed.

'Tell that bitch McShane to open the back door and stand in the middle of that fucking gateway where I can see her … Tell her!' He ground the gun into Toots's ear.

Toots screamed out the message, tears coursing down her cheeks.

'Stop crying, for fuck's sake. I can't think straight.' Reilly looked up but couldn't see Sal anywhere. 'Scream louder. That McShane bitch doesn't seem to have heard you.'

'Yes, I did,' Sal said softly as she opened the back door of the Toyota. 'Stay calm, Toots. This'll be over soon. Don't worry.'

By this time, two other cars had stopped on the road.

'Like fuck it will. It'll be over when I say so,' Reilly growled. 'Now get into the middle of that gateway where I can see you … Go!'

Sal moved away from the back of the Toyota. The driver of one of the other cars came towards them.

'Stay back – he's got a gun,' Sal said softly.

By way of demonstration, Reilly fired off a shot which smashed through the toughened glass of the sunroof. Toots screamed again.

The driver Sal had spoken to hid behind his car while the driver of the other car slammed into reverse and shot backwards down the road. Sal stopped in the middle of the gateway.

'Keep your hands above your head. Right up … Now, keep them there and don't move or this wee cunt gets a new earhole.' Reilly laughed at his own joke.

Reilly pushed Toots into the back, scrambled over her and crawled out through the half-open back door. He kept his eyes on Sal as he reached in, caught the binding around Toots's ankles and pulled her hard out onto the ground. Her tartan skirt had gathered up round her waist, her sweater up under her arms. Reilly made a disgusting slurping noise.

'Very nice!' he said, looking her up and down. 'Right, McShane bitch, help her up and get her into that car on the road. Where's the fucking driver at? Driver, come and give us a hand or you'll get a new earhole too.' Reilly laughed again.

The cowering car driver stood up and came over to where Toots lay, exposed and helpless, on the ground. He and Sal lifted her gently, Sal smiling and shushing while they carried her to his car. Reilly turned back to the Toyota and fetched his jacket from the front and a package from the glove compartment. As he moved towards the other car, a single shot rang out.

Reilly stood momentarily headless before his body collapsed in a bloody heap on the road. The car driver collapsed in a dead faint at Sal's feet, dropping Toots to the ground. She cried out.

'You're safe, Toots,' Sal said soothingly. 'Reilly's dead ... Listen, I need to leave you for a moment. I need to see to Clem.'

Sal ran to where Clem was sitting in the ditch, the snub-nosed Colt in his lap.

'What the hell did you have in that thing?' she asked, giving him a hug.

'Yeah, .38 dumdums tend to make an impression. Jesus, Sal, get the first-aid box. This leg's killing me, and I think I may have broken my left wrist. Is Toots in one piece?'

'Yes, she's fine – physically. But terrified. I'll be back in a minute,' Sal said.

She ran back to the Range Rover to fetch the first-aid box. Clem was worse than he thought he was; there was blood pouring from a wound in the back of his head.

Toots started to cry. The other driver, who had come to, propped her against his car and did his best to make her decent. He had untied her ankles and was working on her wrists. The sound of a fast-approaching siren drowned out his words of comfort.

Sal knelt beside Clem, opened the first-aid box and took out a syringe and an ampoule of morphine.

'Hold on a second, Sal. I need to talk to the senator first. Can you reach me my phone please?'

Sal took out her own phone and hit one of the speed-dial numbers. It started to ring.

'Hello, Mary? Is the boss handy? ... Thanks.' Sal turned to Clem. 'And the needle's going in ... now,' she said.

'Clement, what news?' the senator asked.

'Toots is shook up but okay,' Clem said through clenched teeth. 'Reilly is dead and I hear the cavalry coming. Can you deal with the fallout, please? I'm about to pass out ... need hospital ... Sal ...'

The wail of the siren was now deafening.

'Turn that bloody thing off!' Sal screamed at the young guard who was stepping out of his car.

Clem had dropped the phone on the ground but it was still connected.

Sal lifted the phone. 'Senator, I'll call you later. Clem needs a hospital.'

'God bless you both, Sal. Thank you.'

Chapter 36

At ten minutes to four, Alex saw them arrive on foot, just as he and Peter intended. Two men in business suits appeared around the corner of the lane, their eyes fixed on the Rolls. One of them was carrying a laptop bag over his shoulder.

Alex stayed in the driver's seat and pressed the call button on his phone, establishing the wire connection.

'We're on, and there are two of them.'

The men stopped to have a conversation, and the shorter one, whom Alex thought was vaguely familiar, pointed to the top of the hill where Vem was concealed. Had they seen something? Or was their cover up the same hill?

'Vem, they're looking up at your spot,' Alex said to his chest.

The two men started to walk again and Alex slipped out of the Rolls, closing the door gently behind him. He walked a few paces to the position that would place the two men in Vem's sights. Now he was up close he realised who one of the men was.

'Inspector Sullivan!' Alex said. 'Jesus! Willy was right all along.'

He turned his attention to Sullivan's elegantly dressed companion.

'And who the hell might you be?'

'I am Wesley Shackleton, Commissioner of An Garda Síochána. We're here to place you under arrest for drug smuggling and money laundering, both rackets that your company has been fronting for some years. I understand you wish to hand over a book by way of mitigation.' He paused.

'May I have it please? Assistant Commissioner Sullivan will authenticate it.'

Sullivan lowered the bag to the ground and pulled out the laptop.

'The book please, Mr Casey.' The commissioner extended his hand.

Alex was confused. The two top Garda officers in the country were here to arrest him, and the commissioner seemed so sure, so confident. Could the senator have made a mistake, or had he misled them all, including his own daughter? Vem wouldn't shoot either of these men if it came to a showdown. They weren't the hoods they had expected.

The senator, listening via the phone and radio link, was willing Alex to do the right thing, to trust him – make the right choice.

'Unfortunately, I don't have the book on me,' said Alex.

'Don't get clever with me, Casey,' the commissioner said, a nasty snarl in his voice. 'This is not the time to play games. The book please.'

Sullivan pulled a Ruger SR9 pistol out of the computer bag and pointed it at Alex. As he rose slowly out of his crouch he moved towards Alex, closing any angle Vem might have on him.

'Don't move, Alex. I won't hesitate to use this,' Sullivan said.

'Someone else has the book,' Alex said.

The commissioner and Sullivan saw Peter at the same time, just as he stepped from behind the rain shelter. Sullivan couldn't make his mind up who to point his pistol at, and he wavered between Alex and Peter. Peter had his hands up, the little red book clearly visible in his right hand.

'Throw the book at my feet and don't make another move,' Sullivan barked.

Peter did as he was told. The book landed to the right of Sullivan, forcing him to take a step to pick it up and giving Vem a clear line of sight.

Sullivan hunkered down, placing the pistol on the ground beside the laptop, opened the book at a random page and started pecking away at the laptop keyboard.

While Sullivan was doing this, the commissioner didn't take his eyes off Peter, a nervous tic playing at one corner of his mouth. Peter held his stare, all the more disconcerting because he was unable to blink. Eventually it became too much for the commissioner.

'Get back in the car, driver. We have no business with you. Go on!'

Peter took a step towards the commissioner.

'I told you, get into the car and stay there!' There was a slight tremor in the commissioner's voice.

Peter took another step closer.

The commissioner's right hand came out of his jacket pocket holding a .22 Beretta pistol. 'It may be small but it's effective,' he said.

Peter stood his ground, his dark eyes boring into the commissioner.

Sullivan closed the laptop. 'It's genuine. The master recognised a random sample of codes I entered. We're back in business at last.'

The commissioner visibly relaxed.

'Well, young Casey, you picked the wrong side this time,' the commissioner said in a lighter tone of voice. 'The senator's done for, as is this bastard who I should have finished off twenty-odd years ago.' The commissioner waved his pistol at Peter. 'Hands behind your heads, both of you! Chris, you watch the boy. I'm going to settle an old score for cousin Francis and a few more besides. Hands behind your heads, I said.'

The listeners at the Old House hardly dared to breathe.

Vem, watching from a distance, slowed her breathing in readiness. She had a clear line of sight on the commissioner provided Peter didn't move any closer to him. Peter's hands moved slowly up. Peter's arm now blocked Vem's line. She drew back from the telescopic sight.

Neither man saw the flash of Peter's left hand. Suddenly Sullivan dropped his gun and clutched his throat. There were no shouts or cries, just a gurgling sound like a sink draining. He staggered back, then his scrabbling hands fell away from his throat, revealing the hilt of a knife projecting from it. A look of complete disbelief had spread over his face. His arms dropped uselessly to his sides, and slowly his knees buckled and he sagged to the ground.

The commissioner, mesmerised by what he'd just seen, quickly turned to Peter and fired once … twice … three times. Peter staggered back, regained his balance, and then with a mad roar, lunged forward. He had made no effort to draw his Glock. Vem watched in horror from the top of the hill, unable to get a clear line on the commissioner.

The commissioner fired the last two rounds in his Beretta as Peter closed in on him. One hit Peter in the right shoulder and his arm fell uselessly to his side. The second grazed the side of his head, just above the livid scar.

Rooted to the spot, Alex could only watch in amazement as the roaring mountain hurled himself at the commissioner, who tried to turn and run. Peter caught him by the throat with one hand and half-lifted, half-pushed him back towards the edge of the cliff. Finally Alex found his voice.

'Peter – the cliff!'

But Peter didn't ease his charging push. He seemed to hesitate at the crumbling edge, as though to let the commissioner get a good look down, before he launched himself into the void taking the frantic commissioner with him.

Alex stumbled towards the edge just in time to hear the commissioner's petrified scream cut short by the splash as the two bodies hit the water. Alex dropped to his belly and crawled to the edge to look over. There was nothing to see – just an endless procession of waves crashing against the base of the cliff.

How long he lay there he didn't know. After a time he was aware of someone beside him. He turned and looked into his mother's tearful face.

'Poor Peter ... Poor, loyal, brave Peter,' she said softly. Then she pointed to a small object floating about thirty yards offshore. 'Look, Alex, look out there.'

It was a bottle-green chauffeur's cap.

Chapter 37

The next morning at the Old House, no one seemed sure what to do. It was a beautiful day. Kate and Liz had a swim before breakfast; everyone else was exhausted.

The arrival of an ambulance with Willy, sore but glad to be out of hospital and back among his friends, lifted the mood. Toots, battered and bruised, immediately tried to take charge, stubbornly battling the shock of her own experience. She had the ambulance men set Willy's stretcher bed in a sunny corner of the terrace. The others immediately gravitated there.

Eventually the senator appeared on the terrace to a chorus of good mornings.

'Good to have you back, William,' he said, then turned to Toots. 'I owe you an apology for your traumatic experience, Siobhan. It was careless of me not to foresee the possibility of some sort of attempt on you or William at the hospital.'

Toots gave the senator an affectionate hug. 'No need to apologise, Eugene. You haven't got eyes in the back of your head.'

The senator sat down beside Gran.

'Alexander, Vem, a difficult day handled very competently. Like me, I am sure you will mourn the loss of Peter, but from your description of the final moments, it was of his own choice. He will have wanted to witness the death throes of the man who so barbarously mistreated him. I shall miss him sorely. And Mrs Casey, what can I say? Your advice, indeed your stoical presence, was invaluable, and I trust I may now call you my friend.'

She nodded and patted his hand.

'You will all have heard by now,' the senator continued, addressing the room, 'that Clement was badly injured while rescuing Siobhan. But Doctor Rafferty says that with a few weeks' recuperation he'll be fine.'

The senator gazed out over Galway and the wide Atlantic.

'I'm sure you're wondering what this was all about. I think it's time to tell the whole story. To understand my motivation, this story has to start before most of you were born – let us say in 1960. It is not going to be a political commentary on those troubled years. It is more of a social history – my family background and business opportunities – and it will explain how my story has come to involve each of you. Nor is it going to be a justification for actions and decisions I took during that period. History will decide for itself, of that I am sure.'

Eugene took a sip from a glass of water.

'The O'Gorman family originally came from the west coast – Mayo to be precise. Like so many others during the 1940s and 1950s, low wages and lack of opportunity in rural Ireland drove my parents to Dublin to seek more profitable work. My father had, for some years, been employed as a clerk in a firm of auditors in Westport not too far from here, but was going nowhere. Brighter by half than the partners' sons, he was frustrated by the firm's attitude. He solved the problems, the sons got the credit. Promotion, or the opportunity to "take his letters", were denied him by jealousy and stupidity. So, in frustration he moved to Dublin.

'A lover of the sea and all things nautical, he headed straight for the docks. Deregulation in the transport industry had just been approved in the Dáil. Containerisation was the future. Private road haulage was going to expand rapidly. My father walked on to Pier Nine where a German freighter was unloading forty or fifty small containers – ten feet by eight by eight they were at that time. He took out his pocket book and noted names and numbers on the containers. The idea then was to telephone the various companies and offer his services as their Irish forwarding agent.

'The harbour official in charge of unloading saw him and asked if he *was* the forwarding agent. My father, ever the opportunist, said yes. The official then informed him that another ship was lying off, waiting for that berth. All containers had to be cleared from the area in twenty-four hours. My father toured the docks looking for private hauliers, my mother following him, recording all the details. And so O'Gorman Transport was born. Then the containers he couldn't deliver that day he moved into a warehouse where he had rented space from the Harbour Board. And so O'Gorman Storage and Distribution was born. Port handling, Customs Clearance, bonded warehousing – you name it, it all followed. If it didn't exist or was poorly organised, O'Gorman Enterprises, as the business was then named, stepped in. My father was a millionaire within two and a half years, my mother ever at his side and me at his heels.

'He never carried a piece of paper after that first day, and he taught me to be the same. I've carried that on to this day, thanks to Mary. My father had a motto – "doing the deal is easy; the paper chase makes the money" – and he was right. May I suggest, Alex, that you take that as your motto as well.'

The senator paused for another drink of water.

'That is a brief summary of my business background and perhaps an indication of what motivates me. Now to some difficult truths, none of which were suppressed for anything but the best of reasons.'

Eugene shifted uncomfortably in his seat.

'In June 1960 I was summoned to a meeting with my father and another gentleman at which I was asked to consider a proposition that would, in their opinion, be of benefit to me. I considered their proposition, accepted it, and on the twelfth of July 1960, I married the Honourable Alice Mary Elisabeth Stuart ... your and Dominic's mother, Vem. I was sworn to secrecy, an oath I took willingly when I understood the circumstances. You see, I am not Dominic's biological father. When I married Lady Alice, she was a companion to Lady

Mountbatten. It was in her household that an inappropriate relationship took place between the naïve, trusting Lady Alice and a member of Lady Mountbatten's family. I leave it to others to make assumptions and draw conclusions. I agreed to an arranged marriage to help Alice, and in exchange I got social advancement and business connections. I am glad to say that love came later, although time conspired against us. You see, Vem, your mother died the day after you were born in 1968, the result of a surgical mistake.'

Vem stared at her father, a blank expression giving nothing away.

'I was heartbroken, but did my best to raise you and Dominic on my own. Mary helped too, trying to instil in you both a sense of morality and goodness, determination and integrity. It was your mother's experience that made your association with Sean Casey, and Alex's birth, difficult for me to deal with. After what I had done for Alice, I could not put myself through that again with you, Vem.

'And so, Alex, where does that leave you? Well, that night twenty-two years ago when Vem delivered you to Carmel Street, I had no concerns for your future. Sean Casey was an outstanding individual who had been ill-treated by circumstances. My only fear always has been that the past would hurt you as it did your father. Sean knew he was being watched at that time, but mistakenly thought it was by me. On the night he died, he set off to a meeting he had called, thinking I would be there. In fact, Francis Fitzpatrick's brother, Paddy, was there. Convinced I had set him up, and knowing his life was in danger, Sean killed Paddy and his son, along with another gunman, then mistakenly headed for my house in the Wicklow Hills. I was waiting for Sean when I heard the blast that killed him. Believe me, part of me died with him.'

Alex nodded; he had been told some of this by Gran, but now he was able to fill in a few blanks. Gran didn't say a word. Eugene, determined to see it through, pushed on.

'The deaths of Sean Casey and Thomas Toomey were

devastating for Seamus. From being one of a group of the three most respected people in the republican movement, and the most feared outside it, he was suddenly on his own. I think it would be fair to say that you went astray, isn't that right, Seamus?'

A knowing smile passed between the two men.

'However, an event six months later was to bring Seamus back to me. On the eighth of November 1987, at the annual Remembrance Day ceremony in Enniskillen, an IRA bomb exploded, killing eleven people and injuring over sixty, including many children. It was a heinous crime, even by the movement's murderous standards. That night at a meeting of the war council in Dublin I resigned, withdrew my financial support from the movement and vowed to bring to justice anyone who used violence for political ends. I recruited a strong body of like-minded men under the leadership of Seamus O'Boyle, and for the last twenty-two years we have dispensed summary justice as necessary.

'As of yesterday, we have removed all but two of the leading conspirators in Sean Casey's murder and Peter's torture. They are both in Portlaoise serving life sentences. Should they ever be granted parole, well … that will be a decision for you, Alex. You see, you inherit my crusade as well as my business. You must decide yourself whether to continue it or not. Seamus will explain the objectives, and Mary has all the historical information on file.

'The day after Sean Casey's funeral I went north to close the offshore bank accounts that I used to help some innocents caught up in our political struggle. Unfortunately I arrived in time to attend another funeral. Alfred McNabb, your father, William, was killed as you know when leaving the hospital after visiting you and your mother. Your father and grandfather worked for my father, taking care of the paperwork behind his offshore interests. He trusted them implicitly, a trust that was passed on to me. So imagine my delight when I discover that the man who had frustrated the best computer brains I could employ was none other than the son of the late Alfred Spencer McNabb. I attended Alfred's funeral, bought his shop, and, I am now ashamed to tell you, had his house searched, all to no avail. It took Mouseman, a thirteen-year-old boy, to find his red book and discover its hidden riches. Like father, like son, you didn't touch the money. The threatening emails and the blocks on searching for family names were an attempt to prevent you from finding out that which I have now explained.'

Alex had a look of despair on his face. Mary Lennihan, sensing the mental turbulence that had engulfed him, reached into her briefcase and pulled out a number of hardback exercise books and a bunch of keys.

'What about these, Senator?'

'Ah, yes, Peter's diaries. These are for you, Alex, at Peter's request. I told you he had a great intellect. Well, he was also an avid diarist. These are the current ones, the rest are in his safe at home. They go back to his university days, way before our friendship started, and are a meticulous account of the happenings every day since.'

The senator then passed the bunch of keys to Alex.

'These are for you as well. They are the keys to Peter's apartment in the coach house. I have no idea what is there, but some time ago he asked Mary to give them to you if anything happened to him.'

Alex, dazed, could only shake his head.

The senator suddenly smiled as if a great weight had been lifted. His smile was like a trigger – suddenly everyone wanted to speak, to ask questions. They were silenced by the *whump whump* of a helicopter approaching. It circled the house once, before gently landing on the pad where they had arrived what seemed like a lifetime ago.

The senator and Mary stood up. He shook hands with the men and kissed the ladies, smiling, answering no questions. Mary embraced each of them in turn, giving Gran a special squeeze.

Straight as a ramrod, the senator walked out to the helicopter with Mary beside him, his black malacca cane click-clicking on the stones.

Also by John Bradley

Ballyduff House, or The Haunting of Johnnie B

Johnnie B has bought Ballyduff House, an old bishop's residence in Fermanagh. It's the find of a lifetime for him, and he plans to renovate it. But what he didn't plan on was the ghost.

On Friday the thirteenth, Johnnie encounters Finty, who seeks his help in putting ghosts of his own to rest. The past catches up with the present when Johnnie decides he's had enough and sells the property on.

Ballyduff House, or The Haunting of Johnnie B recounts the events of one weekend in June, a weekend that Johnnie is never going to forget.

Made in the USA
Columbia, SC
25 November 2017